"*The Crooked Staircase* is not as good as the first two entries in the Jane Hawk series—it's better! It has just the right amount of paranoia coupled with electric suspense. . . . This current series comprises the most character-driven narratives [Koontz] has ever written. . . . I join millions of Koontz fans who are waiting patiently for *The Forbidden Door* to be released so we can spend more time with the wonderful Jane Hawk." —*Bookreporter*

THE WHISPERING ROOM

"Koontz has never exactly shied away from complex characters or situations. And this situation gets very complex indeed, as Jane pursues the people behind the conspiracy with the kind of single-minded relentlessness that makes the book absolutely spellbinding. As good as *The Silent Corner* was, this one's even better. . . . Koontz is on another roll with a new series that boasts a juicy premise and a compelling star. . . . Pure gold." —*Booklist* (starred review)

"From exciting to overdrive, there's something dangerous around every corner that will have readers loving the thrills and chills created in a way only Koontz can create. Hawk is one of those rare characters that quickly became a favorite with readers and, thankfully, will continue for a long time to come."
—*Suspense Magazine*

"A deeply layered, satisfying thriller that is character-driven and nearly impossible to put down . . . grounded in many real-world, current issues [but] never loses sight of the classic political/sci-fi/thriller elements that make it so much fun to read."
—*Bookreporter*

"Jane Hawk, the compelling heroine of *The Silent Corner*, returns in another terrifying Dean Koontz conspiracy thriller, *The Whispering Room*. . . . The character of Jane Hawk is arguably the best character Koontz has created. Knowledge of *The Silent Corner* helps put some of the narrative in perspective, but it's not necessary to fall under the author's spell. It's clear that another story featuring her quest for ultimate justice is on the horizon, and hopefully there will be even more after that. Simply put, wow."
—Associated Press

"Master of suspense Dean Koontz has done it again. Written a new series . . . a techno-thriller from the darker corners of his imagination. Meet his latest character, Jane Hawk . . . a resourceful, street-savvy FBI agent who takes a leave of absence to investigate the apparent suicide of her husband [and] discovers [a] conspiracy at the highest levels of government and the tech industry. . . . The action is fast, emotions and tension run high, and there are casualties. . . . Readers are right there with [Jane] as she ingeniously survives a series of close encounters in her quest to unveil the truth one piece at a time. . . . Koontz is writing at his most expressive and compelling as he follows Jane on her calculated yet obsessive journey. . . . Clearly, there is no stopping Jane Hawk."
—*Between the Lines*/Capital Public Radio

"Employing her impressive skill set that combines tech-savviness with physical prowess, [Jane Hawk] methodically pursues the powerful and evil masterminds behind [a] malevolent conspiracy. . . . The results she achieves both satisfy and leave the door open for Jane's promised return. Koontz delivers another winner." —*Library Journal*

THE SILENT CORNER

"FBI agent Jane Hawk goes rogue. . . . She's capable of taking on the opposition single-handedly, with or without her trusty Heckler & Koch handgun. . . . A proven specialist in action scenes, Koontz pulls off some doozies here. . . . The book is full of neat touches. . . . And the prose, as always in a Koontz novel, is first-rate. Perhaps Koontz's leanest, meanest thriller, this initial entry in a new series introduces a smart, appealing heroine who can outthink as well as outshoot the baddest of bad dudes."
—*Kirkus Reviews* (starred review)

"Gripping . . . The paranoia and mystery increase as the story unfolds. . . . Koontz has created such a wonderful character in Jane Hawk [that] readers will clamor for more tales involving Hawk and her quest for justice. Koontz rocks it again."
—Associated Press

"The latest page-turner by Dean Koontz introduces readers to Jane Hawk. . . . An inspired choice for a protagonist, by far the strongest part of a reliably entertaining book by the perennial bestselling author . . . action, zippy dialogue and a winning character at the center of the book, part of a new series by Koontz."
—Minneapolis *Star Tribune*

"Bestselling novelist Dean Koontz is back with a fierce new main character named Jane Hawk. But what's really scary in *The Silent Corner* is Mr. Koontz's chilling villain. . . . In this era of stingy text-message prose, Mr. Koontz is practically Shakespeare. . . . Readers who appreciate heightened expression and super dramatic similes will be thrilled by Mr. Koontz's choices. His authorial individualism continues with a blend of vintage and trendy. . . . But Mr. Koontz is ultra-contemporary, too. . . . [He] makes several points about Jane's antagonists that more than apply to the times in which we are living. *The Silent Corner* brims with both action and emotion."
—Pittsburgh *Post-Gazette*

THE
Crooked
STAIRCASE

DEAN KOONTZ

THE
Crooked
STAIRCASE

A Jane Hawk Novel

Bantam Books | New York

2018 Bantam Books Mass Market Edition

Copyright © 2018 by Dean Koontz
Excerpt from *The Forbidden Door* by Dean Koontz
copyright © 2018 by Dean Koontz

Published in the United States by Bantam Books,
an imprint of Random House, a division of
Penguin Random House LLC, New York.

BANTAM BOOKS and the HOUSE colophon are registered
trademarks of Penguin Random House LLC.

Originally published in hardcover in the United States by
Bantam Books, an imprint of Random House, a division of
Penguin Random House LLC, in 2018.

This book contains an excerpt from the forthcoming book
The Forbidden Door by Dean Koontz. This excerpt has been set
for this edition only and may not reflect the final content of
the forthcoming edition.

ISBN 978-0-525-48369-4
Ebook ISBN 978-0-525-48344-1
International edition ISBN 978-1-9848-1749-5

Cover design: Scott Biel
Cover photograph: Claudio Marinesco

Printed in the United States of America

randomhousebooks.com

2 4 6 8 9 7 5 3 1

Bantam Books mass market edition: September 2018

To Vito and Lynn,
with love, for all the laughter

A shattering of shop windows
The bomb in the baby carriage
Was wired to the radio
These are the days of miracle and wonder . . .
And don't cry, baby, don't cry,
Don't cry
    —PAUL SIMON, "The Boy in the Bubble"

Hateful empty Masks, full of beetles and spiders,
yet glaring out . . . from their glass eyes with a
ghastly affectation of life.
    —THOMAS CARLYLE, *Sartor Resartus*

THE
Crooked
STAIRCASE

PART ONE

Nowhere Safe

1

A t seven o'clock on that night in March, during a thunderless but heavy rain pounding as loud as an orchestra of kettledrums, Sara Holdsteck finally left the offices of Paradise Real Estate, carrying her briefcase in her left hand, open purse slung over her left shoulder, right hand free for a cross-body draw of the gun in the purse. She boarded her Ford Explorer, threw back the dripping hood of her raincoat, and drove home by way of familiar suburban streets on which the foul weather had settled a strangeness, an apocalyptic gloom that matched her mood. Not for the first time in the past two years, she felt as if somewhere ahead of her, reality itself must be eroding, washing away, so that she might come to the crumbling edge of a precipice with nothing beyond but a lightless, bottomless abyss. Silver needles of rain pleated the darkness with mystery and threat. Any vehicle that followed her more than three blocks elicited her suspicion.

The Springfield Armory Champion .45 ACP was nestled in her open purse, which stood on her briefcase, within easy reach on the passenger seat. Originally she hadn't wanted a weapon of such a high caliber, but she had eventually realized that nothing smaller would so reliably stop an assailant. She had spent many hours on a shooting range, learning to control the recoil.

She had once lived in a gated community with an around-the-clock security guard, in a paid-off twelve-thousand-square-foot residence with a view of the Pacific Ocean. Now she owned a house one-quarter that size, encumbered by a fat mortgage, in a neighborhood with no gate, no guard, no view. Starting with little money, by the age of forty she had built a modest fortune as a Southern California real-estate agent, broker, and canny investor—but most of it had been taken from her by the time she was forty-two.

At forty-four, though bitter, she was nonetheless grateful that she hadn't been rendered penniless. Having clawed her way to the top once before, she'd been left with just enough assets to start the climb again. This time she would not make the mistake that had led to her ruin; she would not marry.

On the street where Sara lived, storm runoff overwhelmed the drains to form shallow lakes wherever the pavement swaled. Her Ford cast up wings of water in a false promise of magical flight. She slowed and swung into her driveway. Lights glowed in some windows, controlled by a smart-house program that, after nightfall and in her absence, created the illusion of occupancy and activity. She remoted the garage door and, while it rolled up on its tracks, put her open purse in her lap. She drove inside, the drumming of rain on the roof relenting as the welcome electronic shriek of the alarm system inspired a greater sense of safety than she had felt since setting out for work that morning.

She did not switch off the engine. With the doors still locked, she kept her left foot hard on the brake, her right poised over the accelerator, and she shifted into reverse. She used the remote control again and looked from one of the SUV's side mirrors to the other, watching the big segmented door descend. If someone tried to slip in under it, the motion detector would sense the intruder and, as a safety measure, retract the door. If that happened, the instant the roll-up cleared the roof of the Explorer, she would take her foot off the brake, stomp the accelerator, and reverse at speed into the driveway, into the street.

With luck, she might be quick enough to run down whatever sonofabitch had come after her.

The bottom rail of the door met the concrete with a soft thud. She was alone in the garage.

She shifted the SUV into park, applied the emergency brake, switched off the engine, and got out. The last exhaust fumes threaded the air. The Ford shed rain on the concrete floor and ticked as the engine cooled.

After unlocking the connecting door to the house, she stepped into the laundry room, turned to the keypad, and entered the four-number code that disarmed the security system. At once she reset the alarm to the at-home mode, which activated only the sensors at the doors and windows, leaving dormant the interior motion detectors, allowing her to move freely through the residence.

She hung her raincoat on a wall hook, where it dripped onto the tile floor. Purse slung from her left shoulder, briefcase in her right hand, she opened the inner laundry-room door and went into the kitchen, realizing an instant too late that the air was redolent with the aroma of freshly brewed coffee.

A stranger with a pistol stood at the dinette table on which rested a mug of coffee and Sara's copy of that morning's *Los Angeles Times* with its banner headline JANE HAWK INDICTED FOR ESPIONAGE, TREASON, MURDER. The barrel of the weapon was elongated by a silencer, the muzzle as dark and deep as a wormhole connecting this universe to another.

Sara halted, shocked not merely because her home had been violated in spite of all her precautions, but also because the intruder was a woman.

Twentysomething, with long black hair parted mid-forehead and tucked behind her ears, with eyes as black and direct as the muzzle of the gun, with no makeup or lipstick—and no need of any—wearing wire-rimmed glasses, dressed in a black sport coat and a white shirt and black jeans, she looked severe and yet beautiful and somehow unearthly, as if Death had undergone an image makeover and at long last revealed her true gender.

"I'm not here to hurt you," the intruder said. "I just

need some information. But first, put your purse on the counter, and don't reach for the gun in it."

Although Sara suspected that it would be foolish to hope to deceive this woman, she heard herself say, "Whatever you are, I'm not like you. I'm just a real-estate agent. I don't have a gun."

The stranger said, "Two years ago, you purchased a Springfield Armory Super Tuned Champion with a Novak low-mount fixed sight, polished extractor and ejector and feed ramp, and a King extended safety. You ordered it with an A1-style trigger precisely tuned to a four-pound pull, and you had the entire weapon carry-beveled, all its edges and corners rounded so that it won't snag during a quick draw. You must have done a lot of research to come up with an order like that. And you must have spent many hours on a shooting range, learning to handle the piece, because then you applied for and received a concealed-carry permit."

Sara put the purse on the counter.

"The briefcase, too," the intruder directed. "Don't even think of slinging it at me."

When she did as told, Sara's gaze fixed on a nearby drawer that held cutlery, including a chef's French knife and a cleaver.

"Unless you're a champion knife thrower," the stranger said, "you'll never be fast enough to use it. Didn't you hear me say I don't mean you any harm?"

Sara turned from the cutlery drawer. "Yeah, I heard. But I don't believe it."

The woman regarded her in silence for a moment and then said, "If you're as smart as I think you are, you'll warm up to me. If you're not that smart, this will get ugly when it doesn't need to be. Sit down at the table."

"What if I just walk out of here?"

"Then I'll have to hurt you a little, after all. But you'll have brought it on yourself."

The intruder's face—the strength of its features, the clarity of its lines, its refinement—was as purely Celtic as any face in Scotland or Ireland. But those eyes, so black that the pupils and irises were as one, seemed to belong in a different countenance. The contrast was somehow unsettling, as if the face might be a mask, its every expression unreliable, while the truth that otherwise might be read in her eyes remained secreted in their darkness.

Although Sara had promised herself that she would never again be intimidated by anyone, after a brief staring match, she sat where she'd been told to sit.

2

The tropical stillness of the storm succumbed to a sudden wind that cast shatters of rain against the windows.

Jane Hawk sat across from Sara Holdsteck and put her Heckler & Koch .45 Compact on the kitchen table. Sara looked weary, which was not surprising, considering all that she had been through in the past two years. Weary but not defeated. Jane was familiar with that condition.

"Your Springfield Champion is a sweet weapon, Sara. But don't carry it in your purse. Change the way you dress. Get in the habit of wearing a sport coat. Carry the gun in a concealed shoulder rig where you can draw it quickly."

"I hate guns. It was a big step for me just to get one."

"I understand. But switch to a shoulder rig anyway. And get real about security systems like the one you had installed here."

Skirling wind rattled rain hard against the glass, disquieting Sara, so that she looked at each of the two kitchen windows as if she expected to see some face of inhuman configuration, conjured by the storm.

Returning her attention to Jane, she said, "Get real about my security system? What's that mean?"

"Do you know that all alarm companies in any city or region use the same central station to monitor the systems they install?"

"I thought each company monitored its own."

"Not the case. And certain government agencies have secret—basically illegal—back doors to all those central stations across the country. Do you understand what I mean by 'back doors'?"

"A way into the company's computer the company doesn't know about."

"I used a back door to your security provider and reviewed your account. Learned where your alarm keypads and motion detectors are located, the password you use when you accidentally trigger an alarm and call in a cancellation, the location of the battery that backs up the system during a power failure. Useful stuff for any bad guy to know. Though he'd still need the four-digit disarming code."

Two words belatedly brought a scowl to Sara's face. "'Government agencies'? I've had enough of them. Which are you with?"

"None. Not anymore. Sara, the alarm company isn't supposed to have that disarming code. It's something only the homeowner should know. You should program it yourself with the primary keypad. But like a lot of people, you didn't want to bother following the steps in the manual, so you asked the installer to program it for you. Which he did. And noted it in your account file. Where I found it."

As if the weight of her mistake pressed on her, Sara slumped lower in her chair. "I've been living defensively for a long time, but I don't claim to be perfect at it."

"Maybe you need to be better, but you don't want to be perfect at it. Only the insane are perfect in their paranoia."

"Sometimes I think I've *already* gone half-crazy, the way I live. I mean, the worst happened more than two years ago. Nothing since."

"But in your gut, you know . . . at any time he might decide you're a loose end that needs to be tied off."

Sara glanced again at the windows.

"Would you like to lower the blinds?" Jane asked.

"I always do when I come home after dark."

"Go ahead. Then sit down again."

Having closed the blinds, Sara returned to her chair.

Jane said, "I got in here using an automatic lock-picking gun supposedly sold only to police. Turned off the alarm with your code, reset it in the at-home mode, and settled down to wait."

"I'll change the code myself. But, who are you?"

Instead of answering, Jane said, "You were on top of the world, selling high-end houses, damn good at it, never a complaint from a client. Then suddenly you're hit with three very public lawsuits, all within two weeks, alleging fraudulent activities."

"The allegations weren't true."

"I'm aware of that. Then came a seemingly unrelated IRS audit. But not an ordinary audit. One conducted with the assumption of criminal intent, accusations of money laundering."

The memory triggered indignation that drew Sara up straight in her chair. "The IRS agents who came to pore through my books, they were *armed*. As if I was some dangerous terrorist."

"Armed auditors aren't supposed to flaunt their weapons."

"Yeah, well, they made damn sure I knew they were packing."

"To intimidate you."

Sara squinted as if to focus more intently on Jane's face. "Do I know you? Have we met before?"

"Doesn't matter, Sara. What matters is that I despise the same people you despise."

"Like who would that be?"

From a jacket pocket, Jane produced a photograph

of Simon Yegg and dealt it across the table as if it were a playing card.

"My husband," Sara said. "Ex-husband. The vicious shit. I know why I despise him, but why do you?"

"Because of the crew he hangs with. I want to use him to get to them. In the process, I can make him profoundly sorry he did to you what he did. I can humble him."

3

Tanuja Shukla was standing in the deep front yard, in the rain and the dark, soaked and chilled and lonely and wildly happy, when the assassins arrived, although of course she didn't at once realize they were assassins.

Twenty-five and obsessively creative from early childhood, Tanuja had been writing a novelette in which a rain-drenched night provided atmosphere but also served as a metaphor for loneliness and spiritual malaise. After watching the downpour from a window of her second-floor study, she seized the opportunity to immerse herself in the elements, the better to know what her lead character felt during a long journey on foot in a storm. Other writers of literary fiction with elements of fantasy found most research unnecessary, but Tanuja believed that a skeleton of truth needed to provide the structure underlying an author's muscular invention—the fantasy—and that the two must be bound together by tendons of accurate facts and well-observed details.

Her twin brother, Sanjay, who was two minutes younger than Tanuja and considerably more acerbic, had said, "Don't worry. When you die of pneumonia, I'll finish writing your story, and the last pages will be the best of it."

Tanuja's jeans and black T-shirt were saturated, at first clinging like one of those weighted blankets meant to alleviate anxiety, but then seeming to dissolve so that she felt as if she were unclothed except for her blue sneakers, naked in the storm, vulnerable and alone, exactly how the character in her novelette felt. As she mentally catalogued the physical details of this experience for later use in fiction, she was more content than she had been all day.

The house stood at the end of a two-lane road, on three acres in the eastern hills of Orange County horse country, though there were no longer horses on this acreage. White-painted wire-infilled board fencing encircled the property. Sixty or seventy yards west of the house, a gate of the same materials barred entrance to the long driveway.

The stormfall drummed the earth and chattered like an infinite number of tumbling dice against the blacktop, and on a nearby hundred-year-old live oak, each of the thousands of stiff oval-shaped leaves was a tongue that gave voice to the rain, raising a chorus of whispers that together were like the roar of a distant crowd, all serving to mask the sound of an approaching engine.

Because the Shukla place was the last residence before the blacktop dead-ended in a turnaround, the light approaching from the south tweaked Tanuja's curiosity. No visitor was expected. In the murk, the seemingly soundless conveyance appeared to be borne on a tide of mist that roiled off the pavement, headlights chasing before them flocks of shadows that winged across eucalyptus trees on the farther side of the two-lane road.

The vehicle halted at the gate, not facing inward but athwart the driveway, as though to block that exit from the property.

When doors were thrown open, interior lights came on, defining the proportions of a large SUV. The driver doused the headlights, and when the last door closed, the vehicle as good as vanished.

Tanuja had stood so long in the deluge that her eyes were fully dark adapted. Because the plank gate was painted white, she could see it even at that distance, less as a gate than as some pale and cryptic symbol, a mysterious hieroglyph floating portentously on the night. She also discerned three half-visible figures clambering over that barrier.

Outside of the gate stood a call box on a post. Visitors were meant to press a button and announce themselves, whereupon the gate could be opened from the house. That these new arrivals eschewed the call box and instead climbed the planking suggested they were not visitors, but intruders bent on mischief or worse.

In her dark clothes, with her black hair and maiden-of-Mumbai complexion, Tanuja would be difficult to spot as long as she avoided the outspill of light from the house. She turned and dashed to the massive oak, which gathered rain and channeled it along leafways, from which it drizzled in a hundred thick streams.

She paused and glanced back and saw three big men hurrying up the driveway, their hooded jackets and determined stride suggesting satanic monks abroad on some infernal task.

Hers was not a life of high drama, other than the scenarios that arose in her mind and found expression in her writing. She had not before experienced such hard pounding of the heart as shook her now, as if contained within her breast were both hammer and anvil.

She sprinted from the oak and around the south side of the house, staying clear of the light from the windows. Onto the back porch. Two doors. The first opened into the kitchen, the second into the mudroom, but of course both were locked.

She fumbled a key from a pocket, dropped it, snatched it from the porch floor, and let herself into the mudroom, where she had left her smartphone before venturing into the storm. Slender and athletic, Tanuja was usually as graceful as a dancer. But now, shedding rainwater, she slipped on the vinyl-tile flooring and fell.

A door on the left connected the mudroom to the kitchen, and one directly ahead accessed the downstairs hallway. She thrust to her feet, sodden shoes slipping as if she were a skater on ice, and opened the door and saw Sanjay. He had stepped out of his study and gone into the foyer at the farther end of the hallway, where he just now opened the front door.

Too late to call out a warning, Tanuja hoped that she had misread the situation, that her overactive imagination had invoked menace where none existed.

The first man at the door was known to her: Lincoln Crossley, who lived two houses south of them, a deputy with the sheriff's department. Linc was married to Kendra, who worked as a bailiff at the county courthouse. They had a sixteen-year-old son, Jeff, and a Labrador retriever named Gustav. They were good people, and for a moment Tanuja was relieved.

Rather than wait for an invitation, however, Crossley and the two men behind him crossed the threshold the moment the door opened, crowding Sanjay backward, their boldness disturbing. None of them wore a uniform, and whoever the two strangers might be, Crossley's behavior was not protocol for an officer of the law.

Tanuja couldn't discern what Linc Crossley said or what Sanjay answered, though she heard the deputy speak her name. She eased the mudroom door almost shut, watching through a narrow gap, feeling like a child, a small uncomprehending girl who by accident stood witness to a mysterious and disquieting adult encounter.

Crossley put one arm around Sanjay's shoulders, but in that move Tanuja read some quality darker than neighborly affection. He was much bigger than Sanjay.

One of Crossley's associates drew a pistol, quickly crossed the foyer, and ascended the stairs, apparently with no concern that his boots and jacket streamed water on the carpet and the hardwood floor.

When the third man closed the front door, stepped out of the foyer, and disappeared into the parlor as though on a search, Tanuja opened a drawer in a mudroom cabinet, retrieved a flashlight, grabbed her phone from a countertop, and fled. She crossed the porch, vaulted the railing, and hurried across the backyard, into the wind and rain, not daring yet to switch on the light, her fertile imagination spawning terrors of extreme violence and rape and intolerable humiliation even as it also crafted desperate scenes in which she might by various means save herself and her brother.

4

Long-lingering resentment pinched Sara Holdsteck's mouth and pinked her cheeks, the knuckles bone-white in her clenched fists, as she spoke about what she'd endured more than two years earlier, when she'd been sued by three clients in one week, which turned out to be the least of the assaults against her. Because the woman's anguish at having been betrayed and played for a fool had not faded with time, Jane found it painful to watch her.

Sara's attorney of fifteen years, Mary Wyatt, had

assured her that those legal actions were frivolous, that among the accusers there was an appearance of collusion with intent to defame, and that she should not worry unduly. Three days later, with no explanation, Mary dropped her as a client and declined to accept her phone calls. Another attorney took her on—and the following day changed his mind. While a third lawyer tried to persuade her to settle the suits out of court, a six-unit apartment building that she owned appeared on an EPA list of structures standing on ground contaminated by highly toxic chemicals, and three days thereafter, she received a health-department summons to appear at a hearing into the dangers faced by tenants of her property. By this time, IRS auditors had been in the offices of her accountant for six business days, examining her books in search of evidence of money laundering.

Now she poked a finger at the photo of Simon Yegg on the table in front of her. "It was a Friday evening. This treacherous snake sat me down for what he called a 'come-to-Jesus meeting.' He claimed my problems were the work of friends of his who he wouldn't name. The smug bastard wanted a divorce. He gave me a property-division ultimatum. He'd keep everything he brought into the marriage just eighteen months earlier . . . and take seventy percent of my assets, graciously leaving me start-over money. In return, he'd make the lawsuits go away, have the IRS audit conclude quickly in my favor, and get the apartments taken off the list of contaminated sites."

"You believed he could do all that?" Jane asked.

"Everything happening to me was so bizarre, surreal. I didn't know what to believe. The change in him was shocking. He'd always been so sweet, so . . . loving. Suddenly he was condescending, cruel, contemptuous of me. I told him to get out. I said it was my house before we were married and it would always be my house."

"What happened to make you back down?"

Sara looked at one blinded window and then at the other, not because anything of the night could be seen, but perhaps because she was embarrassed to meet Jane's eyes.

"I didn't know he had three people with him. They came in from the garage. Two men and a woman. He gave me to them, and he left."

"'Gave' you to them?"

Sara opened her fists, regarding her hands as if repulsed by some filth that only she could see. "The men held me down."

After a silence, Jane said, "Rape."

"No. They stripped me naked. Cuffed my hands. Indifferent. As if I wasn't a woman to them. Not a person. Just a thing."

Her voice had gone flat, deflated of all emotion, as if she had so often examined this memory that she'd worn away its sharp edges and its ability to distress her. But the truth of its enduring effect could be seen in the paleness of her lips, the color burning in her cheeks, and the stiffening of her body as if in defense against a hard blow.

"They took me to a bathroom," she continued in a voice eerily detached from the cruelty she described. "The woman had filled the tub with cold water. Also with ice. Cubes from the kitchen icemaker. A lot of ice. They forced me to sit in the tub."

"Hypothermia is an effective torture," Jane said. "Iranians use it. North Koreans. Cubans. When they don't want to mark the victim."

"One man sat on the toilet. One brought a chair. The woman sat on the tub. Edge of the tub. They talked movies, TV, sports, like I wasn't there. If I spoke, she zapped my neck with a Taser, then held my head out of the water by my hair till the spasms stopped."

"How long did this go on?"

"I lost track of time. But it wasn't just one session. They did it to me on and off all weekend."

Jane listed some symptoms of hypothermia. "Uncontrollable shivering, confusion, weakness, dizziness, slurred speech."

"Cold is its own kind of pain," Sara said. She closed her eyes and bent her head and might have been mistaken for a woman in prayer if her hands had not cramped into fists once more.

Jane waited in patient quiet, Sara in the chilly silence of mortification, until Jane said, "It wasn't primarily about the pain. Sure, they wanted you to be miserable. And afraid. But mainly it was about humiliation. Making you feel helpless, submissive, using shame to break your resolve."

When at last Sara spoke, her voice trembled as if the needled cold of that long-ago ordeal pricked her bones again. "The men . . . when they had to . . ."

Jane spared her from the need to say it. "When they had to urinate, they did it in the tub."

Finally Sara raised her head and met Jane's eyes. "I

never could've imagined such a thing, treating anyone with such contempt."

"Because you'd never dealt with their type before. I have."

The character of the tremor in Sara's voice changed, no longer occasioned by a memory of cold or humiliation, but by a virulent and righteous anger. "Will you do to Simon what those three did to me?"

"I don't work that way, Sara."

"He deserves it."

"He deserves worse."

"Will you ruin him?"

"Possibly."

"Take his money?"

"Some of it, anyway."

"Will you kill him?"

"If I force him to tell me what I need to know, other people will probably kill him for ratting on them."

Sara considered that prospect. "What's this all about?"

"You don't want to know. But if you hope to get your self-respect back, entirely back, you need to help me."

Outside, rain and wind. In the mind of Sara Holdsteck, a different but equal turbulence.

Then she said, "What do you want to know?"

5

Tanuja Shukla, thrashed by fear but driven by duty, owing her brother no less than everything, hurrying through the dark stable where no horses had been kept for years, hooding the flashlight with her left hand even though distance and foul weather made it unlikely that one of the men in the house, glancing out a window, would glimpse the pale beam . . . Rain beating on the roof like the booted feet of marching legions, the earthen scent of the hard-packed hoof-imprinted floor, the musty but sweet smell of old straw moldering in the corners of the empty stalls . . .

What had once been the tack room, where saddles and bridles and other horse gear had been stored, now contained a riding lawnmower, rakes and spades and gardening tools. A long-handled axe could serve as a weapon, but it wouldn't be enough to help one slender girl drive off or chop down three men, even if she had the stomach for such violence, which she didn't.

Because the tack room was without windows, she no longer hooded the flashlight beam. She swept it quickly across bags of fertilizer, terra-cotta pots of all sizes, redwood stakes for tomato plants, cans of Spectracide Wasp & Hornet Killer. . . .

From the shelf she took a container of hornet spray. Removed the safety cap. The can was about ten inches tall. Weighed maybe a pound and a half. It contained a lot of poison.

A cadenced wind now brought complex rhythms to the rain as Tanuja returned to the open door of the stable, where she switched off the flashlight and put it on the floor.

Hindu by birth but not by practice, she had not believed in the faith of her mother and father since she'd been ten, which was the year they perished in the crash of a 747 while on a flight from New Delhi to London. Yet now she sent up a prayer to Bhavani, the goddess who was the benign aspect of the fierce Shakti, Bhavani the giver of life and the great font of mercy. *Provide me with strength and allow me to triumph.*

She plunged into the cold rain, vigorously shaking the can of Spectracide as she ran toward the house where Sanjay was perhaps in mortal danger. Sanjay had slid into existence and taken his first breath close behind her, following her from womb to wicked world; therefore, she must always be his *rakshak*, his protector.

6

A crystal bowl, like a Gypsy's instrument of foretelling that had failed to predict the current threat, seemed to float on the translucent milky quartz tabletop, bright with a fullness of ripe roses that shed petals as portentous as blood drops.

Sitting at the kitchen table, held there at gunpoint, Sanjay Shukla was both fearful and exhilarated. He was sufficiently self-aware to marvel that, in such dire circumstances, a thread of delight was woven through his dread.

His sister wrote a kind of magic realism, and her new novel, only in stores three weeks, had earned all but universal critical acclaim. Sanjay, too, had been declared an author of promise for importing into the literary novel certain qualities of hard-boiled detective stories. Sometimes he worried that he'd not experienced enough of the dangers and roughness of the world to be able to write neo-noir fiction as effectively as he wished. Yes, his parents had died when terrorists blew up an airplane. Yes, his and Tanuja's *mausi*—their mother's sister—Aunt Ashima Chatterjee and her husband, Burt, during their guardianship of the Shukla twins, had embezzled two-thirds of the inheritance before their niece and nephew could induce a court to declare them adults at the age of seventeen. But none of that was the kind of noir ordeal that would have made a good movie with Robert Mitchum; therefore, Sanjay often wished that he had more gritty experience of threat and violence.

Now here he was, staring down the barrel of a pistol held by a neighbor who previously seemed as straight-arrow as Captain America. A second gunman, a stranger, stood near the door to the mudroom. A third man, whose caterpillar eyebrows nearly met over the bridge of his nose, placed on the table a small cooler from which he produced a packaged hypodermic needle with cannula and a stainless-steel box about nine inches square, seven or eight inches deep; he handled the box with cotton gloves, evidently because it was cold enough to take the skin off bare fingers.

Sanjay was less alarmed by the pistol than by the syringe. A gun was an easily understood threat, but the needle injected an element of the unknown. It made him think of illness, disease. He wasn't sick, and even if he had been, these men were not here to heal him, which meant they might be here to *infect* him.

That made no sense, but people did a lot of things that made no sense.

Sanjay also thought of truth serum, movie scenes involving interrogation, but that didn't compute, either, because he didn't have any valuable information to withhold from anyone.

He had asked them what they wanted, what they were doing, what this was all about, but they had ignored his questions even though he answered theirs. Maybe they intuited that his answers were not truthful, which was why they responded to his inquiries only with silence. He'd told them that Tanuja was on a date with her boyfriend and that he didn't know when they would return. He hoped that his sister, who didn't currently *have* a boyfriend, who had been outside somewhere, standing in the rain, engaged in one of her eccentric quests for authentic details to enhance her writing, had seen these men coming, realized their malicious intent, and gone for help.

Because conducting an agitated one-sided conversation would only make him seem desperate and likely to make a break for freedom, Sanjay matched their silence with silence and slumped in the chair, as if sliding into hopelessness, just a skinny Indian boy with a pair of *golis* no bigger than chickpeas, if he had any *golis* at all between his legs. The more certain they were that he'd submitted to them, the more likely he might surprise them and escape.

The man wearing gloves opened the metal box, from which wafted a pale odorless mist, as if perhaps the contents rested on a bed of dry ice that began to evaporate when exposed to the air.

The guns and syringe were frightening, but the shared attitude of the three intruders was even more intimidating: the sense of authority with which they invaded the house and forcibly escorted Sanjay to the kitchen and pressed him into this chair and pushed aside the bowl of roses, slopping water on the quartz; the arrogant silence with which they responded to his protests and questions; their faces without expression; their stares direct and pitiless, as though they regarded him as belonging to a different—and inferior—species from them. Linc Crossley was not himself, lacking his usual humor, and there was something machinelike about all of them.

The metal box appeared to contain numerous sleeves of silvery insulation, each perhaps an inch in diameter and seven inches long. As the gloved man removed three of these and put them on the table, his frown brought his caterpillar eyebrows together as if in an act of bristling conjugation.

Crossley put his pistol on the counter by the refrigerator and from a jacket pocket produced a length of rubber tubing of the kind that phlebotomists used as a tourniquet to make it easier to find the vein of a patient from whom blood was to be drawn.

The unhurried movements of the mute and solemn men, like mimes engaged not in entertainment but in the conveyance of some truth with a terrible consequence . . . Razor-keen light gleaming off the edges of the stainless-steel box as it was pressed shut . . . A few last feathery emissions from the smoking ice, as ephemeral as the secrets of the deceased issuing from the death-throttled throats of spirits . . . Moment by moment, the scene became more dreamlike yet hyperreal in its detail.

The gun on the counter seemed to be an opportunity. If Sanjay chose the right moment when the men were distracted, twisted his chair to the left, reared back from the table, bolted up, moved fast, he surely could reach the pistol before the deputy seized it, though it was important to remember that Linc had police training.

Crossley also produced a foil packet that might have contained an alcohol-saturated pad to sterilize the skin before pricking it with a needle.

Sanjay's attention was drawn again to the three silvery tubes. Caterpillar Man peeled open the Velcro closure on one, and into his hand slid a glass ampule containing a cloudy amber fluid.

The fragile thread of delight woven through Sanjay's dread had withered away. In the past few minutes, he had experienced enough threat and violence to inspire his writing for the rest of his career, assuming that he lived long enough to have one.

As Caterpillar Man pierced the membrane of the ampule with the needle and drew the amber fluid into the barrel of the syringe, the man standing near the mudroom holstered his gun and approached, perhaps to restrain Sanjay should that be necessary. He yawned as though he must be so experienced in this work that it bored him.

For an instant, it seemed as if a thick jet of glistering gastric acid erupted from his mouth. But recognizing the smell, Sanjay turned his head to follow the stream of hornet-killing insecticide to its origin.

Only five feet four, a hundred pounds, wet, and no doubt cold, Tanuja seemed to be a towering menace when she entered from the downstairs hall, her pretty face contorted by wrath, as if she were a terrible manifestation of Kali, goddess of death and destruction, minus two of Kali's four limbs, a can of Spectracide held at arm's length. The highly pressurized container did not provide a spray, but instead produced a thick stream that projected up to twenty feet from the nozzle.

Ironically, it was Linc Crossley who had once mentioned that wasp spray and bear repellent were effective home-defense weapons.

The first man, gagging on the insecticide and unable to get his breath because of the volatile fumes, stumbled toward the kitchen sink perhaps to rinse out his mouth, which would make things worse.

Lithe as a dancer, Tanuja pivoted toward Lincoln Crossley, who reached for the pistol on the counter, and she triggered the can again. At a distance of only eight feet, the stream splattered forcefully into his eyes and nose, rendering him temporarily blind and in even greater respiratory distress than her first target.

As the man in white gloves cursed and dropped the ampule with the hypodermic, Sanjay slid out of his chair and under the table and onto his hands and knees, to get out of the line of fire.

Now all three of the men were wheezing, coughing, issuing wordless cries of misery, colliding with furniture and one another.

Pushing between steel-legged chairs, crawling out from under the table, Sanjay heard his sister call his name. He saw her at the door between the kitchen and garage, which was when gunfire erupted. The glass window in the microwave shattered. A round ricocheted off the refrigerator. An upper cabinet door pocked and cracked, and the dishes within exploded in a rattle-jangle of shrapnel.

If not blinded, with tears and insecticide flooding down his face, Linc Crossley must have seen a world blurred beyond all recognition. He drew breath in raw gasps, exhaling explosively as each inhalation contained more suffocating flatus than air, swaying in place as if his legs were rubberizing. Yet he held fast to the pistol, firing at phantoms evoked by his stinging, bloodshot eyes.

Crawling frantically, Sanjay stayed wide of the gloved intruder, who was lying on his right side, bearded with vomit. Hands clutching his stomach, the man now foamed at the mouth as though rabid.

The guy who had been by the mudroom door, having taken a few ounces of the hornet-killing concoction straight in the mouth and having reflexively swallowed it, sprawled on his back, clawing his throat with such urgency that his fingernails scratched bloody furrows in his flesh, perhaps desperate for air, perhaps poisoned and dying. Beside him lay a smartphone, which must have slipped out of a jacket pocket when he fell.

Although frantic to escape the kitchen and the blind man's Hail Mary gunfire, Sanjay had the presence of mind to confiscate the phone on his way to the open door through which Tanuja had vanished.

After dogging it into the laundry room, where his sister had put down the Spectracide and waited at the entrance to the garage, Sanjay clambered to his feet. In his terror, he heard himself praise her with a Hindi expression of their dad's—"*Shabash!*"—which meant "Well done!" Switching on the phone as he followed Tanuja into the garage, he said, "I'll call nine-one-one."

"Screw that," she said. "We're outta here."

7

Now confident that it wouldn't be thrown at her, Jane poured a second mug of coffee, brought it to the table, and put it in front of Sara Holdsteck, the fragrant steam rising in serpentine ribbons.

As she refreshed her own mug, she said, "Though

you've agreed to help me, first there's more you need to hear."

"Which must mean . . . my situation is even worse than I think."

"Simon never told you he'd been married three times before?"

Sara was surprised for a moment—and then not. "He said he'd sworn to stay a bachelor. But with me, he wanted it to be forever."

"His third wife said he has a silver tongue."

"Yeah. And a heart of iron."

Jane returned the Pyrex pot to the coffeemaker. "He seems to choose his wives for two reasons. First, they resemble one another. Slim brunettes with blue eyes, five feet six, give or take an inch."

"The other qualification?"

"Money. They inherited it. Or earned it, as in your case and another. Not enormous fortunes, but serious money. Three other wives with four different divorce attorneys. Yet in every case they wanted zip from Simon, while giving him fifty to seventy percent of their assets."

"After going through one hell or another."

In her chair again, Jane said, "Pretty much the same hell. People sued them, all kinds of federal agencies suddenly came after them, and at the height of the chaos . . . ice-cold baths or the equivalent, and a dose of intense humiliation."

"They all broke like me," Sara intuited, not as if she thought the weakness of the three previous wives somehow exonerated her, but as if depressed by the news of Simon's repeated triumphs.

"Count yourself lucky or wise that you gave him what he wanted after a weekend of abuse. Anyway, your only other choice would have been to kill him."

"I wish I had. But I was a different person then. So timid."

"Not timid," Jane said. "Naïve. His third wife endured eight days. Ice-water baths, brutal sessions in a superheated sauna, sleep deprivation—and then came the vicious gang rapes you escaped, three men at a time and never the same three. She broke. She lives simply now on what he allowed her to keep. She's become agoraphobic, so afraid of the outside world she never leaves her little bungalow."

When Sara drank some coffee, the mug rattled against her teeth.

"I don't know what outrages the other two wives were subjected to," Jane said. "But even with his first, Simon didn't need her money. He was already an entrepreneur with a few highly profitable businesses, largely because of his connections with people in positions of power."

Sara folded her hands around the warm mug and closed her eyes and seemed to be listening to the torrents of rain pummeling the house, but perhaps instead she heard only moments of the past, her ex-husband's sneering voice. In time she said, "I always knew my money was the least of it. What mattered most to him was my total mortification, my shame, my submission. That's why I think he let me live. So he can know I'm out here, changed forever and suffering."

Because Sara was smart enough to understand the implications of two final revelations, Jane gave her facts without interpretation. "Two and a half years after the divorce, his first wife treated herself to a vacation in France, accompanied by her cousin. On their third day in Paris, both women disappeared. Their remains were found two days later, in an abandoned building in an arrondissement where they would never have dared to go, where even police are reluctant to patrol because of the Iranian and Syrian gangs that operate there. They'd been robbed and beaten to death with lengths of iron pipe left at the scene. In the case of his second wife, three years after the divorce, she'd recovered enough confidence to have a boyfriend. They went hiking in Yosemite. At a point where the trail narrowed with a steep drop to one side, maybe one of them slipped over the edge. Maybe the other reached out to halt the companion's fall and was pulled off balance. However it happened, both ended up dead on the rocks three hundred feet below."

Sara seemed to want the coffee only for the warmth that the mug imparted to her hands. "So I've got six months to a year."

"Unless I kill him in self-defense or someone else kills him because of the information I'm able to pry out of him."

"I already agreed to help you."

"I know," Jane said. "I've told you this only because I want you to get more serious about carrying that concealed pistol, about your security system, about your life and how fragile it remains."

8

The rising garage sectional like a mausoleum door setting free those who had been thought dead and entombed, the sudden cataracts of rain against the windshield, the wild night of shaken trees and wet whirling leaves and wind-worked forms of mist galloping out of the west . . . All of it now became a celebration of life.

Behind the wheel of the Hyundai Santa Fe Sport, Sanjay Shukla was intoxicated by their escape but also harrowed by the recent violence. As he accelerated toward the distant gate that would swing open automatically at his approach, he switched on the headlights.

"Lights off!" Tanuja cried with such conviction that he obeyed without question. "They blocked the driveway with their SUV."

"So we pop the brake, shift it into neutral, push it aside."

"But there might be a fourth sonofabitch with it."

"Shit." Sanjay wished he'd thought to take the poisoned man's gun instead of his smartphone.

Simultaneously, he and his sister declared, "The horse gate!"

Sanjay swung the Hyundai off the pavement, left onto the front yard, and rollicked across the uneven lawn, which had been an unmown meadow of tall grass in the days when their father had kept horses.

The equine gate on the south side of the property had been a second construction entrance during the building of the house. It was wide enough for a vehicle. A simple hinged section of fencing gave access to a riding trail that wound through the eastern hills.

In the gloom, the great black limbs of the spreading oaks were unmoved by the storm, but the willowy branchlets whipped the night and cast off beetle-shaped leaves that skittered across the windshield and were flung into flight by the wipers.

The land sloped down, and below them, like the sunken ramparts of some lost city, the faint white boardwork of the ranch fencing welled out of the watery darkness.

Sanjay braked, intending to get out and release the gate, but Tanuja threw open her door—"Got it!"—and plunged into the rain.

As Sanjay watched her ghosting through the murk, Tanuja seemed small, childlike, as though the night was shrinking her, his *chotti bhenji*, his little big sister. Suddenly, he feared losing her for the first time since they'd escaped the clutches of Ashima and Burt Chatterjee to become emancipated minors by order of the court. For the seven years prior to that, they had been two against the world; and so they appeared to be again, inexplicably.

For fraternal twins, they were remarkably alike, slender but athletic, with glossy black hair and eyes darker still. Both were talented guitarists. Both were unbeatable bridge players at fourteen but grew bored with cards at eighteen, when their writing began to consume them. She would marry one day, and perhaps so would he; and while he'd be happy for her, on the day that they parted he would feel as though he'd been cleaved in half.

The gate swung open, and Tanuja returned to the Hyundai. Sanjay drove into the rugged land where the horse trail promised adventure for the equine gentry to which their parents had once belonged. He turned downhill, toward the county road, lights still off, hoping the thousand voices of wind and water would mask their engine noise, in case a guard remained in the SUV at the main gate.

"They were going to inject me. You, too, if they found you."

"I saw the syringe. But inject with what?" she asked.

"With nothing good."

"With this, whatever it is," she said, revealing two of the sleeves of silvery insulation that contained ampules, which she had evidently snatched off the table while Sanjay was crawling under it.

He said, "It's crazy, Linc Crossley being with them."

"It's just as crazy without him."

The land sloped gently westward. A narrowing of the horse trail bracketed them with weeds that tapped and scraped at the vehicle, as if with brittle fingers the resurrected residents of an ancient burial ground were protesting this intrusion on sacred soil.

"Could Ashima and Burt be part of this?" Tanuja wondered.

"What would they have to gain?"

"What little they didn't already steal from us. And revenge."

"Not after eight years. They're lucky they avoided prison, and they know it."

Out of the rain and fog and formless dark, order appeared as two parallel lines. At first pale, perhaps illusory, they acquired reality, crisp edges: the double white line defining the center of the county road.

The slope terminated in the flat expanse of blacktop. Sanjay turned left, away from their house and the SUV that blocked access to it. He braked at once, however, because a Range Rover stood across both lanes, leaving too little room to drive past it either fore or aft. The headlights were not on, but the blinkers silvered the falling rain in front of it and bloodied the rain behind.

Doors opened and two men got out of the vehicle, shadowy figures, solemn and methodical and unhurried, like those who had forced their way into the house.

Sanjay shifted into reverse, backed up at speed, wheeled hard right, fishtailed the Hyundai 180 degrees, braked, shifted into drive, switched on the lights, and fled north, past the SUV blocking their driveway. The road dead-ended in a turnaround, where the fall-off from the pavement was so gentle that there were no guardrails.

"They have all-wheel drive like we do," Tanuja warned.

"But maybe not nerve enough," Sanjay said as they crossed the graveled shoulder and angled down a weeded slope, broomstraw and brambles shredding against the undercarriage.

The mist thickened in the realm below, born out of

the depths, and in its ascent was shaped by the wind into stampeding forms that flung themselves at the Hyundai and flared around it. Phalanxes of eucalyptuses stood guard against descent, penetrated by the herded fog but seemingly impenetrable to all else.

Having walked the land for years, Sanjay knew the architecture of earth, rock, and flora. To him, this wilderness wasn't wild, but a palace of elegant chambers and passageways. He steered between jambs of rock, across a canted threshold of stone, onto a slope of rain-jeweled ribbon grass, and toward the trees, as if the wall they presented was as insubstantial as the fog that seethed between them.

"Sanjay, no," Tanuja warned as he maintained speed.

"Yes."

"Yes?"

"Yes."

"*Jhav!*" she cried, an obscenity he had never before heard her use in any language. She braced herself for impact.

At the last moment, he thought he'd angled toward the wrong point in the tree line, but then the unbroken rampart of forest was revealed to be an illusion. The trees to the left were older growth, twenty feet downhill from the younger specimens to the right; the distance differential made them appear the same size and age, and the abrupt drop in the land hid the truth that one long phalanx was in fact two. The Hyundai plunged. Sanjay swung the vehicle hard to the right. It didn't roll. He drove behind the younger stand of eucalyptus, which was a natural windbreak, three trees deep, rather than a full forest. He continued north along a narrow escarpment, trees to the right, a black void to the left where the land descended—more steeply now—three or four hundred feet to the canyon floor.

They'd had no option other than an off-road escape, but he knew that this escarpment narrowed until it terminated in an out-fold of canyon wall. They needed to go down into less hospitable territory.

Twin luminous globes appeared behind them, haloed in the mist, shimmering witchily in the rain, nothing of their source revealed, like some otherworldly visitation, but of course they were the headlights of the Range Rover.

Sanjay wheeled the Hyundai off the ridge line, into the void.

9

Gaining Sara Holdsteck's trust had taken Jane Hawk much longer than she would require to get answers to the few essential questions that she had come there to ask.

She popped a pill with her coffee.

Sara raised her eyebrows.

"Acid reducer," Jane explained.

"Taken with black, black coffee."

"Coffee doesn't reflux on me. The mess the world's in, the arrogant elitists who screwed it up, who believe in nothing but power, like your ex-husband. *That's* the acid, why I need this."

"You have an extra one of those?"

Jane shook a tablet from the bottle and passed it across the table. "So Simon occupies the house you used to own."

Sara swallowed the pill. "I hear he has a live-in hottie."

"I know about the hottie. But there are some things about the house I couldn't get from research. I need you to tell me."

"Anything. Whatever. But . . . maybe it's time I knew your name."

"Elizabeth Bennet," Jane lied.

"Like in *Pride and Prejudice*."

"Is it?"

"Do you sometimes go as Elizabeth Darcy?"

Jane smiled. "Not that I recall."

"All right, Lizzy. What do you want to know about the house?"

A few minutes later, Jane changed the subject. "I also need some info about certain of his personal habits."

When a sudden acceleration of wind drove raindrops against the house with the hard snap of a nail-gun barrage, Sara didn't startle as before or glance at the blinded windows. In a quiet, steady voice she spoke dispassionately about Simon Yegg, apparently now convinced there was a chance that some justice would be settled upon him.

Jane's last item concerned family. "You ever meet his brother?"

"Simon has a brother?"

"A half brother. Same mother, different fathers."

"His dad died when Simon was eight, his mom six years later."

"No. She divorced the father. He later died in a fire. Mother's not dead."

"Damn. Did the man never say a word of truth?"

"His tongue's not made for it. You know a Booth Hendrickson?"

"Never heard of him."

"He's the half brother. Born in Florida. Raised in Nevada, California. Tall. Salt-and-pepper hair. Pale green eyes. Talks like he's Boston Society. Five-thousand-dollar suits."

"Rings no bell."

"He's very high up in the Department of Justice. Only a couple rungs below the attorney general. Through a network of associates, he seems to have a lot of power in other agencies."

Sara digested that revelation. Her souring expression suggested that she might be glad to have taken the pill Jane had given her. "Other agencies? Like the IRS?"

"Not just the IRS. He's a unique cross-agency player."

"What—he and Simon ruin naïve women and split the proceeds?"

"I doubt Hendrickson wants a dime. He does it for his brother."

"How touching."

"They have different last names. They don't advertise their relationship. Hendrickson has much bigger interests of his own that he wouldn't want compromised by Simon. But they're close, and I was able to link them."

"You said you're after Simon because of who he hangs with. You mean Hendrickson?"

"Yeah. I'm going to get at Hendrickson through Simon. After Hendrickson . . . others just as corrupt as those two." Jane got to her feet and picked up the Heckler and holstered it. "It'll be best for you if you never tell anyone about me or what we discussed."

"Who would I tell? I don't trust anyone anymore."

"That'll change if you let it. You're smarter now about who might be rotten. Just remember the pistol rig, a new security code."

"Code tonight. The rig tomorrow. I won't be going to Paris, either. Or Yosemite."

Jane went to the back door that led to a patio.

Behind her, Sara said, "Oh, my God."

Jane turned. She saw in the woman's face something that was disconcertingly like awe.

"I know who you are. Black hair, not blond. Black eyes, not blue. But it's you."

"I'm nobody."

Sara didn't say that Jane, once a decorated FBI agent, was now at the top of the Bureau's most-wanted list, the object of a media frenzy. She pointed to the banner headline on the *Los Angeles Times*. "There's no truth in the news, is there? Not about you, not about anything. We're living in a world of lies."

"There's always truth, Sara. Under an ocean of deceit, there's truth just waiting."

The woman's weariness gave way to an earnest look, to an air of edgy enthusiasm that troubled Jane. "Whatever they've done, you're taking it to them. Whatever they're hiding, you're digging it up." She rose from her chair. "People, some people anyway, sense we're being manipulated about what to think of you, but we don't know why they want you to be so hated. I wish . . . wish I had what you have, could do what you're doing."

"I'm nobody," Jane repeated, though not in the interest of denying her identity. "I could be dead tomorrow. If not tonight."

"You won't be, though. Not you."

The fervor in the woman's voice, a shining something in her eyes, chilled Jane for reasons she could not entirely understand.

"Yes, me," she said. "Dead sooner than later. Or something worse than dead."

To discourage a response, she stepped outside with her last word and closed the door. She crossed the concrete patio, hurried alongside the house and into the street, toward the car that she'd parked a block and a half away.

The singular chill persisted in her bones, colder than the late-March rain. She cast a shadow under the streetlamps, which was good. The sharp wind stung her face, and the blown rain blurred her vision, which was also good. The darkness—that of the lowering storm clouds and especially that of the star-shot sky fixed eternal above the storm—made her feel small and fragile, which was both good and right.

10

They switchbacked down the canyon slope at precarious angles more felt than seen, in a mist that curdled and became less animate as the wind diminished with their altitude and as the walls of the declivity drew closer on both sides. The special off-road tires churned through sodden weeds and sandy mud, spun and slid sideways on wet layered shale that splintered and sluiced out from under the Santa Fe Sport. Storm runoff followed ancient channels, foaming torrents that, in the crossing, surged against the wheels as though to tip the Hyundai out of Sanjay's control and roll it into ruin. Where there was no shale or stone of any kind, he feared that the hundreds of feet of compacted soil, saturated by hours of relentless rain, would begin to move under their vehicle like an immense beast from a thousand millennia in the past, avalanching them into the lower darkness and burying them there beyond all possibility of escape or rescue.

Despite the focus demanded of him by the terrain

and weather, from time to time Sanjay glanced up-slope, or Tanuja encouraged him to do so, and always above them, finding its way toward them, was the Range Rover with its sinister passengers. If their pursuers were not drawing steadily closer, neither were they falling much behind. As he could see them by the lights that guided them, so the lights of the Hyundai encouraged their pursuit.

When the gauntlet of trees and brush and mud and rushing water had been navigated, they arrived at the canyon's bottom, where thousands of storm spates converged to form a temporary brown river surging and tossing southward. Sanjay switched off the head-lights before turning in the same direction that the river raced.

"Maybe they'll think we went north," he said.

"They won't," Tanuja disagreed, although she was not by nature a pessimist. "Without headlights, we'll have to go slower. They'll catch us sooner."

"I don't intend to go slower, Tanny," he assured her.

In the formation of the river, the descending water had washed debris from its banks, even objects as large as rotting sections of long-fallen trees, which tumbled and wallowed along in the filthy currents. Furthermore, over many thousands of years and countless storms, the land here had been smoothed until the banks, short of flood tide, were almost as navigable as causeways.

Although the Hyundai could no longer be seen by those farther up the canyon wall, Sanjay was at first all but blind, the way ahead obscure. The brown water was dimly visible on their right because of its agitation and its freight of pale flotsam, but also because its churning generated lush garlands of vaguely phosphorescent foam that flowered upon it and gave definition to its sinuous form.

"We'll leave tire tracks in the soft earth," Sanjay said, "but in this rain, those ought to wash away in a minute or two. And where there's scree instead of mud, we won't leave tracks at all. They'll have to go slower than they want, looking for where we might have turned away from the river and gone uphill again."

"Suddenly you've got a *chaska* for danger," Tanuja said.

"I've got no taste for it at all," he objected. "But I sure am obsessed with staying alive."

11

Waiting for the heater to bake the chill out of her bones, Jane Hawk sat behind the wheel of her Ford Explorer Sport, staring at a nightscape distorted by rain shimmering down the windshield. Through that fluid lens, the streetlamps appeared to quiver, receding like great scaffold-mounted torches along some shadowy road that led to Death and onward to Damnation.

She had purchased her current vehicle from an all-cash black-market dealer who worked out of a series of barns on a former horse ranch near Nogales, Arizona. The Explorer Sport had been stolen in the United States and reworked in Mexico, where among other improvements it had been given a purpose-built 825-horsepower 502 Chevy engine.

If you had to go on the run, hunted by law-enforcement and national-security agencies at the federal, state, and local level, it paid to have been an FBI agent who had learned how various criminal enterprises operated and where to find them.

At Jane's request, the navigation system had been stripped from the Explorer. If those searching for her got a lead on the vehicle, a GPS would give them her location with such specificity, mile by mile, that they could take her as elegantly as a bird of prey snatching a field mouse from a meadow. To avoid carrying other locaters, she had no smartphone and no computer.

The hot air streaming from the dashboard vents warmed her but failed to alleviate the deeper chill, which wasn't physical. It had gripped her when Sara Holdsteck regarded her with fervent admiration if not even reverence.

Jane didn't want to be anybody's hero. She had undertaken this fight for two selfish reasons: to restore her husband's reputation, because Nick had *not* committed suicide as the evidence indicated; and to save the life of her only child, five-year-old Travis, who'd been threatened when her investigation of Nick's death led to the discovery of a conspiracy in some of the highest offices of government and industry. The roots of that cabal spread day by day through a nation of people unaware of their extreme peril.

She had accepted that she might die during this endeavor. Even if she exposed and destroyed the conspiracy, she'd almost certainly afterward be murdered as a matter of revenge. Her enemies were people of great power and wealth, unaccustomed to defeat, and they would not endure it with grace. Travis was hidden away with friends, where he wasn't likely to be found; were she to be killed, he would be raised with love and proper guidance.

Her chances of survival, slim as they were, depended on staying tightly focused, on keeping her purpose narrow and her motivation personal, proceeding with confidence tempered by humility. Although the future of freedom hung in the balance, she was no Joan of Arc and didn't want to be weighed down by a grand obligation like the one that had inspired the Maid of Orleans, at the insistence of adoring crowds, to put on armor and pick up a sword. Charismatic crusaders of that kind were doomed even in triumph, destroyed by exalted ambition if not by pride. And what Jane's enemies could do to her, if they brought her down, would be far worse than being burned alive at the stake.

She turned on the windshield wipers and drove away from the curb. A difficult task awaited her, and time was running out.

12

The dreary rain like a forewarning of despair to come, the claustrophobic closed-coffin darkness of the night, the half-seen python-muscled river in its serpentine flow to the right of them like some pagan god of fate whose forward slithery rush compelled them to follow, heedless of all consequences . . .

Tanuja Shukla made no claim to psychic powers. The future was as unknown to her as to anyone. But as they neared the southern end of the canyon, where the surging cataracts would flood between the piers of a bridge and under the county road, the exhilaration of their apparent escape gave way to a vague presentiment of disaster.

Sanjay's strategy seemed to have worked. The imprudent speed with which he'd driven headlong into the gloom had brought them a few rocky moments when the ground under the Hyundai had become briefly treacherous, when they were startled by massive entanglements of tumbleweed and other loose brush, as big as the SUV itself, that blew down from higher ground and against the vehicle with a skreak and clatter as of some beast born of myth and mist. But for several minutes now, the headlights of the Range Rover had not cleaved the night and rain behind them. Their pursuers evidently had turned away from the river to follow a false trail or had fallen so far behind that turnings in the land concealed them.

Yet as Sanjay drove out of the mouth of the canyon, up a slope of gravel, onto the county road, and turned right onto the bridge, Tanuja braced herself for a crisis. It arrived at once in the form of a big Chevrolet crew-cab pickup jacked on outsized tires.

They were headed west, and the truck came from that direction. They had every reason to expect that it would cruise past them, driven by someone as innocent as they were. Instead, it angled to a stop on the bridge approach. The back doors on both sides were flung open, and men jumped out into the rain.

There was no turning back into the canyon. Nor could they do a 360, because less than two miles to the east lay the dead end and the house that they had so recently fled.

If Sanjay had slowed in the face of this emerging threat, they would have been lost. But even as the pickup skidded to a stop and the doors began to open, he accelerated. The Santa Fe Sport shot forward, and for one mad instant, Tanuja thought her brother meant to ram the Chevy head-on.

The man who jumped down from the starboard side of the truck held a shotgun in his right hand. He looked surprised to see their Hyundai rocketing toward him, his face pale and wide eyes glittering with reflections of their headlights. He wasn't fast enough to bring up the shotgun in a two-hand grip and wasn't smart enough to fling himself out of harm's way. The Hyundai clipped the open door, and the door checked the gunman hard, knocking him off his feet and backward as they careened past.

"Holy shit!" Tanuja declared on impact.

The Chevy blocked too much of the roadway, and Sanjay could not get past it on the pavement. He steered down a graveled slope, the angle of descent seeming even more severe than it was because they had lost one headlight in the collision, the single remaining beam lending a cockeyed aspect to all that lay before them. He fought the steering wheel as the back end of the Hyundai slid clockwise. With the vehicle horizontal to the shoulder of the highway above them, at a scary slant that encouraged Tanuja to brace herself in expectation of a roll, Sanjay drove west across the face of the incline, well past the pickup, perhaps out of shotgun range, before angling uphill and returning to the blacktop.

Tanuja looked at the starboard mirror as her brother glanced at the rearview. Speaking over each other, she said, "Here they come, here they come!" as he said, "We can outrun a freaking crew-cab pickup!"

"They're just letting that guy lie there on the road," she said. "Maybe he's dead."

"He's not dead," Sanjay said.

"The door hit him hard."

"Not that hard."

"I don't care if he's dead. He was going to shoot us."

"Who are these crazy bastards?"

"*Rakshasa*," Tanuja said, referring to a race of demons from Hindu mythology, an element of fantasy she had used in a novelette.

"Hoods, goons, torpedoes," Sanjay said, "but working for who, doing what, *why us*?"

"And how the hell did they know where we'd come out of the canyon?"

Bullets of rain fragmented off the windshield as the Santa Fe Sport topped ninety miles per hour and, even with all-wheel drive, seemed to risk hydroplaning off the rain-swept blacktop.

They were still in a rural area, but the road undulated and curved through a miles-long downgrade toward the densely populated lowlands of Orange County. The crew-cab pickup had ceased falling farther behind but wasn't gaining, either, when in the distance a pulsing light quickened out of the dark and mist, the source hidden beyond the far fall of the highway, at first as eerie as an alien close encounter à la Spielberg: white and red, red and blue, white and red. . . .

"Hey, cops!" Sanjay said. "We're okay, Tanny. It's the cops."

"Lincoln Crossley's the cops, a sheriff's deputy, same thing," said Tanuja, and she remembered Linc temporarily rendered sightless by insecticide and firing his gun blindly even though he'd been as likely to hit his two companions as to kill either her or Sanjay. She groaned as a patrol car topped the distant rise, the lightbar on its roof flaring brighter. The siren could now be heard even over the roar of rain and engine. "We are so screwed."

"We aren't screwed," Sanjay disagreed.

"We are so screwed."

"What do you know? You write hopeful fantasy,

magic realism, whatever. *I'm* the noir guy, and I say we're not screwed."

"*Chodu*," she said.

"We are not *chodu*."

"We are so *chodu*," she insisted as the siren swelled louder.

13

The storm relented from a downpour to a fitful drizzle by the time Jane parked around the corner and almost two blocks from her destination in the city of Orange. She walked from there, carrying a zippered tote bag.

If the authorities ever made a connection between her and the metallic-gray Explorer, a vehicle description would be put on the National Crime Information Center website, with an alert to every law-enforcement agency in the nation. Thereafter, she would be in constant jeopardy while driving it. She would need two or three days to get new license plates and a DMV registration from her current source for forged documents in Reseda, north of Los Angeles; it might be safer to abandon the SUV than to use it during the interim between an NCIC listing and the receipt of new plates and documents.

Better, instead, to be discreet, to park out of any line of sight from the place she intended to visit. The guy she needed to see wasn't part of the conspiracy against which she'd set herself. She didn't expect him to betray her. But like snakes molting out of their old skins, people so often shed her expectations of them that she had learned to be ready for anything.

The building was as she remembered it: flanked by parking lots, presenting an imposing two-story Southern Classic Revival face of white-painted brick with raised portico, balustrade, and tapered columns. At nine o'clock, cars stood in both parking lots.

Avoiding the front entrance, she went around the west side of the establishment, where the grand façade gave way to the stucco so prevalent in Southern California that it suggested the primary goals of local architecture must be impermanence and ease of eventual demolition. At the back of the property was a wide detached garage with four roll-ups. Between the structures lay a motor courtyard.

The main building featured an ordinary back entrance, but also a pair of sliding doors behind which lay a freight elevator that was accessible only with a code entered in a keypad. She tried the door at the stoop and found that she didn't need her lock-release gun.

She stepped into a vestibule. A door directly ahead of her would open to a ground-floor hallway, where there would be people whom she didn't want to encounter. She tried the door on the left. Stairs led to the second floor.

Behind the door on the right were stairs to the basement. She descended quickly.

She came into a long corridor. A series of flush-set

eighteen-inch-diameter frosted-glass lenses shed a cold white light with a faint blue tint. The white walls were of a smooth, glossy laminate. Shiny gray vinyl served as flooring and baseboard, curving up to meet the walls. The space had a science-fiction-y feel, as if she'd entered a time tunnel or an interstellar vessel.

The freight elevator access to this level was on her right.

She opened the door across the hall from the elevator, switched on the lights, saw a dead man, and went into that room.

14

As in a vivid but incomprehensible nightmare, the relentless pursuers came from behind them like a demonic posse with a death warrant, and police raced head-on toward them, the modulated siren shrilling. The land was still lonely and forbidding on both sides of the highway. The rain abruptly diminished as though a long drumroll had ended and the pending event to which it called attention would now occur.

Sanjay respected the police and prided himself on remaining calm in difficult situations, but twenty-five years of experience had not prepared him for a night when known reality dropped out from under him as if it had been a trapdoor. Although it wasn't like him to rely on intuition rather than reason, he sensed that the insanity would only escalate from here.

"Hold on," he warned Tanuja as, in the headlights, wet pavement glistened toward a crossroads. He pumped the brakes, made a hard right turn onto the new two-lane, nearly spun out, oriented the Hyundai, and accelerated.

"What are we doing?" his sister asked.

"I don't know."

"Where are we going?"

"I'll know it when I see it."

"Will *I* know it when you see it?"

"Someplace we can get off the road, out of sight."

The blacktop wove through low hills and vales of ancient live oaks immense and spreading, dark and dripping. Numerous curves, in conjunction with the trees, repeatedly screened their SUV from those in pursuit of them.

Although Sanjay knew this back road well, he couldn't think of a bolt-hole anywhere along its course. He was a guy who could focus as tightly as a laser, but he was first to admit he was a poor multitasker. He saw no need to chew gum and play basketball at the same time. He didn't even *like* basketball. He could pilot the Santa Fe Sport at high speed along wet pavement, through treacherous curves, with confidence, monitoring pursuers in the rearview and side mirrors, but an answer to the question *Where next?* eluded him.

As always, Tanuja was a critical component in the two-piece puzzle that was the Shukla twins. She said, "We're coming up on Honeydale Stables. That's the place."

"That's the place," he agreed.

And here came the turnoff to their right, a single-lane driveway of cracked and potholed blacktop lined with oaks, bisecting a once-rich meadow gone to weeds, flanked by ranch fencing collapsed in places by the work of termites, rot, and dry rot.

Sanjay hung a right, killed the headlights. He let their speed fall without using the brakes, and avoided revealing their position with a red flush of taillights in case their pursuers might be closer than he believed they were.

After about thirty yards, the private lane descended, and they were beyond view of the highway behind them, coasting into a valley that lay in a moonless, starless murk. The dilapidated fencing and colonnade of oaks guided them in the gloom, and the wild grass to both sides was not as dark as the pavement.

They passed near the ruins of the once-great house in which the owners had perished in a fire three years earlier: a rubble of broken masonry and infallen timbers. Two stone fireplaces with chimneys stood largely unscathed, oddly threatening in the night, like shrines to a primitive god that had slaughtered his own idolaters.

Wind had been at work on the night of the fire. Flames jumped to the extensive stables, and more than half were destroyed. The owners' breeding horses and the horses of others who'd paid to board their mounts at Honeydale were saved by the ranch manager, but the business died with its owners. After a contentious battle between heirs, the estate was eventually settled, but though the property had been on the market for a year, it hadn't yet sold.

Sanjay drove behind one of the intact stables and parked and switched off the engine. "When they realize they've lost us, they won't backtrack to look. They'll figure we're long gone."

Tanuja rolled down her window. The rain had stopped. The wind had died. Cool night air brought with it a faint scent of char that the recent downpour had stirred from a half-collapsed stable nearby, but she heard neither a siren in the distance nor the growl of engines.

"Who'll believe us, Sanjay?"

"Not the sheriff. Something's corrupt there."

Referring to their parents, Tanuja said, "That's why dear *Baap* and *Mai* left India, so much corruption there, why they brought us here so long ago. I still miss them every day."

Sanjay agreed. "I always will."

The world lay in eclipse under the shrouded sky, and a palpable night tide seemed to pour through the open window, pooling thickly in the Hyundai. Sanjay felt strangely as if he were breathing both air and darkness, but exhaling only air.

"Maybe the sheriff isn't rotten," Tanuja said, "just some of his deputies."

"Or maybe he *is* rotten."

"Most cities in the county have their own police."

"But we don't live in one of those cities."

"Well, we have to go to *somebody*."

Although Sanjay had not started the SUV, although neither he nor his sister had touched any control, the computer screen in the dashboard brightened, startling them. The navigation system became active. A map appeared. It featured a thick serpentine line labeled with the route number of the county road they had recently departed. Leading off the thick line, a thinner one wasn't labeled, although it could be nothing but the private driveway leading to Honeydale Stables. On the map, a red indicator blinked at the end of the driveway and to one side of it, where the Hyundai currently stood.

"What's happening?" Tanuja asked.

Sanjay threw open the driver's door and got out. He took a few steps forward to stand by the front bumper, listening to a stillness disturbed only by the arrhythmic ticking of the cooling engine, the dripping rainwater from saturated trees, and the occasional haunting question of an owl.

As his sister exited the passenger door, Sanjay looked up at the sky, wondering. If someone knew the registration number of this vehicle and therefore was able to obtain the unique signal that its locater broadcast as part of its navigation system, could that someone find them? Did the vehicle's transponder continue to transmit even when the engine was off? Could a satellite serving their navigation system "see" them by that transmission, and could their GPS be switched on remotely to taunt them? He didn't know the answers. But the glowing screen in the dashboard seemed to say, *You can't hide.*

He heard an engine in the distance. More than one.

Tanuja looked at him across the hood of the SUV. "Sanjay?"

As the engine noise grew louder, he hurried around the front of the Hyundai and grabbed his sister's hand. *"Run!"*

15

The cool air carried on it an astringent chemical odor, and under that a fainter and less pleasant organic smell on which Jane chose not to dwell.

The slightly tilted stainless-steel table with blood gutters had been used and methodically scrubbed clean. It stood empty now, as was the clear-plastic collection reservoir under it.

The decedent had been transferred to a second steel slab, this one without gutters, where he lay naked under a white shroud that exposed only his neck and head, and one arm that had slipped out from under the sheet and hung off the table. The hard, pitiless light rendered every enlarged pore as a crater, every wrinkle as a crevasse, so that his pale face had the texture and contours of a track of desert tortured by heat, eroding wind, and tectonic forces. He would look much better in the morning, after the esthetician had painted a semblance of life and an illusion of sleep over his grim features.

Attached to the foot of the table was a file holder.

She found a photograph of the deceased as he had been when alive and healthy, a guide for the esthetician. His name was on the back of the photo: Kenneth Eugene Conklin.

She returned the file to the holder and placed a call with her disposable phone.

In a viewing room upstairs in the funeral home, the proprietor answered. "Gilberto Mendez."

"You once said you'd die for my husband if it came to that. No need to die, he beat you to it, but I could use a little help."

"My God, where are you?"

"Keeping company with Kenneth Conklin."

"I don't believe this."

"I'd put him on the line to vouch for me, but Ken's in a funk."

"I'll be right there."

When Gilberto came through the door a minute later, dressed in a black suit and white shirt and black tie, he looked twenty pounds heavier than he'd been two years earlier, but still in good shape. He had a round, brown, pleasant face. His wife, Carmella, called it a gingerbread man's face. At thirty-six, with receding hair, he'd begun to resemble the father from whom he'd inherited the business.

Closing the door behind him, referring to Jane's jet-black hair and dark eyes, he said, "You aren't you at all."

"It's just a wig, colored contacts, and attitude."

"Well, you've always had attitude."

He came to the farther side of the table, the dead

man between them, and Jane said, "How're you doing, Gilberto?"

"Happier than I deserve to be."

"Makes me feel good just to hear that."

"We're having our fourth baby in June."

"Another girl?"

"A boy. God help him, with three older sisters."

"Like having three guardian angels."

"Maybe you're right."

Jane indicated the graven face of the man on the table. "At your dad's funeral two years ago, you said you were going to sell the business."

When Gilberto smiled, he looked boyish, sweet. Even then, his eyes were the saddest Jane had ever seen.

"I joined the Marines to escape this," Gilberto said. "But the way it turned out, this work is a calling, not just a business. My dad said what it's about, above all else, is preserving the dignity of the dead, about not letting death rob them of it. That didn't make sense to me then. After I'd been to war, it did."

With tenderness, as if he were a nurse and the decedent a sick friend, he lifted the uncovered arm onto the table and pulled the shroud over it.

He said, "Nick never would've killed himself."

"He didn't."

"So this mess you're in, it's because you want the truth."

"I've learned the truth about Nick. It's way beyond that now."

"The things they say about you on the news—

murder, selling national secrets, treason—no one who knows you would believe it."

"There's not much news in the news anymore. The lies they tell don't leave a lot of time for the facts about anything."

"Whose rocks did you overturn?"

She said, "Some of them are in government, some in private industry. They play a lot of the media like so many harmonicas."

From the moment Gilberto had mentioned Carmella's pregnancy, Jane had not been able to stop thinking about the wife, the three young daughters, and the boy waiting to be born.

She said, "You've got so many responsibilities. I never should have come here. I better go."

In a quiet voice, almost a murmur, suited to conversation with grieving loved ones in the viewing rooms on the main floor, he said, "How's your boy, how's Travis?"

After a silence, she said, "He's struggling with the loss of Nick. But he's safe, hidden away with people who care about him."

"It's necessary to hide him, is it?"

"To stop me from investigating all this, they threatened to kill him. But they'll never get their hands on him. Never."

When Jane picked up her tote bag to leave, Gilberto said, "Why do you think *semper fi* doesn't mean anything to me anymore?"

"That's not what I think, Gilberto."

"Always faithful means *always* faithful, not just when it's convenient."

"Family first," she said. "Be faithful to your family."

"Nick was family. Like a brother. I wouldn't be here today if not for him. Makes you family, too. Put down the tote. Respect me enough to tell me what you need from me. If it's too damn crazy, if it's jumping off a cliff, I'll say no."

She did not put down the tote bag. "I was going to ask you to pose as a chauffeur and drive a car."

"What else?"

"We'd be kidnapping this creep who works in the Department of Justice. My only remaining lead. He surfaced in the attack that killed the governor of Minnesota last week. I learned he's coming here when I back-doored the computer of his brother's limo company. He has information I'm going to have to break him to get, but I don't need you for that. You pick him up as if you're his assigned chauffeur, you drive him to me, you leave. That's it—if all goes well. Which maybe it won't."

He said, "I'm a good driver. Never had a ticket."

"Kidnapping, Gilberto. They put you away for a long time."

"I'll just be driving. Playing a chauffeur—a piece of cake. Part of what I already do is be a chauffeur. I drive the hearse."

16

The California live oaks didn't grow close enough together to constitute a forest, but their crowns were of such immense diameter that across the vale and up a long slope, the figuration of their massive limbs arched over Tanuja and Sanjay like the vaulted ceiling of some elaborate nature-built cathedral in which the god Pan might come upon them, goat-legged and horned, playing his panpipes.

But as they hurried away from Honeydale Stables, the closest thing to music was the singing of countless tree frogs that, in Tanuja's estimation, was ominous as never before. Such frogs always celebrated following a rainstorm, but they were acutely aware of intruders in their realm and fell silent during the passage of any human being. This chorus, an almost frenzied jubilation and not once interrupted, seemed to suggest that nature and her creatures knew that the Shukla twins were so soon to be dead that they were already hardly more than spirits and of no concern.

The blessing of a writer's imagination was also a curse.

With only wild grass and no deep brush to hamper them, on terrain presenting no foot-twisting fissures, they were restrained from a flat-out run only by the darkness and the fear of falling off an unseen edge. They reached the top of the ridge in good time and paused and looked back to the south, high enough to see over the trees. For a long moment, gasping for breath, they stared at two sets of headlights in the distance, neither pair of beams currently on the move, both focused on what must have been the Hyundai Santa Fe Sport that they had abandoned.

"Who *are* they?" she wondered.

"Not just sheriff's deputies. Someone bigger wants us."

"Bigger who? Wants us *for what*?"

"Damn if I know, Tanny. But we've got to keep moving."

Together they turned from the southern vista. North-northeast, beyond another ridge, the darkness relented to an eerie light, in fact three conjoined and distorted bubbles of light—one blue, one red, one yellow. The blue like a gas flame but constant in shade and brightness. The red not reminiscent of fire, but intense and darkish and steady like the ruby color of a lit glass cup on a votive-candle rack. A canted brim of canary yellow, as if the blue and red were borne on it like the twin crowns of a tipped hat.

For a moment, it seemed to Tanuja that she was being drawn through this extraordinary and fearsome night toward some ultimate mystery and revelation, as might be a mystified character in one of the stories in her preferred genre of magic realism. But then she realized from where the lights arose. She said, "It's neon glow from Coogan's Crossroads."

The Crossroads was a restaurant, but less a restaurant than a tavern, and less a tavern than a tradition, the iconic gathering place to which the residents of the smattering of tiny communities in the remote east-county canyons were drawn for companionship, especially on weekend nights like this.

"Probably half a mile," Sanjay said.

"We can get help there."

"Maybe," Sanjay said. "Maybe."

"There's sure to be at least a couple people we know."

"We knew Lincoln Crossley—or thought we did."

"The whole world can't have been corrupted, Sanjay. Come on."

With the threat of their pursuers no longer immediate, they descended the ridge, angling north-northeast toward the neon aurora, adopting a less reckless pace overland now that they had a place to go and the hope of help. The clouds were slowly unraveling. Through the ragged rents and thinning veils came a suggestion of moonlight. The only thing that could go wrong now—or so it seemed—was for one of them to stumble in the gloom and fall and break a leg. Sanjay held Tanuja's left arm as together they proceeded with caution.

17

Maybe they kept the dead man between them because Jane still had second thoughts about involving this father of four in such a dangerous enterprise, and because Gilberto, for all his talk of *semper fi* and a debt owed to Nick, had doubts of his own.

Solemn and silent on the table, the decedent was a barrier to impetuous action, a reminder that they might die in the course of a kidnapping. Jane's love for Nick was so intense that his death had not diminished it, and though Gilberto's gratitude and admiration were less piercing emotions, Jane's late husband served as a touchstone by which they both could test their commitment to what was good and true in a world of darkness and lies. But a touchstone had value only if they acted with reason, from a sense of duty, rather than because sentimentality overtook them. Jane knew—perhaps, so did Gilberto—that a touch, a hug, even a handshake in the early minutes of this reunion could twist honest sentiment into sentimentalism, inciting him to make a fateful decision on the wrong grounds.

"I appreciate you'd do this just for me," she said, "just for Nick. But if they discover you helped me, they won't care that all you did was drive. They'll take you out. You need to understand what they've done, what they want to do, how much they have to lose."

She looked at the dead man's face, so eggshell white after his embalming, lips fixed as if they had never formed a smile, eyelids paper thin as though half worn away by all the distressing sights against which, in life, they'd been closed. Nick had been cremated. She preferred fire, too, if after her death a body could be found.

"These bastards, this conspiracy, cabal, whatever you want to call it—they have a computer model. It identifies people likely to steer civilization in the wrong direction, people in the arts, journalism, academia, science, politics, military. . . ."

Gilberto frowned. "Wrong direction? How does a computer decide what's the wrong direction for civilization?"

"It doesn't. *They* decided when they designed the damn computer model. All it does is identify targets. They say, just erase enough carefully selected people, those likely to achieve positions to influence others with wrong ideas, then over time we'll have Utopia. But it's not about Utopia. It's all about power. Absolute power."

Gilberto had come back from war with an enduring sadness from which was born a gentleness and a desire to avoid all conflict. But anger enfolded the gentleness now, and his mouth was set tight when he said, "Just erase. *Erase.* Always the nice words for *murder.*"

"Joseph Stalin reportedly said, 'A single death is a tragedy, a million deaths is a statistic.' You have a problem with that?"

"They're gonna kill a million?"

"Eventually more. Two hundred ten thousand per generation, in the U.S. So eighty-four hundred a year."

"They told you this?"

"One of them did. You'll have to take my word for it. He's not available to confirm it. I killed him. In self-defense."

Although he'd been to war, Gilberto was shaken. War half a world away was different from battles in the streets of his own country. He put his hands on the steel table and leaned into it for support.

Jane said, "The people they kill are on something called the Hamlet list. Once they identify the targets, they go after them when they're most vulnerable. When they're away from home at a conference or traveling alone and can be drugged, sedated one way or another."

"'Sedated'?"

"They don't want it to look like murder. They sedate them and program them to commit suicide. Nick was on their Hamlet list. He cut his throat with his Marine Corps knife, his Ka-Bar, sliced so deep that he severed a carotid artery."

Gilberto stared at her for a long moment, as if to determine what brand of crazy she had embraced. "*Program* them?"

"Life is sci-fi these days, Gilberto. And it's not a feel-good family movie. You know about nanotechnology?"

"Microscopic things. Maybe machines so small they're invisible. Something like that."

"In this case, constructs made from a few molecules. Hundreds of thousands—maybe millions—suspended in a serum, injected into the bloodstream. They're brain-tropic. Once they pass through the capillary walls into brain tissue, they self-assemble into a larger network. A weblike control mechanism. Within hours, total control is effected. The subject doesn't know anything's happened. He seems himself. No one sees anything different about him. But days later, weeks, whenever, he gets a command to commit suicide . . . and obeys."

"If I didn't know you," Gilberto said, "I'd think you were a candidate for a psych ward."

"Sometimes lately, I've felt like one. Nick didn't know what he was doing. Or maybe he knew and couldn't stop himself, which makes me sick." She closed her eyes. Took a deep breath. "Suicides of successful, happy people have soared for two years, people with no history of depression, with every reason to live. Sometimes they take other people with them." She opened her eyes. "You must have seen the story about the woman in Minnesota, Teacher of the Year, not only killed herself but also the governor and forty-some others. I know for a fact she was controlled by these people, as Nick was."

"You have proof of all this?"

"Yeah. So who do I trust with it? The FBI isn't entirely corrupt, but some people in it are part of this conspiracy. Same with the NSA, Homeland Security. They're salted everywhere."

"Go to the press?"

"I tried. Thought I had a trustworthy journalist. He wasn't. I have evidence, a lot of it. But if I give it to the wrong person and he destroys it, everything I've endured has been for nothing. And there's even worse than the Hamlet list. Much worse. Not everyone they inject is programmed for suicide."

"Then what?"

"Some people under their control seem to have free will, but they don't. They're used ruthlessly. As programmed assassins. Others are flat-out enslaved and used as cheap labor."

She hated death, the thief that had robbed her of

her mother and her husband, but when she looked at the corpse between her and the mortician, the cold, wax-pale face suggested an enduring peace that might be envied by those who lived with a nanoweb woven across and through their brains.

"I've seen men guarding an estate of one of the Arcadians—as they call themselves—a pack of men in slacks and sport coats, normal at first glance, but like trained dogs, living in conditions as crowded as kennels. Their personalities and memories wiped away. No internal lives. Programmed to carry guns and provide security, to track down and kill intruders. They're like . . . machines of flesh."

If she had any doubt that he believed her, it was resolved when he made the sign of the cross.

"Machines of flesh," she repeated. "There are high-end brothels for wealthy, powerful people who fund this conspiracy. I managed to get into one—and out alive. The girls are beautiful beyond words. But they have no memories. No awareness of who they once were or of a world beyond the brothel. No hopes. No dreams. No interests except staying fit, desirable. Programmed to provide any sexual pleasure. Totally submissive. Never disobedient. No desire is so extreme they won't satisfy it. They're soft-spoken, sweet, apparently happy, but it's all programmed. They're incapable of expressing anger, sadness. Somewhere deep inside . . . what if there *is* something left in one of them, some palest shadow of real human feeling and awareness, some thread of self-respect, some fragile hope? Then her body is a prison. A life of unrelieved loneliness in a solitary hell. I've dreamed of being one of them. I wake up shaking as if with malaria. I'm not ashamed to say I'm terrified of ending like that, stripped of all free will. Because once the control mechanism assembles in the brain, there's no removing it, no way out except death."

18

A dragon's-egg moon emerged from a nest of shredding clouds harried southeast by a high wind that had no presence here at ground level. The oaks were widely separated now, each the majesty of its domain, black-limbed and cragged and crooked, like the scorched but stalwart survivors of a cataclysm, or oracles warning of some dire event impending. The land grew less hospitable to grass, and the last upslope was patterned with faint tree-cast moonshadows on a carpet of wet pebbles and scraggly clumps of flattened sedge.

In spite of the inexplicable danger in which Tanuja and her brother found themselves, she could not help but see the story potential in this bizarre situation. Even as she hurried toward the crest of the last hill, a novel was germinating, a contemporary take on "Hansel and Gretel," a brother and sister transported from the primeval woods of Germany to the semi-desert wildlands of Southern California, their adversary not a witch who lived in a house made of bread and cake, but instead some fearsome sect or wicked fellowship. What she had always liked most about Hansel and Gretel was that they kicked ass; after Gretel shoved the witch into the oven and bolted it shut, she and Hansel filled their pockets with the vicious hag's fortune of pearls and jewels.

Gasping for breath, she and Sanjay reached the crest, where the source of the red, blue, and yellow auras that drew them through the darkness now flared bright below them. The sole structure in sight, a commercial building made to resemble a log house, advertised itself with a double row of neon tubes around the roofline; and in the enormous sign at the front, the words COOGAN'S CROSSROADS blazed within the glowing outline of a giant cowboy hat.

At least twenty vehicles were parked in front of and beside the establishment. Faint country music found its way into the night from a barroom jukebox.

Tanuja followed Sanjay down a slippery slope of rain-sodden half-collapsed masses of foot-snaring Aureola grass and onto the east-west two-lane that made a crossroads with a north-south route.

As they entered Coogan's parking lot, a few bars of "Macarena" by Los Del Río issued from a pocket of Sanjay's jeans, bringing him to a halt. As the ringtone repeated, he fished out the smartphone that belonged to one of the men who had invaded their house.

"Don't answer it," Tanuja warned.

"I won't," Sanjay said. "I took this so we'd eventually be able to get a lead on who they are."

"Who's calling? What's their number?"

"No ID," Sanjay said.

Although he did not accept the call, a connection was somehow effected. A long chain of binary code, like a centipede racing along a switchback path, flowed down the screen from top to bottom. The code vanished, the blue background blinked to white, and two black lines, labeled with route numbers, portrayed the crossroads at which they had arrived. A blinking red indicator could have represented nothing else but the position of the smartphone.

"Shit!" Sanjay said. "They just located us."

"How's that possible?"

"I don't know."

Tanuja looked toward the north-south route, dark at the moment and untraveled. "They'll be coming."

The building featured a plank porch elevated on two-foot log piers. Sanjay ran to it and threw the phone between two plants in a decorative fringe of cushion spurge, into the dark space far back under the porch.

Engine noise arose and swiftly grew louder. Out of the south, from the direction of the ruins of Honeydale Stables, a wash of light, undulating with the contours of the road, swelled behind a windbreak of eucalyptuses.

Tanuja and Sanjay, of the same mind without the need to speak, ran to one of the parked vehicles—a truck with a thirty-foot bed, tall slat-wood sides, and an arched canvas canopy fitted to a metal frame. They scaled the tailgate and swung into the dark cargo area, where just enough light entered to suggest that they were aboard a landscaper's truck more than half full of large ferns and Rhapis palms growing in soil-filled ten-gallon plastic nursery buckets. They crouched four feet from the tailgate, beyond where the neon radiance might reflect off their faces, the fronds of the young Australian tree ferns cascading over and around them.

A moment later, the engine noise peaked. Headlights swept the parking area, one pair and then another. First past the landscaper's tailgate was a sheriff's department cruiser, employing neither its sirens nor its lightbar, braking to a stop at the steps to the plank porch, where the yellow-striped pavement warned against parking.

Close behind the squad car came the Chevy crew-cab on jacked tires, the front passenger door caved and incompletely closed and rattling, held shut by the man riding shotgun. The pickup pulled into an empty slot between two SUVs. The driver killed the engine and got out with two other men. Evidently the injured man had been left back at the bridge to fend for himself. The driver went around the north side of Coogan's Crossroads, the other two around the south side, evidently intending to rendezvous at the back of the tavern, where there were a kitchen entrance and an emergency exit.

Two uniformed deputies got out of the cruiser and climbed the steps to the porch, stood there for a moment surveying the parking lot, and then went inside.

"We're so *chodu* if we stay here," Tanuja said just as Sanjay said, "They don't find us in there, they'll check these vehicles."

One at a time, they slipped over the tailgate and out of the landscaper's truck.

They expected to be on foot again, a dismal prospect with miles between them and any pocket of civilization in which they might be able to hide and buy time to think. Plus they would be unarmed at night in coyote country, just when those prairie wolves might venture forth, sharp-toothed and merciless, in the wake of the rain.

Then a crackle of police-band radio static drew their attention to the cruiser and alerted them that its engine was idling.

"We can't," Sanjay said.

Tanuja said, "In like three minutes they'll know we're not in Coogan's."

She hurried to the black-and-white, and Sanjay followed.

The window in the driver's door had been rolled down. The voice of a dispatcher sought assistance on an 11-80 in Silverado Canyon, whatever an 11-80 might be.

Tanuja got behind the wheel and popped the emergency brake as Sanjay slid into the other front seat. She reversed away from the tavern.

19

The unforgiving light in the windowless basement room, the air as cool as that in a meat locker, the chemical smell, the underlying odor best left unanalyzed, the funeral director's voice soft with respect and sympathy, and the settled sorrow in his eyes . . .

He repeated what she'd told him regarding anyone injected with a nanotech control mechanism. "'No way out except death'?"

By turning her words into a question, he was asking not for her to confirm the fate of those injected, but for her assurance that she truly believed, even in the face of her massed enemies and the unprecedented threat she had described, that there was a future for *her*, some way out of this other than death. If her sole hope was to save the life of her child at the cost of her own, if her truest analysis of the situation convinced her that she could bring down the conspirators only with a mortal sacrifice, she was not like the Marines with whom he had gone into battle. They had fought for their country and no less for one another, but they also had gone into every fight with the conviction that survival was likely.

As the wife of a Marine, Jane understood Gilberto's concern. A warrior couldn't be without fear, for the fearless were often also reckless, putting the mission at risk. However, neither should anyone enter combat with the expectation of certain death, because no fighter fought well in such a state of diminished spirit.

"I need to live for Travis," she said. "I *will* live for the pleasure of seeing these arrogant creeps ruined, their power ripped from them, imprisoned for life, although I'd much rather see them lined up against a wall and shot. I'm not fearless or nihilistic. I'll make mistakes. But I won't throw my life away—or yours."

"Sorry to make you say it."

"I would have done the same if I were you."

"So who's this Department of Justice guy we're kidnapping?"

"Name's Booth Hendrickson." She zippered open her tote bag and took from it a manila envelope, which she passed to Gilberto. "Study this photo till you're sure you'll recognize him, then destroy it."

"When do you need me for the job?"

"Tomorrow at ten-thirty in the morning, you'll pick him up at the private-aircraft terminal at Orange County airport."

As if the dead man's pallor were caused by what he heard being discussed, eyes closed as though in prayer, he lay between them like some priest without vestments, distressed and rendered supine by the weight of the crimes that they were confessing.

"Our hearse can't pass for a limousine," Gilberto said.

"I'll have a limo for you. His brother owns a limousine company in addition to a lot of other things. He'll feel safe getting in one of his brother's limos, with one of his brother's drivers."

She talked him through how it would be done, then took from the tote a leather shoulder rig with a weapon in the holster, a polymer-frame Heckler & Koch .45 Compact like the one she carried.

"I don't see any way you'll need a gun," she said. "But this is the devil's world, and he never rests. It has a nine-round magazine with semi-staggered ammo stacks. Allows for a nice grip."

Instead of accepting it, he said, "I have a gun of my own. I like the feel of it. I know its quirks."

"But it might be traced back to you. This one has no history. Take it. Use it if you have to."

She put the rig and pistol on the shrouded chest of the dead man. From the tote she took a spare magazine and a sound suppressor for the Heckler. She also put those on the corpse and then added a disposable phone. "You'll need a burner phone during the operation. The number for my burner is taped to the back of yours."

Gilberto said, "Even if you win some kind of safety for you and Travis . . . even then you lose."

"Maybe."

"Because you can't put the nano genie back in the bottle."

"No one could uninvent the atomic bomb, either. But here we still are."

"At least for today."

"None of us ever has more than this moment. Tomorrow becomes today, today becomes yesterday. The best I can do for my boy is give him enough todays that he can make a past for himself that will have had some meaning in it."

She zippered shut the tote bag. She came around the mortician's table and put one hand on the back of Gilberto's neck and pulled his face to hers until their foreheads touched. They stood that way in silence for a long moment. Then she kissed his cheek and left the room and left the building and went into the night, which always held the promise of being the last night of the world.

20

Tanuja was driving fast and well, not perturbed by her lack of familiarity with the vehicle. But the events of the evening were so extraordinary, whipsawing her emotions so violently, she felt almost as though reality was plastic and being remade around her, as easily as she might reimagine it in fiction, the land on both sides of the police car like a black and alien sea, the wild rolling hills not hills at all, but the humped backs of Devonian beasts swimming as they swam four hundred million years earlier.

Because he had written a few stories featuring police, Sanjay knew where to find the controls for the siren and the lightbar. Tanuja used them only in the no-passing zones, when she needed to encourage slower traffic to pull off the road and let her pass.

They dared not use the car for long, and Tanuja wanted to get as deep into the communities of west county as possible. The more populous the territory, the more options they would have, although at the moment she couldn't grasp what one of those options might be.

"We've gotta hole up tonight, think this through," Sanjay said.

"Hole up where, with whom?"

"Not friends. We don't know what we might bring down on them."

"Anyway," she said, "who do we trust? We don't even know *why*."

After a silence, Sanjay said, "Stop at the first Wells Fargo ATM. All I have is like a hundred eighty bucks. You?"

"Not a dime."

"They tracked our car's GPS. So maybe they'll also know when I use a credit card for a motel room."

"Is that possible? Tracking credit-card use in real time?"

"I don't know what's possible anymore, Tanny. It seems like any damn thing is possible. So we need as much cash as we can get."

At 8:50 P.M., after withdrawing six hundred dollars from a Wells Fargo ATM, they found an office complex in Lake Forest that provided a deserted parking lot in which they left the police cruiser. As far as they were able to tell, they abandoned the car without drawing attention to themselves.

Mottled sulfur yellow by the upwash of suburban light, rags of dark clouds unraveled across a sky in which an incomplete moon hung in a strange deformity—or so it seemed to Tanuja—as if the shadow that cloaked part of it was cast by a misshapen Earth. The stars appeared misplaced, arranged in no familiar constellations, and the concrete underfoot seemed to move ever so subtly. In a few minutes, they arrived at a major thoroughfare on which traffic flashed and growled, along which crowded a smorgasbord of fast-food restaurants and a riot of enterprises that included, half a block to their left, a motor inn that was part of a medium-priced national chain and, less than half a block to their right, a less polished motel.

Even from a distance, neither the brand name nor the generic option appealed as a refuge in which to spend the night, and in fact something about each seemed, if not sinister, at least foreboding. Tanuja assumed that this perceived menace was imaginary, a product of her anxiety and the disorientation that arose from being targeted for reasons unknown— until Sanjay said, "Even if we pay cash when we check in, I don't like this. It feels wrong. There must be somewhere else we can go."

21

From the funeral home in Orange, Jane Hawk drove south to a recently annexed portion of Newport Beach that featured several guard-gated enclaves of multimillion-dollar estates. One of these had belonged to Sara Holdsteck until her former husband, Simon Yegg, wrested it from her.

Jane parked at an all-night supermarket in an upscale shopping center. Carrying her leather tote bag, she set out on foot. The traffic whizzing past on the parkway to her left seemed like a sales-lot-in-motion for Mercedes, BMW, and Ferrari.

She walked perhaps a mile and a half along a sidewalk flanked by lush landscaping, encountering neither residences nor businesses, nor other pedestrians. There were only the imposing guardhouse gates fronting the exclusive communities and, between them, glimpses of the moon-washed canyon above which those mansions had been built.

Although the entrances appeared formidable, these communities were not surrounded by complete, uniform barriers. Each homeowner had built an enclosure—iron staves, glass panels, stone—compatible with the design of his house. Where the community's common spaces met the canyon, there was either wrought-iron fencing or nothing at all; if the canyon slope was rugged and steep, it was assumed that thieves wouldn't make the climb to burglarize a house when, should the job go wrong, the only hope of escape would be on foot.

Having left the sidewalk to proceed cautiously along the grassy crest of the canyon, guided by moonlight and, when the lunar lamp was insufficient, by a small flashlight that she hooded with one hand, Jane found an unfenced transit point between the canyon and one of the community's common areas. Less than a minute later, she was on a sidewalk again, on a street behind the guardhouse gates.

She wasn't concerned that she would be suspected of intrusion. There were more than 150 homes in the community; no single guard could be expected to recognize all the residents, not to mention houseguests. If the lone patrol car happened upon her, she would smile and wave and most likely earn a smile and a wave in return.

Thanks to Google Earth and Google Maps, she had

familiarized herself with the layout of the looping streets. She needed only a few minutes to reach the Yegg residence.

The immense Mediterranean Revival–style house was clad in limestone, featured arched windows recessed in carved-limestone surrounds, and had an entrance sheltered by a dramatic portico with massive columns supporting an elaborately detailed entablature.

She approached the front door as though she belonged there. The windows were dark.

According to Sara Holdsteck, when Simon moved in prior to their wedding, he wanted no servants in the house on weeknights or weekends. Two housekeepers worked from eight till five, Monday through Friday. It was unlikely that he would have changed this routine.

With the exception of December, on the last Friday of each month, Simon played poker with four of his friends. The game moved from one of their houses to another on an agreed-upon schedule. In March, the card game occurred elsewhere than here.

Petra Quist, the hottie who currently lived with Simon, a twenty-six-year-old blonde with blue eyes, twenty years his junior, enjoyed a girls' night out on the last Friday of the month. The photos on her Facebook page ranged from icky cute to nearly obscene and featured five other leggy, dressed-to-tease young women, her "wrecking crew," with whom she went shopping and barhopping in a limousine. Judging by the photographs, their revelries weren't hampered by a three-drink limit.

Jane pulled the trigger of the lock-release gun four times before the automatic pick threw all the pins to the shear line and the door opened. She stepped inside as the house alarm shrilled.

She had two minutes to enter the disarming code before the central station would summon the police.

When Sara had signed over the mortgage-free house to Simon, he'd made a point of telling her that he wasn't going to change either the locks or the alarm code. *Anytime you want, kitten, you come back and let yourself in and wait for me and shoot me ten times dead when I come home. Think you could do that, kitten? No, I don't think so, either. You talk big, the self-made real-estate guru, but you're just a big-mouthed bitch, a gutless pussy, a stupid skank who by dumb luck made some money. All you ever were was an okay piece of ass, and now you're past your prime in that department, way past. If you go broke and have to sell your ass, kitten, you won't get any business if you price it more than ten bucks.* Sara remembered his abusive good-bye speech almost word for word, and though more than once she thought about doing what he had dared her to do, she knew that she would ruin her life if she killed him. Or, more likely, the invitation was a trap; he would be ready for her; and she, an armed trespasser, would be shot dead. Nevertheless, his insults still stung two years later—*gutless, stupid, by dumb luck*—and it was clear to Jane that Sara, in spite of her intelligence and fortitude, had internalized those words and could not bleach them from the stained self-image with which Simon had left her.

At the security-system keypad to the left of the front door, Jane entered the four numbers that Sara had given her and pressed the asterisk. The alarm fell silent. Yegg, the arrogant bastard, in fact had so little fear of his former wife that he'd kept his promise to raise no barriers to her return.

After resetting the perimeter alarm but not the interior motion detectors, Jane began to explore the grand house.

As reported in Petra Quist's Facebook postings, the hottie and her crew "rocked the shit out of the club scene" on such nights as this. They didn't stagger home until nearly midnight, and even then reluctantly. She was never later than that, however, because her "nuclear-powered love machine," whom she identified only as Mr. Big, didn't like to come home to an empty house. According to Sara, Simon returned from poker night between twelve-thirty and one o'clock.

Jane figured she had more than an hour to determine where and how she would incarcerate Petra Quist so that she could have some quality time alone with Mr. Big, who might not be so big by the time dawn came.

22

Half a block off the main thoroughfare where traffic whisked brightly through the night, the trees stood wet of bark and dry of leaf half an hour after the passing of the storm. Nothing gurgled in the gutters any longer. The Mission of Light Church stood full of stained-glass glow, and from it issued muffled bursts of laughter and applause.

A church had not been on Sanjay's mind when he'd told his sister that there must be some place other than a motel where they could take refuge. Yet as they stood before it, the warmth of its light, the laughter, and the periodic applause seemed to promise safety. Sanjay, who wrote noir fiction and who, as a writer of conviction, therefore must believe in the essential darkness of the world and life, couldn't quite commit to this church. However, he knew that his magic-realist sister would have no problem believing that here lay safety. He set aside his doubt and bias, putting his sister's welfare first. Besides, he didn't know where else they could go.

They entered the building through one of two front doors that stood open and found the narthex deserted. Likewise, the nave offered empty pews, and no one manned the altar under an enormous white-plastic cross that was lit from within.

Children's voices came from a distance, a flutter of adult laughter, piano music, and then a chorus of youngsters singing.

Sanjay and Tanuja followed the center aisle to the crossing and stopped short of the chancel railing when they saw a bank of open doors to the left. They went to one doorway beyond which, in the north transept, an exhibition hall had been transformed into a makeshift theater.

Rows of folding chairs were occupied by as many as two hundred people. A choir of a dozen kids stood on three tiers to the right of the stage, the piano before them. On the stage were grade-schoolers in a variety of costumes, including three dressed as white rabbits.

Evidently, although Easter was almost two weeks away, they were presenting a production with a holiday theme. At least for the time being, the church had set aside such solemn considerations as crucifixion and resurrection in favor of lighter fare involving rabbits, girls dressed as daffodils, and three little boys costumed as eggs and standing in front of what might have been a papier-mâché chicken three times bigger than they were.

Sanjay saw, to the right, a hallway entrance surmounted by a sign that promised restrooms. The hall appeared to be long, as if it led to more facilities than just the men's and women's lavatories.

He took Tanuja's hand and drew her across the back of the room as music swelled and the rabbits began to caper among the daffodils. The audience was focused on the performers, but if a few shifted their attention to Sanjay and his sister, there was no reason for them to suppose that these two newcomers didn't belong here.

Beyond the restrooms were classrooms where perhaps Sunday school was held and other instructions given. At the end of the hallway, another corridor opened on the left, serving a kitchen and church offices. Last of all, they came to a large storage room with eclectic contents: janitorial equipment, including vacuum cleaners and floor buffers; twenty or more six-foot-long folding tables standing on end, securely racked; a full complement of life-size nativity-scene figures, including three wise men, camels, a cow, a couple lambs, a donkey; and numerous other items.

Sanjay led his sister inside and closed the door behind them. "We'll wait here. The play must be nearly over. They'll all be gone soon."

"You mean stay the night?"

"We have restrooms. Might be food in the kitchen, something the church staff has for lunch or snacks."

"It feels weird to stay here."

"It feels safe, Tanny."

"Yeah, well . . . it kind of does," she agreed.

"We'll have time to think, figure this out."

"But we could hide for a year and figure out nothing. And what if someone comes in here?"

"We'll tuck ourselves in behind the nativity figures. No one will see us unless they come all the way to the back of the room."

They left the light on in order to make their way through the gauntlet of stored items, and they sat on the floor, screened by heavy cast-plastic wise men and camels.

In the distance, muffled piano and choir crescendoed, and after a second of silence, the volume and duration of applause suggested the performance might have come to an end.

23

I n the parking lot of an office complex in Lake Forest, sitting behind the wheel of the abandoned patrol car, Carter Jergen imports the contents of the vehicle's camera archives into his laptop. The fore and aft recordings on police cruisers are intended to protect officers, so the department can easily disprove accusations of police brutality and misconduct of which they are not guilty.

As for the officers who recently used this cruiser, their offense is not brutality. Jergen isn't affiliated with the sheriff's department; ostensibly he works for the National Security Agency, and therefore he lacks direct authority over those deputies, although his federal credentials compel them to assist him. If he *were* the boss of them, he'd charge them with dereliction of duty—with sheer stupidity—for letting the Shukla twins steal their car.

What concerns him most is that both of the deputies who screwed up are among the adjusted people, those who have been injected with nanomachine control mechanisms, which is why they were called to support the conversion crew when everything went wrong at the Shukla house. All of them in fact are adjusted people, though they don't realize it, including Lincoln Crossley and the two men with him, who allowed themselves to be hornet-sprayed by a slip of a girl who is a foot shorter and weighs only half as much as any of them.

Recently, Jergen has begun to suspect that when the weblike control mechanism self-assembles across the brain, something of the adjusted person is lost in addition to his free will. Maybe it isn't lost at once. Maybe it fades away slowly. But it seems to Jergen that at least some of the adjusted are not as intelligent as they were before being injected.

Well, no, perhaps it's not that they're less intelligent. It is rather that the quality of their motivation has changed. They will do what they are instructed to do, but some—perhaps many—seem to lack the interest, the incentive, to do more than required.

Maybe this is not a bad thing. In his estimation, a lot of people are too smart for their own good, motivated by the wrong aspirations and desires, such as money and status and the admiration of others. The new world coming will be shaped by those who, like Carter Jergen, are most equipped to identify and correct all the errors to which human beings are so prone. It is likely the case that a fully corrected civilization can be kept stable more easily if a significant part of its population is motivated to perform only as they are instructed to perform and are shorn of any incentive to achieve more than others. The determination to achieve can, after all, lead to an inclination toward rebellion.

Bathed in the laptop's pale light, scanning through the video from the patrol car's front-facing camera, Jergen arrives at the moment when the Shukla twins walk away into the night, across the lamplit parking lot, onto the public sidewalk. They turn west and hurry out of sight, oblivious that they have left this first crumb of evidence that will make it possible for him to track them down.

Jergen switches off his laptop, closes it, gets out of the car.

Radley Dubose is waiting a few feet away, beside the Range Rover in which the two of them had unsuccessfully pursued Sanjay and Tanuja Shukla into the canyon. Radley appears angry enough and big enough to pick up the patrol car and throw it. He has a square Dudley Do-Right jaw and eyes as feverish looking as those of Yosemite Sam; though Dubose is a graduate of Princeton and dedicated to the cause, Jergen thinks he is cartoonish.

"Whatever you're going to tell me," Radley Dubose says, "don't tell me anything if those little shits disabled the car's cameras and faded away like a couple ghosts. I've had enough of their smart-aleck crap, the insolent little shits. I'd like to shove each one's head up the other one's ass and roll them down the street like a hoop."

"Maybe you'll get a chance to do it," Jergen says. "They went west on foot, toward the boulevard."

They get into the mud-spattered Range Rover. Carter Jergen switches on the headlights, drives out of the parking lot, turns west on the street.

"I mean," Dubose says, "they're two freaking writers, of all things. *Writers.* You and I, we're hard-case pros. We break heads, get the job done. Why do a couple bookworm geeks think they're smart enough to keep pissing on us and getting away with it?"

"Maybe because they can," Jergen suggests.

"Not anymore. Damn if they will. I've had enough. Let's make this happen."

Jergen pulls to the curb and parks illegally just short of the intersection with the boulevard.

They get out of the Rover and stand on the corner, scoping out the situation. The restaurants and bars are open, but the stores in the strip centers and the stand-alones are closed. Traffic races past and brakes and races again, spasming between signal lights at the intersections, fewer vehicles than would have been here an hour earlier, more than will be here an hour from now.

The first thing that intrigues Dubose is a motor inn to the south and a cheapjack motel to the north. "We already got word that sonofabitch Sanjay used his ATM card. He wants to pay cash at a motel rather than use a credit card."

The first thing that intrigues Jergen is the traffic cameras mounted high on a streetlamp, one aimed south, one north. "Maybe they didn't get a room. Maybe they hitched a ride or went somewhere else. Before we start playing gumshoe, squeezing motel desk clerks, let's have a look at the traffic-cam video."

24

Turning on lights ahead of her and switching them off behind, Jane toured the house, feeling oppressed by a surfeit of deeply carved moldings and decorative paneling and crystal chandeliers; exotic silk draperies with swagged valances and tasseled hems; French furniture featuring intricate inlaid patterns and scenes; gilded this and silver-leafed that. Where the floors weren't limestone, they were wide-plank walnut. The many antique Persian carpets—Tabriz, Mahal, Sultanabad—were exquisite. Some lamps appeared to be by Tiffany, others by Handel.

In mad contrast to the overdone but harmonious décor, the riotous abstract paintings might have been by famous artists. Jane didn't know for sure. Like most modern art, they interested her no more than did the wind-tangled rain-compacted sun-bleached trash that time accumulated in vomitous-looking masses along California's cracked and potholed highways, as the once-golden state stewed in government corruption on its way to bankruptcy.

The house had been built by Sara Holdsteck, but Jane suspected that the feverish décor was all Simon Yegg, comprising treasures accumulated from his for-profit marriages.

She found what she needed in a subterranean level too grand to be called a basement. The garage, which could accommodate eight cars, currently housed a

Rolls-Royce, a Mercedes GL 550, a Cadillac Escalade, and a Lamborghini. There were cabinets of tools and a workbench and one of those wheeled boards on which a mechanic could lie to roll under a car, and a hydraulic vehicle lift, suggesting that Simon not only collected cars but enjoyed working on them. The rest of that level was given to a large wine cellar with a spacious tasting room and a home theater that seated fifteen.

The ornate theater came with an authentic French façade, a receiving area with box office, a lobby with candy counter, and the main screening room, which itself measured about thirty-five by fifty feet. Underground as it was, windowless as it was, thoroughly soundproofed to prevent the loudest movie music and sound effects from disturbing people elsewhere in the house, the theater provided the ideal—if inappropriately glamorous—venue for a prolonged and vigorous interrogation.

25

Parked at the corner, the Range Rover is in the spillover zone of the Wi-Fi service established for a nearby office building.

While Radley Dubose stands out on the corner, scowling north and then south and then north again along the boulevard, as though everyone and everything in sight profoundly offends him, Carter Jergen sits in the driver's seat with his laptop. He accesses the National Security Agency's all but infinite virtual storerooms of data at their million-square-foot Utah facility.

Although he is an employee of the NSA with the highest security clearance, Jergen is not at the moment working for the agency or for the existing government of the country. He is serving the secret confederacy that intends to remake the nation into a utopia, and he dares not risk alerting his NSA superiors as to what information he is seeking or for what purpose. Consequently, he enters by a back door established by certain of his colleagues.

In addition to snatching every phone call and text message from the ether and storing them for possible future review, the agency also, among other tasks, coordinates traffic and venue cameras from law-enforcement jurisdictions nationwide. Once having accessed this program, it is possible to select any location within the borders of the United States and obtain a real-time view of events there.

In this case, Jergen does not want to see the current action captured by the cameras mounted atop streetlamps at the intersection directly in front of him. Instead, he seeks the archived video that will show what happened there a few minutes after the Shukla twins abandoned the patrol car.

In recent years, traffic cameras have become ubiquitous. Many reasons are put forth to explain the need for them. To study vehicle flow and design more efficient intersections. To discourage drivers from running red lights when a video record is being made to provide evidence of the violation. To preserve the security of the citizens in a time of terrorism. *Yada, yada, yada.*

There is some truth in all the reasons that are given. But from Jergen's perspective, the best use of this ocean of archived video is to find people who don't want to be found, in order to do to them what they don't want done.

And here—*ta-da!*—are the Shukla twins on the laptop screen, standing on the northeast corner of the intersection in time past, exactly where Radley Dubose stands in time present. The dangerous young authors regard the street with confusion and indecision and fear, rather than with Dubose's smoldering rage.

26

Considering its metal shelves packed full of everything from cleaning supplies to bibles, its wooden creche containing a swaddled baby Jesus with a bent halo wired to his head, its plastic livestock with unlikely expressions of adoration, and its life-size figures staring with realistic glass eyes, the windowless storage room was a strange place in ordinary times and downright eerie at the moment.

When the last voices faded, when no more doors were slammed, after no further car engines rumbled to life in the parking lot, when silence endured for two minutes, three, Sanjay and Tanuja rose from their concealment behind the camels and passed among the wise men.

Sanjay eased open the door and saw a pitch-black hallway brightened only by the light that spilled past him and imprinted his shadow on the floor, a swollen and distorted silhouette, as if it might not be just a shadow, but instead the image of some entity that possessed him, here revealed. He leaned out and looked toward the junction of corridors. The darkness and silence were complete.

"I think we're alone."

Tanuja said, "Did you notice a rectory next to the church?"

"No. Maybe. I don't know."

"If there is, we don't dare turn on lights near any windows. The minister or someone might see."

In case of an earthquake, there was an emergency flashlight plugged into a wall outlet by the door, perpetually charging. They were most likely distributed throughout the building.

"It's too bright," Tanuja judged.

"Candles," Sanjay said. "A church can't be without candles."

They found two shelves of boxed candles: long tapers for the altar, others of various sizes. Crates of china and glassware that were evidently used at church dinners. They put a fat candle in each of three drinking tumblers.

"There ought to be some matches in the sacristy," Sanjay said.

"And in the kitchen," Tanuja suggested. "The kitchen is closer, and that's where we're going, anyway."

Sanjay switched on the emergency flashlight and hooded the lens with one hand and led his sister along the hallway, past the church offices, to the kitchen, while she carried the three candleholders.

The two kitchen windows featured blinds. Sanjay drew them all the way down. With the flashlight, he searched the drawers for matches but found a butane lighter with a long flexible-metal neck.

Tanuja put the glasses on the kitchen table, and Sanjay lit the candles with the torchlike spout of butane flame. Then he switched off the flashlight. The amber glow that fluttered from the burning wicks was subdued and surely didn't leak around the edges of the blinds enough to be noticed from outside.

They had not eaten dinner yet when Linc Crossley and his two associates had come calling, and the subsequent events of the evening had stropped a sharp edge on their hunger.

The first of two Sub-Zero refrigerators was mostly empty except for bottled water and Diet Pepsi. Among other items, the second fridge held sliced ham, baloney, various cheeses, tomatoes, mustard, mayonnaise, lettuce, and a half-empty bag of sesame-seed rolls—the sandwich-makings for one or more church-office employees.

In one of the Sub-Zero's vegetable drawers, a bottle of good champagne lay hidden beneath a package of romaine lettuce, as though its presence in the church kitchen must be an embarrassment. Or maybe it had been nestled there for a surprise birthday celebration, because in another drawer, under two packages of bean sprouts, were four champagne flutes.

Sanjay said, "Grab two glasses. I'll open the bottle."

"Should we?" Tanuja wondered.

"Why shouldn't we?"

"We're not out of the woods yet."

"Think of it as a restorative."

"We don't even know whose woods we're in."

He took the bottle to the sink, in case it foamed upon being opened. "If I have to eat baloney, I'm washing it down with this."

Tanuja said, "Maybe there's not even a way out of these woods."

"The woods metaphor has been exhausted," Sanjay declared as he peeled the foil off the wire muzzle that caged the cork. "We're Hansel and Gretel, and you know how that story goes. They find their way out of the woods, their pockets stuffed with pearls and jewels."

Putting the champagne flutes on the table, Tanuja said, "We're reversing roles again. I'm all noir, you're Mr. Optimistic."

Sanjay twisted the wire off the cork. "Whoever is after us, they're not as bad as a wicked witch. They're not *supernatural*."

"They're *something*," she said. "They're not just any standard-variety sociopath. They've got weird mojo."

The cork squeaked against the glass. The hollow

pop, in other circumstances festive, didn't sound so festive now. The bottle spewed laces of foam that fizzed in the stainless-steel sink.

Sanjay poured the champagne. "We have some mojo of our own. We'll trick them into the oven and roast them all."

"*Chotti bhai*, the Hansel-and-Gretel metaphor has been way exhausted."

"I'm your little brother only by two minutes, *bhenji*. Old enough to drink." He put down the bottle and raised his glass. "To the indomitable Shukla twins. We are survivors."

Her eyes were wide in the candlelight. "No joking, Sanjay. I'm scared."

He was pained to hear those words, but it half broke his heart that, in truth, he could do nothing to reassure her. He could only clink his glass against hers and drink.

After a hesitation, she sipped her champagne, too. Then she proposed a second toast. "To dear *Baap* and *Mai*, always with us."

He did not believe that their long-dead father and mother were always with them, but he never said otherwise to his beloved sister. "Always with us," he agreed, and together they sipped the ice-cold and delicious champagne.

27

After a hesitation, the Shukla twins had walked north on the boulevard and continued to the far end of the long block. The high-definition video from the camera at the first intersection allows Carter Jergen to frame distant objects and enlarge them without a significant loss of clarity. On his laptop, he watches Sanjay and Tanuja turn right, east, and out of sight.

With Radley Dubose aboard again, hulking in the front passenger seat and glowering like an Orc displaced from Tolkien's Mordor, Jergen drives to the next cross street and turns east at the corner as the twins had done. Again he parks illegally at a red curb.

When he has the name of this street and marries it with the boulevard, he is able to access the NSA-archived video from the four cameras that monitor the intersection.

"What we've got here," Jergen says, "is the only bird horror that Hitchcock left out of the movie."

Dubose groans. "Airborne diarrhea."

"Plenty of it," Jergen confirms.

Birds frequently perch on the cameras, and the earlier models don't have spiked cowls to thwart them. If in the vicinity there are trees that produce berries, the droppings are so acidic that they etch the plastic bubble serving as a lens shield. Even after a heavy rain washes off the mess, the camera is peering through a cataract. Of the four traffic cams at this intersection, those aimed north and east provide only a milky blur of shadowy shapes.

"High-tech craps out," Dubose says. "So much for government. You see a private-sector answer?"

"There's sure to be one," Jergen says.

The next intersection to the east involves secondary streets, where there won't be traffic cams. Carter Jergen laments that a nation drowning in debt has its priorities so woefully wrong. It struggles to maintain five-thousand-acre wind farms and in-depth research on the pernicious effects of loud dance music on the early sexual maturation of preteen girls, but is unable to install quite as many millions of high-definition video cameras as are required to maintain surveillance and control of a large and restive population.

Street parking is not allowed in this block. Jergen cruises slowly along the curb, surveying enterprises on both sides, enduring the horns of impatient motorists.

"Assholes," Dubose grumbles. "They have another lane, room to go around us, but they gotta make a statement. If only this heap had a sunroof."

"Why a sunroof?"

"If I stood up and shot one of the noisy bastards, that would give the rest of them something to think about."

"You like those old Warner Brothers cartoons?" Jergen asks.

Squinting through the windshield at the businesses

ahead of them, Dubose says, "What shit are you talking about?"

"Bugs Bunny, Daffy Duck. I loved all that when I was a kid."

"Never seen them. Being a kid never interested me. Didn't have time for it."

"There was this character, Yosemite Sam, he wore a big cowboy hat, always sure that shooting a problem would solve it."

"Had his head on straight," Dubose says. He leans forward in his seat, his Dudley Do-Right jaw thrust at the windshield, his brow furrowed, bird-dogging a prospect. "Here's a nice little paranoid corner grocery."

The last business on the south side of the block is less a grocery than a convenience store. Jergen pulls off the street and into a parking space. At the peak of the roof above the front doors, a cluster of security cameras maintains surveillance of approaches from the east and west as well as from the street directly in front of the premises. There will be an additional camera or two inside.

"Sure as shit," Dubose says, "something's wrong when QuickMart has the scene scoped better than the NSA and Homeland Security combined," and Jergen has to agree.

28

Although Jane didn't expect Petra Quist to return until almost midnight, she finished touring the house, stopped in the kitchen to leave an item from her tote, extinguised the last of the lights that she'd turned on, and by 11:10 was standing in the foyer, next to one of the windows that flanked the front door. At 11:15, far earlier than she had anticipated, a superstretch black Cadillac limo turned off the street and into the circular driveway.

Jane stepped back from the window and watched as the chauffeur came around the front of the vehicle. He opened a back door and offered a hand to help the passenger disembark.

In a short, sleeveless dress, wearing neither a coat nor a wrap in deference to the cool weather, Petra Quist emerged from the car. Although she appeared to be all long legs and slender arms, she came forth with none of the swanlike grace that could be seen in some of her Facebook photos, but instead like a marionette whose wooden joints were in need of some oil. When she turned from the driver and started up the portico steps, however, she repressed a girls'-night-out stagger and achieved that other kind of avian elegance common to cranes and storks, moving with a studied fluidity punctuated by fraction-of-a-second hesitations, as though her limbs might lock. It was evident that she expected the driver to be watching her with barely constrained desire.

Maybe the chauffeur was in fact riveted by her fashion-model legs and schoolgirl butt. More likely, he observed her with concern that she might fall upon the steps, bruising her face or splitting her perfect lips. In that case, he would be in deep trouble with the owner of the limousine company, who happened to be Simon Yegg, this girl's "nuclear-powered love machine."

Petra negotiated the steps with her chin high, as she might hold it when bringing a martini glass to her mouth.

Jane picked up her tote bag and backed away from the entrance, into the open doorway of the nearby study, which smelled of leather upholstery and cigars cuddled in a humidor. She set the tote aside.

From the sound of it, the party girl had difficulty inserting the key in the lock. Then the deadbolt clacked open and the alarm sounded as she stepped inside.

Closing the door, Petra said, "Anabel, follow me with light," and the foyer chandelier brightened above her.

Sara Holdsteck had failed to mention that the computerized systems of the house responded to voice commands preceded by its customized identity— Anabel. Evidently this feature had been added since her ex-husband had forced her out. Interesting. And curious.

"Anabel, disarm security. Five, six, five, one, star."

A disembodied female voice said, *"Control is now disarmed."*

When Petra began to sing Rachel Platten's "Fight Song" and started across the foyer, Jane stepped from the darkness of the study. Pistol held at her side, muzzle toward the floor, she said, "Petra Quist, formerly Eudora Mertz of Albany, Oregon."

The party girl halted among the prismatic patterns cast on the marble floor by the immense crystal chandelier, likewise prismed herself, as though she might have been pieced together from glass. Wings of golden hair framing her face. A complexion as smooth as the petals of a cream-colored rose. Blue eyes so boldly striated that they gleamed like faceted jewels. In the short, custom-fitted dress that matched her eyes, with a Rockstud Rolling purse from Valentino slung over her shoulder, she stood with one leg before the other, as if frozen in mid-stride.

Jane said, "Voted most popular girl in the senior class. Main squeeze of Keith Buchanan, high-school football hero. Then you're off to New York and modeling jobs. Three years later, it's L.A. and commercials for national brands, occasionally an acting gig."

If Petra was surprised or fearful, she didn't show it. Her expression said, *I'm dangerous* and *I'm too cool for your school*, a look that was perpetually popular in the high-fashion magazines.

"Two years in L.A.," Jane said, "then you're in Nashville, playing guitar and singing in the starter clubs. Eighteen months later, you're back here, just south of true La La Land, twenty-six years old and . . . doing what?"

Petra issued a sigh of impatience. "You've got no

reason to be pissed at me. If Simon dumped you, chickee, save your ammo for him."

"Maybe I will. But I want you out of the way when he comes home. You and I, we're going down to the theater."

"Screw that. I need a drink."

Jane raised the pistol. She had fixed a sound suppressor to it, not because a shot was likely to be heard beyond the walls of the mansion, but because the average person found a pistol even more intimidating when it was fitted with a silencer, announcing that the bearer of the weapon was a professional and not to be resisted.

Either because an evening of drinking with the girls had rendered Petra incapable of discerning a threat or because even sober she would have more attitude than common sense, she said, "If you want to have a bitch contest, honey, you better go into training for a year. Then come back, and we'll get it on."

She turned away from Jane and sauntered toward the living room archway, moving as seductively as when she climbed the portico steps with the chauffeur watching. No doubt, from experience, she knew that some girls coveted her no less than did most men. Perhaps she hoped that Jane was one such whose desire would make her vulnerable.

As Petra stepped out of the foyer, lamps bloomed with light in the living room.

In other circumstances, with the clock ticking toward Simon's arrival, Jane would have overpowered Petra the moment the woman disarmed the security system. She would have taken her by surprise with a spray bottle of chloroform, of which she had a supply that she'd derived from art-store acetone and janitorial bleaching powder. Because she hoped to pry certain information from this woman, however, she needed her to be clearheaded, or at least no more muddle-brained than an evening of club-hopping had already left her.

Trailing Petra across the living room, Jane said, "I'm not one of Simon's girls, and this has nothing to do with you."

"Oh, good. Then piss off, why don't you?"

"But if you force me to it, I'll hurt you."

"So you'll double-cap me? Two shots in the back of the head? Why should I care? I'd never know it happened."

"You're drunk."

Petra Quist said, "I'm best when I'm drunk. Don't think I'm not. You hear a slur in my voice? No, you don't. Vodka clarifies. Peter Parker is bitten, so then he's Spider-Man and all. Ice-cold Belvedere and an olive—that's my spider bite."

As Jane followed the woman through open double doors and into a hallway, a series of crystal ceiling fixtures brightened, a spectrum of primary colors burning bright along the sharp edges of the pendants.

"Don't be stupid," Jane said. "Don't push me like this."

"Kiss my ass. You probably even want to kiss it."

In training at Quantico and during her busy years in the FBI, working cases involving Behavioral Analysis Units 3 and 4, which dealt mostly with mass murders and serial killings, Jane had known all kinds of hard cases, men and women, and ultimately cracked every one of them. But there was something different about Petra Quist, something new and disturbing. The woman's restiveness under these circumstances was not entirely related to how much she had drunk, and dealing with her successfully might require understanding the deeper reason for her mulish—and reckless—stubbornness.

Still walking in front of Jane, Petra said, "Why don't you grab my hair, throw me down, kick me in the teeth, bust me up? Are you all bullshit and no balls?"

The vast kitchen—maple cabinets, black granite countertops, stainless-steel appliances, designed to accommodate a caterer with a platoon of cooks and other staff—welcomed Petra with sudden light.

"Or maybe you don't want to bruise my pretty body before you get a chance to use it."

Jane watched in silence as the woman—no, the girl, perhaps in some way even still a child—took two martini glasses and a cocktail shaker from a bar-supply cabinet. A bottle of dry vermouth from another cupboard. A jar of olives from the second of four Sub-Zero refrigerators. One by one, she placed the items on the first of two large center islands.

"Or maybe you're some kind of prig," Petra said, pausing to look Jane up and down. "Some tight-assed prude, you don't do girls, don't do boys, don't even do yourself. Well, chickee, you better damn well drink, 'cause I won't even *talk* to some self-righteous teetotaler let alone get naked with her. Or him. Or it."

She turned away from Jane and went to the fourth

refrigerator. She opened the door and withdrew a tall chilled bottle of Belvedere.

As the refrigerator door swung shut, Petra returned with the vodka and stopped near the island and cocked her head, regarding Jane with perplexity and disdain. "Girl, you're fully bitchin' top to bottom. A face for the movies, a goddess body and all. But here you are, no makeup, lifeless hair, dressed one step up from thrift-shop chic. Do you work just hours and hours every day, trying so hard to look ordinary? Are you so screwed up, you *want* to be homely? You must have some crazy damn story. I want to hear your story and all. Tell me your story." With that she spoke to the house computer: "Anabel, lights out!"

In the last luminous moment between the command and the response, Jane saw the girl swing the Belvedere, and in the instant that darkness fell through the kitchen, she heard the glass shatter against the granite top of the island. The broken rim of the thick-walled long-necked bottle would make a disfiguring, even deadly, weapon.

29

Here in the final hours of Friday, just one employee staffs the QuickMart. According to the clip-on badge attached to the pocket of his white shirt, his name is Tuong, and he tells them his last name is Phan, so he's Vietnamese American, a neat well-barbered young man of perhaps twenty-two, soft-spoken, polite. Carter Jergen imagines that Tuong, like so many of his ethnicity, works hard at two jobs and intends one day to have a business of his own. Though he might just as likely be working his way through his sixth year in college, aiming for an MBA or an advanced degree in computer science.

Whatever Tuong's flaws may be, stupidity isn't one of them. In spite of his humility, his keen intelligence is so obvious that it's almost a visible aura. Nor does he have any animus toward authority, because people of his community generally go to college to acquire useful knowledge, not to learn how to man the barricades in a rage against whatever. When Tuong insists that he has no idea as to the location of the security-system video recorder, Jergen does not for a moment doubt him.

Radley Dubose, however, would not trust the pope's description of the weather if they stood together under a cloudless sky that the pontiff called sunny. Not for the first time, hulking on the public side of the cashier's station, Dubose shakes his NSA credentials in Tuong's face, as a painted-and-feathered shaman might shake a brace of dried snake heads at the superstitious members of his flock to scare them into submission. He warns of the dire consequences of refusing to cooperate with federal agents in urgent pursuit of a terrorist.

In fact, the cables from all the security cameras, inside and outside the convenience store, are buried in the walls. Dubose himself is unable to follow them to the recorder.

He bullies the clerk. "It'll be in a back room, in the office or storeroom or something. It'll be as obvious as a cockroach on a wedding cake."

"We don't sell wedding cakes," says Tuong.

As if Dubose doesn't grasp that the American-born clerk's first language is English, which maybe he does not, his response is thick with frustration and contempt. "Of course you don't sell wedding cakes. It's a freakin' convenience store. I'm talking metaphor."

"Or was it simile?" Tuong wonders.

"Was it what?"

"Anyway," Tuong says, "we don't have cockroaches. We receive only praise from the health inspector."

Entertained by this confrontation, Jergen plucks a candy bar from a counter display, peels back the wrapper, and takes a bite with a pleasure akin to that of sitting stage-side in a fine dinner theater.

"This isn't about cockroaches, it's about—"

Daring to interrupt the big man, apparently having as much fun as Jergen, Tuong says earnestly, "It's about *not having* cockroaches. We are very proud of our cleanliness."

Dubose's fists are like two five-pound hams at the ends of his arms. "I'm going back there and look for the recorder. Understand me?" Before the clerk can respond, Dubose says, "You have a gun under the counter?"

"Yes, sir."

"Do you know how to use it?"

"Yes, sir."

"Do you know how to leave it right the hell where it is?"

"At all times," Tuong says, "that's what I prefer."

"Let me tell you, boy, if you ever pull a gun on a federal agent, you'll be in a shitstorm."

"I will let you tell me."

"Tell you what?"

"About the shitstorm."

Dubose looks as if he will tear out Tuong's lungs through his esophagus. "Time's wasting. I don't speak stupid, and I can't wait around for a translator. I'm coming back there."

Tuong Phan watches deadpan as Dubose steps to the end of the service counter, opens a gate, and goes through a door to a hall that serves whatever rooms lay beyond the clerk's domain.

He looks at Carter Jergen. "I'll call Mr. Zabotin and ask him where the recorder is."

"Who's Zabotin?" Jergen wonders.

"Ivan Zabotin owns this QuickMart franchise and three others."

"Give him my congratulations on keeping this place cockroach-free," Jergen says and takes another bite of the candy bar.

Tuong Phan smiles and picks up the phone.

30

Faux frost of moonlight crystalizing on the window glass, green numbers softly glowing on the oven clocks like some enigmatic code by which the immediate future might be read . . .

Otherwise, this seemed to be the ultimate darkness, the outer dark of souls in oblivion, the air scented with spirits, shards of glass splintering under Petra's shoes with a sound like grinding-gnashing teeth. Thin cries issued from her each time she slashed savagely, blindly with the broken vodka bottle, counting on her familiarity with the kitchen layout to give her the advantage until, by some stroke of benighted luck, she might find a face and gouge it and permanently blind her adversary.

In the first instant of darkness, Jane had chosen not to fire her pistol. Even at close range, she was less likely to hit than miss, while the muzzle flare would reveal her precise location. Besides, she didn't want to kill this drunk and disturbed party girl unless she had no other choice.

Instead, she backed off and shouted to the house-control system that had so readily obeyed Petra—"*Anabel, lights on!*"—though to no effect. Quickly, by touch, she found the second large granite-topped island and sprang onto it, out of the pathways that the other woman knew so well. Three feet above the floor, at the approximate middle of the seven-foot-long,

five-foot-wide slab, Jane poised on one knee, as if gen-
uflecting, left hand flat on the polished stone to provide a sense of stability in the disorienting blackness.
With the Heckler in her right hand, she strained to
listen as someone sightless might listen to the nuances
of sound that escaped the notice of the sighted.

In the cloud of astringent vodka fumes, Petra Quist
cast aside any remaining prudence and forethought.
Her anger escalated to an animal frenzy. She struck
out even more wildly, grunting and cursing and fling-
ing at Jane every obscene name in the vile lexicon
shared by the worst woman-hating men. The thick,
weaponized bottle clinked, clanked, clinked as it
rapped off one thing or another, and then cracked
harder against granite, spalling off chips that spilled
across the polished stone with a faint, brief burst of
fairy music.

When Jane sensed that her stalker had passed by,
she pivoted toward the ranting voice. Having recalled the precise wording with which Petra had first
commanded the house, she rose to her feet as she
said, "Anabel, follow me with light," and a bright
downwash cast away all shadows.

At a corner of the island, Petra glanced up in surprise, her face distorted by rage. She remained beautiful, although this was far different from the comeliness
that had turned heads during an evening of club-
hopping. This was instead a terrible and fearsome
beauty, as Medusa might have looked under her serpent tresses just as, by her stare alone, she excited a
man into stone.

Jane kicked, and the party girl cried out when her

right forearm took the blow. The broken bottle flipped out of her grasp, its glass teeth glittering as it arced onto a gas cooktop, where it fragmented and rattled down into the cast-iron drip pans.

The would-be slasher collapsed onto her back, rolled over, and scrambled up even as Jane came off the island and slammed into her, driving her backward into one of the refrigerators. Petra didn't know how to fight, but she knew how to resist furiously: twisting, as torsional as an eel; clawing violently if ineffectively, her nail-shop acrylics snagging and snapping off; thrusting her head forward, trying to bite Jane's face.

A knee driven into Petra's crotch didn't half paralyze her as it would have a man, but a blow to the pelvis bruised her vulva and sent such a shock through her body core that she shuddered and briefly lost the ability to resist. Jane upswept a forearm under that perfectly molded chin, the full brute force of her shoulder hard behind it. Petra's eyes rolled to white like those of a doll, and the back of her head rapped the refrigerator door, whereupon Jane stepped back just enough to allow the woman to slide down the stainless steel and sit on the floor, chin on her ample breasts, unconscious.

31

Perhaps the presence of Radley Dubose standing at the front counter in QuickMart does not discourage incoming customers as much as would a blood-smeared clown with a chain saw, but Carter Jergen suspects that the number of those who suddenly decide to shop elsewhere is only slightly fewer than would have been put off by a psychotic circus performer. Radley is big; he appears arrogant and angry; and although he doesn't telepathically transmit the words *National Security Agency,* anyone with a minimum of street smarts realizes that he possesses the legal authority to kick ass and a desire to do so as often as possible.

Ivan Zabotin, owner of the franchise, prefers not to have Tuong Phan, the clerk, deal with people as important as federal agents. He takes twenty minutes to get from his home to the market, however, and though he is apologetic, his expressed regrets only further incense Dubose.

Zabotin is a small man with a large head and delicate hands, which makes him seem strangely like a bearded child. Speaking clear but accented English, having emigrated from Russia, where his parents must have been oppressed by the Communists and where he apparently came of age in the marginally less dangerous society that followed the collapse of the Soviet Union, he obviously fears and distrusts government. As he asks to see their credentials, studies that ID, and then escorts them toward the office at the back of the building, he smiles nervously and nods and is deferential without being so meek that his respect might seem to have an underlying note of mockery.

"Over there in Mother Russia, you were what?" Dubose asks. "Some kind of oligarch?"

"'Oligarch'?" the startled Zabotin echoes. "No, no, no. No, sir. My people, our living blood was sucked out by the oligarchs."

"You own a lot of franchises," Dubose says. "So how does that happen if you didn't arrive in America on a three-hundred-foot yacht with a billion dollars in dirty cash?"

Zabotin's legs seem to go weak, and he pauses at the door to the office. "My wife and I arrived with less than little. Worked hard, saved, invested. A Quick-Mart franchise is not a billion."

"You have four of them," Dubose says in the grave accusatory tone of a Star Chamber judge, as if the well-known cost of such a franchise is a quarter of a billion.

Zabotin turns to Jergen, seeking relief from this unreason, but Jergen meets the stare without expression. Because neither he nor Dubose can convincingly fake sympathy, they never play good cop, bad cop. The best that Zabotin will get is indifferent cop, bad cop.

Anxious to hurry them out of his establishment, Zabotin sits at a laminate-topped office desk and boots up the computer, explaining that the security-system recorder is shelved in the walk-in safe, but the video from any of the six cameras can be accessed from here and played back on this monitor.

Jergen specifies the three exterior cameras mounted above the front entrance to the store and gives Zabotin the precise time at which the Shukla twins, on foot, turned the corner from the main boulevard earlier in the evening.

On the desk stand framed photos of the owner and a woman who is most likely his wife, as well as others of their daughter, two sons, and the family dog. Among the photos are also a cast-plastic model of the Statue of Liberty and a brass holder with a six-by-four-inch starched-fabric flag that is always at full fly.

While the proprietor seeks the requested video and Jergen stands at his side to watch, Radley Dubose, brow furrowed, picks up the framed photographs one at a time. He intently studies the faces of the wife and children, as if committing them to memory.

Zabotin is acutely aware of Dubose's interest in his family. His attention flickers between the screen and the big hands that seem almost to fondle the photographs.

Before Dubose puts down the photo of Zabotin and his wife, he licks the thumb of his right hand and carefully smears it across the glass over her face, as if to clear away a smudge and have a better look at her. But then, one by one, he returns to the pictures of the daughter and those of the two sons, all of them seemingly under the age of eleven or twelve, and he repeats this unsettling act in a ritualistic manner, licking the thumb and wiping it over each face, as if by an unspoken bewitchment he is marking not merely their images but they themselves, asserting some occult power over them.

Dubose's behavior so disturbs Ivan Zabotin that his fingers fumble on the keyboard, and he must correct his errors en route to summoning the needed video.

Although Jergen finds his partner cartoonish, he is also never less than intrigued by the man. Sometimes Dubose might be Yosemite Sam, but at other times he more resembles a character from one of those edgy comic books like *Tales from the Crypt*.

And here, on the screen, out of the west and out of the recent past, come the fugitive brother and sister, approaching hand in hand along the sidewalk, both of them looking this way and that, as if expecting to be assaulted from one quarter or another, as indeed they ought to expect.

When they pass beyond view, Zabotin finds them in the video archives of the second camera, which covers the parking lot and the street beyond it, then locates them once more in the east-facing-camera. They walk away into the dripping night, pause at the nearby corner to wait for the pedestrian-control signal to flash from DON'T WALK to WALK, and then continue east across the intersection. On that southeast corner, they stop for a moment, perhaps surveying the way ahead, considering their options.

Judging by the absence of business signs and a convocation of shadows in that next block, the commercial area gives way to some kind of mixed-use zone.

The twins enter a crosswalk again, proceeding to the northeast corner of the four-way intersection, where they continue directly east, past what appear to be two stately old houses.

Although Zabotin has sprung for high-definition cameras, they are intended only for short-range surveillance. As the Shukla twins venture farther from the QuickMart, they seem to deliquesce as if they were never of real substance, but only a pair of rain spirits now dissolving in the aftermath of the storm. The many reflective wet surfaces of the newly washed scene, flaring and scintillant in the rush of vehicle headlights, conspire with the shadows, which swell and shrink and shiver in the same sweeping beams, transforming the fugitives from flesh into fading mirage.

In the last moment of visibility, the twins appear to turn left, off the sidewalk, moving toward a puzzling geometry of colored lights that are not a business sign.

"Scan backward and play those few seconds again," Carter Jergen says. Zabotin does as told, and Jergen reviews that brief piece of video not once but four times before, at his direction, the Russian émigré freezes the image at the penultimate moment. Jergen taps the screen with a forefinger. "These look like car shapes. But what are those weird lights beyond them?"

"Stained glass," Zabotin says. "Church windows."

"What church?"

"Mission of Light."

Jergen looks at Radley Dubose, and the big man says, "Why would they go to ground in a church?"

"People in trouble have taken sanctuary in churches as long as there've *been* churches."

Dubose shakes his head. "Not anybody I know."

Eager to be done with this, Ivan Zabotin swivels in his chair to face Jergen. "Sir, Mr. Agent Jergen, what else, what anything, can I do for you?"

"You've been very helpful, Mr. Zabotin. All you need to do now is forget we were ever here. This is a matter of national security. Were you to discuss our visit with anyone, even with your wife, you could be charged with a felony." That is bullshit, but Zabotin pales. "A felony punishable by up to thirty years in prison."

"Thirty-five," Dubose amends.

"Nothing happened here, nothing to tell anyone," Zabotin assures them, his brow now stippled with tiny beads of perspiration.

Jergen and Dubose leave the QuickMart mogul at his desk and return to the front of the store.

At the cash register, Tuong Phan reminds Jergen, "You owe for that candy bar you ate."

"I didn't like it," Jergen replies, and he takes another of the same from the counter display. "It tasted like shit."

Outside, he throws the unwrapped candy bar in a trash can.

"It really tasted that bad?" asks Dubose as they head to the Range Rover.

"No, it was good," Jergen says. "But I have to watch my waistline."

32

Time in flight, the longest clock hand having swept away almost half of the current circle of sixty, the witching hour aloft on its broom and fast approaching . . .

In the kitchen, a built-in secretary provided a place to plan menus. A wheeled office chair was tucked into the knee space.

Jane rolled the chair to the unconscious woman, wrestled her into it, and secured her wrists to the chair arms with two heavy-duty hard-plastic zip-ties taken from the tote bag.

The chair's five legs radiated from a center post. She zip-tied each of Petra's ankles to the post.

There could be no automatic assumption of sisterhood in this world of deceit and violence, and only those who had the most shallow understanding of human nature could assume otherwise. Yet Jane took no pride or pleasure in what she had done to Petra Quist, even if the girl-woman had tried to do worse to her. Any predator sharp of tooth and claw did not require great courage when chasing down a lamb, merely persistence and a little luck.

Petra wasn't exactly a lamb, though neither was she the dangerous wolf that she pretended to be. Her carefully crafted tough-bitch image served as her armor, but her only weapons were attitude, a fearsome disregard for consequences, and what seemed to be an unquenchable, empowering anger.

When Jane was done with her, Ms. Quist might have no armor anymore, nor any weapons. If from this night forward she had to face a world of rapacity and depredation without her usual defenses, she might not last long; in which case, though Petra had to an extent spun the thread of her own fate, Jane would have some responsibility for turning her loose disabled.

In the end, there was no rational choice other than to accept whatever guilt might accrue to her by doing whatever must be done to Petra Quist in an effort to save Travis, as well as the innocents on the Hamlet list. Jane had no illusions that anyone got through this world unstained by the experience, especially not her.

The mansion featured two elevators, one in the front hall, the other in the spacious butler's pantry between the kitchen and the formal dining room. She rolled Petra into the latter, and they rode down to the subterranean level.

On poker nights, the man of the house—what passed for a man—usually arrived home between twelve-thirty and one in the morning. An hour would be enough for Jane to deal with this girl-woman and be ready to handle Simon Yegg.

But what if Petra had returned early because she knew that he would not be out as late as usual? Instead of an hour or more, Simon might come home in half an hour. Perhaps in mere minutes.

When Jane wheeled her captive out of the elevator,

the virtual servant, Anabel, brought up the lights. The marquee blazed with hundreds of small bulbs, and the name of the home theater—*Cinema Parisian*—flowed above the marquee in blue neon cursive.

She maneuvered the office chair through the double doors with no problem, though it didn't move as well in the carpeted reception area as it had on the limestone floors. She pushed it past the box office, through an archway, and parked the unconscious woman by the candy counter in the lobby.

Each of the wheels featured a flip-down chock that prevented it from moving. She engaged them all, so that Petra would not be able to roll anywhere if she regained consciousness.

At the lobby door, Jane said, "Anabel, lights out."

Absolute darkness collapsed upon her, but she manually switched on only the theater-lobby lights before leaving Petra there alone.

She took the stairs rather than the elevator to the main floor, turning on lights as she needed them.

She revisited the kitchen only to get her leather tote bag. No need to mop up the shattered glass, the lake of vodka. Simon would not enter the house via the garage and would not ascend from there to the kitchen either by the stairs or the elevator; therefore, he would have no chance to be alarmed by this mess.

According to Sara Holdsteck, Simon's most recent wife, he always reserved one of his limousine company's cars and chauffeurs on poker night, because he enjoyed a few glasses of Macallan Scotch with the game. The car would return him to the front door, as the other limo had delivered Petra, and if all went well, Jane would be there waiting for him.

In the foyer, she used the keypad to set the security system's perimeter alarm and turned off the chandelier and stepped to one of the tall, narrow windows that flanked the front door.

The street and lawn and phoenix palms enrobed in shadows, the curve of driveway trimmed by low lamps and hemmed with scallops of light like a radiant silken garment, the portico subtly though dramatically illuminated, everything as hushed and still as in a painting, an air of expectation over all . . .

Carrying the tote, Jane doused the main-floor lights behind her as she returned to the theater lobby in the basement.

Petra Quist had come awake. In her restraints, she was as fetching as any object of desire in any bondage freak's best dream—though not a fraction as sweet as any of the offerings in the nearby candy-counter display case.

As though her situation did not concern her, she wore attitude like a porcupine's quills. "You're good as dead, you piece of shit."

"Yeah, well," Jane said, "we're all as good as dead. Some of us just go sooner than others."

She moved a small padded bench away from a wall and positioned it in front of Petra and sat on it.

"Bad as I'm hurting," Petra said, "Simon's gonna hurt you ten times worse."

"Did I hurt you? Really? Where did I?"

"Go screw yourself."

"That's not advice I'd give *you* until there's been some time for the bruising to diminish."

Petra spit at her but missed. Viscous saliva quivered on the bench upholstery. "You think you're really something, you know, but you're not."

"I'm something. You're something. We're all something. Though we can't always be sure what."

They stared at each other in silence for maybe half a minute.

Then Jane said, "How much do you hate Simon?"

"You're so full of crap. I don't hate him."

"Of course you do."

"He's good to me. He gives me everything."

"So how much do you hate him?"

"Why would I hate him?"

Jane said, "Why wouldn't you?"

33

Although it had been wreathed in brightness on the QuickMart video, the church now stands dark from foundation to bell tower to spire. Not a single vehicle remains in the parking lot.

Some lights glow in the rectory next door, however, and a hooded porch lamp hangs over a plaque that welcomes visitors.

MISSION OF LIGHT CHURCH
*"I am come that they might have life,
and that they might have it more abundantly."*
RECTORY
REV. GORDON M. GORDON

As Carter Jergen rings the doorbell, Radley Dubose says, "There better not be any damn sanctuary going on here. These Shukla brats have jerked us around long enough. Anyway, they can't get sanctuary in this place. There's nothing Hindu about this joint."

"They aren't Hindu," Jergen reminds him.

"Their parents were."

"Your parents were something, too."

"My mother was an Adventist for a while."

"And look at you."

"Yeah, but Hindu's different. It sticks."

"It doesn't stick."

"It sticks," Dubose insisted.

"Let's just be cool with this guy," Jergen says. "Ministers, they're trained to make nice. This can be smooth and quick."

Dubose stands in silence, like the stone representation of some Norse god of storms that might abruptly come alive and emblazon the night with thunderbolts.

"Smooth and quick," Jergen repeats. "Everybody making nice."

A man in his fifties answers the door. He wears suit pants and a white shirt with the sleeves rolled up and a loosened necktie. His full head of graying hair is well styled, and he sports a deep tan that, at this time of year, must have come from a machine. His smile is the kind that has closed a thousand deals.

The guy looks less like a man of the cloth than like a real-estate salesman, but Jergen nevertheless asks, "Reverend Gordon?"

"At your service. What may I do for you?"

Jergen and Dubose go into their spiel—a matter of national security, fugitives suspected of terrorist connections, time is of the essence—and present their credentials.

The reverend's smile phases to a solemn expression. He ushers them into the quiet house and along a hallway and into a parlor, his bearing as somber as it might be when someone arrives with news of a parishioner's untimely death.

Gordon M. Gordon perches on the edge of a brown tufted-leather armchair, while Jergen and Dubose sit forward on a sofa, as if all of them might at any moment drop to their knees.

On the table beside the armchair stands a glass containing what appears to be whisky and ice. On a footstool, a hardcover book lies open, facedown, not a theology text, not a volume of inspirational essays, but a John Grisham thriller.

Reverend Gordon sees Jergen notice the drink and the novel. "For some time now, I've been afflicted with insomnia. Well, since Marjorie passed away two years ago. That's my wife, as fine a woman as ever lived. Married thirty years. A glass of spirits and a good tale are the only things that relax me enough that I can sleep."

"Well, sir," Jergen says, "neither Scotch in moderation nor any amount of Grisham is a vice. I'm sorry to hear about your wife. Thirty years is a long blessing, though."

"It is," the reverend agrees. "It's a long blessing."

"I was going to ask if Mrs. Gordon might be off to bed, because what we've come to discuss isn't for everyone to hear."

"Not to worry, Mr. Jergen. The children are gone. I'm alone except for Mr. Grisham and a sip of Scotland's finest."

A tad too brusquely, Dubose says, "There was a well-attended event at the church earlier this evening. What was that about?"

"The first Easter-season play. A silly one, pure fun, for the children. Nearer the Sunday, we'll have a serious Passion play."

Jergen holds out his smartphone, on which he has summoned a photo of the Shukla twins. "By any chance, sir, did you see these two at the performance?"

Leaning further forward on the armchair, Gordon squints at the phone. He smiles and nods. "Yes, a handsome couple. Quite striking. I didn't see them until more than halfway through the evening, as they were getting up to visit the restrooms. I didn't know them, but I assumed they were guests of one parishioner or another."

In a moment of well-rehearsed cop theater, Carter Jergen gives his partner a dour and meaningful look, and Dubose returns it. When they are sure the reverend sees The Look and is intrigued, a little alarmed, they turn to their host, frowning. Jergen says, "Reverend, it's important to think about your answer and be sure it's accurate. Did you see these two leave the church after the performance?"

"No. I realized later that I never learned who they were with or if they might be interested in joining the Mission of Light."

"So they could still be in there?"

The minister may understand the meaning of life, but Jergen's simple question apparently mystifies him. "In the church? Why would they be in the church?"

"Seeking sanctuary," says Dubose.

"Hiding out," Jergen clarifies.

As if he briefly forgot what they'd said on his doorstep that gained them entry, Gordon opens his eyes wide and furrows his brow. "Oh my. Fugitives with suspected terrorist ties?"

Dubose says, "Do you lock the church at night?"

"Yes. The church, the attached chancellery and event building. It's necessary these days. There was a time, in my youth, when the front doors of churches were open twenty-four hours a day. But these days, open doors invite vandalism, even desecration."

"We need to search the place." Dubose sounds impatient, but he's mostly acting as if he agrees with Jergen that this will go smooth and quick if only they just give Gordon the chance to be as nice as his bible tells him to be. "We need the keys."

"Just us?" Gordon asks. "Shouldn't we involve the police?"

"Local police don't have national security clearance," Jergen says. "Neither do you. Agent Dubose and I will conduct the search."

"What—the two of you alone? Isn't that dangerous?"

As he and Dubose get up from the sofa, Jergen says, "It's what we do. Don't worry about us. May we have the keys, Reverend Gordon?"

The minister glances at the whisky, forgoes a taste, gets to his feet, fishes a set of three keys from a pocket, but hesitates to relinquish them. "What if they've got guns?"

Jergen holds out one hand for the keys. "We don't believe they're armed."

"Yes, but what if they are? Couldn't a SWAT team seal off the building and wait them out? Wouldn't that be safer?"

"Preacher, listen, just give us the keys," Dubose says in a tone of voice that always makes him look even bigger than he is.

"If someone were shot," says Gordon M. Gordon, "that would have terrible ramifications for the Mission of Light. Bad publicity, lawsuits, liabilities."

Reaching under his coat to draw a pistol from the belt holster in the small of his back, Dubose says, "The only liability at the moment is you," and he shoots Gordon once in the head.

The reverend seems to fold down into a pile as if he is not a thing of flesh and blood, but an inflatable figure like those that some people add to their Halloween decorations—Face Wound Guy—to terrify the kiddies. He lies billowed and folded with an incurvate countenance, between the armchair and the footstool, taking up less space in death than seems consistent with his size when alive.

Carter Jergen indicates the gun. "Is that a Glock twenty-six?"

"Yeah. Loaded with full-jacket hollow-points."

"Obviously. But there's something different about the grip."

"A Pearce grip extension. It really improves the draw speed."

"It's a drop gun?" Jergen asks, by which he's inquiring if the pistol has no history and therefore can't be traced.

"For sure. We give it to that little shit Sanjay Shukla, and when this is done, Preacher Gordon is just one more kill credited to our writer friend." For the moment, Dubose returns the compact auto to the small of his back. "I tried to let the talky sonofabitch preacher make nice with us."

"I know," Jergen says. "You gave him every chance."

"It was up to him."

"It always is," Jergen says as he picks up the keys that were dropped by the dead man.

Dubose says, "You touch anything?"

"Just the doorbell. And I already wiped it."

Taking one last look at the dead man, Dubose declares, "After all *this*, the Shukla brats damn well better be hiding over there at the church."

34

The theater lobby was about twenty feet square and drenched with ornamentation. The concave ceiling featured coffers brightened by trompe l'oeil paintings of dawn skies ablaze with cerulean blue, coral, and golden light. Each luminous figuration on the chandeliers was of creamy glass shaped like some large-petaled mythical flower. Gilded bronze appliqués and alabaster inlays brightened columns of black marble surmounted by highly ornate capitals. The walls were paneled with ruby silk.

Surrounded by this excess of French décor, dressed for bad electronic dance music in a twenty-first-century hook-up bar, Ms. Petra Quist sat erect in the office chair, as if it were a weird minimalist time machine that had transported her to Paris in 1850.

"I don't hate Simon," she repeated.

Sitting face-to-face with her captive, Jane said, "I despise him, and I haven't even met him yet."

Looking as if she might spit again, but subverting the urge into a sneer of contempt, Petra said, "Maybe you've got an anger problem."

"You're right about that," Jane agreed. "Some days I think I don't have nearly enough of it."

"You're a seriously crazy bitch, you know?"

"I respect the opinion of an expert."

"What?"

"Come on now, girl. Simon is a slimeball, and you know it."

"If you really never met him, what's your problem?"

Instead of answering, Jane said, "So Sugar Daddy gives you everything, huh? Money, jewelry, clothes, limousines to ride around in, all the usual compensation."

"Compensation? What's that supposed to mean?"

"Doesn't matter what I mean, what I think. What matters is if you're clear-eyed about your situation or deluded."

Although only twenty-six Petra had been drinking for enough years and in enough quantity that she'd developed a tolerance for booze that allowed her to rock the clubs with her girl crew for six hours and, though hammered, nevertheless appear almost sober. But the conversation had quickly gotten too complex and too intense for her blood-alcohol level. "'Situation'?"

Leaning forward, with genuine—if vinegary—sympathy, Jane said, "Are you so easily deceived, you think your relationship with him has a long, rosy future—or do you realize you're a whore?"

Considering the dictionary of crude obscenities that this girl had hurled at Jane while raging after her with a broken bottle in the kitchen, her reaction to this comparatively genteel insult was proof that she did indeed harbor illusions about how Simon Yegg regarded her. Hatred knotted her lovely face. Unshed tears of hurt and anger shimmered in her eyes. She spat at her captor again and missed as before.

"If you keep that up," Jane said, "you'll dehydrate. Do you know dehydration kills?"

Petra sprayed words instead of saliva. "Who do you think you are, bitch? What gives you a right to judge me? If there's a worn-out stinking skank sitting here, you're it."

"He's never going to marry you, girl."

"Shows what you know. He's getting me a ring. He says he's not the marrying kind, never has been, but I've melted him, melted his heart. So shut your ignorant, filthy mouth and just go away."

"As for his not being the marrying kind," Jane said, "I'm sure his four wives would agree with him."

More martinis than were prudent now required Petra to process any fresh bit of important data through a brain that effortlessly produced obscenities and lies and self-deceit but that needed to explore a new fact in the manner that a lifelong blind woman, by touch alone, might feel her way to an understanding of the purpose of a mysterious artifact. She moved her tongue around her mouth as though searching for words and finally found a few. "What a load of crap, four wives, you think I'm stupid?"

"He marries rich women and takes them for most of what they have, breaks them psychologically if he can, and throws them away."

Although Petra interrupted with expressions of disbelief, Jane told her about Sara Holdsteck, the ice-water baths, the contempt of the men urinating in the tub, the Tasering, and the rest of it. "Other wives were gang-raped by his associates. To break them, make them relent. He didn't really need their money. He's rich himself. It's some kind of sick sport to him."

"There aren't four ex-wives," Petra insisted. "There aren't four or forty or even one. You're a liar, that's all."

"One of them is agoraphobic, so afraid of the world, she can't leave her little house. Two of the others were eventually murdered, maybe because they started to regain their self-esteem, work up the courage to confront him about what he'd done."

Petra closed her eyes and sagged in the office chair. "You're such a rotten liar. Just a lying liar is all you are. I'm not gonna listen anymore. Not letting you in my head. I'm deaf. Stone deaf. Go away."

"Your life depends on listening, girl. I'm using Simon to get at his half brother, a very bad guy with powerful allies."

"He doesn't have a brother, half or whole."

"A miracle—she hears. His brother is named Booth Hendrickson. They don't advertise it, because Booth and his pals push government business to Simon's enterprises. The limo company is the least of it, but he has a fat contract to drive Justice Department officials and other D.C. muckety-mucks when they're in Southern California."

Eyes tight shut, lips pressed together, Petra Quist pretended deafness, twenty-six years old going on thirteen.

"You think you won't tell me what I want to know about Simon, but you will. One way or the other, you will."

Petra's pout and a tremor at one corner of her mouth suggested less fear than self-pity.

Jane said, "When, through Simon, I get at Booth, which I will, and when I get from Booth what I need to know, which I will, these people are going to be in a desperate cover-their-ass mode. Simon's going to think you didn't do enough to resist me. More important, he's going to realize, because of me, you know too much. If he doesn't slit your throat, kid, he'll pay the guy who does."

"Things are so damn good, the best ever, ever-ever, and then *you* come along. It's not right. It's not fair. What is it with you, you're so hateful?"

"My husband was a fine man. Nick. My Nick was the best. These power-crazy people killed him."

Although Petra clung to denial, the weight of detail in Jane's story seemed to have loosened the knot of her disbelief. Eyes still closed, she shook her head. "I don't want to know. What good does knowing do me?"

"My little boy's in hiding. They'll kill him if they find him."

"Unless you're as crazy as you sound and none of this is true."

"It's true. Open your eyes and look at me. It's true."

Petra opened her eyes. If there was anything to be read in them other than self-pity and hatred and anger, Jane couldn't see it.

"Whoever you are, you're a liar. And if you aren't, which you are, but if you aren't, shit, then whether I spill to you or don't, I'm dead."

In other words, she had just said, *Show me a way out, give me hope, and maybe I'll help you.*

"Simon keeps big money in the house, in a safe somewhere," Jane said. "His kind always do."

"I don't know about any big-money safe."

Jane waited a beat and let a note of tenderness into her voice. "There've been times I've been lost, there seemed no obvious road ahead. But a lost girl, any lost girl, she doesn't need to be lost forever. I'll make him tell me where the money is. I don't need it. After I'm done here, you take the money and go."

"Go where? I got nowhere to go."

"A couple hundred thousand, maybe more. With that, you can go anywhere you want, somewhere you've never been and nobody knows you. Stop being Petra Quist. You changed your name before. Change it again. And stay the hell away from men like him. Find a new way."

"What new way?"

Jane leaned forward on the padded bench and put her left hand over one of the child-woman's zip-tied hands. "A new way to be. The way you are, even if I'd never shown up, chances are you'd be dead by thirty. You said Simon's good to you, gives you everything, he's sweet. But you've had moments—haven't you?— moments when you sensed real evil in him, violence."

After a hesitation, Petra broke eye contact. She tipped her head back and gazed up at the trompe l'oeil cloud forms, through which a colorful dawn broke perpetually.

Even in an interrogation more intense than this one, even when physical threats and worse were involved, the objective was always to persuade the subject rather than to force submission by fear of brute force. In nearly every inquest of this nature, there came a point when the examinee was ready to cooperate but hadn't said so, when in fact the decision to provide the information remained as yet more subconscious than fully realized. The interrogator needed to be able to recognize such a moment and not step on it with additional questions or, worst of all, with intimidation, because until the subject had come all the way into the light, she could so easily change her mind and stay on the dark side.

Still searching the faux clouds, Petra said, "Sometimes he hurts me, but he doesn't mean to."

35

The candle flames twisted and unfurled and fluttered in the cheap glassware, the soft amber light ceaselessly ebbing and flowing in waveforms across the table in the church kitchen, their pale reflections quivering in the brushed stainless steel of the nearby refrigerator, like a trio of spirits writhing in some visible but inaccessible dimension parallel to the one in which Tanuja and Sanjay lived.

The twins sat catercorner to each other as they ate ham-and-cheese sandwiches slathered with mayonnaise—two each, for they were ravenous—and potato chips. Their flight from a nightmare posse had been bizarre and terrifying as they'd raced from the eastern canyons into the heavily populated cities of mid-county and the coast. But now that they had found sanctuary, however temporary, the experience seemed less terrifying than fairy-tale spooky, less bizarre than fantastic, like some adventure concocted by a modern equivalent of the Brothers Grimm—or at least so it seemed to Tanuja. As in all such tales of fantasy, they had come to that moment of respite in which the most humble circumstances seemed all the warmer for being unpretentious and in contrast to the extraordinary drama that had preceded it, when homely food seemed to be the most delicious meal ever put before them because it had been earned by their cleverness and bravery.

During the first sandwich, such was their extreme hunger and their desire to steep in the coziness of this haven that they barely talked. As they ate the second sandwiches more slowly, they could hardly *stop* talking. Rehashing what they'd been through. Speculating on the meaning of it. Considering their options.

Throughout their conversation, on the table lay the two ampules that Tanuja had scooped up after she had felled Linc Crossley and his two henchmen with insecticide. Within those glass containers, in the candlelight, the cloudy amber fluid glimmered like some magical elixir that would grant them extramundane powers.

The pulsing candle flames created an illusion of shifting currents within that elixir, but there was real movement as well. The tiny particles clouding the fluid were falling out of suspension and adhering to one another in tangled threadlike formations that kept slowly dissolving and re-forming in new configurations. Here and there along the threads were what at first appeared to be knots but that, on closer inspection, almost seemed to resemble elements on a silicon microchip. These, too, dissolved even as others similar to them began to accrete elsewhere in the web of threads.

Sanjay pondered the ampules. "Maybe this stuff was stored in that container of dry ice to keep it stable. When it warms up, it starts doing this."

Leaning into the candle glow, Tanuja said, "Yeah, but what exactly is it doing? Turning putrid or something?"

"It kind of looks like all the tiny particles are trying to come together to form something. Though how could they do that undirected?"

"Form what?"

Sanjay frowned. "They were going to inject me with this."

"Form what?" Tanuja repeated.

"Something. I don't know. Nothing good."

While making the sandwiches, they had found a bar of dark chocolate and had at once determined to save some of the champagne to have with it.

When Tanuja had eaten her share of the candy, as her brother poured the last of the champagne in her glass, the aromatic bubbles fizzing, she said, "I need to use the ladies' room."

He pushed his chair back from the table to accompany her.

"No, no," she said. "Not unless you need the men's. I remember the way. Enjoy your chocolate, *chotti bhai*."

She rose from her chair and picked up one of the tumblers that contained a candle. "When I get back, we absolutely have to decide what we do in the morning. I won't sleep tonight if we don't have a plan."

"We could have the plan of all plans," Sanjay said, "and I doubt I'd sleep, anyway."

At the doorway to the hall, she glanced back and saw her brother leaning over the ampules, peering intently at the contents. By some trick of candlelight, the tangled threads within the amber fluid appeared to cast the faintest web of trembling shadows across his sweet brown face.

36

"Hurts you?" Jane said. "How does he hurt you?"

With her head still tipped back, face turned to the coffered vault of the theater lobby, Petra Quist closed her eyes, and behind the lids they moved as if following events in a disturbing dream.

"He doesn't mean to. He just, like, you know, he gets too excited. He's like a boy sometimes, the way he gets so excited."

"How does he hurt you?" Jane persisted.

"I'm a little drunk. I'm dead tired. I want to sleep."

"How does he hurt you?"

"It's not like he really hurts me."

"You said he did. Sometimes."

"Yeah, but I mean . . . not bad, not so it marks me."

"How? Come on, girl. You want to tell me."

After a silence, shaped by tension yet as still as kiln-fired porcelain, Petra spoke softly, though she didn't whisper. Her voice grew quieter than before and somehow distant, as if the essence of her retreated from the outer regions of her body, from the world of ceaseless sensations assaulting her five senses. "He slaps me."

"Your face?"

"It stings but never marks. He never marks me. He never would."

"What else?"

"Sometimes . . . one hand around my throat. Holding me down."

"Choking you?"

"No. A little. But I can breathe. It's scary, is all. But I can breathe a little. He never marks me. Never would. He's good to me."

Thunders of silence suggested an inner storm, and the blank upturned face served as a mask behind which anguish hid. She was drunk, and she might be tired, but in spite of what she said, she didn't want to sleep. Her silence was not a final statement, but instead a pause for gathering.

"Sometimes he calls me names and, like, says things he doesn't mean, and he's so . . . rough. But only, you know, because he gets so excited, is all. He never marks me."

Jane said, "All this, holding you down by the throat,

slapping you, being rough . . . you mean it's during sex."

"Yeah. Not every time. But sometimes. He doesn't mean it. He's always sorry afterward. He buys me Tiffany to apologize. He can be so sweet, like a little boy."

This troubled child in a woman's body had made revelations that Jane could use to push some of Simon's buttons in an interrogation, although nothing yet with which she could effectively whipsaw him.

Bound by more than zip-ties, by ligatures of times past, trapped between the idea of a thrilling libertine life and the grim reality as she lived it, head tipped back and slender throat exposed to Jane, Petra now disclosed a fact that might be used to break her cruel lover, though she didn't understand the importance of it.

From the internal distance into which she had retreated, her voice came colored by melancholy. "Funny how things are. You figure nobody can really hurt you anymore, you've been hit with it all. And then some stupid thing that shouldn't matter does. Like, it's not when he's rough that hurts me, you know, not hurts me so it matters. What hurts me is the weird thing, when sometimes he forgets my name and calls me by hers, and she's just a damn machine."

37

Into darkness Tanuja carried light, the glass tumbler warm in her hand, luminous candle-cast shapes without form pulsing on the hallway walls, ahead of her absolute blackness beyond the reach of the humble lamp.

This building drew into it the hush of the church to which it stood connected, the quiet of those empty pews and that shadowed altar. The only sounds were the faint squeak of her sneakers on the waxed-vinyl floor and the occasional sputter as the candle flame found impurities in the wick.

The restroom doors did not feature automatic closures. The one at the women's lavatory stood half-open. She pushed it wider and did not close it after she crossed the threshold.

In this smaller space, with reflective glossy-white laminate walls and mirrors, more light seemed to swell from the candle, and the shadows largely retreated. There were two sinks in a cove on the left side of the room, two on the right, and four enclosed stalls against the back wall.

She went to the cove on the right and set the candle on the counter between those two sinks. In addition to the back wall, the side walls of the cove were also lined with mirrors, each reflecting the reflection in the other, flickering candles ordered to infinity.

Tanuja went into the nearest stall. Just enough candlelight bounced off the low ceiling to provide guidance. She tended to business and flushed the toilet.

She returned to one of the sinks and cranked on the water and pumped liquid soap from the bottle. The water was hot, and from her lathered hands rose the rich orange fragrance of the soap.

When she turned off the water and pulled a couple paper towels from the dispenser, she looked at her face in the back mirror, half expecting the stresses of the night to have visibly aged her. Food and drink had done their job, however, so that she didn't even appear tired.

The candle before her and its legions of reflections rendered her eyes less dark adapted than they had been in the hallway. When movement in the back mirror suggested a presence behind her, she thought at first it must be illusory, nothing more than shadow and light dancing to the soundless rhythm of the throbbing candle flame.

But her confusion lasted only a moment. Whether he had entered through the open door to the hall while the water rushing into the sink masked his arrival or whether he had been in one of the other stalls, he was there and he was real. A youngish man. Blond hair that looked almost white in the spectral light. He loomed less than an arm's length away, and though she wanted to believe that he was an innocent parishioner who, for whatever reason, had remained behind after the play, she knew that he was no one that benign.

She started to turn but felt the poles of a handheld Taser pressed hard into the small of her back. Although the cold steel pins failed to pierce her T-shirt, the garment didn't provide enough insulation to protect her, and she received a shock that disrupted nerve-path messaging throughout her body.

The sound that escaped her was like the faint lament of some small night creature seized in the talons of an owl. She seemed not to collapse so much as shiver to the floor, as if unraveling from her bones, there to shudder uncontrollably and gasp for breath that her lungs would not expand to receive.

The attacker pressed the Taser to her abdomen and shocked her again, and pressed it to her neck for a third blast, which was when she passed out.

38

Turning her face to Jane and opening her eyes, Petra Quist said, "Anabel. Sometimes in the sack, he calls me Anabel, just like the house computer. Weird, huh?"

"Have you asked him why?"

"He doesn't know why. He says it doesn't matter, it's nothing. But it's something to me."

Leaning forward, touching the girl's hand again, Jane said, "Sometimes they hurt us most when they don't know they're hurting us at all. In fact, that's why it hurts—because they don't even know us well enough to understand."

"That's some true shit. How can he be in my arms—in *me*—and call me, you know, a machine name?"

"Do you know, with the program he has," Jane explained, "each homeowner can customize the service name of the house computer?"

The party girl's blue eyes were clear, her stare direct, but she was still peering at the world from the bottom of a martini glass. A frown of puzzlement. "What's that mean or matter?"

"He could name it anything from Abby to Zoe. So he named it after some woman he knows."

Whatever might happen here in the next few hours, Petra must realize that she had no future with Simon, and yet she reacted in a proprietary manner. "What damn woman? Why didn't he tell me about the bitch?"

"If I were you, I'd ask him. Hell, I'd *make* him tell me. But, listen, sweetie, maybe this is important. Exactly when does he call you Anabel?"

"I told you, like only sometimes in the sack."

"When he climaxes?"

"No. Well, I'm not sure, but I don't think ever then." Her gaze turned to the zip-tie that secured her left hand to the chair. "When he slaps me, clamps a hand around my throat, when he's rough . . ."

Her voice feathered away into silence, and it seemed as if her mind had taken wing through a dark woods of memory.

In time, Petra said, "Yeah, when he calls me Anabel, there's always this anger. It's a little scary, but it's not me he's angry with. I always thought he was angry with himself. For not, you know, being able. Mostly he's super ready, though sometimes not. But I'm hearing him now, how he sounds, and maybe it's not all anger, maybe mostly hatred. So bitter how he says her name, and then he's rough with me, and if he's rough enough, then he's ready and able."

"Able to get an erection," Jane clarified.

"Poor Simon," said Petra with seeming sympathy. "How awful for him when he's got trouble with it."

39

In the wake of some nameless catastrophe that had extinguished the lights of the city and its surrounding settlements, fires leaped in man-made craters, and undulatory ashes rose on hot currents into a night watched over by a sinister smiling moon, but mostly there was darkness and smoke and a greasy odor not to be contemplated. Bier carriers bore the deceased upon their weary shoulders and Brahmans officiated in the otherworldly light, as sweating cremators in loincloths stoked the flames. Here in the *shamshan ghat*, where dead bodies were burned, uncountable mourners roamed less than half-seen, to whom Tanuja must be as shadowy as they were to her, cries of grief issuing from their shadow mouths. She was in Mumbai again, not as a child, but as a woman, yet somehow it was the night her parents had perished in the plane crash. And though the plane had gone down far from India, she *knew* they were inexplicably here, among these victims of this unnamed cataclysm. Although they must be dead, Tanuja grew ever more desperate to find dear *Baap* and *Mai*, for it was urgent that, in death, they reach out to Sanjay, as she at the moment could not, reach out and warn him that he was in great peril.

Waking from the dream, she needed a moment to realize she was lying on the restroom floor. She smelled hot candle wax and orange-scented soap.

The man who had Tasered her stepped into view and stood over her and reached down, offering assistance. She didn't want to touch him, but when she shied from his hand, he seized her by the wrist and yanked her into a sitting position.

"Get off your ass," he said, "or I'll drag you out of here by your hair."

She found her strength, rose, swayed, regained her equilibrium, and put one hand to her neck to learn the nature of something that constricted her. A collar. Her attacker pulled on a lead, and the collar tightened. While she had lain unconscious, he'd put her on a leash, as if she were a dog.

After seven years during which she and her brother had been ensnared by their aunt and uncle, the devious Chatterjees, freedom was no less essential than air to Tanuja Shukla. She prided herself on being a woman who coped with any situation, who was not easily alarmed. But a fright akin to panic now seized her. Heart knocking as though she'd run miles, she fumbled for the clasp on the collar but could not release it.

"Leave the candle," her captor said. "Don't think

you can throw it in my face. We're going to the kitchen. You know the way."

As they approached the open door to the hallway, she shouted a warning to Sanjay, and her keeper slapped her hard upside the head. She cried out again—"*Sanjay, run! Run!*"—and the man whipped the end of the leash across her face.

"Don't be stupid," he said. "It's too late."

Stepping out of the restroom, Tanuja hoped desperately he'd not meant that her beloved brother had been captured, but instead that Sanjay had already escaped, that it was too late for them to get their filthy hands on him.

With the lavatory behind them, darkness shrouded the first hallway, which seemed like a passage to *jahannan*, where demons bred and all hope must be shed. She knew they entered the intersection of the two halls when to the left she saw a doorway defined by a faint aura of wick light: the kitchen.

When she crossed that threshold, her keeper at her back, she saw this was indeed *jahannan*, and she wept silently at the sight of Sanjay sitting at the table in defeat. His shirt was torn, his hair disarranged, as if he'd struggled against the hulking man who stood beside his chair. In the glow of the two remaining candles, Tanuja could see the collar around his neck, the leash drawn taut down the back of his chair and tied securely to the stretcher bar between the two back legs.

40

"I'm sorry about this, but it's necessary," Jane said as from her tote bag she withdrew a prepared ball of gauze and a roll of duct tape. "Although I don't think Simon could hear you from the foyer upstairs, I can't risk you calling out a warning. Once I've got him in the theater, I'll come back and strip off the tape, take out the gag, so you'll be more comfortable."

"You can trust me," Petra said. "I get it now—my situation."

"That sure was quick, huh? 'I was blind, but now I see.'"

"I'm not scamming you. I really get it. The only way out for me is your way."

"I believe you *do* get it, kid. But you've got Simon under your skin."

"No. That's over."

"He hits you, chokes you, gets rough with you in I don't know what other ways, but when you're sitting here alone, without me to focus you on that one way out, you'll slip loose from your common sense and drift back toward him."

The girl was sufficiently self-aware not to argue. She said only, "Maybe not."

"'Maybe' isn't good enough."

As though a hangover now pincered its way through her skull hours ahead of schedule, the girl's face paled under its light coat of foundation and powder blush. She had lip-printed the most recent martini glasses with much of her Maybelline; and the natural pink of her mouth now grayed a little as if with the memory of her night on the town, of all that she had drunk and said and done.

"Later," Jane promised, "when I've opened his safe and put his money in front of you, I'll let you have a look at him and decide whether you want him . . . or the cash and a new start. I can try to trust you then. Because when I've finished with him, I think you'll rather have the money."

"What are you going to do to him?"

"That depends on Simon. Whether it's a cakewalk or a firewalk is up to him. Now let me put this gauze in your mouth. If you try to bite me, I'll slap you harder than Simon does, and I'll damn sure leave a mark or three."

Petra opened her mouth, but then turned her head aside. "Wait. I have to go potty. I need to pee."

"There's no time for that. You'll have to hold it."

"How long?"

"Until you can't anymore."

"That is so wrong."

"It is. It's wrong," Jane agreed. "But with Simon arriving soon, that's the way it has to be."

"You're a total bitch."

"You've said as much several times before, and I haven't once disagreed—have I? Now open your mouth."

Petra took the gauze gag without trying to bite.

Jane patched the girl's mouth shut with a rectangle of duct tape and then wound a longer strip twice around her head to secure the first.

41

The creep who collared Tanuja was no prize, but he didn't scare her as much as did his partner. The bigger man stood maybe six feet five and weighed about 230 pounds, but it wasn't just his formidable size that disturbed her. His cold stare impaled her with his contempt. He was graceful for such a giant, but his every move was oiled with arrogance, as if during all the years since he had been born into the world, he'd never seen one smallest reason to doubt he was superior to everything and everyone in it. He radiated a potential for sudden violence no less than did a tiger with its ears pricked and nostrils flared and fangs bared as it watched a lame gazelle.

The dishes, champagne glasses, and ampules having been cleared from the table, they were replaced now with rubber tubing to be used as a tourniquet and foil-wrapped antiseptic wipes with which to sterilize the point of injection.

Tanuja sat catercorner to Sanjay, as she had when they'd been eating, now bound neck to stretcher bar as he was. Her dear *chotti bhai* said he was sorry, as though by some mistake solely his, he'd brought these two down on them.

The giant advised them to be quiet if they didn't want to have their tongues cut out, and although the threat was over the top, no feverish imagination was required to envision him fulfilling it with the deft use of a scalpel.

The smaller man, blond with blue eyes, had a prep-school air, though he appeared to be in his thirties. Now he placed on the table an insulated cooler identical to the one that Linc Crossley's buddy with caterpillar eyebrows had brought to their house earlier in the night. After slipping his hands into a pair of cotton gloves, the preppy took from the cooler two hypodermic syringes, a few plastic-wrapped objects that Tanuja could not identify, and then a nine-inch-square stainless-steel box that was maybe eight inches deep. When he opened the lid of the box, dry ice exhaled a frosty breath that winnowed away in the warm air and candlelight.

Tanuja felt as if she were dreaming a nightmare that she had dreamed before.

From the steel box, the preppy withdrew six insulated sleeves with Velcro closures. He shut the box and stripped off the gloves.

Sanjay tried to pull away when the big man began to tie the tourniquet around his right arm, but resistance only earned him a blow to the face with the heel of the giant's hand, which snapped Sanjay's head back and stunned him as might have any other man's point-blank punch with a tightly closed fist.

Tanuja saw a thread of blood issue from one of her

brother's nostrils. She tried to get up, but the leash secured her to the chair so that she couldn't stand.

The preppy turned on the kitchen lights so that his partner might better see the target blood vessel in Sanjay's arm.

With the efficiency of a trained phlebotomist, the big man used the hypodermic needle to insert a cannula in the vein, then set the needle aside. He punctured the seal on the first of the cold ampules and fitted it to the valve on the cannula. He held the ampule in an elevated position and opened the valve to whatever setting might be required. By intravenous infusion, the cloudy amber fluid began to move from the glass ampule into Sanjay's bloodstream, its nature unknown, its purpose unfathomed.

Tanuja urgently wanted to know *what*, to understand *why*, but there was no point in asking, for these men would not tell her, and there was nothing to be gained by screaming because no one would hear her in time, nor any way to resist that would long forestall whatever fate filled those ampules. She felt ten years old again, in fresh receipt of the news of their parents' long fall from the sky, in the shadow of her smiling aunt Ashima Chatterjee, for whom a sister's untimely death was less a grievous loss than a golden opportunity. As a child, she had found the world mysterious and forbidding, wound through with more darkness than light, had perceived threats coiled everywhere from the attic to the space under her bed, from an open woods at noon to the front yard at night. Sanjay, too, had early on been of a noirish sensibility, and yet it was because of him that Tanuja had over time been

able to put her countless fears behind her, to recon-
ceive the world as a place of wonder brimming with
magical possibilities, to have such conviction in that
revised conception that her career as a writer flowered
from it. By his kindness, by his caring, by his patient
and wise instruction, her little brother, with two minutes less experience of this life, had been her therapist,
her spiritual guide, teaching her the truth and power
of free will to make of this world more than it seemed
to be, more even than it was, and thereby purge the
darkness of all threat and find in it as much magic as
in the light. Only a year or so ago, she had realized
that Sanjay's noirish point of view had remained, primarily, the way he perceived this life; though he believed in free will and was never in a mood as dark
as any in his writing, he didn't see a world with wonder brimming and magical possibilities, as he had so
passionately, persistently encouraged her to see it. In
a family with too much stoicism, with too little love
expressed—and, following the plane's fall into the sea,
with no love at all—Sanjay openly adored his sister;
he was troubled that so much frightened her and so
little enchanted. One day he resolved to banish her
fears and see her grow in happiness. He had pretended that the vision of a wondrous world, full of
miracles and marvels, was his to share, and he had
championed it with such enthusiasm that his pretense
had become her truth, her unshakable conviction. She
and Sanjay had been conceived in the same moment,
had come into the world together, and she could not
imagine her life unspooling past the moment when
her *chotti bhai* no longer breathed. As she watched the

third ampule drain through the cannula into her brother's arm, Tanuja welcomed the infusion of the remaining three into herself, for regardless of what might now have been done to Sanjay, she must follow him into the unknown and, if given the chance, be for him what he had always been for her.

The hateful *rakshasa* finished the first phase of his demonic task by removing the cannula from Sanjay's arm. He didn't bother to press a Band-Aid over the needle puncture, but allowed a button of blood to form in the crook of the elbow and a scarlet thread to slowly unravel from it, like a misplaced stigmata.

Tanuja didn't resist—nor did she allow them the satisfaction of seeing her fear—as the preppy applied the tourniquet to her right arm. He palpated the visible veins to find the most generous one and swabbed the skin with the sterilizing pad.

The big man came around the table, carrying another cannula, the second hypodermic, and three large ampules.

42

At twenty-three minutes past midnight, headlights swept off the street and arced onto the circular driveway, followed by a gleaming black Cadillac limousine with heavily tinted windows. The long car motored to the portico with surprisingly little engine noise, as menacing as it was elegant. The quiet limo seemed even somewhat eerie at this hour and in these circumstances, as if skull-faced Death had traded in his classic horse-drawn carriage for a modern conveyance and would step out with a silver scythe, wearing not a hooded cloak but a Tom Ford suit.

Standing back from the foyer window, Jane Hawk watched as the chauffeur opened a starboard door and Simon Yegg appeared. He was attired not in a suit but in red-and-white sneakers, tan chinos, a brightly striped rugby shirt, an unzipped leather jacket, and a pink baseball cap with a large number three on it: a forty-six-year-old white guy who thought he could pull off the look of a cool black rapper half his age.

The limo glided away as Simon unlocked the deadbolt. The alarm sounded as he stepped into the house.

Jane stood on the hinge side of the door, concealed from him.

"Anabel, disarm security. Five, six, five, one, star." The alarm fell silent, and Anabel informed him that it was disarmed, whereupon he said, "Anabel, follow me with light."

As the chandelier brightened, Simon Yegg closed the door and saw Jane holding the six-ounce plastic bottle at arm's length. She sprayed his nose and mouth with chloroform, and he dropped with a swish of clothing, like a basketball through a net, although when he hit the floor, he had no bounce in him.

She hadn't been able to use chloroform with the girl because she'd needed to interrogate her in a timely manner. She had hours to devote to Yegg if she needed them.

Chloroform was highly volatile. To be sure that he remained unconscious, she put a double thickness of paper towels over his face, trapping the fumes. He wasn't having a breathing problem.

At the security-system keypad, Jane set the alarm in the HOME mode. She returned to the front door, engaged the Schlage deadbolt, and peered out the window. The limousine was long gone. In the pale penumbra of a streetlamp, a slinking coyote turned its luminous yellow eyes toward the house, as if it sensed her watching.

Muscular, five feet ten, weighing about 180 pounds, Simon posed a greater logistics problem than had Petra Quist. There were always ways to accomplish such tricky tasks, however, and in this case, the problem himself had thoughtfully provided her with the solution. From the garage, she had earlier brought up the mechanic's sled. She rolled it to his side and locked the wheels.

A hundred and eighty pounds of inert Yegg was a lot of dead weight. Getting him onto the board required treating him as if he were several loosely connected sacks of potatoes, and after four or five minutes of struggle, she got the job done.

The board was too short to hold all of him. His legs were off the sled from mid-thigh down, but the drag factor wouldn't slow her too much.

To prevent his arms from sliding off the board, she undid the belt on his Gucci chinos, shoved his hands under the waistband, and cinched the belt tight. He lay there as if fondling himself.

To fashion a pull for the sled, she had employed

one of the extension cords that she'd found stored in a garage cabinet. After flipping up the built-in chocks on the wheels, she pulled Simon Yegg to the main elevator, leaving the baseball cap on the foyer floor.

Descending to the basement, she lifted the paper towels and checked the color in his face and made sure he was still breathing well. Then she replaced the towels and lightly spritzed them with more chloroform.

In the theater, the carpet somewhat resisted the squeaking wheels, and when Jane pulled the sled into the lobby, Petra sat up straight, eyes wide. The girl worked her jaws, perhaps trying to shift the wad of saliva-soaked gauze in her mouth. She made urgent noises that, through the duct tape, were not words.

Jane propped open the door between the lobby and the theater. She maneuvered the sled into the main room.

There were three rows of chairs, five per row, but they were neither traditional theater seats nor in harmony with the French theme. These adjustable loungers, upholstered in leather, appeared more conducive to sleep than to cinema.

The rows of chairs were flanked by wide aisles. Because the floor sloped down to a stage and a big screen—currently out of sight behind a burgundy-velvet curtain trimmed with enormous tassels—gravity more than overcame the impediment of the carpet.

Between the front row and the stage, an eight-foot-wide flat area extended the width of the theater. She parked the sled there, where earlier she had left three more extension cords, the workbench stool from the garage, a Bernzomatic butane lighter with a long flex-ible neck that she had found in a kitchen drawer, and half a dozen sixteen-ounce bottles of water.

She passed the first of the extension cords under the sled and used it as a rope to secure Simon Yegg's upper arms to the board. In similar fashion, she strapped down his waist and then his legs. The rubber on the cords didn't allow knots to be drawn as tight as she preferred them; therefore, with the butane lighter, she fused them into knots that couldn't be undone, using some of the water in one of the bottles each time the melting rubber began to flame.

She plucked the paper towels off the wife killer's face and tossed them aside. A faint moist residue of chloroform lent a sheen to his upper lip, which evaporated even as she watched, and a few tiny drops of dew sparkled in his nose hairs. Simon would regain consciousness in ten to fifteen minutes.

43

After Tanuja Shukla receives her nano-machine control mechanism, Carter Jergen gathers up the empty ampules and other debris, and he returns everything to the cooler, leaving no signifi-cant evidence behind.

He goes to the women's restroom and returns with the candle glass that was left there. He sets it on the table with the other two and turns off the overhead fluorescents, preferring to pass the waiting period in this softer and more atmospheric light.

Dubose stands by the kitchen sink, smoking a joint, taking deep breaths and holding them and expelling them less with a sigh than with a gruff bearish exhalation, all the while watching the girl.

Jergen supposes he knows what that means. This waiting period isn't likely to be as tedious as it has been during other recent conversions.

He settles at the table with his iPad and goes online to explore hotel possibilities for a Caribbean vacation that he's hoping to take in September.

But for Dubose's smoking and what little noises Jergen makes, the church kitchen is quiet. The twins now understand that any question will receive a blow rather than an answer, as will any comment or argument. They are powerless, and they are acutely aware of it. All the Shukla moxie has evaporated. They don't know what the injections have done to them, and fear of the unknown is paralyzing. If they aren't in despair, if they haven't utterly abandoned hope, they are despondent, with no current capacity for hope. Part of the reason they do not speak is no doubt because they fear that their voices will sound weak and lost, that hearing themselves will only further discourage them.

Sooner than Jergen expects, Dubose pinches out the remainder of the joint, drops it in a jacket pocket, and crosses the room to the girl. He unties the leash from the stretcher bar and tells her to get up. When she hesitates, he jerks hard on the leash, as if he's an impatient child and she's a pull toy that's wedged immobile.

She rises from the chair, and her brother says anxiously, "What's happening, what're you doing?"

Jergen leans forward, grabs the kid's left ear, twists it hard enough to crush a little cartilage and make his point. Sanjay tries to pull his head away, but Jergen won't allow that.

As Dubose leads the girl toward the hallway door, she looks back and says her brother's name, not as if calling for his help, but as if saying good-bye. Then she and Dubose are gone.

When Jergen lets go of the ear, Sanjay tries to thrust to his feet, as if there might be some slightest chance that the leash will snap or the collar come undone, or the dinette chair disintegrate as he thrashes valiantly in it. He transitions directly from despondency to that energized form of despair called desperation. Although he surges from stoic immobility into a screaming rage, his fury will not gain him anything, for he is furious less with Dubose than with himself, with his helplessness, which will endure for the rest of his life.

Jergen puts aside his iPad to watch Sanjay, who for the moment is more entertaining than any Caribbean vacation.

In but a minute, Sanjay exhausts himself and sags in the chair, slick with sweat. He is like a horse that, having been thrown into a panic by a snake, has stamped and reared so often, to no avail, that it has no strength remaining for anything other than the tremors coursing through it from throttle to thigh, its blind terror otherwise expressed only in its eyes, which seem to swell in their sockets, encircled by an extraordinary field of white, the irises like twin craters in twin moons.

Such are Sanjay's eyes when Carter Jergen says, "In a way, she did this to herself, to you. The two of you were on the Hamlet list to be adjusted, but you weren't near the top until her novel was published three weeks ago. *Alecto Rising*. The response of certain critics and too many deeply affected readers led the computer to move you to the top of the list."

Jergen is not sure that Sanjay can make sense of what he hears, so deeply is he sunk in misery, his mind turning round and round on a descending spiral path of grief and guilt. But Jergen and Dubose have won the day, and there's no point in achieving a win if you can't have some fun with it.

"Her novel will inspire the worst ideas among impressionable younger generations. The computer identifies it as potentially a dangerous iconic work. So it's fitting—don't you think?—that the two of you will now be tasked with discrediting it and all your other writing, ensuring that every word the two of you have put on paper will go out of print forever."

Sanjay's gaze fixed on the nearest of the candles, the faux fire bright in his eyes, which might never again be alive with a true fire.

"It used to take eight to twelve hours after injection for the control mechanism to fully form across the brain. Only in the last few days have we been using a new version of the secret sauce that completes the job in four hours. Millions of brain-tropic molecular machines swimming upstream toward those three pounds of tissue in your skull. Sanjay Shukla is only secondarily the body in this chair before me. The essential you is those three pounds. Can you feel those millions of invaders swimming through you and at the same time *toward* you? I am fascinated by it all. I wonder . . . when they pass through the walls of cerebral capillaries and into the very tissue of the brain, when they begin to link up and form a web across the various lobes, in the final hour of your independence, before everything settles down up there, will you feel as if spiders are creeping inside your skull?"

Sanjay's eyes turn from the candle and meet Jergen's stare. In a whisper, he declares, "You're insane."

"Sticks and stones," Jergen replies.

"Evil," Sanjay says. "Not all madmen are evil, but all evil men are mad."

Jergen smiled. "You shouldn't speak so disparagingly of someone who will shortly be your absolute master."

11

Jane returned from the theater to the lobby and released the chocks on the wheels of the office chair. She rolled Petra Quist into the theater and parked her in the shadows behind the back row of seats, where she could see and hear what was to come. Then she fixed the wheels in place once more.

After unwinding the duct tape, Jane waited while the party girl worked the sodden mass of gauze between her teeth and expelled it into her lap.

Considering that Simon Yegg made a habit of hurting her and that she claimed to be over him, Petra seemed unduly worried about his well-being, almost breathless with concern. "My God, what've you done to him, did you kill him already, his *face* was covered, wasn't his face covered?"

"It's not covered now," Jane said, directing Petra's attention to her nuclear love machine below, bound like Gulliver in Lilliput. She had adjusted the theater lighting so that only the stage and the area immediately in front of it were illuminated. "He's just asleep, recovering from an encounter with chloroform."

"What are you going to do to him?"

"Not a fraction of what he deserves."

"He's not all bad. I mean, he's not so nice sometimes, but he's not a hopeless shit."

Jane said, "Listen, I've brought you into this so you can hear him and maybe learn something. Lying down there, Simon's not at an angle where he can see you even if he turns his head, even if you weren't in the dark up here. Among other things, you'll learn what he really thinks about you. It'll be worth hearing. But if you can't keep your mouth shut, I'll gag and duct-tape you again."

"No. Don't. I can't. I thought I was gonna puke and choke on it, you know."

"Then be silent."

"Okay. I will. But please, please, *please* let me go potty."

Those blue eyes were so pellucid that they seemed like windows to a soul in all its truth, but artful cunning was required to meet eye to eye for as long as this and seem guileless. Jane put a hand to her captive's head, and the girl flinched. She wanted only to smooth the disarranged hair back from Petra's forehead, which she did before saying, "Sorry, but I don't trust you yet. In spite of all your attitude, you have so little self-esteem that you'll go on needing Simon until you have even less respect for him than you have for yourself."

Sudden color pinked the girl's pale cheeks and her chin thrust forward. She seemed about to pull the trigger on her temper. But she restrained herself, opting for a look of pitiable distress. "I *really* gotta pee."

"It's not my chair," Jane said, "so have at it."

45

Sanjay Shukla finds no hope in the candle-light and yet another reason for despair in Carter Jergen's eyes, and so he turns his attention to the open door through which Radley Dubose led Tanuja.

In a voice breaking with anguish, he says, "Where has he taken my sister?"

"If Pastor Gordon has an office here," says Jergen, "it's a cozy space with all the amenities. He didn't strike me as one of those clergy who believes there's any point to a vow of poverty. Mainly, my partner will want a nice big sofa."

The thin sound that escapes the younger twin suggests an intensity of grief that Jergen has never heard before.

"You don't have to worry that I might have any such intentions, Sanjay. That good old boy was raised in backwoods West Virginia. I wasn't. Oh, yes, he was accepted at Princeton and earned a degree. But the standards expected of Princeton grads, if any standards are expected at all, are magnitudes below those of Harvard alumni. I'd rather be partnered with one of my own kind, but I must admit he does keep things interesting."

The girl's first cry seems to issue from a greater distance than is in fact the case, and it sounds like the forlorn voice of some exotic night bird, though lonelier and eerier than a loon's call and more miserable than the moaning of an ibis.

Jergen's buttoned-up old-school father, Carlton, has long been a member of New England's preeminent bird-watching club, one of his many cultured interests. Inevitably, some of the elder Jergen's deep knowledge of all things avian has rubbed off on his son, although by his university days, Carter's interests were quite different from those of his old man.

Tanuja's protests no longer sound birdlike in any way, nor distant. They are shrill and terrible. She is apparently resisting with all her strength, though considering Dubose's size and the ferocity of his appetites, resistance is futile.

Kicking violently at the floor, Sanjay rocks the chair

backward from the table and attempts to stand, but the taut collar-and-leash tether makes it impossible for him to unbend his body from a sitting position and thrust to his feet. He can neither release the collar nor reach far enough behind and down to the knot at the stretcher bar. The chair topples onto its side, bearing him with it. He yanks on the arms of it as though he will break them off with his bare hands, but the frame of the chair is welded steel. The minimal restraint allows the illusion of easy escape; therefore, the truth of his helplessness is all the more frustrating. He is furious in his anguish, in his excruciating grief, managing to rattle the chair in a half circle to no useful purpose. Throughout this, he never shouts or screams, but grunts and hisses and snarls in this dumb-animal striving, breathing ever more noisily, until at last he is no longer able to deny his impotence. He lies on his side in the cage of his chair, immobilized and weeping miserably.

If the sister continues to make any noise, her protests are of little volume and contained within some room farther along the hall, where what was inevitable has come to pass.

Carter Jergen rises from his chair and stands over Sanjay, gazing down at him. "It's not as bad as you think. It won't haunt you the rest of your life. You won't forever be eaten by guilt. In fact, though your sister is traumatized and filled with shame now, she'll have entirely recovered by dawn. No trauma, no shame. Once your control mechanisms self-assemble and you've become adjusted people, I only need to tell you and her to forget everything that occurred

tonight, and all of it will be gone from memory—
including me, including my partner and what he's
done. A thing that can't be remembered . . . well, that's
as good as if it never happened."

46

Cinema Parisian. The area in front of the
stage and the apron of the stage itself
lighted as if for live entertainment to precede the
movie, the front row of seats in half light, the second
row in shadow, the third in darkness draped . . . And
at the highest point of the theater, shrouded in gloom,
the lone member of the audience, Petra Quist, perhaps a candidate for redemption, perhaps beyond
reclamation . . .

Jane placed the workshop stool beside the mechanic's sled and sat there as Simon Yegg muttered,
his facial expression morphing to reflect the rapidly
changing circumstances in one of the vivid and macabre dreams that sometimes made an ordeal of chloroform sleep.

He startled awake, blinked at her towering over
him, mumbled, "No," and closed his eyes as though
he could refuse this reality and receive another. He
repeated this exercise—"No . . . no . . . no . . . hell, no"—
each time becoming more aware of his hard circumstances, testing the extension cords that bound him,

until he came to the realization that there was but one world for him, whereupon he said in rapid order, "This sucks. Who're you? What's this about? You're the walking dead. You realize that? You're as dead as dead gets."

Jane said, "Given your situation, you talk some amazing trash. But I guess maybe you've got a good reason to pretend you're full-on macho."

He clearly didn't like what she said, but he failed to comment on her implication. "You can't scare me. I don't scare. You got me good. That was smart the way you got me like this. Real smart. So let's deal. You want money. Everyone wants money. So okay, I got money. Though you should live long enough to spend a dime."

After a silence, smiling as if he amused her, Jane said, "Maybe I'm not here for money. Maybe this is about the Hamlet list."

"The what?"

"Maybe it's about these bastards who call themselves the Techno Arcadians, like thirteen-year-old nerd boys meeting in a clubhouse in a tree."

"You sure you have the right address, honey? Maybe this would make sense to somebody next door, but it's just noise to me."

His confusion seemed genuine. His brother—Booth, big man in the Department of Justice—had been steering government business to him for years, but that didn't mean he trusted Simon enough to involve him in the conspiracy that had killed her Nick.

She said, "Or maybe I'm here on behalf of your ex-wives."

He didn't need to hesitate to formulate a deceitful comeback. "They took me to the cleaners. What more could they want?"

"*They* took *you*? Not the way I hear it."

"Everybody has her story." He realized that in addition to the cords binding him, his hands were in his pants and cinched tight under his belt. "I got a circulation problem here. My fingers are numb."

"Word on the street says it's not your fingers that's numb."

"What does that even mean?" he dared to ask. "Are you a crackhead bitch? You freebasing cocaine or something? You've maybe got a psychological problem, honey. Don't bring me that. I'm no psychiatrist. Let's get this done, let's talk money."

Trammeled beyond any hope of escape, flat on his back, gazing up at her on the high stool, he had to be disoriented. On the ladder of fear, other men might have been on the step labeled DREAD or even TERROR. Simon didn't appear to have gotten as high as MILD DISQUIET. Techniques for managing fear and subverting it into positive energy could be taught, but Simon's attitude and responses did not suggest he'd been through such instruction. Instead, his apparent confidence was in fact unalloyed arrogance, and his fearlessness more likely had its roots in solipsism, the belief that in all of the world, he alone was truly real, the center of the universe and its only story, while other people were just furnishings, mere provisions of which he could make any use he wished. In her serial-killing and mass-murder cases with the Bureau, she had encountered more than a few sociopaths like him. Because of his delusional view of reality, there were strings she might use to manipulate him; however, it was necessary always to recognize his twisted genius and his cunning, for such a man could be dangerous no matter how thoroughly he had been tied down and immobilized.

"'Everybody has her story,'" Jane quoted him. "Except your first ex, Marlo, who has no story these days because she was beaten to death in Paris."

"I loved that girl. She was my world, she truly was. She was sweet, but she had no common sense. What the hell was my Marlo doing in a radical Muslim neighborhood, anyway? Looking for a rich sheik?"

"And Alexis has no story anymore, either. She was pushed off a cliff in Yosemite. Three hundred feet is a long way to fall knowing you'll be dead on impact."

"Pushed? Who ever said pushed? She and some idiot boyfriend were hiking on an insanely dangerous trail. They were casual hikers. They didn't have the skills for it. Made me sick when I heard about it, just sick to my stomach, heartsick. I was in Hawaii at the time. Ruined Hawaii for me. Sure, our marriage didn't work out, and that was mostly my fault. I'm not proud at some time - thinking with my little head instead of my big one. I'm no choirboy. But I loved that girl, and it hurts me, hurts me bad, her life was cut so short."

Jane had the urge to get off the stool and step on his throat, put all her weight into it, and hear his esophagus collapse with a satisfying crunch. Such was the response that his kind too often elicited, because his mission in life wasn't what he thought, wasn't to be the unconquered hero of an epic story of power and triumph; his role was to anger others and dispirit them and, if possible, foster in them a desire to descend to his level and tempt them to act with a viciousness equal to his. She did not crush his throat, but the desire to do so remained.

"I guess it also hurts you when you think what's happened to your ex Dana, how she's totally agoraphobic now, so afraid of the wider world that she can't leave her house, lives such a prescribed existence, she's more isolated than a nun in a cloistered order."

Somehow, by attitude alone, Simon almost succeeded in making it seem that *he* was in the higher position, looking down on *her*. "Don't be such a snarky bitch. It's tiresome. If you know Dana, you know what a tragedy that is, not just the whole agoraphobia thing, but Dana herself. I mean, she's smart as a whip and so compassionate. She loves people, all people, not the tiniest bone of prejudice in that girl. But for all her virtues—and there's a lot more than I've mentioned—in spite of her many virtues, she's always been a little off. You hear what I'm saying? I fell hard in love with her—who wouldn't?—so I didn't see the problem for a while, but then it became undeniable. She was always a little off true north, like only two or three degrees off, but over time it gets worse, until she's not going anywhere on the compass that people like you and me would recognize, she's off into some weird territory. I feel so bad for her."

He paused in his odd mix of encomiums and self-justifications to cock his head and regard Jane from a slightly different angle, like an earthbound broken-wing bird turning one eye toward the sky to calculate the likelihood of single-wing flight. After a moment of silence, he said, "You're not here about Dana or Alexis or Marlo. My Sara sent you, didn't she?"

"Sara Holdsteck, wife number four? I know that part of your history, but I've never even spoken to her," Jane lied.

Briefly—but only briefly—puzzled, he said, "This isn't about any ex-wife. So is it Petra? No, it can't be. Don't tell me Petra's brought in some radical-feminist muscle to break some money out of me. I wouldn't have figured Petra capable of that kind of thing."

"Why wouldn't you think her capable of it?"

He shrugged as best he could in his restraints. "She's a fun kid, and she's smart enough, but she doesn't have it in her to look out for herself."

"Yeah? Well, a little earlier tonight, she came at me with a broken vodka bottle, tried to slash my face."

"No shit? She really did?" He appeared delighted by the image that those words had painted in his mind. "Of course, after a girls' night out, she would've been drunk. And she can always hold her own when it's just girl on girl. You gotta tell me, sugar, what'd you do to piss her off?"

"I liked *bitch* better."

"What?"

"Don't call me *sugar*."

"Yeah, you're one of those types. I get it. But what did you do to piss off Petra?"

"I needed her to tell me some things about you, and she didn't feel in a mood to cooperate."

"Where is she now?"

"Dead," Jane lied. "She came at me hard, and I shot her."

"You're shittin' me."

"Her body's in the kitchen."

"Damn, that's some of the sorriest news I've heard in a while. She was really hot. The word *hot* doesn't do her justice. She was a fine, fine piece of girl." He sighed and shook his head. "You're not here because of the wives, and not here because of Petra. You're here for you. So then why all this talk, talk, talk, talk? Let's do business."

"What did you mean, Petra can 'hold her own when it's just girl on girl'?"

"What's it matter now?"

"Humor me. I'm the curious type."

"I never been tied up for a gossip session before. Okay, all right. With a guy, any guy, she was like putty, just rolled over no matter what. Did what she was told, drunk or sober or in between. Did what she was told, took what she was told to take, and *liked* it. Never complained no matter what."

Jane leaned forward on her stool and peered down as if to read him more closely. "No matter what? So did you hit her?"

" 'Hit her'? Hell, no. I can get all the girls I want without ever hitting them. What's wrong with you talking trash like that? We're making progress, correcting the record, slowly coming to terms, and now you dis me like this. *'Did you hit her?'* I don't take offense easy, but that one's over the line. Did you come here just to insult me, or you want something worth the risks you've taken?"

Jane got off the stool. She walked away from him and then back toward him, rolling her shoulders, stretching her neck. "Two things I want. First, tell me where the cash is. And don't play any games with this, because I'm not Petra. I don't roll over."

"Maybe I look stupid right now, but I'm not. I give you one wrong number, you'll come back here and start cutting me or using a pair of pliers on my balls. I got no leverage. All I want is we do our business and get you gone."

After he told her where to find the safe and divulged the combination, she said, "You just want me gone, but what about Petra? Will you hang that murder on me?"

"There won't be a body by tomorrow morning," he said. "It'll be ground-up sludge poured in a pond at a sewage-treatment plant. She's the kind no one'll miss. Even those dumb-ass bitches she goes club-hopping with—in a month they won't remember her name. So she went off to Puerto Vallarta or Vegas or Mars with some other stud, just slutting her way to an early grave. So what? Who cares? Nobody. She's nothing."

She had parked Petra in the back of the theater because she wanted her to hear the truth of Simon from his lips, in the hope that the girl might ask herself what had gone wrong with her that she'd involve herself with such a man. But in Petra's fragile condition, Simon's acid contempt might do her more harm than good, and it was regrettable that she'd had to hear it.

Jane asked, "You sure you can get the sewage-treatment-plant thing done?"

"Haven't you been telling me how I'm great at

making women go away? And does it seem like I worry about cops? Let me tell you, honey, I'm so connected I could get a police escort to that sewage plant."

Jane knelt on the floor beside him. She could see that he preferred her at a distance. "I'm curious about something."

"You're a damn cat with all your curiosity."

"Why did you name the house computer Anabel?"

"What's that got to do with the price of beans? Go get the money you came for, honey."

"Money honey. Rhymin' Simon. Of all the names in the world, why name the house computer Anabel? It's a simple question. Isn't that a simple question?"

"Nothing about you is simple, is it? I didn't mean *honey,* it's just how I talk. I'll go back to *bitch,* make us both happy. Okay, all right. The system doesn't come with a set name. You have to give it one. I could've called it anything."

"But you called it Anabel. Your mother's name is Anabel. Does it make you feel special to be able to tell your mother what to do, and she always obeys?"

For the first time, he was nervous. In spite of his solipsism, perhaps he began to be troubled by the thought that even if he was the only *real* person in existence, even if the universe had been created solely as a vehicle for him to tell his story, his fate could take an unexpected turn for the worse.

47

Still kneeling beside Simon Yegg, Jane pressed one finger to the dimple in his chin. "Just like that actor back in the day, Kirk Douglas. When you were little, did your mommy put her finger in your chin dimple and call you adorable?"

As he had said, he wasn't stupid. He knew where this must be going, and it was forbidden territory.

His expression did not betray the anger that he wanted to conceal from her, but his eyes belied the impression of unconcern and self-control that he worked hard to project. Thus far they had been as opaque as the eyes of a ventriloquist's dummy, but now they revealed an inhuman fury. If he had not been tied down, he would have killed Jane to prevent her from pursuing her current line of inquiry.

She wiped her chin-probing finger on his rugby shirt. "Tell me now, how much do you hate your mother?"

"You're off true north yourself. You're totally off the map. My mother's a great lady."

"How much do you hate and fear your mother?" she persisted.

"Just shove it, shut your mouth. You don't know her."

"But I know *about* her. Four husbands. Each an effete wuss, a trust-fund baby from the day he was born.

Each of them had just scads and scads of inherited wealth."

"You don't go there. You don't go to family, ever."

"Four divorces, she gets everything she wants. More than she wants. They give her whatever it takes. They're in terror of her."

"They all loved her," Simon insisted. "Not a one of them ever said a word against her, not one word, not ever."

Flat on his back, he suddenly couldn't swallow his saliva as fast as it formed. He choked and coughed. Strings of spittle sputtered between his lips, spattered his chin.

Jane watched this brief episode with interest, because it had meaning for her.

The three pairs of salivary glands in the mouth secrete three pints of saliva every day. The purposes of saliva are to moisten food for swallowing, help keep teeth clean, convert complex starches into sugars, and minimize acidity in the mouth. The production of this fluid can be accelerated by the sight or smell of delicious food, also by nausea, among other things. Although it's frequently written that someone's mouth went dry with fear, it is more likely that extreme fear, which contributes to acidity in the mouth, will trigger a sudden flood of saliva, which is a balancing alkaline.

Jane said, "In the years following those divorces, one of her husbands committed suicide. The note he left behind claimed he had come to hate himself for his cowardice and weakness, so he believed he needed to suffer. He made his death especially hard for himself by using a barbed-wire noose. Another took a vacation to Jamaica—where his body was found hacked apart with a machete, pieces of it arranged in various elaborately drawn voodoo veves in an old Quonset hut used for occult ceremonies. Another, your father, died during an evening at a friend's house, when a home-invasion robbery went bad. His friend was shot to death, and he himself was burned to death when the intruders, who were never caught, set the place ablaze to cover their crimes. You'd be amazed, Rhymin' Simon, at how much security her remaining ex has, even though your dear mom is now seventy-five and he's eighty-six. Why, the president of the United States doesn't have that much security."

Simon swallowed hard, licked his wet lips. "You're taking facts and making them into something they're not. It's all distortion."

"If you don't hate and fear your mother, why did you tell your wives she was long dead? I know you told Dana, because I talked to her, so I figure you told the other three the same."

He sounded tubercular, words rising like bubbles through the saliva that slurried down his throat. "You get away from me, stay away from me." He turned his face from her. "I won't listen anymore."

"Every one of your four wives was the image of your mother. Uncannily like her."

"You're talking shit now, crazy shit now."

"All of them the same height and weight, all with raven-black hair, all with blue eyes—just like your mother in her youth."

There on the floor before the stage, the lightfall favored his supine performance as he turned his head toward her again, his face a mask of astonishment and abhorrence. Words eluded him as he worked his mouth in search of them.

Sociopaths were good actors. Lacking all feelings other than self-love, they were nevertheless able to fake a panoply of emotions that in other people were real. This man wasn't half as accomplished a thespian as others Jane had known. However, his stifled speech and his nuanced expression of shock far exceeded the highest level of performance of which he'd previously shown himself capable. Although he surely knew that he was doing to wealthy women what Anabel had done to wealthy men, Jane could believe that he might not have been consciously aware of choosing only mother figures to abuse and break and loot.

Sociopaths were as efficient in the human ocean as sharks in their water world. They were humming engines of need, untroubled by any doubt about their rightness and imbued with such a strong sense of superiority that they could not conceive that failure might be a possibility. They were empty vessels. Their minds were hollow spheres of certitude. Yet each of them believed he had more facets than a treasure of well-cut diamonds and was certain he knew those countless aspects of himself in full detail, though all he—or she—knew was what he wanted and how to get it with ruthless action.

Therefore, this first crack in Simon's armor, this rare moment of psychological insight that badly rattled his self-image, was an opportunity Jane must seize before he repaired it with the mortar of delusion.

She pressed him: "Petra's the same weight, height,

body type as your mother. Blue eyes like your mother. She's a blonde, but there are times—aren't there?—when she wears a wig for you?"

The wig was a guess; Petra had not mentioned it. Simon's eyes widened with further shock, his face twisted with hatred and alarm, his slack mouth spilled forth a thin drool, proving the truth of what she'd said.

"You can't be a man with it unless you hit them or break them or steal from them. All you can do with it is pee. Your hands are in your pants, and your fingers aren't numb, so why don't you feel for it, see what condition it's in, if you can even find it."

He choked on excess saliva and coughed, coughed, and found the words that had eluded him, all of them obscene, vicious, a torrent of invective.

Jane rose from beside him and sat on the stool once more. She gazed down at him not with an expression of disgust, but with an indifference that would nettle him more, as if she had considered stepping on him, yes, but had decided that crushing him wasn't worth soiling her shoe.

His curses dried up, and he lay in wordless passion of the darkest character. Theater light pooled in his baleful eyes, fading their color. Yet his gaze seemed to sharpen the longer he regarded her, as though in his helplessness he sought to tap the godlike power that every sociopath believed would one day manifest in himself, and behead her with his stare.

"Two things," Jane reminded him. "The money is the least of them. The second thing I want is your brother, your half brother, Booth Hendrickson."

If Simon was surprised, he didn't show it, and he

remained silent. Perhaps he understood that his fearlessness had been revealed as pretense, that he had been diminished in her eyes and would be further reduced in her estimation if, when speaking, he again became intemperate.

Even though he was lying in bonds, he needed *her* to be afraid of *him*, not because he was formulating a plan to exploit her fear and turn the tables on her, but because he needed to believe that when he wanted to disquiet other people, he could alarm them enough to elicit their respect. Being an evoker of apprehension was a core part of a sociopath's self-image.

She said, "Your brother's flying in from D.C. on an FBI jet he commandeered for his work at the Department of Justice. He'll land at Orange County airport, the private-plane terminal, at about ten-thirty tomorrow morning. One of your company's limos will pick him up. Don't deny it. Researching you, I hacked your company. I saw the booking for him. So what I want is . . . you pull your scheduled chauffeur off the job, and I'll supply the driver."

He said, "No."

"No? You really think *no* is an option?"

"Time comes, I'm gonna put a hand up your snatch and rip your guts out through it."

"So you skipped high-school biology, huh?"

He sheathed his dagger eyes.

"Anyway," she said, "your hands are still in your pants. Find any little thing yet? Maybe if you think about punching your mother in the face, that'll work better than Viagra."

He hated her too much to keep his eyes closed. The

sight of her filled him with homicidal fantasies, one of his favorite forms of entertainment.

From the breast pocket of her sport coat, Jane removed a microcassette recorder smaller than a pack of cigarettes. "Everything we said is on this."

"Why do I give a shit? I'm telling you, I'm wired into so much protection, the cops will shine my shoes if I ask."

"Maybe I know cops who don't shine shoes. Cops or no cops, I'll hand a copy of this to your mom, in another recorder, ready to play. She lives under her maiden name—Anabel Claridge—half the year on an estate in La Jolla, half on a waterfront estate in Lake Tahoe, Nevada. When I give it to her, I'll suggest if she gets a gift box on Mother's Day, she should call the bomb squad to open it."

Throughout their tête-à-tête, Simon's complexion had been florid to one degree or another. Now he paled.

"I could leave you like you are for the weekend," Jane said, "and be in La Jolla in little more than an hour. Your mommy would be able to have a listen over and over again before you'd have a chance to explain yourself. Do you think you might get just a spanking, or do you maybe wish you had presidential-level security like the one of her four husbands who's managed to stay alive?"

He needed only a moment to consider the situation. "What're you going to do to Booth?"

"Just ask him a few questions."

"If you do anything to him, the biggest damn hurt you can imagine is gonna come down on you. I don't know his world, what he does in it, and I don't want to know. But he's in with the biggest movers and shakers, and they look out for their own."

"I'm trembling."

"Yeah, well, I'm serious. You're gonna be one sorry-ass bitch if you so much as muss his hair."

Jane got off the stool. As she explained how she expected him to assist her, she walked slowly twice around the mechanic's sled, studying him as if he were some bizarre sea beast that she had found on the beach.

When Jane was finished with her explanation, Simon said, "I need to piss."

"This theater," she said, "is the swankiest urinal in California."

48

In the garage, to the left of the workbench, stood a sixteen-foot-long bank of seven-foot-tall cabinets, a single built-in unit with four doors. Behind the first three doors were shelves stocked with parts and supplies for the repair and maintenance of Simon's car collection. Behind the fourth, an empty space without shelves offered only a pole near the top from which coveralls and other garments might be hung, though nothing hung there now.

Jane stepped in front of the open door adjacent to

the empty unit. In her right hand she held a plastic thumb-size electronic-key blind-stamped with the word HID, the initials of the company that had provided it. She'd found the key in Simon's desk, just where he had promised it would be. Holding it at arm's length, she pointed it at the cornice rail of the cabinet, above the open door, and moved it left to right until a single *beep* signified that a code reader had approved the key. A series of concealed lock bolts clacked open, and the side walls of the cabinet whisked pneumatically out of the way, to the left, taking with them the loaded shelves, which now filled the previously empty fourth unit as if they had always been there.

When Jane stepped into the now empty third space, her weight triggered a lock release, and the back wall of the cabinet—inch-thick steel clad in wood—whisked to the right, revealing a walk-in safe about fourteen feet from front to back and twenty feet from side to side. Overhead lights brightened automatically as she entered the vault.

Three walls were lined with two-foot-deep shelves, and in the center of the space stood an eight-foot-square work island with a stainless-steel top. Some of the shelves were unused, but others held cardboard file boxes, guns, ammunition, cartons containing she knew not what, and the two high-end four-inch-deep titanium-alloy attaché cases stored where Simon had said they would be.

She put the cases on the work island and opened them using the combination locks. Each contained banded ten-thousand-dollar stacks of hundred-dollar bills, each bundle vacuum-packed in waterproof plastic using a FoodSaver sealing appliance.

In weeks past, she'd invaded a few homes of the self-described Arcadians and always found cash, on average two hundred thousand per residence. Usually there were forged passports as well, in a variety of names, and credit cards to match.

Considering that they were people of extreme arrogance who saw themselves as the rightful makers and rulers of a brave new world in which they could murder those whom they deemed bad influences on the culture and enslave hundreds of thousands if not millions of others with nanomachine brain implants, Jane found it telling that they all took the precaution of squirreling away the cash and credentials to support a hasty exit from the country, to get them to wherever they had secreted fortunes to sustain them in the aftermath of failure. Under the egoism that armored them, beneath the layers of pride and conceit and disdain, at the center of the rotten fruit that was their hateful conviction, nestled a seed of doubt.

Simon Yegg apparently wasn't one of the Arcadians. He didn't resort to noble talk about saving civilization as a justification for using people. He just ruthlessly used them. Maybe intuition warned him that the consequences of his actions required that he be prepared to flee the authorities in some crisis. Or maybe his half brother had hinted at possible ugly consequences of the work in which he was involved. For whatever reason, Simon had stashed passports and other forged ID in

each attaché, and he'd set aside more get-out-of-Dodge
cash than any Arcadian: $480,000, half in each titanium
case.

49

With Sanjay Shukla strapped in it, Carter
Jergen turns the dinette chair off its side
and tips it up onto four feet once more. He spends the
next two hours alternately using his laptop to scout
possible Caribbean vacations and studying the young
writer, who sits in wet-eyed silence when he isn't weeping. The tears seem excessive, but perhaps a successful writer must be more sensitive than makes sense to
a nonwriter. Growing bored with the Caribbean, Jergen opens himself to a more exotic getaway in the
South Pacific and begins to investigate Tahiti.

At last Radley Dubose returns with Tanuja. After
what must have been a vigorous workout, the big
man ought to appear sated, a little loose in the joints,
his eyes heavy-lidded, his face softer in the afterglow
of such a release. But Dubose looks as edgy as ever
and remains darkly energized, still the West Virginia
golem that he has always been, as if shaped from
mud, invoked with life by some ill-advised ceremony,
and sent forth on a mission of revenge.

The girl seems weary but not broken. Her hair is in
disarray, one sleeve ripped off her T-shirt, the collar

torn along the stitch line. When leading her to a seat at the table, Dubose jerks too hard on her leash. In a furious silence, she pivots to him and strikes his massive chest with her fists, tries for his face but fails to land a blow there. He grabs her by the neck, jams her in the chair, and ties her leash to the stretcher bar.

For his part, Dubose is amused by Tanuja's rebellion. He seldom either laughs or smiles, and now his amusement is conveyed to Jergen only by raised eyebrows and a shake of the head. He leans against the counter by the sink and fishes the half-finished hand-rolled cigarette from his jacket pocket. He preps the joint and fires it and takes a deep drag, staring into space as he did before the idea of doing the girl began to be irresistible.

Now that Tanuja is seated within the candlelight, Jergen sees that her lower lip is swollen, blood coagulated in one split corner.

When she speaks to her brother, however, her speech is not thick from the injury. Softly and with grave tenderness, she says, "Sanjay? *Chotti bhai* . . . ?"

He cannot look at her. He sits with his head bowed, and when she says *chotti bhai*, whatever that means, his weeping, which has recently been quiet, becomes a wretched sobbing.

"*Chotti bhai,*" she repeats, "it's all right."

"No," Sanjay says. "Oh, God, no."

"Look at me. You have no blame," she says. When he can't bear to face her, she says what sounds like "*Peri pauna.*"

This so affects Sanjay that he gasps and looks up at

her and says, "*Bhenji*, no. I don't deserve your respect or anyone's."

"*Peri pauna*," she insists.

Curious, Jergen says, "What does that mean—*peri pauna*?"

The girl turns her head to stare at him, and though she is shackled to the chair, the ferocity in her eyes and the loathing in her voice chill Jergen when she says, "Go fuck yourself, you disgusting pig."

This elicits a small laugh from Dubose, and though the chill lingers in Jergen's bones, he smiles and nods and says, "Indulge yourself in a little rebellion." He consults his wristwatch. "You don't have much more time for it."

50

Earlier, leaving Simon Yegg firmly bound at the foot of the stage, Jane had rolled Petra Quist out of the theater and into the lobby once more. Although the girl had not wet herself, she no longer professed an urgent need to pee. She hadn't been voluble and challenging as before, but reserved, taciturn. And sober.

Now Jane returned with a black-and-yellow four-wheeled Rimowa suitcase that she had taken the liberty of packing with a couple changes of clothes and what she thought were the essential items from Petra's share of the master-bathroom drawers. She stood it by the candy counter. She also brought a pair of sneakers, socks, jeans, a sweater, a leather jacket, and Petra's purse, all of which she put in the half bath adjacent to the lobby, so that the girl could dress in more practical gear for what might lie ahead.

Jane brought as well one of the titanium attaché cases that contained $240,000. She placed it on the upholstered bench in front of the office chair to which Petra remained shackled.

She would keep the second case. The quest for truth upon which she had embarked was also a kind of war, and wars were expensive.

She sat on the bench beside that treasure.

In the short and sleeveless dress, Petra still appeared to be all long legs and slender arms, but she did not, as before, evoke thoughts of fashion models and party girls. Her powerful sexuality—bestowed so generously on her by nature, which she so diligently maintained and enhanced—had for the moment ebbed. Time seemed to have carried her backward through its forward flow, washing from her all iniquitous experience and corruption, so that she had become a gangling, awkward child.

She sat with head half-bowed, eyes open but perhaps seeing some memory of another time and place. A bluish bruise shadowed the line of her jaw on the right side of her face and half her chin, no doubt a result of the blow she'd taken from Jane's forearm when she'd been jammed against the refrigerator in the kitchen.

"Some people," Jane said, "will tell you Simon is

a vicious swine, a woman hater, a sleazy thief, a self-absorbed narcissist, and they're half-right. He's all those things, but he's something worse."

Petra said nothing.

"He's one of those dangerous people that we call sociopaths. He fakes being human, because he lacks all the emotions you and I feel. He cares only about himself, and if he felt he could get away with it, he would commit any atrocity you can imagine, without remorse."

There seemed to be no anger in this girl, no bitterness arising from how dismissively Simon had spoken of her. Rather, she appeared to be shaken by the realization of how naïve she had been. Perhaps she thought it not possible to imagine a way forward. Events had unmoored her. She must feel adrift.

"Some believe sociopaths are born that way," Jane said, "and others believe they're made that way by dreadful parenting. Nature or nurture. I think it's both. Some are born that way, and some are made. In Simon's case, I suspect he was born sociopathic, the son of a sociopathic mother—and then made worse by her. Now he knows you told me stuff about him that he didn't want known. If I turn him loose after this thing with his brother is done, and if you're still where he can find you, he *will* kill you, Petra. And he will make it a very hard death."

After a silence, the girl met Jane's eyes. "Do you think it's true what he said about Felicity and Chandra and them?"

"Felicity and Chandra who?"

"My crew, you know, my girlfriends. He said if I go

missing, like, in a month they won't remember my name. That's shit for sure—don't you think?"

Jane considered her words carefully. "Remember your name? Of course they will. Miss the free limo, yes. And I bet you buy a lot more drinks for them than they buy for you, so they'll miss that. But care that you're gone? What do you think?"

Petra broke eye contact. Glanced at the door to the theater.

"Sweetie," Jane said, "it's not that you aren't memorable. God knows, you'd be hard to forget. But tell me true . . . if one of them dropped out of your crew and just went away, would *you* care?"

The girl opened her mouth to respond, frowned, said nothing.

"A life of superficial pleasures can be exciting, a lot of fun, even thrilling. For a while. But if you party every day, they soon aren't parties anymore. They're desperation. And if all you do with your friends is party—then your friends are really strangers."

Petra closed her eyes and hung her head, perhaps thinking about what might have been, what had been, and to what end her twenty-six years now pointed.

She whispered, "Where do I go from here?"

"I don't know. And no one can tell you where. You've got to find the way yourself. But this may help."

The sound of the latches opening on the attaché case raised Petra's head and opened her eyes.

"It's nearly a quarter of a million dollars," Jane said.

Regarding the cash with a solemnity that defied

interpretation, the girl at last said, "What if all that money . . . undoes me?"

"Simon's not going to report it stolen."

"No, I mean what if I take it and . . . slide back into all the usual shit, not with Simon but with some other guy?"

"If you can ask that question, then you probably won't slide."

"No guarantee, though."

"Life doesn't come with one." Jane closed the case.

From her tote bag, she removed a pair of scissors. She cut the zip-tie binding the captive's right wrist to the arm of the chair.

"I'm not your enemy, never was. Now that you're not drunk, I'm counting on you to remember that." She gave the scissors to Petra. "Just the same, I'll move back a ways while you free yourself. Use the half bath to freshen up and change clothes. I'll wait."

As the girl cut the plastic strap on her left wrist and then leaned forward to feel under the chair for the ties that bound her ankles, she said, "That stuff about their mother made me half-sick, you know? I feel dirty if I was like her to him. Is the brother that twisted?"

"You don't want to know about the brother," Jane said.

Getting up from the chair, putting the scissors on the bench beside the attaché case, Petra appeared unsteady, muscles cramped. "I guess I don't want to know your name, either."

"You've got that right."

51

In the church kitchen, the silence of grief and the stillness of dread, the brother's guilt and the sister's forgiveness no longer spoken but palpable, two of the three dwindling candles guttering in their glasses, flames twisting and leaping as if to take flight from their wicks and morph into butterflies, lambent light and rippling shadows tattooing ever-changing patterns across the faces of the twins, faces as spectral as any appearing in a séance . . .

As if he is the Last Judgment embodied in a dark and fierce form, Radley Dubose comes to the table and speaks to Carter Jergen. "It might have happened by now. Let's try the trigger and be done with them if we can."

Those adjusted persons injected with previous iterations of the command mechanism have been accessed and controlled by the phrase *Play Manchurian with me,* a reference to the famous 1959 novel by Richard Condon, a thriller about brainwashing. That was a little joke of Dr. Bertold Shenneck's, the recently deceased genius behind this application of nanotechnology.

Jane Hawk has learned that unlocking sentence. Therefore, all the adjusted people thus controlled are being reprogrammed as quickly as possible. For new conversions, a fresh set of triggering words is installed with the latest generation of the command mechanism.

From across the table, Jergen regards the twins and says, "Uncle Ira is not Uncle Ira."

He doesn't know who chose these new key words. The sentence is from *Invasion of the Body Snatchers* by Jack Finney, a 1955 novel, twice filmed well, about an alien life form that perfectly mimics specific people, takes their place, and disposes of them. The analogy is not as apt as is the reference to the Condon novel, but not every Arcadian is as keen of wit as the late Dr. Shenneck.

Sanjay responds a fraction of a second before Tanuja, but both say, "Yes, all right," which is the correct programmed response.

The brain implant has self-assembled, and the twins now possess only the *illusion* of free will.

"Lovely," says Jergen, pleased that after the long pursuit and so much inconvenience, the conversion of the Shuklas into adjusted people has ended well.

Brother and sister appear to be as alert as ever, but they are in a kind of trance, where they will remain until Jergen or Dubose releases them with the words *Auf Wiedersehen*, which in German mean "until we meet again."

Jergen says, "You must do precisely as you're told. Do you understand?"

The twins reply—"Yes"—in unison.

Dubose releases them from their collars and leashes.

As instructed by Carter Jergen, the Shuklas wash the dishes and glassware they used for their dinner and put everything away. They neither speak to each other nor exchange a glance, as efficient as two ants operating according to genetically prescribed roles.

"We're going to drive you home now," Jergen tells them.

"All right," they reply.

One of the candles gutters out. Jergen extinguishes the other two, and the Shuklas carry the warm glasses out of the building, so that nothing too unusual will be found in the morning, thus focusing the attention of the police largely on the rectory, where Reverend Gordon M. Gordon's material body lies in the absence of his soul.

52

Dressed more demurely in jeans and a sweater, Petra Quist was once more graceful, her brief regression to childlike awkwardness behind her.

She wheeled the Rimowa bag with her right hand and carried the attaché case in her left, preceding Jane into the garage and to the Cadillac Escalade, the least attention-getting vehicle in Simon's collection. She loaded the suitcase through the tailgate but put the money on the front passenger seat.

"Use the Cadillac only for a few hours," Jane advised, "until you're where you can rent a car. You should be safe then. I'll make sure Simon doesn't even think about looking for you. His brother and the people the brother's involved with—they don't have a reason to be interested in Simon's ex-girlfriend. They're no threat to you."

Petra regarded Jane for a long moment, her expression that of someone puzzling over the meaning of a line spoken in a foreign language. "I tried to slash you with a broken bottle."

"You were drunk."

"But I would have . . ."

"I more than paid you back. How's your jaw?"

Petra touched the bruise with her fingertips. "Not too bad. But the thing is, like, I don't know how to say thank you."

Jane smiled. "Yes, you do. Don't backslide. Find a new way. Be truly happy. If I were you, I'd stay away from the glamorous places, the glamorous businesses you've been in. That's not life. It's only an imitation of life. Find a place that's real, some town that looks like it came out of a fifties sitcom, with people who might even be who they seem to be."

"Never before in my whole life did anyone do something for me without wanting something bigger in return."

As Petra walked around to the driver's door and opened it, Jane followed. "You don't mean never in your life."

"I do, I mean it, and it's true."

Hearing a trace of melancholy in the girl's voice, Jane found it necessary to say, "None of my business, but do you know . . . when it all started going bad for you?"

"Oh, yeah. Yeah. I know the year. I know the day, the hour. A long, long time ago."

"Maybe it's good that you know. If it was a mystery, if it was forgotten . . . well, you can't exorcise a demon if you don't know its name."

"And even then, maybe you can't exorcise it."

"Maybe you can't. But you don't know till you try."

Petra nodded. She started to speak, stopped herself. Then in a voice thick with emotion that she was clearly intent on repressing, she said, "Nice shoes."

"They're nothing special. Just Rockport walkers."

"Yeah, I know. But they're tough, they last, they do the job."

Jane said, "All you can ask of a shoe."

Looking up from the Rockports, Petra said, "I'll never forget this. This, right now."

"Neither will I," Jane said.

Petra got in the Escalade and closed the door and started the engine. Using a remote control, she raised the segmented roll-up.

With the engine noise racketing off the low concrete ceiling and the walls, Jane watched the Cadillac cruise out into the night.

53

In a trance state, the twins are told by Radley Dubose to sleep until they are awakened by their names. They sit in the backseat of the Range Rover, in their safety harnesses, eyes closed. Her head is tipped slightly to the right. His chin rests on his chest. Although they must be exhausted after such a long and stressful night, theirs is a most unnatural sleep, commanded upon them, and perhaps their dreams, if any, are of a kind that no one but adjusted people can experience.

Jergen drives east, out of the more populated cities of west county, toward the rural hills and canyons in the east, taking the Shuklas home.

Their Hyundai Santa Fe Sport, which they had abandoned at the burned-out ruins of Honeydale Stables, had earlier been returned to the garage at their house. A crew had removed every trace of the events in their kitchen, including the liberal splashes of hornet-killing insecticide that the girl had used to free her brother from Lincoln Crossley and the others.

Soon the twins will begin the final chapter of their lives, a murderous frenzy that will make big news and imprint their names on the public mind as the names of monsters. Tanuja's recent novel, which is not a best-seller yet but has generated buzz and has the potential—according to the Hamlet-list program—to shape an entire generation's moral perspective, will be forever anathema, despised and unread.

Jergen glances at Dubose. "You mind telling me something?"

"She was good. Lubricious, you would say at Harvard."

"I assumed she was good."

"So why ask?"

"Why not wait for her control mechanism to be operative?"

"Spare me the phony New England gentility."

"I don't know what you mean."

"Son of a Boston Brahmin, so refined that he's mystified by the crude behavior of the backwoods boy."

"Once she was adjusted, she would've obeyed your every command. You could have avoided the struggle."

Dubose turns and tilts his bearish head and regards Jergen from under a ledge of brow, his expression so rich with sarcasm that no words are necessary to convey his meaning.

"So I guess I'm to infer," says Jergen, "that the struggle made it better for you."

"There you go."

"Well, I don't know."

"You never had it that way? Don't bullshit me."

"Never," says Jergen. "I like things easy."

"But the way she is now, it'd be like doing it with a robot."

"A very attractive robot."

"Then when we get them back to their place, go for it."

"No offense, Radley, but not just after you've been in there."

This elicits from Dubose a rare laugh, low and sour. "Isn't it a little weird to be so fastidious after everything we did tonight?"

"Well, just the same, I'll pass. Anyway, we only did our job."

Dubose says, "Making the world a better place."

54

Jane Hawk had slept late Friday morning and taken a nap in the afternoon, in preparation for all that she'd done in the past twelve hours. By four-thirty Saturday morning, after saying good-bye to Petra Quist, she wanted a few hours' sleep to be ready for Booth Hendrickson when he arrived in Orange County from Washington, six hours hence. But she was wound tight, not in the least drowsy.

Simon Yegg, with no hope of freeing himself, marinated in his own juices in the theater. She had no need to watch over him.

In the kitchen, cautious of the shattered glass, she found another bottle of Belvedere, Coca-Cola, and an ice maker full of cubes in the shape of half moons. She built a drink and carried it into the study, where she turned on the desk lamp.

Near the lamp stood an iPod. She considered reviewing its playlist, but music might mask other sounds that she needed to hear.

She was an accomplished pianist, as had been her murdered mother, and as her mother-murdering father still was. Just recently, he'd toured to the acclaim of adoring fans when, if the truth were known, he ought to have been rotting in prison for the past nineteen years. To Jane, music had always been nearly as essential as food—listening to it and bringing it forth from a Steinway. She might have tried to make a career of recordings and concerts, except that a grand piano, with its lid raised by the prop stick, too often reminded her of an open coffin, her mother's coffin, an association not conducive to a performance of concert-hall quality.

She didn't need analysis or Freudian jargon to understand why she had chosen instead a career in law enforcement.

As she sipped the vodka and Coke, she withdrew half of a broken cameo locket from a pocket of her jeans: a woman's face in profile, carved from soapstone, embedded in a silver oval. Her lovely little boy, Travis, found it on the water-washed stones beside the creek behind the house where he was being secretly sheltered by friends.

Travis had convinced himself that the woman on the locket was the very image of his mother. To him it was an omen of her ultimate triumph and return to him, but also a talisman that would protect her from all harm as long as she carried it.

To Jane, this piece of a locket with half a hinge attached was enchanted and precious not because she believed that it had magical powers, but because it had been given to her by her child, Nick's son, who had been conceived in love and brought into the world with the hope he would find in it the wonder, the joy, and the truth of things that make a life worth living. When she held the locket and closed her eyes, she could see Travis as clearly as if he were in the room with her—the shy little boy who shared the precise shade of his father's blue eyes, with tousled hair, a sweet smile, and the intelligence that sometimes made him seem like a little man waiting patiently to be done with childhood.

Maybe it was the vodka or maybe the locket that soon settled a calm on her. When she finished the drink, she returned the cameo to her pocket and set the alarm feature on her wristwatch. She rose from the desk and turned off the lamp and stretched out on the sofa.

She asked that her dreams, if any, be bright visions of her child. But for a girl who had, at the age of nine, discovered her mother's bloody corpse in a bathtub and almost nineteen years later found her husband in a similar condition, dreams were more often dark than bright.

55

More than forty thousand feet above the surface of the earth, with the sun behind the plane, a distant and receding darkness in the west beyond the curve of the planet . . . The reassuring drone of two powerful Rolls-Royce turbofan engines, almost ninety thousand pounds of craft and fuel cruising well in excess of five hundred miles per hour, a grand defiance of gravity . . .

The scrabbling multitudes of humanity toiled far below, feverish in their often pointless and nearly always misguided strivings, unaware of the change fast coming to their world.

This is a thrilling time to be alive, especially if you are Booth Hendrickson, the lone passenger in a Gulfstream V configured to carry fourteen in addition to crew. He finds it rewarding to be known by the grandees of Washington and their grubbing minions not merely as an attorney highly placed in the Department of Justice, but also as a go-to man who can arrange discreet off-the-record meetings between highly placed officials in any of the security services and law-enforcement agencies, and with selected other pooh-bahs in the maze of bureaucracies. It is even more satisfying to be within the inner circle of the Techno Arcadians, of whom 98 percent of those grandees, minions, and pooh-bahs are ignorant, his power in fact far greater than they know.

Not a little of the satisfaction comes from the perks that he is able to bestow upon himself, such as this splendid aircraft. The Gulfstream is owned by the FBI and, as specified in the original appropriations bill, is intended especially to facilitate urgent investigations involving acts of terrorism. Such is Hendrickson's authority that he needs merely to claim—without supporting details or documentation—that his business is both urgent and related to uncovering some nefarious scheme involving white supremacists or Islamic radicals, and the jet is his.

He has just received a late breakfast prepared and served by the steward. A crab omelet made with duck eggs. A serving of sliced potatoes deep-fried in coconut oil. Buttery baby carrots al dente and flavored with thyme. Brioche toast.

The food is delicious, but the wine disquiets him. When making flight arrangements the previous afternoon, he'd specified Far Niente chardonnay for breakfast. He is served instead a pinot grigio of only moderate distinction, and it is a shade too sweet to accompany the omelet.

Although the steward is apologetic, he has no explanation for how this could have happened. There is no chardonnay aboard, and Hendrickson must make do with the pinot grigio. Instead of the two glasses that he might have allowed himself, he drinks only one.

He is not a superstitious man. He does not have any regard for portents of calamity, for omens foretelling either good or evil. He doesn't accept the existence of gods or fate, or luck. He believes only in himself, in the efficacy of raw power, and in the plastic nature of a material world that can be bent to a strong man's will.

Nevertheless, as he finishes breakfast with mandarin orange slices under shavings of dark chocolate, the disquiet inspired by the wine only grows. He listens to the Rolls-Royce engines for any change in pitch that might suggest some mechanical problem in its early stages.

After the meal, when he tries to work on his laptop, he can't resist consulting a variety of sources for weather reports, in expectation of turbulence ahead. Hour by hour, all the way across the country, although he repeatedly counsels himself that this apprehension is groundless, he can banish it only temporarily.

He finds himself repeatedly reviewing news stories about the recent bizarre death of a billionaire who was a founder of the Arcadians. He revisits digitally archived evidence of Jane Hawk's presence at the site in San Francisco where the death of that man occurred in spite of heavy security. Because this is evidence that he has studied previously and from which he can't possibly gain new insights, he must admit that this bitch of bitches has gotten under his skin.

When Hendrickson arrives in California, as he disembarks from the jet at the private-craft terminal at the Orange County airport and sees his limousine and driver waiting on the tarmac, which his status allows, his apprehension swells into alarm. His half brother, Simon, seems to have sent him a subtle message that all is not what it appears to be.

In fact, it is so subtle that no one else would recognize it as a warning, a shrewdly conceived and softly rung alarm only brothers might hear. And perhaps only brothers who had survived a mother like theirs and been bonded by the experience.

Suddenly the situation requires vigilance, tactical elegance, and cunning. Hendrickson acknowledges some fear, but he is also electrified by the possibility that Jane Hawk has made a grave mistake. If someone is trying to get at him through Simon, it is surely Jane Hawk, because she recently became aware that Hendrickson is a Techno Arcadian, one of the most effective spears of the revolution.

If he plays this right, if he stays calm, stays cool, he may be the one to kill her.

PART TWO

Migraine Jane

1

At eight forty-five that Saturday morning, Gilberto Mendez—former Marine, mortician, about-to-be chauffeur impersonator—had parked his Chevy Suburban in a quiet residential neighborhood, under a lacy pepper tree beaded with tiny pink corns, where he could be sure there were no traffic cameras.

He wore well-polished black shoes, a black suit, a crisp white shirt, a black tie, and a double-peaked black cap with a short bill. The pants were of a suit purchased a month previously, but the matching coat was from two years earlier, when he had been forty pounds above his ideal weight instead of just twenty. The extra room in the coat allowed for the concealment of the shoulder rig and the Heckler & Koch .45 Compact that Jane had given him.

Setting out on foot for a public park five blocks

away, he thought that he looked somewhat out of place, though none of the people he encountered—sweating runners, smiling dog walkers, kids on skateboards—gave him a second look.

The sky was the very blue of the birthing blanket that his wife, Carmella, had purchased in anticipation of their fourth child, whom she now carried into her third trimester. The rain of the previous night had washed a brighter green into the trees, more dazzling colors into the flowers, and the lawns were almost as unreal as artificial turf.

This was a wonderful day to be alive, which was a thought that perhaps occurred to a mortician more often than to people in other lines of work. In a certain Middle East hellhole, he had known a day when a devout chaplain questioned the value of it or even the value of all days that time had thus far dealt out or ever would. Gilberto was not as devout as that good man, yet there were moments in even the most terrible hours when he saw the beauty of the world that the worst of humanity's actions couldn't obscure—an enchanting pattern of purple shadow and soft light on the stone floor of an ancient courtyard, a white bird in flight against a golden dawn—and such moments assured him there would be days when all darkness, not just that of night, would remain at bay. Although he carried a firearm into this bright morning, it was a wonderful day to be alive, in part because he would again fulfill that sacred warrior's pledge—*semper fi*—made not just to country, but also to freedom and to comrades in arms.

The park contained a playing field on which a group of young girls were already darting through a game of soccer. Majestic old oaks, crowned like a conclave of kings, shaded tables and benches on a picnic ground. In a parking lot by a lake shimmering as if it were a pool of mercury, the white Cadillac stood where Jane had promised he would find it. With whatever explanation, the owner of the limo company had ordered an employee to leave it there.

The vehicle wasn't locked. After putting on a pair of driving gloves to ensure he would leave no fingerprints, Gilberto opened the door, lifted the floor mat, and found an electronic key taped there. When he settled behind the wheel, he hesitated to close the door, ostensibly because a newly sprung breeze stirred the jasmine espaliered across the wall of a nearby park-maintenance building and carried its fragrance to be savored. In truth, he delayed because it seemed that when he closed the door, he might be shutting himself off from his future, from his wife and daughters, from the unborn son he might never see.

The scent of jasmine, however, was the olfactory equivalent of a white bird in flight against a golden dawn. He said, *"Semper fi,"* and closed the door and started the engine.

2

At eight-thirty that morning, Jane Hawk had been awakened by the alarm function of her wristwatch. She got off the sofa and went to the window in Simon Yegg's study. She stood for a while in the early light, which elsewhere fell on her child and on the grave of her husband, and to her it was the light of a love that conjoined them regardless of distance and time, in life and death. She felt no need for further sleep, nor any weariness.

In the bathroom connected to the study, she washed her face and adjusted her raven-haired wig. She removed her colored contacts and floated them in solution in their carrying case, and with the end of that eclipse, her eyes were bluer than oceans when she met them in the mirror.

She went downstairs to the theater, where Simon lay bound and reeking of urine. As if emptying his bladder had stimulated his liver to produce a flood of bile, his face swelled with rage, both pale and florid like the mottled scales of some exotic serpent. His bloodshot eyes welled with such festered and virulent malignity that they could not have appeared more alien if they'd had the vertical irises of a snake's eyes.

At the sound of her approach, he spewed bitter curses and threats. When she stepped into view, Simon strained mightily against the restraints that had foiled him all night, rattling the wheeled board under him.

As she stood over him, watching, he seethed at her, told her what parts of her anatomy he would cut off while she still lived and into which of her orifices he would cram what he butchered from her.

Strangely, his ordeal had only strengthened his sociopathic certainty that he was the axis around which the universe turned, that he couldn't die because his death would be not just the end of him, but the end of all. The suffering that he currently endured was perhaps, to his way of thinking, some test of fortitude prescribed by the unknown masters of the game of life, and he would pass it and triumph and break her as she could never hope to break him.

His fury seemed demonic and therefore inexhaustible, and it burned undiminished when he recognized the crucial change in her appearance, though he was stricken speechless. Her height, her strong but slender form, and her raven hair were as before, but he evidently didn't recognize her similarities to his mother until her eyes, too, were as those of Anabel.

"Blue," he said, as if some alchemic wonder had been performed, a base substance transmuted into the equivalent of gold. And though fury still drew his face taut and made his jaw muscles bulge, though his pulse was visible in his temples, he continued to be silenced by whatever psychotic computations consumed him.

"I came to tell you," Jane said, "that if anything goes wrong with this and it turns out your brother was alerted by some trick of yours, there will be consequences. At the very least, I'll come back here with a hammer and kneecap you. If anything bad happens to the friend who's helping me or if Booth calls down the troops on this place, I'll take the time to shoot off your pecker, and I'll be smiling all the way out of the house as I listen to you screaming down the path to Hell."

So many conflicting emotions contested with his anger that his face had a kaleidoscopic quality, features shifting ceaselessly into subtle new arrangements. His eyes were slitted and glassy, feverish, avoiding her now, settling on various points within his view but fixing on nothing for longer than a second.

Jane ceased to be able to read him. As if it were a moon within his skull, Simon's mind had turned toward her its cold and cratered dark side, on which no light reflected.

He lay in tortured silence until she had nearly reached the back of the theater, and then he called to her as if her name were the same as a smutty word for *vagina*. He made an obscene promise of extreme and personal violence, but she was not moved because she had heard the same from others who, like him, were all talk and no performance.

3

When Booth Hendrickson disembarks from the Gulfstream V and sees the white Cadillac limousine awaiting him in the Southern California sun, the vehicle is both an affront and a warning.

In his estimation, a *white* limo is for weddings, proms, and bachelorette parties, for bar mitzvah boys to horse around in with their friends between the synagogue and the reception that follows.

People of accomplishment and serious purpose should be met by a black car with windows tinted even darker than the law allows—and in his case, always by a stretched black Mercedes. Simon's contract with the Department of Justice requires that his stable include two Mercedes limousines for those of high rank who might have business between San Diego and Los Angeles.

Hendrickson is certain that Simon would never offend him like this. Therefore, the car is more than just transportation. It is a message to the effect that the morning will not unfold as expected.

Beside the prom wagon stands a chauffeur, not either of the two usually sent for him, both of whom are also unofficial muscle. This guy wears a black suit, as all Simon's drivers are attired. However, he also wears a black two-peaked cap with a short shiny bill, though those who have driven Hendrickson previously wore no hat. He also sports a pair of wraparound sunglasses, which ordinarily a driver would not put on until behind the wheel, if at all.

The inescapable conclusion is that the hat is meant to conceal the driver's hairline, which can be a helpful identifying factor if later one needs to look through mug books of suspects' photographs. The sunglasses are part of his disguise as well, a simple way to conceal his eye color, to make it difficult to discern and remember the set of his eyes, the shape of his nose.

"Mr. Hendrickson?" the chauffeur inquires.

Resisting an urge to lament the car, Hendrickson says, "Yes."

"My name is Charles. I hope you had a restful flight, sir."

"Good weather all the way."

Charles opens the rear door of the limo. "If you'll wait in the comfort of the car, sir, I'll get your luggage from the steward."

"I have only two bags and a laptop. I've been sitting all the way across the continent. I'd rather stand a few minutes and enjoy the fresh air."

"Yes, sir, of course," Charles says, and proceeds to the jet, where the steward has appeared at the top of the portable stairs.

As far as the open door allows Hendrickson to see, no one waits for him in the passenger compartment of the limo. He warily surveys the tarmac surrounding the private-aircraft terminal—the parked planes, the variety of battery-powered service vehicles attending them, mechanics and luggage handlers and embarking passengers—seeking those who might be shanghaiers in league with the chauffeur, but he sees no one who appears particularly suspicious, because *all* of them look suspicious.

A few people notice him, which means they are *not* individuals of concern. Any operative who has him under surveillance will be at pains to avoid looking at him. No doubt he attracts their interest because he's tall, handsome, with a stylish mane of salt-and-pepper hair, the very image of success, authority, and erudition.

Inevitably, he thinks back to the missing chardonnay and the inappropriate pinot grigio. Could it be that some drug was given to him in the wine? To what purpose? Perhaps it is some new delayed-effect sedative that requires five or six hours to work, that will drop him into a sudden, helpless sleep when he's in the limo and at the mercy of the driver. Or perhaps the damn stuff lingers in the system an inordinately long time; so that when he unwittingly drinks another doctored beverage hours later, the two will combine in his blood to form both a sedative and a truth serum, compelling him to divulge all his secrets while in a drugged sleep.

That scenario might seem unlikely, even absurd, to a layman unfamiliar with the technological advances that have occurred in the fields of espionage and national security during the past decade. But Booth Hendrickson is well aware that, week by week, the unlikely is waxing into fact, and the impossible is waning into the probable.

He regrets not having bodyguards.

For three reasons, he doesn't travel with security. First, in spite of all his power, his face is unknown to the general public. He doesn't need to worry about being accosted by some deranged proponent of limited government or an earnest but disturbed advocate for the proposition that animals should be allowed to vote, or any of the other human debris that is becoming an ever larger part of the population. Second, the men on a security detail might testify in court about where Booth goes and with whom he speaks; a man in his position can't risk constant witnesses. Third, he carries a gun, knows how to use it, and has confidence in his innate—if untested—talent for physical violence and derring-do.

Anyway, fretting about the pinot grigio is most likely a step too far into the paranoia zone. For all her cleverness, Jane Hawk can't have breached the security around the Bureau's jets, which are hangared in a location unknown to most agents. Besides, providing pinot grigio in place of the wanted chardonnay only calls attention to the substitution; if Hawk or anyone else meant to drug him, they would have used the chardonnay.

Unless . . . unless a difference in the acid-alkaline balance between the chardonnay and the pinot grigio makes the former an inappropriate medium for the drug.

The chauffeur and the Gulfstream steward together transfer the luggage from the jet to the trunk of the limousine, except for the laptop, which is given to Hendrickson at his request.

He watches the two men with an eye for any evidence that they have known each other prior to this encounter, for any small sign of familiarity that indicates collusion. He sees none, but that might mean only that they are well practiced in deceit.

This is a world of dissemblers and imposters, and Hendrickson's mission particularly requires him to swim in a sea of duplicity and subterfuge. Paranoia isn't only justifiable but essential if he is to survive. The trick is not to allow healthy paranoia to escalate into panic.

The steward wishes him well before departing, and the chauffeur steps to the open rear door of the limousine, intending to close it once Hendrickson has entered the vehicle.

"Charles," Hendrickson says, "I'm sure you know the itinerary and schedule."

"Yes, sir. First to Mr. Yegg's house for lunch. Then to Pelican Hill Resort at three o'clock for check-in."

He can conceive of no excuse to avoid boarding the limousine. And if it is in fact Jane Hawk at work here, he must go along with this to some extent and not fumble the opportunity to capture or kill her.

As he settles in the plushly upholstered seat, the door closes with a solid *thunk*.

4

J ane, in Simon Yegg's study, at his desk, using his computer, entered the telecom company's network by a back door.

Just then her disposable phone rang.

She picked it up from the desk. "Yes?"

She recognized Gilberto's voice when he said, "He's landed. I'm watching the plane be taxied onto the apron."

"You have the remote?"

"It was in the cup holder where you said it would be."

"Let's make it happen."

The mortician hung up, and Jane returned her attention to the computer screen, to the exquisite architecture of the telecom provider's integrated systems.

Before she'd gone on leave from the FBI following Nick's death, she had known a sweet, funny, white-hat hacker who was employed by the Bureau—Vikram Rangnekar. From time to time, Vikram took a ride into black-hat territory when instructed to do so by the director or by some highly placed person in the Department of Justice. In spite of Jane being a married woman, Vikram had an unrequited crush on her and delighted in showing her what he had created—"my wicked little babies"—with the sanction of his superiors.

Although Jane had been a by-the-book agent who

never resorted to illegal methods, she couldn't resist learning who was corrupt over at Justice and what they were up to. She allowed Vikram to take her on tours of his black-hat installations, which was, for him, the equivalent of a male peacock spreading and shaking its magnificent tail of iridescent feathers. Some of his wicked little babies were back doors by which he could easily and secretly invade the computer networks of every major telecom provider. By various means, he'd installed a rootkit, a powerful malware program, in each of those companies' systems. The rootkit functioned at such low levels that Vikram could navigate those networks without leaving tracks; and the most skilled IT-security specialists would be unlikely to detect his activity even while he was buccaneering through their systems.

He had shown Jane how to exploit those back doors, and for all his peacocking, he had received only a kiss on the cheek—which it seemed was more than he'd expected.

Because every computer had an identifier built into it and could be located in real time by track-to-source programs, she did not own a laptop or other computer, not since she had gone on the run. For the same reason, she used only disposable cellphones.

Two days earlier, in short sessions, sitting at the public-access computers in a series of libraries, she had opened Vikram's back doors and had gone searching those company records for Booth Hendrickson's telecom accounts. The Department of Justice provided a smartphone for him, and he owned a second that he paid for himself.

Now, with Simon's computer, Jane entered those account files and deleted Hendrickson's private number, terminated it with extreme prejudice, which should at once have caused a cascade of changes through the strata of the company's system, resulting in immediate deactivation of the number and cancellation of service. She turned her attention next to the account provided to him by the Department of Justice.

5

As the Cadillac limousine pulls away from the terminal, Booth Hendrickson requests that the driver close the partition between himself and the passenger cabin. Booth needs to make an urgent phone call, for which he requires privacy.

If the driver is an imposter and if he suspects that perhaps Booth has identified him as such, he nevertheless complies with the request.

Booth and Simon have different worthless fathers, therefore different surnames. They have taken pains to obscure that they are half brothers, lest some diligent inspector general at Justice—or at another department where Booth exercises authority—might one day discover that tens of millions of dollars in public funds have been, by contract, funneled into Simon's various enterprises by his kin, in violation of several federal statutes.

He and Simon tend to discuss everything face-to-face. When they speak by phone, which is rare, they either rely on disposables or Booth uses his personal smartphone, never the one provided by the Department of Justice.

Now he discovers that the preferred phone is not working. The screen brightens but is blank: no telecom name, no signature music.

With no other choice, he tries his business phone, but with the same result.

He is not carrying a disposable.

The days when limousines provided a phone in the passenger cabin are long gone.

As the Cadillac slows to a stop at a traffic light, Hendrickson tries the door beside him. Of course it's locked. Safety regulations and insurance-company provisions require that a limousine driver control the locks on the passenger compartment when the vehicle is in transit and release them only when parked, lest some idiot drunk or willful child should open a door and spill out into traffic.

Although Booth has his laptop, he entertains no illusion that he will be able to send a text message precisely as, by chance, they pass through the spillover zone from an unsecured Wi-Fi network. And even if he can send a text message, no one will read it in time to help him, as Simon's house is but fifteen minutes from the airport.

He withdraws the pistol from the shoulder holster under his suit coat.

6

As Simon earlier revealed to Jane, the limo driver customarily brought Booth directly into the garage, rather than drop him at the front door. The brothers were discreet about their relationship and preferred that Booth not be seen by neighbors.

Jane carried her tote down to the garage. She didn't turn on the lights, but found her way to the workbench with her small LED flashlight. She put the tote on the bench and took the spray bottle of chloroform from it and slipped the bottle into a jacket pocket.

A stepladder hung on the wall. She took it down and opened it under the ceiling fixture that would light automatically when the garage door began to ascend. The fixture was a high-security model, sealed so that the cover could not be unscrewed. She retrieved a hammer from the tool collection, climbed the ladder, smashed the hard plastic fixture, and smashed the LED bulb beneath. After putting the ladder and hammer away, she used a push broom to sweep the debris into a corner.

She opened the door on the section of the storage cabinets that stood empty, through which she'd earlier accessed the vault where the attaché cases of cash had been stored. She didn't step inside right away, but switched off the flashlight and waited in the dark for the sound of the limo in the driveway.

In all likelihood, Hendrickson would have a gun.

Jane and Gilberto were armed as well, but the last thing they wanted was a close-quarters firefight.

So she had a plan. Plans were comforting. As long as you always remembered that even the best plans seldom unfolded as intended.

As soon as Gilberto drove into the garage, he would use a remote control to close the big door, and he'd get out of the limo, leaving the engine running and the ventilation system set not on air-conditioning or heat, but on fresh air. As the segmented door lowered, the incoming sunshine would diminish, and he would proceed to the front of the vehicle, open the hood, and switch on his own small flashlight.

Because the passenger-compartment doors would be locked with the master control, Hendrickson would be unable to exit the limo.

When the big door fully closed, the subterranean garage would fall into complete darkness. At that point, Jane would step out of the cabinet and make her way to Gilberto.

Because of the privacy panel between the passenger compartment and the driver's seat, Hendrickson would not be able to see what was happening at the front of the Cadillac. At that moment, if not before, he would know that he'd fallen into a trap, but he wouldn't be able to see anyone to shoot at through the side or rear windows.

He might start firing wildly, blowing out windows, but that seemed unlikely. He would want to conserve his ammunition for the moment when he finally had a target.

By the time Jane arrived at the car, Gilberto would have identified the air intake for the ventilation system. She would spray most of the remaining chloroform into that aperture. Maybe the concentration of the chemical within the vehicle would not be such that Hendrickson would entirely lose consciousness, but it was all but certain that he'd at least be disoriented and easily disarmed.

But now, no slightest thread of light was woven through the black fabric of the garage. Jane stood in the dark, and the dark stood in her, the latter being the darkness of both her past actions and lethal potential. And looming over all was the other darkness that her restless mind could not escape considering: the darkness beyond the world, into which had been taken her mother and her husband, perhaps there to await her, into which she'd sent bad and brutal men, perhaps there to await her.

7

South of the airport, the limousine accelerates on MacArthur Boulevard, past business parks where some of the nation's most successful corporations have offices. The grounds are beautifully landscaped. But seen through the heavily tinted windows, the trees lack full color, and the lawns appear bronze. The sleek glass buildings darkle skyward and seem to torque, as if some heretofore unknown cosmic force is passing in waves of distortion through the world, leaving behind a grim new reality.

Booth Hendrickson is accustomed to having subordinates at his disposal: armed men comfortable with extreme violence; platoons of attorneys to use the law as a bludgeon; entire bureaucracies adept at destroying his enemies with ten thousand paper cuts.

Sometimes in the act of coitus and more often in dreams, he thinks of himself as a cunning wolf in human form. Although he has no doubt that he is always the leader of those with whom he runs, he is no lone wolf and is at his best in a pack, where there is power in numbers and a shared sense of purpose, rightness, destiny.

The pistol in his hand, a Kimber Ultra CDP II in 9 mm, weighs less than two pounds even with eight rounds in the magazine and one in the chamber. It is all he can rely on in the absence of a pack.

He moves from the forward-facing seat to the longer starboard-facing bench on his left and slides toward the driver's compartment.

When the limo stops at a traffic light, if he fires four times through the partition, into the back of the chauffeur's head . . .

No. If he kills the driver, Booth will remain trapped in this locked compartment. Lacking a foot on the brake and with a corpse slumped against the steering wheel, the car will drift into oncoming traffic.

Maybe he can break out the privacy panel in the center of the partition. Reach through and put a gun to the driver's head. Demand that he unlock the doors.

But what if the panel doesn't give easily? What if it doesn't give at all? Or what if he can break out the panel—but the instant that he reaches through, the alerted driver Tasers him to shock the pistol out of his hand or slashes him with a knife?

He puts the Kimber on the seat.

He tries both of his phones again. Neither works.

The limo is cruising at fifty miles per hour, maybe faster. In minutes they will be at Simon's house.

If Jane Hawk is there—and she will be there; he's certain now that she will be there—she'll interrogate him. She's captured and grilled several other Arcadians, individuals who seemed too cunning to be taken prisoner, too tough to be cracked, and she's broken them all, gotten from them what she wanted.

She's even gotten to David James Michael, the billionaire who was a founder of the Techno Arcadian movement, although he had been wrapped in multiple layers of security. If she can take down D.J. in spite of all his resources, she can get her hands on anyone.

Until now, Hendrickson has never felt more than fleetingly vulnerable in his adult life, not since his mother ruthlessly forged him throughout his childhood. She has made him into the closest thing to one of Nietzsche's race of supermen that any mortal can be. Anabel has bent poor Simon, cracked him, almost broken him. Made of far stronger stuff than his half brother, Booth was the ideal base material she needed to shape a son of steel.

In addition, he hasn't felt vulnerable because he has never imagined that Jane Hawk can know of his role in the conspiracy. He now realizes there's one way she might have deduced his involvement. But that is for later consideration.

If she captures him, she will not break him. Not *him*. If she is an irresistible force, she will find that he is an immovable object.

Nevertheless, he prefers to escape her clutches and avoid the unpleasantness that other Arcadians have experienced at her hands. The only reason to let himself be taken to her is to kill her. But he isn't likely to be able to do that when she has orchestrated his abduction and enjoys the advantage.

He pockets the dead phones and picks up the pistol just as a cloud moves off the sun and a stream of warm light pours through a cutout in the limousine roof. The square of glass—or acrylic—hinged on one side and seated in a rubber gasket to seal out foul weather, is not a sunroof, but an escape hatch.

Some years earlier, a party of six or eight women, out for a birthday celebration, had instead been chauffeured into tragedy, not in one of Simon's cars, but in that of another company. A fire had broken out in the undercarriage and in a flash penetrated the passenger compartment. For whatever reason, the driver had not pulled off the highway fast enough in response to the women's screams, had not been quick enough to unlock the doors. In less than a minute, all were afire; none survived. Since then, new limousines in California were required to have escape hatches.

Exiting by that route will be fraught with risk. Besides, he regrets that he is wearing a suit, a shirt, and a tie by Dior Homme, with Paul Malone shoes, an ensemble that cost him more than $5,400. Some if not all of these garments will be damaged.

He holsters the pistol.

Once more the limo slows, possibly for a red traffic light.

In expectation, Hendrickson rises from the seat and stands in a crouch, swaying with the movement of the vehicle, getting a grip on the handle that will release the escape hatch.

The car comes to a full stop.

He twists the handle. The hatch drops open.

When he stands to his full height, his head and shoulders are out of the limo. He straddles the cabin, one foot on a seat, one on the bar, rattling the glassware and dislodging cubes from the ice bin as he thrusts farther out of the car. Gets his arms through the hatch. Levers up. Drags himself onto the roof.

8

Until the words HATCH RELEASE appeared on the dashboard display simultaneously with a triple-beep warning sound, Gilberto Mendez had no indication that his passenger suspected he was being abducted. Gilberto put down the privacy panel and turned and saw kicking feet disappear through the ceiling. He heard Hendrickson on the roof, heard

him coming off it and down the starboard side of the
car.

Although stopped at a red light, five vehicles back
from the intersection, in the middle lane of three lanes
of traffic, Gilberto threw open the door and got out,
reaching under his suit coat to put a hand on the
Heckler & Koch. Crazy as it would be, he nonetheless
expected a worst-case scenario: Hendrickson coming
around the car with a gun, a public shootout.

But then he saw the man on the farther side of the
limousine, dodging between two sedans in lane number one, hurrying forward between the waiting vehicles and the sidewalk.

9

Booth Hendrickson is on the run in a Dior
Homme suit and Paul Malone shoes, already
gasping for breath, his dignity offended, nauseated by
the thought of being captured, of being subjected to
torture and mockery.

Once the venomous Hawk bitch gets to them, powerful and well-protected Arcadians like Booth Hendrickson have been found dead in a long-abandoned
rat-infested factory, dead in their own heavily guarded
residences, shattered and dead on a public street after
a nine-story fall. There's nothing supernatural about

her; she's just a pleb like billions of others, just a good-looking piece of tail who suffers from the delusion that she was born with rights other than those that her betters choose to bestow on her, polluting the world with her every breath. The only reason she's been able to take down so many of Booth's associates is because she's gone bat-shit insane with revenge. Insanity makes her bold, fearless, unpredictable. That's Hendrickson's analysis—although, in the quick, maybe her kind of insanity is just as fearsome as any supernatural power.

He hurries uphill, along the line of vehicles waiting to turn right at the intersection. He tries the front passenger door on a Tesla, startling the driver. Locked. On to a silver Lexus SUV. Yanks open the door. A little girl holding a plush-toy toad regards him wide-eyed. No good. Booth slams the door. He looks back and across lanes to the Cadillac limo, where the driver stands watching, not yet coming after him.

He moves on to a brand of car he doesn't know—maybe a Honda, maybe a Toyota; he has no interest in brands that aren't advertised in the luxury-oriented magazines he reads—and he opens the front door. The driver is a twentysomething woman in jeans, cowgirl shirt with decorative stitching, red neckerchief, and something like a half-size Stetson—a cowboy hat *in a car*—and she appears frightened.

Flashing his Department of Justice ID, he says, "FBI," because no one is impressed by the letters *DOJ*. Anyway, the DOJ oversees the Bureau. "I need your assistance—I need your car," he declares as he clambers into the passenger seat and pulls shut the door.

Her fright instead proves to be righteous indignation when she snatches from the dashboard a bobble-head statue of some cartoon character Hendrickson doesn't recognize and starts bashing him with it. *"Hey, hey, hey, get out, get the hell out!"*

Infuriated that she would resist a legitimate law-enforcement official, he tears the bobble-head out of her grip and throws it into the backseat as with his right hand he draws his pistol. The traffic light turns green and car horns blare. He demands, *"Turn right. Move, move, move!"*

The chauffeur appears at the driver's door, and Booth squeezes off a shot, blowing out that window.

Because she hasn't seen the chauffeur, the cowgirl thinks her assailant has fired a warning shot to force her cooperation. She shouts—*"Shit!"*—and tramps on the gas and takes the corner in a wide turn.

10

Of all the people in the numerous vehicles lined up in three lanes, many must have seen Hendrickson bail out of the limousine and try to jack a car—an extraordinary moment of street theater—but no one other than Gilberto made any effort to intervene. An effort that nearly got him shot.

Speckled with window glass, dodging cars as impa-

tient motorists swerved around him, he hurried back to
the limo and got behind the wheel and pulled shut the
door. He set out in pursuit of the yellow Subaru that
Hendrickson had carjacked.

When he turned off MacArthur Boulevard onto
Bison, he saw the Subaru ahead of him, closer than
he expected, moving erratically from lane to lane.

The burner phone that Jane had provided lay on
the seat beside him. Driving with one hand, he keyed
in the number of *her* burner.

She took the call. "Yeah?"

"Somehow he knew. He went out the emergency
hatch in the roof."

"Where are you?"

"He carjacked this woman. I'm following. On Bison,
headed toward Jamboree."

"She'll have a phone," Jane said.

"Yeah. You better split."

"Splitting," she said. "Call you in a few minutes."

11

The cowgirl is agitated, which is understand-
able, and she's frightened, which she ought
to be, but more than anything, she's angry, glancing at
him with exasperation so hot that he can almost feel it.

"Make a U-turn," he tells her. "Here, do it, *here!*"

She swings the car toward a break in the median, and now they are heading back down Bison toward MacArthur Boulevard, where the traffic light ahead of them is red.

"You trashed my window. That's gonna cost me."

Her purse is resting between her thigh and the console. When Hendrickson takes it, she tries to snatch it back.

He raps her knuckles sharply with the barrel of the pistol. "Just drive, damn it."

"That's my money, you can't have it."

"I don't want your money. I'm FBI."

"Gimme my money."

"I only want your phone. *I'm FBI!*"

"Get your own freakin' phone."

"Keep your hands on the wheel."

She grabs for the iPhone.

He jams the pistol against her neck. "Are you stupid?"

"You kill me, who drives?"

"I will, sitting in your blood."

"You're no FBI."

"What're you stopping for?"

"You think maybe for *the red light*?"

"Screw the red light. *Keep going.*" When she doesn't tramp the accelerator, he moves the pistol from her throat to her temple. *"Now, bitch!"*

Six lanes of traffic, three westbound and three eastbound, flash past on MacArthur. She lays on the horn as she takes the plunge, as if anyone will hear it in time to stop. Although Booth commands her to do this, he at once regrets his imprudence, fording this Amazon of traffic not with the stout heart of an adventurer, but in sudden fright. His alarm is so primitive that a hurtling eighteen-wheeler seems like a living leviathan that will scoop them into its maw and swallow them. Horns blare, brakes shriek, but they reach the farther shore after just two near misses, so maybe his luck is changing.

"Take 73 south," he orders.

"Why? Where?"

He raps the side of her head with the barrel of the pistol hard enough to hurt, to knock a little sense into her. "You don't need to know where. Faster, damn it, *put the pedal down.*"

As they descend the entrance ramp to State Highway 73, he quickly makes a call with her iPhone, keying in the emergency number for a multi-agency task force dubbed J-Spotter, which is coordinating efforts to apprehend Jane Hawk. It's a rare example of cooperation between five entities that otherwise jealously guard their jurisdictions: the FBI, Homeland Security, the NSA, the CIA, and the Environmental Protection Agency. Their vast combined resources—money, personnel, satellites, aircraft, vehicles, armaments—in combination with local police departments, allow them to put a team in the vicinity of any Hawk sighting anywhere in the country within half an hour, perhaps in some locations as soon as ten minutes.

"FASTER!" Hendrickson shouts.

"I'm already speedin'."

"Doesn't matter. I'm FBI."

"That's steamin' bullshit," she says, but she's sufficiently frightened of the gun to put the car up to eighty.

The heads of the five agencies in the coalition aren't aware that the impetus to create J-Spotter came from Techno Arcadians in their ranks, and that members of the conspiracy fully control the task force. While the stated purpose of this effort is to arrest Jane Hawk and prosecute her for murder, treason, and other trumped-up charges, the Arcadians intend to inject her with a control mechanism to learn who might have been assisting her, and then kill her in such a way as to make her death appear to be the result of natural causes.

When Hendrickson's call is answered on the second ring, he announces himself not by name but by a seven-digit identifier. He specifies the guard-gated community in which Simon lives, gives the address of the house, and finishes by saying, "Blackbird is there now but not for long."

Their code name for Jane Hawk is *Blackbird*.

"I'm five minutes out. Get me backup."

Booth Hendrickson relishes—thrives on—the power and the perks of his position. But he delights as well, perhaps equally, in the trappings of such clandestine work, the code names and passwords and hush-hush and hugger-mugger, the secrets within secrets, the ciphers and signals and signs. There's a quality of *play* about it all, which is exhilarating to one who, throughout his blighted childhood, was never allowed much playtime.

When he terminates the call, he tucks the iPhone in

a coat pocket, which incenses the cowgirl. "That's my phone. I paid for that phone."

"Be good, you'll get a new one free from the government."

"I want that one. Gimme it."

"Take the next exit."

"Hey, asshole, this is America."

"America is over and done," he declares, putting the gun to her head again.

"The hell it is."

"Take this exit!"

12

Jane had been in the blind-black garage when Gilberto Mendez called. Having carjacked some woman, Hendrickson would most likely get his captive's cellphone, which upended the entire plan.

A minute later, upstairs in the kitchen, she recovered the lunchbox-size Medexpress carrier she had left there on first touring the house and once more hurried to the garage, where she switched on the lights.

Although she'd come to the house on foot, she didn't have time to hike out of the community and all the way back to her Explorer Sport, which she'd left near an all-night supermarket in a shopping-center parking lot.

Rolls-Royce, Lamborghini, Mercedes GL 550.

In a workbench drawer, Jane found the key to the Mercedes SUV.

From the perfboard display of tools, she took two screwdrivers, one with a regular blade, one with a Phillips head.

13

With State Highway 73 behind them, racing west on Newport Coast Drive, weaving lane to lane, the cowgirl leans into the steering wheel, jaws clenched as though she's afflicted with tetanus. As argumentative as she has been, she is that silent now.

Her silence is at first welcome, but then suspicious. Booth Hendrickson dislikes her even more than he dislikes other people, and he attributes her silence to the feverish scheming of a birdbrain twit.

"Don't do anything stupid," he advises.

"Fascist bastard."

"Just drive. Get around these cars. Lay on the horn."

She hammers the horn but says, "Nazi turd."

Hendrickson doesn't take such insults lightly. No one has ever called him a fascist or a Nazi until now; those are words *he* uses against others. "Honey, if you dress like a rodeo shitkicker, better not be calling other people names."

"Communist bloodsucker."

"What's with the ridiculous half-size Stetson?" he counters. "Couldn't you afford the grown-up cowgirl look?"

"It's a uniform, you asswipe. I work in a theme restaurant. And I recognize your type."

"My *type*?"

"Big-talkin' cheap-tippin' Commie-Nazi jerk."

He wants so badly to hit her with the pistol, break out a couple teeth, but instead he snatches up his Department of Justice ID and shakes it at her and says, "Take the next right turn."

"You ever really work a day in your life?" she asks. *"Right turn!"*

She brakes hard, fishtails the car, slides onto the new street, as if she's the offspring of demolition-derby drivers. "You sucked on your mama's teat till you could suck on a government teat."

If they weren't one minute away from the front gate to the guarded community in which Simon lives, one minute away from nailing Jane Hawk, he would shoot this impudent bitch. Instead, in a voice he wishes were more in his control, he says, "Drive as if your life depends on it."

14

Jane, in the stolen Mercedes SUV, thirty seconds from the front gate, was brought to a halt by a double-hopper truck pulling into the street from a vacant lot where excavation was under way for the construction of a house. Each of its twin hoppers was mounded with a few tons of dirt that inescapably reminded her of recent graves not yet grassed. The driver had to maneuver the big vehicle back and forth to get it fully into the uphill lane, and only then did Jane have room to risk oncoming traffic and get around the behemoth.

She topped the hill, crossed the crest, and sped down the other side, into the exit lane for the front gate. The electronic eye that monitored oncoming vehicles seemed slow on the uptake, so that she came to a full stop before the barrier began to roll aside. Trees had recently been trimmed, and a fragment of a yellowed palm frond had blown into the recessed track, so that the gate wheels stuttered against it, chewed at it, and finally began to roll through it.

Jane believed that, with free will and fortitude, anything within the laws of nature could be accomplished. She did *not* believe in luck, good or bad. But at moments like this, when obstructions were repeatedly raised at the most inconvenient times during the most urgent tasks, a chill of recognition whispered through her, for she discerned intention behind the impediments put in her way, could *feel* the mystery of the world's dark governance beyond what was to be seen.

She drove through the open gate, past the guard-house, between flanking colonnades of towering palm trees, fast along the entry drive that connected the community to the public road. She arrived at the stop sign just as the yellow Subaru appeared to her left, coming downhill at high speed.

15

By the Subaru's erratic movements, Gilberto had deduced that, in spite of Hendrickson's gun, there must be a continuing battle of wills being fought between him and the driver, if not also to some degree an ongoing physical contest. At first, he'd been able to see the woman and her kidnapper seeming to strike each other. But then the bright-yellow car spun 180 degrees on Bison and plunged recklessly through the cross traffic on MacArthur Boulevard. By the time he followed in the limo, with a modicum of caution, onto State Highway 73, they were well ahead of him. Although the Subaru didn't weave from lane to lane as before, it sometimes drifted onto the shoulder before returning to the pavement.

Rather than try to close the gap that had opened between him and the car, Gilberto remained as far back as he dared, hoping that Hendrickson might not realize he was being tailed. There was every reason to expect that, having split the scene in such a dramatic fashion, the man assumed his escape to be complete and was too preoccupied with his resisting hostage to discover otherwise.

Gilberto considered using his burner phone to call 911 and report the carjacking. But he would be siccing the cops on a kidnapper that he himself had kidnapped. There were maybe ten thousand ways that could go wrong for him.

Besides, he quickly realized that Hendrickson was heading toward the southern end of Newport Beach, where Hendrickson's brother lived in one of the several guard-gated communities in a neighborhood known as Newport Coast. He was trying to get to Jane before she ghosted away from Simon Yegg's place.

Gilberto considered phoning her, decided against it. She'd be moving fast, her hands full. Anyway, she didn't need a warning. She already expected that Hendrickson would have used his hostage's phone to report her location to the battalions searching for her.

When the Subaru left State Highway 73 at Newport Coast Drive without reducing speed, in fact accelerating with much blowing of its horn, Gilberto closed part of the gap between them.

16

In his phone call to Jane, Gilberto hadn't mentioned the make or color of the car that Hendrickson had jacked. But as she braked at the stop sign and saw the lemon-yellow Subaru streaking along the descending curve of pavement, coming in from her left as fast as any angry hornet, there was about it an aura of menace, a threat of ruin, that spoke to the ear of her intuition. And behind it, farther uphill, in immediate confirmation, came a white Cadillac limousine.

If Hendrickson at first intended to have his captive driver swing hard right into the entrance lane, he must have recognized the GL 550 as from his brother's collection. The car braked and began to turn, but then corrected, aiming for the Mercedes.

Jane reacted just quickly enough, shifting into reverse. Brief banshee wails issued from the tires of both vehicles as the Mercedes smoked backward on the blacktop and as the Subaru imprinted skid marks before rocking to a stop athwart the two-lane community drive.

Gun in both hands, Hendrickson erupted from the car, clearly intending to open fire on Jane, but only then becoming aware of the limousine, a juggernaut in the wake of the Subaru. He squeezed off two shots at the Caddy. Starburst pocks appeared in the smooth sweep of windshield. A third round entirely dissolved the glass.

Jane put the Mercedes in park, exited fast and low, using the door as a shield, drawing her Heckler.

Hendrickson hitched and stumbled sideways, out of the path of the incoming limo.

The grinding of disc brakes and the shriek of tires molting skins of rubber on the pavement raised the expectation of a violent crash. But the impact of car and car was almost discreet: a crisp crumpling of metal, the crack of fractured plastic, the tinkle of shattered headlights cascading across the roadway.

As Jane came out from behind the open door of the Mercedes, she was relieved to see Gilberto scramble from the limousine, his pistol in hand. Two of them against Hendrickson, drawing down on him from different directions. The bastard would have to surrender.

Good. The last thing she wanted to do was kill him. She had other uses for him.

As Hendrickson reeled away from the crash and regained his balance, Jane was about to order him to drop the gun when the driver of the Subaru—booted, jeaned, wearing a rhinestone-cowboy shirt—intervened. Something like a scaled-down Western hat fell from the woman's head as she launched at Hendrickson and leaped onto his back. Her long legs clamped around his middle, as if this were a rodeo ring and he the bull that must be ridden. The impact staggered him, almost took him to his knees, and the gun flew from his grip. His rider pulled fiercely on his mane of hair with her left hand and pounded on the side of his face with her right.

Gilberto scooped the weapon off the blacktop before Hendrickson could retrieve it.

Jane holstered her pistol and withdrew the bottle of chloroform from a jacket pocket.

If Hendrickson had ever been trained in physical combat, he remembered nothing he'd been taught. Bent under the weight of his assailant, he weaved in a circle, trying to reach back and tear her off, like some mad turtle offended by its own shell. His strength quickly deserted him, and he collapsed onto his side, taking his rider with him.

Even as Hendrickson went down, Jane dropped to her knees before him. He rolled his head and glared up at her, his patrician features distorted so grotesquely by rage that he resembled a gargoyle fallen from a high parapet. His mouth twisted in a snarl, but before one word of invective could escape him, she sprayed him with chloroform, and he passed out.

17

As if he'd read Jane's mind, Gilberto hurried to the GL 550, boarded it, pulled a U-turn, and reversed toward Jane where she knelt beside Hendrickson.

Having been witness to car crash, gunfire, and struggle, the guard in the community gatehouse, about seventy feet away, might already be on the phone to the police. If Hendrickson had reported Jane's where-abouts with his hostage's cellphone, far more danger-ous specimens than the local cops were on the way.

Hendrickson had no sooner passed out, nose and mouth wet with chloroform, than the scrappy girl in Western garb, clambering over him, extracted an iPhone from one of his coat pockets.

"I need that phone," Jane said as the GL 550 braked behind her.

The cowgirl said, "I worked hard for it. You ever work hard or you just shoot people for what you want?"

"I'll buy it," Jane said, putting up the tailgate of the 550.

"Buy it? Like that makes any sense."

The girl stepped aside while Jane rolled Hendrick-son onto his back and Gilberto took hold of him by the ankles.

"Ten thousand bucks." Jane and Gilberto lifted Hendrickson into the back of the SUV. "Throw in that red scarf, and I'll pay cash."

"It's not a scarf, it's a neckerchief. What're you doin' with that bastard?"

"You don't want to know." Jane asked Gilberto to get three packets from the attaché case on the front seat.

The girl glared at Hendrickson in the cargo space of the SUV. "He belongs in jail, what he did to me."

Gilberto appeared with three banded blocks of cash and gave one to the girl at Jane's direction.

"Ten thousand for the phone and the neckerchief," Jane offered.

The girl's eyes narrowed with suspicion.

"It's real, and it's not hot money. You'll have to trust me."

"Who trusts anyone anymore?" Nevertheless the girl handed over the iPhone. She slipped off the kerchief and surrendered that, too.

"This other twenty thousand," Jane said, as she put the scarf over Hendrickson's face and sprayed it lightly with chloroform, "is for saying my friend here wasn't Hispanic. He was a tall, blond white dude. And this wasn't a white GL 550, it looked silver. And this guy wasn't chloroformed. We abducted him at gunpoint."

Although she took the twenty thousand that Gilberto offered, the girl appeared fretful. "What's it called—lying for money?"

"It's called politics," Jane said. "Better hide the cash."

As Gilberto hurried to the driver's door and Jane closed the tailgate, the girl stuffed two packets in her bra and shoved the third down the front of her jeans, into her underpants. "If you're gonna hurt that Commie-Nazi piece of shit, hurt him some for me."

"Deal."

"Who are you, anyway?"

"Dorothy," Jane lied.

The girl said, "I'm Jane."

"Of course you are," Jane said, climbed into the passenger seat, and closed the door.

18

They drove north on the Pacific Coast Highway, where ragged blankets of grass and scrub covered the sandy soil to the left of the road. Beyond that rough and prickly shore, a pale beach smoothed into a sea glinting with infinite knives of sunlight, but shadowed by its ceaseless heavings.

In Corona del Mar, with the sea lost to sight, they heard the first siren, saw the flashing lightbar atop a southbound Newport Beach police cruiser. Traffic deferred to it, and the siren waned.

The residential neighborhood west of the Coast Highway was known as the Village: picturesque streets of lovely houses leading down toward a bluff where parks overlooked the ocean. Gilberto pulled to the curb in a quiet block, and while he remained behind the wheel with the engine running, Jane got out with the two screwdrivers she had taken from the garage at Simon Yegg's house.

Border to border, from sea to shining sea, police cars and other government vehicles had for some time been equipped with 360-degree license-plate-scanning systems that recorded the numbers of the vehicles around them, whether parked or in motion, transmitting them 24/7 to regional archives, which in turn shared the information with the National Security Agency's vast intelligence troves in its million-square-foot Utah Data Center.

Authorities could track a fugitive by a license-plate number if the vehicle happened to be scanned often enough during its journey from point A to point Z. Now that Jane's original plan had been upended by events, she and Gilberto needed to transfer Booth Hendrickson from the Mercedes to Gilberto's Chevrolet Suburban and then ditch the superhot GL 550. But they didn't dare do so if a series of scans would later allow the Arcadians to connect the two vehicles and put the entire Mendez family on a kill-or-convert list.

Driving without the SUV's tags, they were at some risk, but the alternative was more certain to lead to disaster.

An ordinary screwdriver was sufficient to detach the license plates. Jane removed them boldly, without looking around furtively, as if she had a perfectly legitimate reason for doing so.

More sirens arose in the distance. The sky resounded with the *chop-chop-chop* of the rotary wing of a helicopter. In fact, when she looked up, she saw one helo to the west, following the shoreline, a standard police aircraft, and a larger chopper—with a military profile—coming in from the northeast, both heading south toward Newport Coast.

She got into the Mercedes. She tucked the license plates and the screwdrivers under the seat. "Let's scoot."

This vehicle was still a deathtrap. They had to be rid of it soon. The authorities would quickly learn that she had escaped in Simon's GL 550. Ten minutes after that, by satellite, they would be tracking its position by the locater built into its GPS.

19

Like a vision out of Edgar Allan Poe's most fevered and eerie imaginings, the three-story building thrust against the sky as if it were the House of Usher heaving up from the tarn that once claimed it, a night scene concurrent with the bright daylight all around, yet resistant to the sun's revelation. Hulking, shadow-filled and shadow-casting, soot-stained and fissured, its shattered windows looking in upon cavernous darkness, partly collapsed yet looming with menace, it was like some haunted palace through which a hideous throng stormed ceaselessly in silence.

The high school had been the site of a Saturday night rally for peace, even though the nation wasn't at war with anyone other than stateless bands of terrorists. In the eight months since the event, how and why a peace protest could have turned violent hadn't been explained to anyone's satisfaction. There might have been a speaker who, while supportive of the crowd's antiwar sentiment, did not a hundred percent agree with their assessment of those groups and individuals most despised as warmongers. In these days of desperate and unreasoned passions, even a well-meaning speaker might inadvertently enrage a crowd with a few ill-chosen words. Some said the flashpoint had something to do with Israel. Others said it was about the dissing of a champion of some South American revolution. Still others insisted that it hadn't been political at all, that a contingent of racists had infiltrated the gathering and seized the sound system to spew their hate, though some survivors had no such memories. As yet no definitive answer had been provided regarding the identity of those who'd brought Molotov cocktails and quantities of jellied gasoline to a peace rally or why so many attendees were carrying guns at an event intended to promote brotherhood and understanding. If a gymnasium that seated twelve hundred hadn't been two hundred people over that capacity, if some of the doors serving it had not been blockaded, the death toll might not have reached three hundred. If the fire alarms had worked, first responders might have arrived in time to save most of the building. In spite of state and federal investigations, the many mysteries of the Independence Day Rally for Peace had grown deeper and more complex with time.

Jane knew nothing of the truth of this place, but she suspected that several adjusted people, brains webbed with control mechanisms, perhaps among those named on the Hamlet list, had been sent here to commit suicide and to take with them as many others as they could. The Techno Arcadians' strategy involved disguising their operations as the work of terrorists and madmen, seeding social chaos so the public would cry out for order. This would allow a steady ratcheting up of security measures and rights restrictions until such a day that even those who had not been adjusted with brain implants would celebrate the firm but enlightened rule of their betters.

Construction fencing surrounded the school and its immediate grounds, but the fabric privacy panels attached to the chain-link had in many places been slashed away by the curious. Signs that warned of toxic chemicals and of the unstable nature of the ruins had been defaced with obscene suggestions.

The building should have been demolished. But although the ruins had been combed repeatedly for clues, the ongoing federal investigations required that the site be preserved to avoid the destruction of possible evidence.

The school backed up to a football field flanked by stadium seating beyond the view of the street. Gilberto drove the GL 550 across that weedy, untended expanse of ground, gaining speed until he rammed the gate in the fence, broke the cheap hinges, and slammed through the rickety barrier. With shattered headlights and a buckled hood, the Mercedes came to a stop on the former faculty parking lot, where the undulant blacktop had been deformed and imprinted with fern-like patterns by the heat pouring off the burning building.

They were about half a mile from the residential street on which Gilberto had parked his Suburban earlier that morning.

"There's a shortcut," he said. "I won't be as much as ten minutes, maybe a couple minutes less."

Together, he and Jane propped the damaged gate in place. It looked reasonably intact in the unlikely event someone chanced by.

She returned to the Mercedes and opened the tailgate and took Hendrickson's pulse, which was steady if somewhat slow. She lifted the red neckerchief and watched his eyes moving under their lids. He muttered wordlessly and yawned. She replaced the cloth and sprayed it lightly with chloroform.

The sun was still forty minutes below the summit of the sky, but the shadow cast by the school seemed longer than it should have been this close to noon. She heard traffic noise in the distance but nothing nearby, no trilling bird, no settling noises in the ruins. Even the damaged Mercedes and its cooling engine failed to make a sound, as if three hundred casualties in one blazing hour had left this area forever a dead zone.

In Newport Coast, they would have found and freed Simon by now. They would know that two vehicles were missing from his collection. They would have determined that Jane Hawk and a male accomplice had departed the scene in Simon's Mercedes. Thereafter, it would take only a few minutes to get the registration number of the vehicle from the DMV and cross-check with the manufacturer's records to obtain the unique signal of the GPS.

It was too much to hope that the minor damage caused by the impact with the gate in the construction fencing had disabled the GPS to the extent of silencing the transponder by which the Mercedes could be tracked. The wolves would soon be coming.

20

Tanuja Shukla woke, opened her eyes without lifting her head from the pillow, and saw it was 11:19 A.M. on Saturday. The clock must be wrong. She never slept so late. Besides, she remained tired to the bone, as though, after an exhausting day, she had been asleep only two or three hours.

She was wearing her wristwatch. She never wore it to bed, but there it was, on her wrist. The watch and clock concurred.

She threw back the covers and sat on the edge of the mattress. Her pajamas were damp with sweat and clung to her body.

A soreness at one corner of her mouth. She put a hand to her lips. Dried blood crumbled against her fingertips.

For a moment she was mystified, but then she remembered the fall.

Last night. Standing in the wet dark. Soaked and chilled and lonely and wildly happy. Cataloguing the details of the foul weather as well as her physical and emotional responses to it, the better to write about the journey of the lead character in her novelette. The storm spoke through the medium of the nearby ancient oak, each leaf a tongue empowered by raindrops, the tree telling the storm's story in a chorus of soft clicks and hisses.

When she had returned to the house, she'd slipped

on the rain-puddled glossy paint of the back-porch floor. Slipped and fell face-first into . . . into one of the rocking chairs. The arm of one of the chairs. Stupid of her. Clumsy. She would need to eat and drink with care for the next couple days.

Now, as she got up from the bed, she felt sticky, dirty, and sore in places that the fall did not fully explain. An odor clung to her separate from the stale smell of her night sweat, a malodor that was familiar, disturbingly familiar . . . but her past experience of it—where, when?—eluded her.

As she went into her bathroom, step by step, the odor became a stink, became a stench, and incipient nausea slid around the walls of her stomach. She had felt dirty a moment earlier; but she felt *filthy* now. She was overcome by an urgent desire for a shower, an almost frantic need to be clean.

The compulsion was peculiar. But it meant nothing. Nothing at all.

Standing in a forceful spray of water as hot as she could tolerate, scrubbing herself with a soapy washcloth, she winced at the pain in her breasts and discovered they were bruised. She must have fallen more fully into the chair than she remembered.

When she felt clean at last and the threat of nausea had passed, she continued to linger there, eyes closed, turning slowly, letting the hot shower melt some of the soreness out of her. The sound of the rushing water returned to her a memory of the previous evening's storm: the sky black; the rain like an inkfall where there was no light to color it; the old oak an elaborate black figuration against the deeper black of the night; and sudden movement that was also black on black, *three robed and hooded figures hurrying through the downpour, like a scene from some film concerning medieval monks engaged in an urgent mission during apocalyptic times.*

Tanuja's breath caught in her chest, and she opened her eyes, half expecting to see those monks gathered around the shower stall, three walls of which were glass. Of course, no hooded figures stood watching her.

Such an odd moment. But it meant nothing. Nothing at all.

After she'd blown dry her hair and dressed, she went in search of Sanjay. She found him in his study, where the door stood open to the hall. He sat at the computer, his back to her, hunched over the keyboard, typing faster than she had ever before seen him type, as though a scene from his current novel in progress flowed from him on a tide of inspiration.

To write fiction well, long periods of intense concentration were nearly as important as talent. She and her brother so respected the creative process that neither would interrupt the other during working hours except for matters significant and urgent.

She went to the kitchen. As she fitted the paper filter in the coffeemaker, she detected an astringent chemical odor, the source of which was not at once evident. By the time she put the coffee and a half teaspoon of cinnamon in the filter, the smell so bothered her that she prowled the room in search of its origin.

The kitchen was sparkling, in fact cleaner than she recalled leaving it the previous night. The offensive odor was not strong, but waned and waxed and waned again. Indeed, it wasn't entirely a bad smell. There was in general a lemony fragrance, like that of the antibacterial spray she used to wipe down the counters, but under it lingered a persistent acridness.

She was drawn to the quartz-topped table, where red roses—the stems cut short in a low arrangement—filled a crystal bowl. Neither of the odors came from the flowers, and yet the blooms fascinated her.

She stared at the coagulum of blood-red petals for a long moment . . . until her gaze was drawn to an unlikely object lying on the table beside the bowl. A hypodermic needle. The barrel of the syringe was filled with a cloudy amber fluid.

It was an exotic item, but at the same time curiously familiar. A sense of déjà vu overcame her, and the feeling that some moment of a forgotten dream had here manifested in real life.

When she reached for the syringe, it ceased to be there on the table, and her fingers closed only on each other.

In that instant, she recognized the chemical odor as that of insecticide, specifically Spectracide hornet spray.

Mystery solved. Except that hornets were not in season. Well, yes, but she and Sanjay did sometimes use the spray for ants.

As for the syringe . . . how strange. But it meant nothing. Nothing at all.

Tanuja returned to the coffeemaker. She filled the Pyrex pot with water to the ten-cup level, because when Sanjay smelled the coffee brewing, he would want some, too.

In a few minutes, the kitchen grew redolent of the fine Jamaica blend, and Tanuja breathed deeply of the wonderful aroma while she cracked eggs for an omelet. She wanted some potatoes as well, and bacon, and toast. She was ravenous.

21

At one time there had been security cameras, because in recent decades too many schools were not merely centers of education, but also dens of drug dealing and violence. In the aftermath of the fire, however, there were no cameras intact and no electricity to power them.

Nevertheless, Jane felt watched, and she studied one broken-out window after another, searching for a faint human form in the charry darkness beyond. Her intuition, which she trusted implicitly, told her that no one lurked in the building, but she scanned the windows anyway. Months of being on the run, with enemies who commanded a panoply of surveillance platforms ranging from simple traffic cams to satellites in orbit, had brought her to that point at which healthy stage-one paranoia could metastasize into a cancerous stage four, which might paralyze her or lead her into fatal misjudgments.

When Gilberto returned in eight minutes, Jane dragged open the damaged gate in the construction fencing to admit him. He backed the Suburban up to the Mercedes GL 550. Together they moved Hendrickson from one vehicle to the other. She also transferred her tote, the attaché case packed with money, and the Medexpress carrier that she had for a while stowed in one of Simon Yegg's refrigerators.

As Jane closed the tailgate, a sudden siren coiled through the morning, close and spiraling louder, surely within a block of the school, much too close for them to escape without being seen. Once spotted, the Suburban would inevitably later be identified, because it would be tracked from the school by Arcadian operatives able to review archived video from traffic cameras, its ultimate destination uncovered. When the vehicle was associated with Booth Hendrickson's abduction, with Jane, it would incriminate Gilberto and bring hellfire upon him and his entire family.

Their eyes locked, and they froze in anticipation, as though they stood on a hangman's platform with rope around their necks, waiting for trapdoors to fall open beneath their feet. The siren Doppler-shifted to lower frequencies as the cops or paramedics, or whoever they were, passed the school and raced away to whatever crime or car wreck they had been summoned.

Gilberto drove and Jane sat in the backseat, the better to monitor the unconscious captive lying in the cargo area.

"I called Carmella," Gilberto said. "She's taken the kids to visit her sister in Dana Point. They'll stay the weekend."

"I'm so sorry. This is exactly what I didn't want—bringing all this right into your home."

"Not your fault. What happened happened. There's no other option that makes sense."

"I'm still trying to think of one."

They crossed the rutted and weedy football field, circled the farther stack of bleachers, turned left into an alley, and slipped away into the suburban sprawl. For the moment, they had eluded the agents of Utopia who would, without hesitation or remorse, kill them in the name of social progress.

She could think of no viable option other than the one Gilberto offered her. How strangely apt it was to find herself harried to a mortuary, to seek refuge with the dead, while in her hands she held the life of this man Hendrickson, who had ordered and/or assisted in uncounted murders.

22

Sanjay Shukla sat at his computer, in a condition he'd never known before, not merely inspired to write but *impelled* to write, as though he'd been bitten by some exotic mosquito that carried not any wasting disease, but instead a communicable need to create. No, not just a need. The word *need* implied a lack of something, a deficiency that he might or might not fill. The extreme urgency with which he was motivated to string together words into sentences allowed no choice between might or might not, but incited him to write as if his very existence depended on the quality of what he created. He was gripped not by the need to write but by the *necessity*, for there was no alternative to writing. He pounded the keyboard as if fever-driven, raining a tropical storm of words onto the screen, with none of his usual careful crafting.

He had awakened from a half-remembered dream seething with kaleidoscopic images of menace and horror. He had at once been obsessed with writing a story about a man who'd been obliged to protect an innocent child and failed to do so, by his failure allowing the child to perish. He had no complete story in mind. He knew only that when the child perished, so did *all* innocence in the world, whereupon civilization fell into a darkness that would never know a dawn.

The narrative flowed from him without a conventional structure, a stream-of-consciousness rant in the voice of the father who had failed the child. Although Sanjay strove to bring coherence to the story, the English language became a wallow of vexatious snakes that he could not wrangle into a satisfying story. Nevertheless, he wrote at a blistering pace for an hour, two hours, three, until the tips of his fingers were tender from the force with which he'd struck the keys. His neck ached, and a heaviness gathered in his chest as if his heart had swollen with retained blood.

He stopped typing and sat in bewilderment, for how long he did not know, until he smelled coffee brewing, bacon frying. The aromas stirred him as if from a dream, as if he had never fully awakened when he had gone from his bed to his office chair. He saved what he had written and got up and went into the kitchen.

At the cooktop, using tongs, Tanuja turned bacon in a frying pan. She looked at him and smiled. "Omelet in the warming drawer. I've made enough for two. The toast is about to pop up. Butter it, will you? Plenty of butter on mine."

Sanjay meant to say that he was starving, but instead he said, "I'm so empty."

If she thought his statement strange, she didn't remark on it, but said, "We need to eat, that's all, just eat and get on with it," which seemed to him nearly as peculiar as the words that he had spoken.

The toast popped up.

He buttered it.

23

The mortuary cosmetician was at work in the basement. The assistant mortician and his intern had driven the decedent from the previous night's viewing to the cemetery, where a graveside service would soon be under way. No other viewing had been scheduled until six o'clock this evening. The place was as quiet as a funeral home.

After stripping off Hendrickson's suit coat and shoulder rig, they strapped him to a gurney on which cadavers were transported, and they wheeled him through the back entrance, into the vestibule. With Gilberto at the head of the gurney and Jane at the foot, they bumped it up the stairs to the family apartment on the top floor.

The sleek and airy modern décor was in stark contrast to the ornate moldings, heavy velvet draperies, and neo-Gothic furniture on the ground floor.

As they wheeled Hendrickson through the living room and along a hallway, Jane said, "What's it like to live with the dead?"

"Same as it is for everyone else," Gilberto replied. "Except we *realize* we live with them—all of us are the dead in waiting, but most people put it out of their mind."

"The kids ever have nightmares?"

"Yeah, but not about the dead."

She left him in the kitchen with Hendrickson and

returned to the Suburban to get her tote, the attaché case, and the Medexpress carrier.

When she returned to the kitchen, Gilberto had adjusted the gurney, jacking up the back end, so Hendrickson remained strapped across his arms and legs, but reclining at a forty-five-degree angle rather than lying flat.

"A mortician doesn't need this feature," Gilberto said, "but they make gurneys mostly for the living, and this is how they come these days. Useful for you, I think."

She checked Hendrickson's pulse, but she didn't at once take the red neckerchief off his face.

Gilberto made coffee, strong and black, and poured it for himself and Jane, without sugar.

Carmella had left a homemade ricotta pie to cool on a wire rack. Jane ate a large slice as a belated breakfast, while Gilberto adjourned to another room to speak with his wife by phone.

By the time Jane finished eating, Hendrickson was muttering to himself. She washed her plate and fork, put them away, refreshed her mug of coffee, and took the scarf off his face.

When he opened his pale-green eyes, he was still floating on currents of chloroform, unaware that he was strapped down, in no condition to puzzle out her identity, not even fully aware of his own. He smiled dreamily up at her as she stood beside him. In a lotus-eater voice of indolent contentment, he said, "Hey, sexy."

"Hey," she said.

"I got a use for that pretty mouth."

"I bet you do, big guy."

"Bring it on down here."

She licked her lips suggestively.

He said, "Uncle Ira is not Uncle Ira."

"Who is he, then?"

Hendrickson smiled patronizingly. "No, that's not what you're supposed to say."

"What am I supposed to say, big guy?"

"You just say, all right."

"All right," she said.

"Blow me, gorgeous."

She puckered up and blew in his face.

"Funny," he said and laughed softly and drifted off into the shallows of unconsciousness.

Half a minute later, when he opened his eyes again, they were clearer, but he still smiled at her and recognized no danger. "I know you from somewhere."

"Want me to refresh your memory?"

"I'm all ears."

"You people killed my husband, threatened to rape and kill my little boy, and have been trying to kill me for months."

Slowly his smile faded.

24

While Sanjay and Tanuja ate a late breakfast together at the kitchen table, their conversation ranged over a wide spectrum of subjects, as usual, including the novelette that Tanuja was in the middle of writing. Coming in from researching the rain the previous evening, she had slipped and fallen, and now she chewed her food judiciously, on the left side of her mouth, to give the split lip a chance to heal. Sanjay asked how she felt. She said she felt fine, that at least she hadn't broken a tooth. She asked what had happened to his right ear, which was when he realized that something must be wrong with it. As if the injury hadn't existed until she spoke of it, he felt a soreness, the heat of inflamed tissue. He touched the helix of his ear, the outer rim; and under the skin, loose fragments of broken cartilage ground together like shards of glass. He winced when his touch induced a throbbing in the flesh, and for a moment it seemed not to be his own hand torturing the ear but the hand of some man seated near him, though no one else was present except he and Tanuja. In his mind's eye, he saw *an unfamiliar kitchen, dark but for the quivering light from three sinuous tongues of candle flame. In that strange place, Tanuja stood in a doorway, looking back at him with something like sorrow, as she was led away . . . led away, leashed and collared like a dog.* The image assaulted Sanjay vividly, and yet flickered out as if it had been an illusion of shadow and candlelight. A still small voice said that it meant nothing, nothing at all. When he tried to summon that other kitchen to mind again, he couldn't. He must have said something or his face contorted in a grotesque expression, because with concern his sister asked what was wrong. He assured her nothing was wrong, nothing at all, just that the injury to his ear puzzled him, as if he'd been sleep-walking, fell, and injured himself without waking. This led to a discussion of somnambulism, which Tanuja had once used as a plot device. By the time they moved on to another subject, the source of his injured ear no longer mattered to either of them because it meant nothing, nothing at all.

After breakfast, Tanuja retreated to her office to work on the novelette, and Sanjay returned to his computer. A leisurely meal with his sister, accompanied by a spirited conversation, always inspired him when he returned to writing, but not today. Something had been different about their colloquy this time. He had not felt fully engaged, and she seemed distracted, too. It was almost as if there was something that she needed to tell him, but she could not bring herself to speak of it, though each had always been frank with the other, each a sympathetic sounding board.

Troubled, he called to the screen the stream-of-consciousness pages he'd written earlier and began to read them. The text was so feverish, nonlinear, and bizarre that he couldn't imagine a magazine that would be interested in it, and there was no market for a book-length manuscript of this nature. Although he strove to make of his work a kind of art, he wrote to entertain, and he did *not* write what would not sell. Yet he had done just that this morning, not merely as an exercise, but with *passion*. And now, as he read the pages, this story of a man who failed to save a child and by his failure in some way brought an end to all innocence—and freedom—seemed to be some kind of allegory, a symbolical narrative in which nothing was what it appeared to be, written in a deep code, *which even he, the writer, could not translate.* Spiritualists believed in something called automatic writing, when a medium opened the door of his mind to any spirit that wished to communicate by way of him; what then flowed from pen to paper or keyboard to screen was the work not of the medium, but of an unknown entity speaking through the veil between the worlds of the living and the dead. But Sanjay wasn't a spiritualist and didn't believe in automatic writing; he could not account for these pages with that explanation.

The more he read, the more he was affected by what he read, and the more urgently he felt impelled to continue writing this . . . this testament, until he came to a moment in the narrative that he did not recall writing, that affected him more powerfully than either the words or the action could explain. The two lead characters, man and child, were born to parents who had emigrated from India. As the child lay dying, he said to the man who had so utterly failed him, *"Peri pauna,"* which meant "I touch your feet," which was something that you said—and did—to someone you venerated, for someone who had earned the greatest respect, for someone before whom you felt such profound love that you humbled yourself completely.

Sanjay's eyes were hot with tears. The screen before him blurred. For a while, he wept quietly, prodigiously, struggling to understand what this incomplete story, this flood of words might mean.

It seemed there would be no end either to his tears or to his desperate desire for enlightenment. But eventually the well of tears was drained, and his burning eyes were as dry as they were sore. His need to understand what he had written faded. It had meant nothing, nothing at all. He sat staring at the screen, at the lines of words that had a short time ago seemed to be crazed poetry crammed full of mysterious meaning expressed in elaborate patterns of symbols. Now they were just words, a witless gush of language, perhaps resulting from a low-grade fever related to an infection, perhaps suggesting a transient ischemic attack, one of those ministrokes caused by a temporary interruption of blood supply to a part of the brain, rare in someone his age but not utterly without precedent.

Nothing. The words meant nothing. Nothing at all.

Sanjay deleted what he'd written.

He opened another document. The manuscript he had been working on for three months.

To settle himself into the mood of the novel and the voice of its narrator, he read the most recently composed chapter. Soon he had recaptured the feel of it. He wrote a new sentence. Another. Eventually he had a paragraph that worked well, and he was doing what he most enjoyed, the work he felt born to do.

If there had been a ragged strangeness about the morning, his memory trimmed it into the neatness of ordinary experience.

The next paragraph began with an elegant metaphor that surprised and pleased him, and already he was in the flow—

His smartphone rang. He took the call.

A man said, "Uncle Ira is not Uncle Ira."

"Yes, all right," said Sanjay.

"I will tell you what must happen this evening, and you will receive these instructions with equanimity. You will be neither afraid nor despairing. You will listen without emotion and will not ever question the rightness of what must occur. Do you understand?"

"Yes."

"When I end this call, you'll have no conscious awareness that it ever took place. You will return to whatever you were doing when I phoned. But you will act according to the instructions that you've been given. Do you understand?"

"Yes."

The man spoke for several minutes. He concluded with the words "*Auf Wiedersehen*, Sanjay."

"Good-bye," he replied.

The next paragraph began with a metaphor that surprised and pleased him, and already he was in the flow, himself again and back in form, in a dance with his favorite partner—the English language.

25

The black hair is the only element of disguise, and her blue eyes are as striking as Booth Hendrickson has heard them described by others who have been in her company and survived.

A solemn-looking block of a man, the chauffeur himself sans cap and sunglasses, in his unfortunate off-the-rack black suit, sits in a dinette chair. His hair is black, as are his eyes, and the coffee in his mug is so dark that it might have been water dredged from the river Styx. Clearly he is meant to be intimidating, the crudest kind of muscle, a high-school dropout with an IQ barely high enough to allow him to drive a car and pull a trigger. Booth Hendrickson can't be intimidated by such a man, who would no doubt define *faux pas* as "the father of my enemy." He has used dozens like this thug and, when necessary, has gotten rid of them to avoid any link between himself and what he's ordered them to do. Intelligence and wit will always triumph over brute strength; intelligence, wit, and powerful connections, the last of which Booth has in abundance.

Again, he looks up into the eyes of Jane Hawk and meets her sky-blue stare and this time does not look away. "I phoned in your location, Simon's house. Maybe you skipped minutes before the hammer came down, but they're tracking you a thousand different ways and closing fast."

"A thousand, huh? Surely that's hyperbole."

He smiles. "I like to hear pretty girls use big words. Which improve-your-vocabulary-in-thirty-days course did you take? Did it include the term *lèse majesté*? If not, you would be well advised to look it up."

"A high crime committed against a sovereign state. Treason," she says. "But it isn't applicable. You Techno Arcadians aren't a sovereign state. You're seditionists, totalitarians drunk on the promise of absolute power. *You're* the treasonist."

That she knows they call themselves Techno Arcadians disturbs him, but he's not surprised that she has clawed this fact out of one of the people she's kidnapped and interrogated.

With the slightest theatrical touch, she takes an iPhone from a jacket pocket and places it on the table as if it's a Fabergé egg.

Evidently she wants him to ask about it, but he will not. They are in a contest of wills, and he knows how to play these games.

He says, "Who's accused of treason and executed for it depends on who controls the press and courts. You don't. Anyway, treason in pursuit of a perfect society is heroic."

Her puzzlement is exaggerated, a mocking expression. "A perfect society with people enslaved by brain implants?"

He smiles and rolls his head back and forth on the gurney. "Not enslaved. They're given peace, released from worry, given direction they can't otherwise find in their lives."

As she unzips a leather tote bag that is standing on the table, Booth glances at the iPhone, wondering what she wants him to ask about it, so that he might ask something entirely different, if he mentions it at all.

The phone becomes a secondary consideration when, from the tote, she extracts a large pair of scissors and smiles as she works the gleaming blades.

She says, "Given direction, huh? Are there a lot of people who can't figure out how to live their lives—they're adrift, lost?"

"Don't play devil's advocate with me, Jane. You know as well as I do, millions waste their lives with drugs, booze. They can't find their way. They're indolent and ignorant and *unhappy*. By adjusting them, we give them a chance to be happy."

"Really? Is that what you're doing, Boo? Giving them a chance to be happy? Gee, I don't know. It still looks like slavery to me."

He pretends disinterest in the scissoring blades. He sighs. "Candidates for adjustment aren't chosen by race, religion, gender, or sexual orientation. No particular group is targeted. It can't be slavery if the purpose of every adjustment is to increase the amount of contentment and happiness in the world."

"So you're quite the humanitarian, Boo. Maybe even a Nobel Peace Prize in your future."

Booth intensely dislikes being called Boo. That is a nickname with which he'd been mocked in his youth. She may have discovered this or intuited it. She thinks that by needling him, ridiculing him, she can unnerve him, just as she will try to unnerve him with the scissors and perhaps other sharp instruments. But he endured so much mockery as a child that he is inured to it. And as for being cut or tortured, she will discover that he has more courage than she supposes and the endurance of stone. Besides, he knows she prides herself on operating as much as possible within traditional moral boundaries and will not stoop to physical torture.

"Not every 'adjusted' person is on your Hamlet list," she says. "But those who are—exactly how are they made happier by killing themselves?"

"I don't select them. The computer does."

"The computer model."

"That's right. It selected your husband because he was likely to have a wrongheaded political career after leaving the Marines."

"Who designed the computer model?"

"Some exceedingly smart people."

"Like Bertold Shenneck and David James Michael."

"Smarter than you and me, Janey," he assures her, though he is an intellectual equal to those men and certainly her superior.

She says, "Shenneck, Michael—both dead. How smart could they have been?"

He does not deign to answer that snarky non sequitur.

He realizes they have taken off his suit coat. It lies jumbled on a counter, where it has been tossed as if it's a rag. They should have had enough decency to ensconce a Dior suit coat in a closet, on a hanger. The wide strap across his thighs will surely leave severe wrinkles diagonal to the pleats in his pant legs.

Using the scissors to point at the iPhone on the table, Jane Hawk says, "Are you wondering about the phone?"

"What's to wonder about? It's just a phone, Janey."

"It's the one you took from the woman you carjacked."

Booth shrugs in his restraints, but a sudden excitement stirs in him, which he must conceal.

"You used that phone to contact your people and call them down on me," she says. "Now I have the number you inputted."

"Which is worth nothing to you."

"Really? Nothing? Think about it, Boo."

He's thinking about it, all right. When he called J-Spotter, the team automatically stored the number of that phone. Now that he has gone missing, they can use the number to quickly obtain the unique locater signal the phone produces. It is essentially a GPS transponder that will allow them to track her to this place sooner than later.

She looks at the chauffeur and works the scissors, and he smiles at her, as if he knows what's coming.

She moves closer to the gurney, clicking the scissors, trying to get Booth to ask what she's going to do with them, but of course he does not ask.

When she pulls on a thick lock of his hair and cuts off a three- or four-inch length, Booth is surprised and displeased. "What the hell?"

"To remember you by," she says, but then drops

the hair on the floor. "Though I'm afraid I've spoiled your perfect . . . What do you call it?"

"What do I call what?"

"Your 'do. Your stylish hairdo. What do you call it?"

"Don't be ridiculous."

"Do you call it a haircut?"

"I don't call it anything."

"No, you wouldn't call it a haircut. Too common. You probably call it a coiffure. A man of your stature goes to a coiffeuse to be coiffed."

A small laugh escapes the black-suited thug, whether genuine or part of a practiced routine is hard to tell.

"How much do you pay when you go to the coiffeuse, Boo?"

"Mockery doesn't work with me," he assures her.

"Do you pay a hundred dollars?"

Booth does not reply.

"I've insulted him," she says to the thug at the table. "Must be two hundred at least, maybe three."

Booth realizes he is staring at the iPhone on the table. He looks away from it, lest she see his interest.

She turns to him again. "How much do you pay the coiffeuse to cut your hair?"

She wishes to define him as a shallow elitist, and he refuses to be that person, for he is *not* that person, not of that class, not of her class, either, not of any class, above all concepts of class, caste, and echelon. He says nothing.

In an instant, she goes from ice to fire, her face contorted by rage and flushed with hatred. With sudden fury she snarls, *"What do you pay for a haircut, ass-hole?"* As she speaks, her right hand arcs high and then down, driving the scissors into the two-inch-thick vinyl-covered mattress, so close to his face that he startles in spite of himself. Vinyl and dense-foam padding split as flesh might, and the points of the blades rap against the steel substrate as if against bone.

She wants him to believe that the death of her husband and the peril in which her child lives and these long months on the run have driven her to the edge of sanity, that she might snap, butchering him before she quite realizes what she's done. But he knows her too well to be conned by this performance. He has reviewed in detail the cases she solved while an agent of the FBI—a record of brilliant deduction, wise strategies, and smart techniques. For months, she has eluded capture even though the combined resources of federal, state, and local law enforcement have been committed to the search for her. Her sanity is a stone that can't be cracked.

Nevertheless, as the scissors flash past his face and gouge the mattress, he glances at the iPhone, attempting by an act of sheer *willpower* to summon the SWAT teams that surely must be en route.

She leans toward him, her rage gone as abruptly as it came, her unblemished face serene and exquisitely erotic in its serenity. Her lips are eight or ten inches from his when she presses the closed blades of the scissors against the lower lid of his left eye. The steel is cold and the point pricking.

In almost a whisper, she says, "Do you know why

I put the phone on the table, Boo? Hmmm? To give you hope. So that when you hoped, I could take your hope away from you. Like you've taken hope from so many people. I hammered a screwdriver blade into the charging port of that phone, Boo. Split the battery. No juice. No locater signal. No one's tracking it. No one's coming to save you."

Her eyes are at least three shades of blue alternating in the striations of the irises, those thin circular layers of muscle like the folds of Japanese fans, the kitchen fluorescents treating each grade of pigment differently, so that her stare seems radiant not by reflection, but because of some internal light. Her pupils are black holes, their gravity alarming.

She still speaks softly, but now as tenderly as a lover. "Tell me, Booth, what else must I take away from you in order to make you talk? Your eyes—so you can see no evil? What a terrible, terrible loss, considering the delight you take in seeing the evil you do."

She moved the scissors to his lips.

"Your lying tongue? Then you'd have to answer all my questions in writing while swallowing so much blood."

She takes the scissors away from his lips but doesn't press them to another part of him. Instead, she startles him by reaching back with her left hand and caressing his crotch, fondling his package through his suit pants.

"Do you go to Aspasia, Booth?"

The elegant and highly secret houses of pleasure, reserved for the wealthiest supporters of the Techno Arcadian mission, are called Aspasia, named after the mistress of Pericles, the famous statesman and mayor of Athens, circa 400 B.C. Booth is disquieted to learn that she knows about Aspasia, as closely guarded a secret as any the Arcadians keep.

"There are four of them," she whispers. "Los Angeles, San Francisco, New York, Washington. Have you tried them all, Booth? I've spent a little time touring the Aspasia in Los Angeles."

The revelation that she has been in one of these highly secure palaces of Eros alarms him, and he tells himself that she is lying.

"The twin colonnades of magnificent phoenix palms that flank the long driveway," she says, "the courtyard with its swimming pool as big as a lake. Tens of millions of dollars of art and antiques. So much marble and granite and gilding. It's all so classy that dirty little perpetual adolescents can go there and feel like big important men."

She is not lying. She has been to Aspasia. The truth of her mood is not in the softness with which she speaks and the tenderness with which she teases him through his pants; the truth is in her stare, her eyes now radiant with fury. What she saw at Aspasia has not merely outraged her; she clearly found it an abomination, for she is filled now with loathing, and the light in her eyes is the light of abhorrence.

"One of the girls in Aspasia is a gorgeous Eurasian, maybe eighteen, nineteen. Her name is LuLing. Well, you know, that's her whore name, given to her. She doesn't remember her real name or what she once was, doesn't remember her family, nothing of her past. She doesn't even possess the *concept* of a past or a future. All that and more has been scrubbed from her mind. She lives only in the moment, Boo. Smiling and attentive, without any inhibitions. You might call her a blithe spirit if there was any spirit left in her. She lives only to submit to those who use her, to satisfy their every desire. Cool, huh? Just thinking about it should fill out the pouch in your briefs, Boo."

He dares not speak. He believes now that he has misjudged her capacity for . . . cruelty.

Her soft voice fades to a breathless whisper. "Do you have extreme desires, Booth? Do you like rough sex? Rougher than rough? Do you like to hear them cry?"

Bravado and ostentatious assertion of his superiority have in the past always gotten Booth through tight passages. His mind races now as he considers what to say and do.

Her face six inches from his. Her hand still moving sensuously over the crotch of his pants. Her warm breath on his face. "Mama's boy is terrified of me, isn't he? If he wasn't, there'd be at least some stiffening of his little man, but there's none at all. Terror is a good thing if it makes you face the truth. Agree to tell me everything I want to know about the Arcadians, because if you don't, not even *your* mind is dark enough to imagine what I'll do to you."

If he rats out the Arcadians, they will surely torture and kill him as a turncoat. His fellow conspirators are infinitely more bloody-minded than this bitch, who is still more of a straight arrow than not. In the past few months, she's given him lots of headaches, some of them as fierce as migraines. Maybe she's capable of greater cruelty than he thought, but she will not—unlike certain of his associates—cut out his tongue or cut off his balls. She terrifies him, yes, but bravado and reliance on his superiority are, now as always, his best hope.

Fear has flooded his mouth with saliva, and he puts it to good use, spitting copiously in her face from a distance of six inches.

He expects her contained fury to erupt, expects to be slapped and clawed, but her face is still serene, and she doesn't touch him.

She remains bent over him for a moment and then slowly rises to her full height. She stands in silence, staring down at him without expression.

Perhaps a minute passes, during which she does not wipe her face. Pearls of spittle glimmer on her cheeks, her chin, and a slimy silvery string depends from the tip of her perfect nose.

She turns away from him and goes to the sink, but she doesn't pull a paper towel from the holder and blot herself or turn on the water. She stares out the window.

Her reaction is so unexpected that Booth's dread grows with the continued silence. He is reluctant to look away from her, but then he rolls his head to the right on the gurney and regards the thug in the black suit, who stares back with eyes as black as those holes in desert sand from which tarantulas burst forth.

Jane Hawk turns from the sink and says to her companion, "I'm going to use the bathroom. Quiet him for me while I'm gone."

"Chloroform?" he asks.

"No. Gag him. Tape him."

She doesn't look at Booth again but walks out of the kitchen, his spittle still wet upon her face.

Her words replay in Booth's memory. *Not even your mind is dark enough to imagine what I'll do to you.*

26

In her office, Tanuja Shukla sat at the computer, moving her lonely character, Subhadra, through a night of wind and rain, on a journey ominous and mysterious but ultimately magical. The sentences failed to form with the usual felicity, but there was satisfaction in the struggle.

Her smartphone ringtone was a few bars of "What a Wonderful World." She smiled and let the music repeat, as she usually did, while she sang, "I see skies of blue and clouds of white." Then she answered it.

A vaguely familiar man's voice said, "Uncle Ira is not Uncle Ira."

"Yes, all right," Tanuja said.

She listened to what must happen that evening, and she said she understood, that she would act according to instructions.

After he was finished, the caller said, "*Auf Wiedersehen*, sweet lips."

"Good-bye," she said and put aside her phone and returned to the novelette in progress.

After a moment, she sang, "I see trees of green and red roses, too," as she reached for the phone. But the music did not repeat. No call was incoming. Either the caller had let it ring once before hanging up or Tanuja had imagined the ringtone.

She stared at the phone in puzzlement for a moment. Then she shrugged and returned to her story about Subhadra in the storm.

Now and then, she absentmindedly touched the wounded corner of her mouth, but the bleeding had stopped hours ago, and her fingers always came away dry.

27

In the half bath, at the sink, Jane washed her face with soap and water and rinsed it and dried with a guest towel.

She leaned against the vanity, staring into the mirror, into her eyes, which lately seemed alien to her, and she wondered if she could really do what she intended to do.

Even as a young girl, she had never spent a lot of time gazing into mirrors. She could see too much of her mother in her face, so that her reflection was a reminder of grievous loss. Not least of all, the image in the looking glass reminded her of the confusion and self-doubt and fear and cowardice that had paralyzed her when, as a nine-year-old child, she hadn't been able to accuse her father of murdering her mother, though she'd had good reason to believe—no, she had *known*—that he'd killed her and staged it as a suicide. We grow, we change, we labor to maturity, to what little wisdom we might ever acquire, but always in the mirror is who we were as well as who we are, a harking back and, yet again, a quiet reckoning.

The problem this time was not cowardice. No courage was needed to do to Booth Hendrickson what she intended. Instead, ruthlessness was required. She needed a hardened heart, if not hardened to all the world, at least to those who lacked the ability to see their own humanity in others, who preyed on others, who recognized no right to life except their own, for whom power was no less essential than air and water. The world had always been acrawl with their squamous kind in nuisance numbers, but these days they flourished as never before, after centuries of compounding technological advances had put into their hands more power than kings of old had dreamed, power that should be entrusted only to benign gods.

She could not interrogate Hendrickson using the techniques she had found successful with other subjects. His arrogance was both a suit of armor and a fortress. The deepest roots of his psychology, like those of his brother, were snarled in a Gordian knot first tied in his earliest childhood and elaborated on since then; the man now in his forties might appear to be a mighty oak, but he was rotten at the core, all his limbs and branches deformed—and leafless, if it could be said that leaves were a sign of health. He was a maze of deception, a primal forest of deceit, and she could trust the answers he gave her only at considerable peril.

With such a man, she had no choice but to be extraordinarily cruel. Of course, uncountable psychopaths resorted to that same rationalization.

She closed her eyes and tried to call to mind her son as she had last seen him: in the ranch-fenced exercise yard adjacent to the stable at Gavin and Jessica Washington's place, where he was hidden away and safe; dappled by sunlight and oak-leaf shadows; standing on a low stool, grooming the mane of the Exmoor pony named Hannah that Gavin and Jessie had recently bought for him; his hair dark and tousled, like his father's, and stirring in the light breeze; his eyes the blue of hers, although clear with an innocence that she had lost long ago.

In the past, at the end of each of her infrequent visits, he had walked with her to her car and watched as she had driven away. But he could no longer bear parting in that manner. On this most recent occasion, soon after Jane's arrival, he'd made it known, through Jessica, that when the time came for his mother to leave, she should just pretend that she was going out to sit on the porch or into the next room to read, something like that, without saying the word *good-bye*.

And so she had stood for a while, watching him groom Hannah, talking about how quickly he was becoming a confident rider under Gavin's tutelage, about how smart Hannah was and about how much the pony enjoyed the company of the German shepherds, Duke and Queenie. As always, a moment came when the deep-heart sorrow of leaving him seemed to double in weight each minute she delayed, so that if she didn't go right then, she would never go. But she had learned too many secrets, done too much harm to too many people whose wealth and power were exceeded by their arrogance and by their cherished and implacable malignity. If she walked away from this grim fight, her enemies would never stop hunting for her, and they would eventually find her. Finding her, they would also find him. No foreign country was far enough away, no lifestyle too humble, no false identities too cleverly woven to thwart them in their search, not when they had numerous eyes in the heavens, maybe a hundred million cameras here below, and the growing Internet of Things that would one day give them undetected access to every room on earth. And so . . . and so she kissed Travis's cheek as he stood grooming Hannah, and she said that she was going for a walk, and she went into the house by the back door and out the front door and to her car and away, the road before her blurred and darkling as if storm-swept, though the day was blue and bright.

Now, in the Mendez family's half bath, she regarded her mirror image and knew that, without doubt, she would be able to commit the horror she had been contemplating. In the defense of the innocent—not just her son, but also the uncounted others whose souls had been or would be harvested by the Arcadians—she would incur no mortal stain requiring that she stand before the judgment of eternity.

However, she would be a fool if she believed that the act she was about to commit would not haunt her for the rest of her life. And she was no fool.

28

In this season, the cooler mornings were for horses, and like other mornings with horses, this last Saturday in March provided idyllic hours of peaceful rhythms, simple nature scenes, and graces abundant, with no jarring note or alarming turn until they stopped for a creekside lunch in the shade of cottonwoods.

Saturday morning, little more than an hour after first light, Gavin Washington had saddled the stallion, Samson, and young Travis had sat smart upon the pony, Hannah, and together they had ridden into the eastern hills of Orange County, where the chaparral was green from all the recent rain. There were still a few clouds in the wake of the previous night's storm, but they were unraveling like cocoon silk, as if the sky were some great blue-winged wonder that had emerged from them.

They didn't talk much when they rode, because

horses were a kind of meditation, which Gavin had long appreciated and which the boy was learning. For a while they proceeded at a slow walk, with just the clop of hooves, the rattle of dislodged gravelstones, the creaking of the leather saddles, and the occasional whispering of a fitful breeze through sage and feather grass, *Avena* and long-stemmed buckwheat. Rabbits startled off the trail into the brush, and lizards watched wall-eyed from perches on sun-warmed rock.

They picked up the pace to a full walk when they turned north to put the morning sun on their right, but Gavin was not yet ready to let the boy ride at a trot except in the fenced exercise yard on their property.

High overhead, red-tailed hawks were gliding on the rising thermals, hunting mice and like creatures condemned to the rough life of the land-bound. The aerial ballet of those predators could be mesmerizing, and Gavin warned Travis to give equal attention to the trail ahead. Although west-leaning shadows of brush and rock still patterned the ground, the day was now warm enough for rattlesnakes.

They turned into an eastward-leading canyon, the walls of which sloped gently to a creek too swollen with recent rains to allow Travis to attempt his first fording. But the gentle grade of the ascending canyon floor offered an easy trail, and on their left, the ceaseless slide of surprisingly clear sun-spangled water over smooth stones was pleasing to both the eye and ear.

Past eleven o'clock, they came to an open grove of cottonwoods and dismounted and walked the horses to the creek and held the reins while Samson and Hannah drank, for the water was clean enough to give Gavin no reason for concern. There had been so much rain this season that the earliest storms had washed the stony creek bed clean of silt and debris.

They let the horses graze the sweet grass that flourished in the open grove and beyond, perhaps not just because of the seasonal rains but because of some aquifer under the canyon floor. They put down a blanket and sat in the shade to eat chicken sandwiches and drink iced tea from thermos bottles.

"Aunt Jessie does good sandwiches," the boy said.

"The entire reason I married her," Gavin said, "was her sandwiches, her homemade ravioli, and her peach pie."

Travis giggled. "That's bushwa."

"Oh, is it? Since when did you become a bushwa expert?"

"You married her 'cause you love her."

Gavin rolled his eyes. "What man wouldn't love a woman with such sandwiches?"

He heard a curious buzzing noise in the distance, like a power tool of some kind, but when he cocked his head to hear it better, the sound faded away.

"How's your sunscreen holding up, Travis?"

"I'm not burned or nothing."

"We'll apply some more before we set out for home."

Gavin was from birth as dark as fire-scorched mahogany, but the boy had Celtic in him and needed to culture a spring tan slowly.

"I wish I was black like you."

"Tell you what—we'll make you an honorary brother tonight after dinner."

"How's that work?"

"We put some Sam Cooke on the stereo and some shoe polish on you, and we say the magic words."

"That's so silly."

"I'll tell you something true that'll sound even sillier."

"Like what?"

"There used to be whales swimming around these parts."

"More bushwa, Uncle Gavin."

"All this parched land and even far east into the true desert used to be a great, deep sea."

"When?"

"Well, not last month. But four million years ago, for sure. They found baleen whale fossils in these parts. If you'd been out here eating chicken sandwiches four million years ago, you might have ended up like Jonah in the belly of Leviathan."

The buzzing noise returned, and this time it grew steadily louder.

"What's that?" asked Travis.

"Let's have a look."

Gavin got up and moved through the open grove, away from the creek, to the tree line. The buzzing seemed to originate overhead. Using his hand as a visor, he shielded his eyes from the sun, but he didn't need to search the heavens for the sound.

Cruising at perhaps fifteen miles an hour, the quadcopter drone came from the east, below the canyon wall, like a ten-pound insect, a camera slung beneath it on a stabilization gimbal.

Although these canyons and hills seemed remote, they were not far from civilization. Many of Orange County's scores of cities extended fingers into wild territory. On the other hand, he and Travis were not just around the corner from a housing tract of a thousand homes. They had never encountered a drone out here before.

There were numerous legitimate purposes for the intrusive damn things. Realtors filmed for-sale properties with them, and surveyors made good use of them. But this was permanent open space, land that would never be given over to houses or office buildings or shopping malls.

"What's it doing?" Travis asked as the drone approached.

They were standing in the last shade of the trees. Gavin said, "Step back," drawing the boy with him deeper into the cover of the cottonwood branches, where they lost sight of the buzzing craft—and could not be seen.

"What's it doing?" the boy asked again.

"Probably some techno geek playing with his newest toy."

"Way out here?"

"Better out here, where he won't screw up and fly it into someone's car windshield. Come on, let's get back to lunch before ants get what's left of our sandwiches."

They returned to the blanket in the cool shade.

The open grove allowed space between the trees. If the drone had flown directly over the woods, the grazing horses might not have been entirely screened from above.

Gavin could still hear the buzzing craft in the distance. He finished his sandwich in two bites and then brought the horses to a nearby tree. He tied them to lower branches, where they now stood in full shade.

"Don't want them getting overheated," he told the boy. "We have brownies for dessert, if you're interested."

"I would've married Aunt Jessie just for her brownies."

"Back off, cowboy. I saw the lady first."

Gavin could hear two drones now, one more distant than the other. One perhaps tracking south to north, the other east to west. There might even have been three.

"There's more of them," Travis said.

"A whole damn club of geeks maybe having themselves some kind of tournament," said Gavin, leaning back against a tree trunk, pretending to be unconcerned.

He wondered why he needed to pretend. His explanation was most likely the correct one. His and Jessie's friendship with Nick and Jane had been a relatively short one and discreet. In the two and a half months they had been sheltering Travis, not one of the legions searching for the boy's mother had connected them to her.

In fact, if those hunting for Jane *had* suddenly linked

Gavin and Jessica to her, the bastards wouldn't be chasing him and Travis with drones. They would be at the house right now, with Jessie in custody, waiting for man and boy to ride home, into their clutches.

29

When Jane entered the kitchen, Gilberto Mendez had not returned to his dinette chair and coffee. He stood by the sink, his spine straight and shoulders back and face solemn, perhaps as he stood at the entrance to one of his viewing rooms when he welcomed mourners to their last sight of a loved one.

Booth Hendrickson was still strapped to the gurney, in a three-quarter sitting position. Gilberto had stuffed a roll of gauze in his mouth and firmly sealed his lips with duct tape.

Even denied his voice, the Department of Justice magnifico was able to convey his contempt by keeping his chin raised, his eyes narrowed, and his brow smooth. Jane sensed that, behind the tape, his mouth was puckered in a pout of pure disdain.

She stood beside the gurney, staring at him, testing her conviction, giving herself one last chance to take another course rather than the one to which she had committed earlier. But she had no second thoughts.

"I thought Shenneck and D. J. Michael were the two heads of the snake, but they're gone and the snake is still alive. I need to know the true power behind these Arcadians of yours, the one who sits on the ultimate throne. I need to know a lot of other things."

Hendrickson shook his head, no, playing the tough guy who would deny her even in this moment of his extreme peril.

"I could interrogate you like I have others, but you're as good a liar as the devil himself. I can't afford to be deceived, sent on some wild-goose chase or into a trap."

If it might be possible to convey a smirk with one's mouth concealed, Hendrickson smirked.

"There's only one way I can trust what you tell me."

He raised an eyebrow.

"In January, we were still living in our house in Virginia, two months after Nick died. A scary thing happened. I'm at the computer, researching strange suicides. Travis is in his room, playing with LEGO blocks. I don't realize some sonofabitch used a lock-release gun to get into the house. He's in my boy's room with him."

Hendrickson's brow was not as smooth as it had been.

"This guy charms Travis with funny stories. Sends him to me to ask what 'natsat' means, then 'milk plus.' I think it's some little kid's game. But they're words from *A Clockwork Orange* by Anthony Burgess. It had a big effect on me in college, helped me go FBI. Travis comes in again, says Mr. Droog is in his room, so then I get it. In the novel, drug-crazed ultraviolent thugs are called droogs. Travis says Mr. Droog is going to teach him a fun game called rape."

Hendrickson's eyes were pale-green pools of venom.

"So I keep Travis close, get my gun, search the house, find no one, just the open back door," Jane continued. "Just then the phone rings. It's Mr. Droog. He tells me if I keep investigating Nick's death and all these suicides, they'll snatch my boy and ship him off to ISIS or Boko Haram to be used as a sex slave until those savages get tired of passing him around. He says they might even do the same with me, so my son and I will have to witness each other's abuse and degradation."

She closed her eyes and took a deep breath because speaking about this, especially to this man, stirred in her a lust for violence that she dared not indulge.

She looked down on Hendrickson again. "This Mr. Droog had a distinctive mid-tenor voice, certain speech patterns that I told myself I'd never forget. Never. And I haven't forgotten you, Mr. Droog. When you came fully out of the chloroform, by the time you told me how much you liked to hear pretty girls use big words like *hyperbole*, I knew you. I knew you."

She went to the refrigerator and took from it the Medexpress container and brought it to the table. An inset digital display on the face of the carrier read thirty-nine degrees Fahrenheit, which was the interior temperature, well within the preservation zone for the contents.

From her leather tote, she took a length of rubber tubing to be used as a tourniquet, a foil-wrapped sterile wipe, and a hypodermic syringe.

Through gauze gag and duct tape, Hendrickson

made interrogatory sounds that might have been words forming an urgent question.

Jane opened the Medexpress container. The Cryo-MAX modular cold packs were still largely frozen.

She took from the container three generous ampules of cloudy amber fluid nestled in insulated sleeves, each bearing the same batch number, intended to be injected in the same session. They were some of the samples that she had taken from Bertold Shenneck's house in Napa County, earlier in the month, when she and an ally invaded the weekend-getaway home of the inventor of the nanomachine control mechanism.

She had wanted the samples as evidence. They were more than evidence now. They were an invaluable tool and a terrible justice.

The sounds Hendrickson produced were no longer interrogatory, but instead exclamatory, a muffled but strenuous protest.

"I do regret this, but there's no other way with you," she said. "No other way to get the truth, and I desperately need the truth, Mr. Droog. Fortunately, Shenneck gave me what I need to squeeze the truth out of you."

He began to thrash in his restraints, rocking the gurney, but there was no escape from the straps.

She waited until he'd exhausted himself, and then she picked up the scissors and began to cut away the right sleeve of his white shirt.

He tried to resist, but was ineffective.

The cut sleeve came away and slithered to the floor.

Gooseflesh stippled his bare arm. His pale forehead glistened with a fine beadwork of sweat.

30

This must not be allowed to happen. This is an outrage. He is who he is, and he is *not* a candidate for adjustment.

No one has told him that she might have ampules containing control mechanisms. Which means no one knows about them.

It's known the crazy bitch took money from Shenneck's safe in the Napa house, and it's suspected she made off with his research files on flash drives, because he worked when in Napa as well as when in his labs in Menlo Park. But no one knows she's gotten her hands on ampules containing control mechanisms.

Shenneck wasn't supposed to have those in such an unsecured location. They should have been stored in Menlo Park. What the *hell* was the demented asshole thinking? The recklessness, the arrogance, the sheer *stupidity*! The syphilitic sonofabitch probably meant to use them on his hot wife, Inga, as domineering a witch as ever rode a broom. Maybe he meant to convert her into his personal version of an Aspasia girl.

This is intolerable. Unthinkable. This must not be allowed to happen. He is who he is. He is who he is, and she's a vulgar pleb, operating out of her league. She's gotten this far on sheer dumb luck, that's all.

As she unwraps the hypodermic, it occurs to Booth that perhaps some Arcadians know she's in possession of control mechanisms but haven't told him. Depending on what cell you're in, what position you fill, you're told only what it's deemed you need to know. But he thought he knew everything, the ultimate insider. If someone decided that such knowledge was reserved for those above his station . . . There is no honor anymore. No integrity. Treachery is everywhere. Machinations, hollowness, treachery, and ruinous disorders! *This can't be allowed to happen.*

31

Jane unwrapped the hypodermic needle. She prepared it and the cannula.

She tied the rubber tube around his biceps and drew it tight. With one fingertip, she palpated the veins in his forearm until she found one suitably prominent.

She tore open the full packet and used the antiseptic wipe on the injection site.

Sounds of an entirely different character than before issued from Booth Hendrickson, a miserable beseeching noise.

The fingers of his upturned hand were spread and trembling, reaching out as best the strap allowed, much as a penniless and frightened beggar might seek alms.

She met his intense stare, and with his eyes he implored her not to continue, seeking the mercy that he had never extended to anyone.

The muffled cries escaping him now were as pitiable as the whimpers of a gravely injured dog.

Gilberto came to Jane's side. "I'll do it. I have training."

"No. Not you. Not this of all things," she murmured. "This is only on my shoulders, no one's but mine."

As Jane prepared the first big ampule for intravenous infusion, Hendrickson began to cry like a frightened child lost and alone in a dark woods. The woods were his life as he had made it for himself, and the dark was the darkness of a soul so long untended that the wick of it had withered until it couldn't be lit to bring forth any guiding hope.

She hesitated to administer the first ampule. She shuddered violently, as though an icy and invisible presence had for a moment occupied the same space in which she stood before moving through her on its way into some nameless void.

The human heart was deceitful above all things, hers no less than any other. In this perilous mission in which she found herself, the days were hard and the nights were lonely, and only two motors drove her onward: first, her love for her child and for her lost husband; second, the conviction that in the perpetual struggle of good and evil, the latter must be resisted without fail. But there was a temptation to use the weapons of evil against it, and in so using them to risk becoming the very thing that she was sworn to resist. She couldn't say without doubt that her heart yearned more for justice than for vengeance, and it was in the self-deception regarding motive that the long descent of the soul began. In the end, she could only depend on her belief—and her heart's faith—that her love for Travis and Nick was greater than her hatred for Hendrickson and his allies, because love and only love inoculated her against evil's infection.

In memory she heard Mr. Droog on the telephone that day in January: *Sheerly for the fun of it, we could pack the little bugger off to some Third World snake pit, turn him over to a group like ISIS or Boko Haram, where they have no slightest qualms about keeping sex slaves. Some of those badasses . . . are terribly fond of little boys as much as they are of little girls. . . . You're more to my taste than your son, but I wouldn't hesitate to pack you off with him and let those Boko boys who swing both ways have a twofer. Tend to your own business instead of ours, and all will be well.*

Now she met Hendrickson's pale-green eyes again and said, "Come Hell or not, you *are* my business."

It was no small thing to deprive a man of his free will, even if he believed that denying others autonomy over their minds and bodies was his right as well as the road to Utopia.

She served the first course of the three-ampule infusion and then the second.

Because a scream would no longer avail him of any hope of rescue and because she sensed that it was her obligation to regard his face complete, even to receive his bitter curses, as she reduced him from a man to a marionette, she stripped the duct tape from his mouth and allowed him to expel the sodden wad of gauze.

He didn't curse her, after all, didn't speak or ever weep.

When she opened the valve to feed the third dose

into the cannula, she met her captive's eyes once more. He appeared to be horrified, stricken. But then a subtle change came over him, and it seemed that in his eyes welled something like awe, as if he were gazing up not at a motherless widow desperate to save the life of her child at any cost, but as if she were some fierce aboriginal goddess, embodiment of ultimate power, figure of mystery and wonder. And there was about him an air of deliverance, as though his lust for power, which would now never be fulfilled, could as well be satisfied by *giving* himself to power, as though his burning desire to have every knee bend before him was but the mirror image of his heart's other and equal desire to live on his knees and kiss the ruler's ring.

A fresh chill gripped Jane, but instead of shivering her as had the previous one, it coiled in her bones to stay awhile.

PART THREE

Alecto Rising

1

Gavin and Travis, facing each other from opposite ends of the blanket, each with his back against a tree, finished the brownies and sat listening to the canyon wrens issuing a long series of clear whistles that cascaded through the cottonwood shade. Man and boy were comfortable with each other in conversation and in silence.

In less than three months, Gavin had come to feel not just protective of Travis but also fatherly toward him. And Jessica was as smitten with him as if she had conceived him and brought him into the world. Any wound that Travis suffered would be their wound. If anything happened to him in their care, the years that remained for them would be years of grief aging into settled sorrow, and even the bright moments of life would be shot through with shadows.

The boy said, "I'm kind of gettin' sleepy here."

"Take a nap, kiddo. We're not in a hurry to be any-where."

"You sleepy?"

"Nope. The only way I can sleep is hanging by my toes from an attic rafter."

"Batman," Travis said, for now and then they played a little game in which Gavin said something ridiculous about himself and the boy had to guess what secret identity he was claiming.

"That one was too easy. While you nap, I'll work up one that'll stump you."

Travis curled on his side, on the blanket, and let out a long sigh of weary contentment.

From time to time, Gavin heard the buzzing of a drone, mostly in the distance. Though the aircraft surely had nothing to do with him and Travis, he didn't want to ride out of the cottonwoods until he hadn't heard one of them for at least twenty minutes or half an hour.

He suspected that the boy knew as much and was feigning sleep, so that Gavin didn't have to keep making excuses for why they were not starting the return trip home. Travis had inherited his parents' good looks; he would be a heartbreaker when he grew up, but he would never break any, because he'd inherited their intelligence as well, and for a kid so young, he under-stood the concept of consequences, that one person's wrong action produced another person's pain. He had already been cured in the brine of grief, and a conse-quence of *that* was a regard for the feelings of others that few children had at his age and that some people never acquired. He'd make a hell of a Marine if he ever followed in his father's footsteps.

Gavin Washington had been an Army man. He and Jessica had met Nick and Jane at a fundraiser for the Wounded Warrior Project in Virginia, fifteen months earlier. Their friendship formed quickly, effortlessly, for they recognized in one another shared attitudes and convictions without the need to explain themselves.

Sometimes it seemed to Gavin that they were brought together by providence, in preparation for all the crap that was coming fast in Jane's life. Because both Gavin and Nick were spec ops guys, they shared an ingrained preference for discretion, for maintaining a low profile. Neither the Hawks nor the Washingtons were much interested in social media; there were no Facebook postings to link them, no Instagram or Snapchat accounts. They corresponded a little by snail mail, which left no indelible digital trail, and they spoke on the phone, but not often. Their friendship flourished face-to-face at weekend-long events for veterans' causes in which Jessie had become an activist following the end of her own Army career. When Jane needed somewhere to hide her boy, family and friends with obvious connections could not provide her with a safe, secret redoubt. There had been only Gavin and Jessica, a continent away, but willing.

The thing that most troubled Gavin about the drones was the length of time they cruised the area. Maximum flight duration for one of that size was probably fifteen minutes, half an hour with a backup battery. He'd first heard these craft an hour earlier, and still the buzzing came and went. Of course if there *was* a tournament involving a club of enthusiasts, they would have brought numerous replacement batteries.

The wrens of both varieties were tireless in their singing. The rasping, scraping screech of a red-tailed hawk in triumph from time to time confirmed a good day's hunting.

By contrast, in a silence came a large swarm of butterflies, Sara Orangetips, white with black and fiery-orange markings on their wingtips, harbingers of spring, lilting through the air like notes of a song translated from music into the hush of Lepidoptera. Their phosphorescent whiteness made ghosts of them in the shadows, but their true beauty flared as they danced through shafts of sunlight.

Perhaps twenty minutes after the most recent buzz of a drone, Travis sat up into that delicate, busy flocking. Yawning elaborately to prove that he'd been asleep, he held out his hands, onto which a few butterflies alighted and flexed their wings and tasted his skin before taking flight once more.

In ages past, various Indian tribes that roamed this territory had spoken of these butterflies as spirits that entered this world from another to celebrate the spring. Most said that they were omens of good luck and of healthy children soon to be born, although there had been a tribe that saw them as omens of death.

Getting up from the blanket, Travis said, "Time to go home?"

They had more than a two-hour ride ahead of them.

Reluctantly, Gavin rose to his feet. "Yeah, I guess we better scoot."

The Sara Orangetips did not follow them when

they rode out of the cottonwood grove and westward down the canyon.

Gavin wondered to himself, *Which are we leaving behind—death or good luck?*

2

I n the ceiling light box, one of the fluorescent tubes faintly buzzing; fan-driven heat whispering out of a wall vent; refrigerator motor softly humming: a mechanical yet forlorn chorus . . .

Faster than a cube of ice becoming water in the summer sun, Booth Hendrickson transformed from a vain master of the universe into a willing and obedient prisoner. With the infusion of the third ampule, his terror and horror faded with an alacrity Jane could not comprehend. The inevitability of his oncoming conversion into an "adjusted person," as he had once so arrogantly named them, seemed entirely to quell his anger, to bleed away any thought of vengeance. More surprising than that, with all options other than conversion denied him, his fate apparently did not depress him, but instead appeared to float him into a tranquil harbor. He relaxed in his restraints and closed his eyes and spoke quietly, less to Jane than to himself, words that might have seemed despairing but were in fact given an inflection that made of them an expression of contentment, "So here I am—it's lovely, isn't it?—after all these years, back here of all places, here in the dark alone."

Jane looked at Gilberto, whose frown mirrored her own.

Hendrickson said, "I think to myself, I play to myself, and nobody knows what I say to myself."

The hundreds of thousands—maybe millions—of tiny brain-tropic nano constructs teeming through his blood would take eight to ten hours to reach their destination, pass through capillary walls into brain tissue, and self-assemble into a control mechanism by virtue of Brownian motion. Hendrickson could not already have been in any way affected by their presence in his bloodstream. His inexplicable contentment, mere hours away from the loss of his free will, seemed to confirm a psychology so twisted, so tortured, that unraveling the reason for this complacent acceptance might be impossible.

On the other hand, he was a prince of deceit. Jane had to assume that, even with Hendrickson's future in chains from which no mortal power could free him, he was nevertheless scheming to use these last few hours to ensure her death, although he would have nothing to gain from it.

He opened his eyes and looked up at her with no evident animosity. "Why wait for the control mechanism to be in place? Interrogate me now. I'll tell you everything you want to know."

"The lies you want me to believe."

"No, listen. Later, when you have total control of me, you can ask some questions again, check those answers against what I'll give you now. You'll save a lot of time that way."

"Why should you care if I save time?"

"I don't care. But I'd rather not spend these next eight hours just . . . waiting. The newest iteration of the mechanism installs in four hours. I didn't know you'd taken ampules from Shenneck's house. Maybe no one knew. They torched the house so fast, to cover what happened there. But what you took in Napa, what you injected into me, that's an older version. Takes eight to ten hours. I might go a little crazy—don't you think?—a little crazy just sitting here waiting to feel it come together inside my skull."

Jane could imagine her anguish in his situation, and what she had done was a moral weight on her. She felt no guilt, but she recognized a responsibility to ease whatever foreboding he might feel during these hours of transition. Sympathy for the devil. Always dangerous.

When first waking from the chloroform sleep, still under the influence of it, he had revealed something that he wasn't likely to remember having disclosed. She tested him. "Last week I learned the access sentence that brings an adjusted person under my control. So you people must've been busy reprogramming them."

"Play Manchurian with me," he said. "That's the one you know. Lots of plebs are accessed with that sentence."

" 'Plebs'?"

"Plebs, plodders, rabble, two-legged cattle. Just other names for the adjusted people."

His contempt for them seemed undiminished even though he was about to join their ranks.

"How many of them are there?" she asked.

"Plebs? Right now, over sixteen thousand."

"Dear Lord," Gilberto said, and he went to sit at the table.

"And what's the new access sentence?"

Hendrickson didn't hesitate. "Uncle Ira is not Uncle Ira."

She had a clear memory of their conversation as he had first come out of the chloroform, not fully conscious:

Hey, sexy.

Hey.

I got a use for that pretty mouth.

I bet you do, big guy.

Bring it on down here. Uncle Ira is not Uncle Ira.

Who is he, then?

No, that's not what you're supposed to say.

What am I supposed to say?

You just say, all right.

A few exchanges later, he had dozed off once more.

Now that he'd passed her test, maybe she should invest minimal trust in him. But first she pressed him on his more recent, cryptic statements. "You said here you were again, here of all places, in the dark alone." She quoted the rest as she remembered it. "'I think to myself, I play to myself, and nobody knows what I say to myself.' What is all that? What does it mean?"

Neither the soft voice in which he answered nor his childlike entreaty was characteristic of him. "What I said—all that stuff is of no importance to you, only to me. So don't make me talk about it now. Leave me a little dignity. If you really want to know . . . wait till you control me. And then after I've told you, just please make me forget I ever did."

Over Hendrickson had settled a hybrid mood that Jane could not fully read. A melancholy that his circumstances could well explain. But also a note of what seemed like a sentimental harking back. A wistful regret. And a curious sort of longing.

His lotus-leaf eyes were without their former power, and his pride gave way to something almost like humility, his manner that of a mendicant.

"All right," she said. "Let's see if we can fill those hours for you—but only if we fill them with the truth."

3

Gavin Washington let Travis lead the way home on his Exmoor pony, the better to watch over him. The boy wore his riding helmet, which he disliked. But he wouldn't be receiving his longed-for cowboy hat until he'd had a few more weeks of experience in the saddle.

Samson was a bit restive about the slow pace and would have liked to gallop full-out or at least canter. But the stallion was always mindful of the signals from his reins and his rider's legs.

Following the pleasant midday warmth, a late-afternoon cooling had begun. Thin high clouds seemed not to drift through the sky, but instead to form on it like a skin of ice crystalizing on the surface of a pond, glazed patches reaching toward one another with growing fractal fingers that blurred away the blue. The fitful breeze had become constant, though it hadn't swelled into a wind, rippling the sage not yet in bloom, shivering the spidery late-winter flowers of coombe wood.

Gavin remained alert for drones. Sometimes he thought he heard one in the distance, but getting a directional fix, before the sound faded, was hampered by the clatter of horseshoes on the stony soil plus the creak and clink of tack.

By the time they came out of the wildland to the gate at the back of their property, near four o'clock, Gavin no longer had any concern about the drones, which must have been flown by hobbyists. He could hear an aircraft circling high over the valley; but he hadn't detected even a suggestion of the comparatively shrill motor of a drone in almost an hour and a half.

They watered the horses at the trough and led them into the stable and removed their saddles. They conducted them into their stalls and put on their feed bags.

Later, after the horses had been fed and the tack had been properly cared for, when Gavin came out of the stable with the boy, the growl of an airplane crawling the sky caused him to search for a dark shape against the hoarfrost clouds. The craft wasn't within view, perhaps off to the north, and he assumed it was not the same plane that he'd heard earlier.

4

After Jane hobbled Hendrickson's ankles with a pair of cable zip-ties, allowing him to walk only in a shuffle, she freed him from the gurney. With pistol drawn, Gilberto accompanied the captive to the bathroom and a few minutes later returned him to the kitchen table. Jane used another two zip-ties to link Hendrickson's ankle fetters to the rear stretcher bar of the chair in which he sat.

She put her minirecorder in front of him. Wearing a PatrolEyes camera around her neck, with a spiral-bound notebook and pen, she sat directly across the table from him.

Her purpose was only in part to learn whom she needed to pursue to break the command structure of the Arcadians. In addition, his insider's testimony should be useful in the eventual prosecution of these conspirators, and it might later help exonerate her of the criminal acts she'd been falsely accused of committing.

Gilberto sat witness. His pistol lay on the table, well out of Hendrickson's reach, in case he still had tricks to spring on them.

A fresh pot of coffee, slices of Carmella's ricotta pie, and Hendrickson's new meek demeanor gave the proceedings an almost cozy context that felt surreal. At times the exchanges between Jane and Hendrickson grew eerie, as he seemed eager to please her not in the way a defendant might want to please a prosecutor or judge, but with the disturbing subservience that a child, browbeaten from the cradle and for years thereafter, might respond to a tyrannical parent.

In curious little ways, he seemed to regress from adulthood as the interrogation entered a second hour. He asked for another slice of pie and, eschewing the fork he'd used with the first serving, he broke off pieces of the treat and ate them with his fingers. He had been drinking coffee black but now wanted a lot of cream and four heaping spoons of sugar, essentially making another dessert of the brew. At times in the third and fourth hours, his attention drifted away from her; for ten seconds, fifteen, half a minute, he fell silent and stared into some private elsewhere. Always, Jane could bring him back to the issue at hand, but she had the impression that Hendrickson was slowly becoming dissociated from the reality of a life of submission into which he was sliding.

She wondered if something might be going very wrong with the nanomachine implantation. As it self-assembled its cerebral web, might it be causing subtle brain damage akin to a stroke?

But his speech wasn't slurred. Neither were there signs of weakness or paralysis. He didn't complain of numbness, tingling, vertigo, or impaired vision.

He was more likely undergoing a psychological rather than a physiological fracturing.

Supposing he was telling the truth, he'd already given her a treasure of information, though his revelations were limited because of the structure of the Arcadian cabal. In the classic tradition of spy networks and resistance movements, they were organized into numerous cells, each with a limited number of members, and those in one cell didn't know the identities of those in others. Access to the complete roster of Arcadians remained a privilege of those at the very top of the pyramid. Hendrickson, for all his former power and posturing, didn't know how far up in the Arcadian architecture his position might be. Considering his grandiose opinion of himself prior to the infusion of a control mechanism, he'd likely imagined that he was closer to the pinnacle than was the case.

What she was getting from him, however, gave her tools to use and new people to go after. She had thought that the now-deceased billionaire David James Michael had perched at the top of the Arcadian pyramid, and she had taken enormous risks to get at him. For the first time since the shocking events in D. J. Michael's penthouse in San Francisco, she might have a chance to tear apart the Arcadian nest and pull from it a writhing tangle of these vipers, bring them into the sunlight of revelation that they shunned with vampiric dread.

Interrogation could be an exhausting process, especially for someone who was betraying every associate with whom he was entwined in criminal activities. It was no less tiring for the interrogator. Shortly before five o'clock, Jane called for a break. She'd had little to eat in the past twenty-four hours and needed to refuel to sharpen her concentration.

"I'll get some takeout," Gilberto said. "There's a good place down the street."

"Protein," Jane said. "Don't load me up with carbs."

"It's Chinese."

He suggested some dishes, and Jane approved.

"You?" Gilberto asked Hendrickson.

The captive didn't answer. He sat with his hands upturned on the table, staring at his palms. The faintest smile suggested that he wasn't reading his future, but perhaps remembering things that his hands had touched and done to his satisfaction.

"Get him what we're having," Jane said. "He's in no position to be picky."

5

Subhadra labored through an eternal storm, or so it seemed, for the novelette would advance only grudgingly. Tanuja pushed with all her creative energy, as if the narrative were a boulder and she were Sisyphus being punished for trickery, fated never to get the great stone to the top of the hill before it rolled down yet again.

At precisely 4:45 P.M., she suddenly knew intuitively that she was nearing a breakthrough with the story. But she needed to step away from it and do something else for a while, something fun, and let her subconscious wrestle with the novelette. She saved the document and switched off the computer.

She always worked by intuition. Whether it was a novel or a shorter piece, she didn't outline a plot, and she didn't produce character sketches before beginning the story itself. She just started to write, guided by the still, small voice of intuition, which was like an open phone line to a higher power, one infinitely more creative than she could ever hope to be.

Like an open phone line, yes, except it didn't speak to her in full sentences, but instead in isolate images and dreamflow scenes of action and hieroglyphics of emotion and enigmatic lines of blank verse that she then had to translate into comprehensible English, into meaningful fiction. But this time, the still, small voice of intuition was in fact a voice that spoke coherently: *Saturday night is for fun, go have fun, forget about Subhadra and her storm, dress up, go out, there is fun to be had, do whatever you feel you must do to be happy, and tomorrow you will write your best work ever.*

Initially, the clarity and specificity of that inner voice was strange, disturbing, but then not so much, and then not at all.

She pushed her chair away from the desk and got up. She left her home office without bothering to turn off the lights.

The time had come. There were actions to be taken. What those actions were did not matter. She did not need to think about them. They would come naturally to her. Intuitively.

She went upstairs to her bedroom. On a shelf in her

walk-in closet rested a small black-lacquered box with silver hinges. She had never seen it before, yet she had known it would be there.

This did not strike her as peculiar. There were actions to be taken. What they were would become clear to her as she took them.

She carried the box to her vanity and opened it.

The first item that she extracted was a necklace of miniature human skulls carved from bone. Gleaming black onyx filled the eye sockets. The craftsmanship was exquisite, the skulls more beautiful than frightening. The box also contained four lovely gold bracelets fashioned as cobras.

Durga, the Goddess Mother of the Hindu pantheon, was maternal and kind and the source of much life, but she also had dark aspects. The most fierce of those was her incarnation as Kali, often depicted as wanton, naked but for the darkness in which she wrapped herself, wearing only gold bracelets and a necklace of human skulls.

In this religion, no separation existed between the sacred and profane. All things on the earth were aspects of the divinity. Kali, an aspect of Durga, had several aspects herself, one being Chandi, the Terrible One. The Chandi aspect of Kali was often depicted with her four arms raised—instead of Kali's usual eight—hands gripping a sword, a noose, a skull-capped staff, and a severed human head. Of all the divinities, only Kali had conquered time, and she was, among other things, a slayer of demons.

Tanuja Shukla did not share her deceased parents' Hindu faith; but she hadn't forgotten it, either. She sometimes employed Hindu mythology in her stories, as metaphor, for color, to evoke a sense of mystery, but never to endorse it. If she could have believed in a goddess, it would have been in the most benign Durga, not any of her less compassionate aspects, not Kali.

But the necklace was quite beautiful. She draped it across her breast and reached behind her neck to click the clasp.

6

Hendrickson—hobbled ankle to ankle, zip-tied to his chair, hands palms-up on the table—at first sat silently as Jane paced the kitchen. She massaged her trapezius muscles and rolled her head side to side to work a stubborn soreness out of her neck.

The light at the windows would last an hour and a half; but the overcast would steal the golden radiance and scarlet dusk that could make a California day's end so enchanting. Following the events of the morning and afternoon, and considering those to come, nature's loveliest pyrotechnics couldn't have bewitched Jane, anyway. Her mood matched the gray skies.

At the table, Hendrickson muttered. When she asked what he'd said, he only smiled at his upturned palms. His expression had no dangerous edge; it was wistful, pensive. She suspected that he hadn't heard her, so lost was he in thought.

She continued pacing and, not for the first time, regarded her reflection in the brushed stainless-steel door of the refrigerator. Her form was warped and blurred, her face a mask of shadows from which all features had been shorn, as though she had died and become a revenant.

At the table, Hendrickson said, "Now is it true, or is it not, that what is which and which is what?"

She went to the table and stared down at him.

His gentle smile was a storybook thing, the smile of a cat who learned to be friends with a mouse, the smile of a mouse who won his prize of cheese, the smile of a boy who survived a fearful adventure and sat now hearthside and home again. Jane was creeped out by it.

Tethered to the chair as he was, he could make no move against her. Even if he had not been shackled, she could have handled him, taken him down.

Nevertheless, she wished that Gilberto would return soon with dinner.

7

At 5:15 P.M. precisely, Sanjay typed THE END in small caps, although he had not reached the end of the novel that he had been writing for the past three months. Neither had he arrived at the conclusion of a chapter or even the bottom of the current page. He wondered at the words, almost deleted them, but then left them dark upon the white screen and saved the document.

The time had come. There were actions to be taken. What those actions were didn't matter. He didn't need to think about them. They would occur naturally to him. Like his sister, Sanjay was an intuitive artist whose finest fiction was not first designed and then constructed according to blueprints. Writing was always work, always, but when he surrendered himself to the currents of creative energy that flowed from the mysterious headwaters of intuition, the source unknown and unknowable, he was at his best. Therefore, the time had come. The time not just to write intuitively, but to *live* intuitively. The time to do whatever occurred to him, without first considering where his actions would lead.

He left the room without switching off the lights.

In his bedroom, he changed into black jeans and a black shirt. Black socks and black rubber-soled shoes. He took a black sport coat from his closet but did not put it on.

Leaving the lights on behind him, he went down the hall and into Tanuja's bedroom.

She was standing beside her vanity bench, waiting for him, as he had known she would be. She was quite beautiful, dressed all in black, wearing a necklace of skulls and gold bracelets fashioned as cobras. She wore black eye shadow and black lipstick and black polish on her fingernails.

They did not speak. There was no reason to speak. The time had come. There were actions to be taken.

Sanjay sat on the vanity bench. Tanuja knelt on the floor before him and began to paint his fingernails black.

Never before had his fingernails been painted. This seemed an odd thing for her to be doing and a peculiar thing for him to allow. His uncertainty—for it was not a strong enough feeling to be called doubt—lasted only until she had painted the thumbnail on his right hand and the nail of the adjacent forefinger, whereupon nothing had ever seemed more natural than this.

After his nails were black and gleaming, as he waited for them to dry, his sister applied black eye shadow to his upper and lower eyelids. She painted his lips black, and this, too, was as it should be, so that he said nothing, nor did she.

8

Numerous one-pint white boxes of Chinese takeout stood on the kitchen table. *Foo yung loong har,* which was lobster omelet with chopped onion. *Subgum chow goong yue chu*—fried scallops with mixed vegetables. Fried prawns. Shrimp balls. Chicken with almonds. Sweet and sour pork.

There were noodles and rice. Jane ate a little of the

latter, none of the former, but indulged in every variety of protein.

At first Gilberto seemed to have over-ordered, but his appetite was as hearty as Jane's. Halfway through the meal, she wondered if they might come to blows when they got to the last white box.

Hendrickson disliked everything he tasted, except the noodles, and he wasn't enthusiastic about those. He dropped the chopsticks, with which he was having considerable trouble, and said, "All I want are some cookies."

"There are no cookies," Jane said.

"Why aren't there cookies?"

"Eat what you have."

"It's all weird stuff."

"You've never eaten Chinese food?"

"I've eaten it, but I don't like it."

Chewing chicken and almonds in a delicious soy-and-sherry sauce, Jane studied him, wondered about him, wondered what else he was becoming on his way to being an adjusted person.

He shied from the intensity of her stare and lowered his eyes to the chopsticks that he had discarded.

Gilberto said, "We have some cookies. Lemon drop cookies, also chocolate chip. Carmella made them."

"That's what I want," said Hendrickson.

"All right with you?" Gilberto asked Jane.

Hendrickson was a condemned man, perhaps only three hours from the moment when Brownian motion jiggled into place the last piece of the nanomechanism. Then spider-web filaments would light up across the surface of his brain as well as deep into the tissue of it, and he would at that moment forget what had been done to him and would be himself in every way except the one that mattered. But which self would that be? The arrogant, vicious Arcadian or an earlier version of Mama Hendrickson's boy, his psyche having collapsed so completely into a past condition that no command mechanism could restore him to full wicked maturity and his job at the Department of Justice? If so, would that be dying twice, long before the death of flesh and bone, whenever that might come?

In any event, a condemned man always received what he ordered for his last meal.

"Give him the cookies," she said.

"And a Coke, please," Hendrickson said, glancing apprehensively at her, then smiling timidly at Gilberto. "Cookies and a Coke would be nice."

Suddenly Jane could eat no more. She set aside the container of chicken and almonds. A few low waves of nausea washed through her, then quieted away.

While Gilberto got the cookies, Jane fetched two cans of Coca-Cola from the refrigerator, one for Hendrickson and one for herself. She got two glasses and scooped a little ice into each one and put them on the table.

"Gilberto, please tell me you've got some vodka I can add to mine."

Thank God, he said yes.

9

Leaving the lights on in the upstairs and downstairs hallways, Sanjay and Tanuja went to the kitchen. He carried his sport coat, and she carried her black purse.

To his eye, the key to the Hyundai Santa Fe Sport glowed as if with supernatural power, as might have the sword of destiny locked in stone, which only good King Arthur had been able to draw from its granite scabbard. It dangled from a peg in the perfboard beside the door to the garage, like a lynchpin holding the kitchen together—the kitchen, the house, the lives they'd known—as though everything would, upon his taking possession of the key, blow away like so many dead leaves in a wind, revealing the truth of the world behind all of humanity's illusions.

Together, he and Tanuja went into the garage.

The vehicle was spotless, gleaming as it had on the showroom floor when they purchased it. For some reason, he expected it to be spattered with mud and the spokes of its high-end custom wheels to be entangled with torn weeds.

For a moment, in his mind's eye, he clearly saw the Hyundai in exactly that filthy condition, but also with a broken headlight and a damaged front fender on the passenger side.

He stared at the SUV in bewilderment. A still, small

voice deep within him said this meant nothing. Nothing at all. His confusion quickly passed.

Tanuja accompanied him to the back of the Hyundai. He put up the tailgate, and they looked into the cargo space.

Sanjay hadn't expected to see two 9 mm Smith & Wesson pistols, but when he saw them, he didn't find them in the least remarkable. In fact, he knew that each gun weighed a mere twenty-six ounces, had a barrel length of three and one-half inches, and featured a white-dot front sight and a Novak Lo-Mount Carry two-dot rear. Stainless-steel slide. Alloy frame. The recoil would be quite manageable.

There was one shoulder rig, into which Sanjay shrugged. He adjusted the straps. He slipped into his sport coat.

Tanuja put her pistol in her purse.

Beside each firearm were two spare ten-round magazines. She dropped one in each front pocket of her sport coat, and her brother did the same.

Also in the cargo space lay a long orange extension cord neatly coiled and beside it an electric reciprocating saw with a twenty-four-inch blade. They would leave those items untouched until they reached their destination.

Sanjay closed the tailgate. He drove. Departing, they left all the garage lights on and didn't close the big door.

10

Part Cherokee, part Irish, part Hawaiian—the last of those including genetic slivers of various South Pacific and Asian ancestors—Jessica Washington, with her Cherokee complexion and sable hair and almond eyes of shamrock green, was a woman of many parts, including two sets of legs.

When she ran for exercise or competed in a 10K run, she wore the legs with flexible blades for feet. Now, as she prepared dinner and put it on the table with the help of man and boy, she wore more traditional prosthetics.

At the age of twenty-three, nine years earlier, she had lost her legs from the knees down while serving in Afghanistan. She'd been Army, like Gavin, but a noncombatant. Roadside IEDs were equal-opportunity destroyers, however, indifferent to issues of gender, race, religion, and nationality. Gavin had met her following the loss of her legs, and they had been married for eight years. They rarely spoke of her disability or her difference except when one of her prosthetic limbs needed to be repaired or replaced.

Gavin had established a solid post-Army career writing military nonfiction and, more recently, a series of novels featuring a cast of Special Forces operatives. He'd not landed on the bestseller list yet—and maybe he never would—but he was doing all right. Jessie had proved to have considerable organizational skills working as a volunteer advocate for wounded veterans. Their lives were happy and full, especially full since Travis had come to live with them.

This evening, it was the boy's turn to say grace. For a five-year-old, he made of the duty a detailed expression of gratitude that always brought a smile to Jessie. He thanked God not just for brisket of beef and au gratin potatoes and sugar snap peas and baked corn and dinner rolls and iced tea and carrot cake, but also for Exmoor ponies and Sara Orangetip butterflies, for Bella and Samson and Hannah, for red-tailed hawks and canyon wrens and baleen whale fossils, for Gavin and Jessica, and last of all for Jane, which was when, as always, he ceased thanking God and required of the Big Guy a term upon which any future statements of gratitude would be conditioned: "And thank you for my mom, the best mom ever, so you have to keep her really safe and bring her back to us really soon, like not a year from now but like really, really soon."

They had music while preparing dinner—classic Sam Cooke—and soft piano during the meal. As the men cleared the table and loaded the dishwasher, Jessie stepped onto the back porch for fresh air, which smelled of jasmine and oak mast. The German shepherds, Duke and Queenie, followed her. Only then, with no screening music, did she hear an airplane cruising the night at altitude.

At various times during the day, with Gavin and Travis off on their ride, as Jessie had been about one chore or another, here and there on the property, she had heard a plane, surely not always the same one. The valley was as rural as anywhere in this sprawling county of three million souls. It wasn't near a major airport. No takeoff or landing paths bisected it. Jets of all sizes crossed the valley, but at such high altitude they could hardly be heard. There were private craft at times, prop planes bound for days of pleasure in farther places, businessmen headed for distant conferences or scouting possible real-estate ventures from the air. But she could not recall a day in which, as today, there seemed to be a constant coarse drone of aircraft.

In fact, it might not just have *seemed* so, but might have *been* so. She had played music at times other than dinner and had been performing tasks that took her full attention or that were noisy enough to mask the sound of a plane.

The dogs had scampered away not merely to have a last pee of the day, but also to patrol the yard, the stables, and the freestanding garage. By their nature, especially between sunset and sunrise, shepherds were diligent guardians of their family.

The breeze had gone to bed with the sun. In the stillness, there were occasional early season tree toads making themselves sound as big as frogs, an owl on an oak-branch perch, calling *hooo-hooo-hooodoo-hooodoo*, as if warning of some dark magic at work in the night— and the plane just clear enough to be tracked as it droned east to west and then turned south. Her military experience allowed Jessie to reach certain conclusions with confidence: that the current aircraft was a twin-engine model, larger than the light planes sold by companies like Cessna and Piper, and that it was being flown above three thousand feet, perhaps to avoid unduly disturbing the residents of the valley—or to avoid, as much as possible, raising suspicion in those with reason to be wary. The engine noise dwindled toward the south, and when it seemed within a minute of fading beyond hearing, it changed in character. Jessica listened until she was sure that the craft had turned east. If in a few minutes it changed course northward, there could be little doubt that it was circling the valley.

She opened the kitchen door. Travis had begun to wipe crumbs off the dinette table with a damp dishcloth, after which he would dry the table with a dish towel. Diligent about the simple chores he was given, the boy focused intently on the table, his face serious and his tongue protruding between his teeth. Just then turning away from the dishwasher, Gavin saw Jessie in the doorway. She gestured at him to join her on the porch.

11

Hendrickson dunked the lemon drop cookies in his Coke. But he ate the chocolate chip cookies dry, taking small bites all the way around the circumference of each one and then around again, until there remained just the center, a miniature cookie, that he could pop into his mouth whole. He ate more of these treats than anyone but a hyperactive child or a fat man of gargantuan appetite could have consumed, and all the while he did not look at either of his captors, did not speak a word.

Jane nursed her vodka-and-Coke, watching Hendrickson gimlet-eyed, wondering if his apparent regression into childlike behavior was real or feigned. If it was a performance, what did he have to gain by it? Nothing that she could imagine. If he'd decided not to tell her more about the Arcadians or about his work on their behalf, he didn't need to fake a psychological implosion; he could simply clam up. He knew she wasn't capable of physically torturing him. Anyway, when his control mechanism began to function in a few hours, she could demand that he tell her all, and he would not be able to resist. Which argued that whatever was happening to him must be real, either triggered by his terror and despair over his coming enslavement or as a consequence of the nanoconstructs failing to properly assemble without causing brain damage.

She worried that a mental collapse might render him a poor subject for interrogation even after the control mechanism had fully and correctly inserted itself. What good would it be to insist he divulge what he knew if mentally he had regressed to some childlike condition in which he remembered nothing past the age of ten?

She decided to press him for more information now. "You've told me all the names in your cell. But as connected as you are, there must be other people you *suspect* of being Arcadians."

"You said I could have cookies."

"And you have them."

"But I need another Coke."

"I'll get it," Gilberto said.

To Hendrickson, Jane said, "Talk to me while you eat."

"Okay. If you say so. But what happened to Simon?"

"Your brother? I left him alive."

"But what happened to him? What did you do?"

"What do you care?"

He lowered his voice almost to a whisper and spoke with evident distress. *"I need to know."*

As Gilberto returned with a cold can of cola and put it on the table, he looked down upon Hendrickson's bent head for a moment and then glanced at Jane as though to be sure that she realized how disconnected their captive had become. With a nod, she assured him that she understood.

If Jane had become for Hendrickson the symbol of ultimate power, and if he had, as she'd earlier thought, always been a man who longed for greater power at the same time that he yearned to submit to it, then she was best advised to keep him fearful of her.

"I broke Simon. Broke him and made him cooperate in your kidnapping. I left him tied up in his fancy theater, lying in his own piss."

He said nothing and put down a half-eaten cookie.

"What do you think about that?" Jane prodded.

Hendrickson muttered something.

"I can't hear you," she said.

He whispered, "Simon was always the strong one."

"I wasn't that impressed with your Simon." She

paused for vodka-and-Coke. "Come on now, tell me, who do you *suspect* might be Techno Arcadians?"

After a silence, he said, "Well, first of all, there's one more I *know* is."

Jane frowned. "You said you'd named all you knew."

"I named everyone in my cell."

"Who is the other?"

Hendrickson licked his lips. He glanced at her and quickly away. "Anabel. My mother. She's one. One of them. She was Bertold Shenneck's first investor. Even before D. J. Michael. She's one. Anabel."

12

When Gavin came onto the porch, Jessie was already standing in the backyard, gazing at a starless sky in which the moon's ascent could be confirmed by only a pale shapeless blur pressing against the crackle-glazed cloud cover like some spirit at a winter-frosted window. He went to her.

"Hear that?" she asked. "It's heading east, but I think it's been circling."

Wearing her standard prosthetics, she stood with her legs more widely spread than she would have if they had been real, to ensure her balance. Her hands were fisted on her hips, and as she peered into the obscure heavens, her posture and expression were a challenge, as though she had taken umbrage at some injustice and, having brought it to the attention of a higher power, was waiting now for a cosmic correction to be effected. Jessie had high expectations of everyone, including Providence and herself, and this was one of the things he most loved about her.

He listened until he determined that the aircraft had changed directions. "Sounds northbound now."

"Bet it turns west in a couple minutes. Thinking back on it, maybe there's been a plane up there all day."

"It would have to refuel. Change crews."

"So maybe there's been two of them, spelling each other."

Every time an owl hooted from its oak-tree perch, mourning doves sheltering in the stable eaves cooed nervously, though their fragile but deep-set nests put them beyond reach of the larger, predatory bird.

As Gavin listened to the plane, the disquiet of the doves infected him, though his foreboding arose from a threat more serious than a great horned owl.

"I guess I know what you're thinking," Jessie said.

"I guess you do."

According to Jane, in the vicinity of all major cities that might be subject to a terrorist attack, the National Security Agency likely maintained surveillance aircraft staffed and ready to take off at a moment's notice. They were equipped to seine from an ocean of telecom signals only those carrier waves reserved for cellphones, even specifically for transmissions from disposable phones, burner phones, within a fifty-mile radius. They were fishermen netting data out of a sea of air, able to use an analytical scanning program to search for references to an impending attack—the names of known terrorists, key words in English, Chinese, Russian, and various Middle Eastern languages—and then use track-to-source technology to pinpoint the location of those burner phones.

Jessie said, "What if . . ."

"Yeah?"

"If the analytical program was customized to search for names like *Jane*, *Travis*, *Nick* . . . for words like *Mom* and *love* and *Dad* and things like that, could they nail us if she calls our burner?"

"Us *and* her. But first they'd have to suspect the boy's in this area. How could they?"

He and Jessie rarely took Travis off the property. And as far as anyone knew, he was their nephew, Tommy, staying with them while his exhausted parents looked after his eight-year-old sister who was fighting cancer. There were only two known photos of Travis, both frequently shown on TV, one from when he was only three. The other, more recent, didn't provide a clear image of him.

"Anyway," Jessie said, "if somebody thought they recognized him and reported him, this place would already be crawling with Feds."

"Not if maybe they checked out our story about a nephew and found it was bogus. And then discovered a link between us and Jane. They'd wait for her to call us."

"It'd be pretty damn expensive to pull a couple of these surveillance planes out of San Diego or L.A. just for this."

"Your tax dollars at work. Anyway, say they get her burner location."

"Say."

"And say she doesn't know they have it. So she doesn't throw it away after calling us."

"They could get to her fast."

"Considering what's at stake, they'll put any resources they have into finding her." He cocked his head and turned one ear to the northbound plane until he said, "Getting louder. I think it just turned west."

About two feet long from tail to ear tufts, with a four-foot wingspan, the great horned owl sailed off the oak branch and swooped down the darkness, beautiful and pale and terrible. It came toward Jessie and Gavin, eyes luminous yellow in a catlike face, passed low over them, and glided lower still. From among the carpet of crisp oak leaves, the bird snatched a soft, warm vole or a field mouse or another small earthbound creature born to the short life of easy prey.

The owl vanished into some high roost to consume its catch in silence, but overhead the aircraft grew louder and nearer in its patient patrol.

Gavin wondered if the drones, earlier in the day, had not been searching for them—because their location was already known—but instead had been meant to spook them just enough so that they might call Jane's burner phone to ask her advice.

"If she calls us," Jessie said, "we warn her and hang up. But if this plane is what we think . . ."

"They'll know we're on to them," Gavin said, "and they'll be all over this place in ten minutes."

He put two fingers in his mouth and whistled loud, and the dogs came running from out of the darkness.

"So we go?" Jessie asked.

"We go. And if it's a false alarm, we come back."

She took his hand. "I don't think we'll be coming back soon."

13

An imposing house at the end of a cul-de-sac. Soft contemporary architecture. Black slate roof, smooth rather than textured stucco, honed limestone paving, enormous sheets of glass on the view side of the residence. Palm trees and ferns. Beds of anthuriums with red heart-shaped spathes like bursts of blood in the landscape lighting.

Sanjay Shukla parked at the curb near the residence.

Tanuja was living her recent novel, or perhaps researching a sequel, much as she had when she stood in the rain to catalogue the feelings of her character Subhadra in the novelette she'd not yet finished writing.

Alecto Rising, her recently published novel, magic realism with a comic edge, had received kind reviews. It concerned a young woman named Emma Dodge into whom was manifested one of the Furies, Alecto. In classic mythology, Tisiphone and Megaera and

Alecto, daughters of the earth goddess Gaea, punished crimes in the name of the victims. In Tanuja's story, Alecto descended to the earth because current-day crimes were so horrible that humanity risked annihilation if criminals were not taught to fear again the justice of the gods. Being a pagan goddess, Alecto preferred swift and harsh retribution, bloodier than not, but Emma Dodge, a twenty-eight-year-old personal shopper with a stubborn streak, at first bewildered to be sharing her body with a violence-prone divinity, had ideas of her own. In the novel, Alecto taught Emma the value of a moral code and respect for higher powers, while Emma put Alecto through an enlightenment less destructive than that of the eighteenth century, and together they devised lesson-teaching punishments as effective as evisceration but less lethal. In his usual acerbic way, Sanjay called it *Death Wish Meets Pay It Forward.*

A Mercedes sedan and a BMW were parked immediately in front of the Chatterjee residence. On the last Saturday of every month, Aunt Ashima and Uncle Burt invited the same four guests to dinner and an evening of cards. Justin Vogt, the attorney who had advised them during their management of the Shukla Family Trust, following the death of *Baap* and *Mai* in the plane crash, who had helped them protect the funds they had looted from it, and his wife, Eleanor, would be there. So would Mohammed Waziri, the accountant, and his lovely wife, Iffat.

As Tanuja got out of the Hyundai, the skulls strung round her neck clicked softly, one against another.

The house faced onto a canyon that declined to the

sea; and the sea had effused a fog into the canyon, so that the darkness of that void had given way to a pallid and amorphous mass that now began to overflow, questing between the houses with its many ghostly hands.

She drew a deep breath of the pleasantly cool night air and surveyed the street, which curved around an oval island—planted with japonica bushes and three mature coral trees—before doubling back on itself.

Of the six houses on the cul-de-sac, four were dark, including two immediately to the east of the Chatterjee property and the one adjacent to it on the west side.

For a moment, Tanuja came unmoored from her purpose and did not know why she found herself in this place. *Alecto Rising* was written and published, and she had no need to research it. Anyway, how was it possible to research what it felt like to share one's body with a pagan divinity? Such a thing could not be researched, only imagined.

From the nearby canyon rose the ululation of coyotes in the frenzied pursuit of prey. She had heard these cries often before. Although the sound always had the power to ice the spine, the chill she felt this time was not related to pity for whatever terrified creature might be fleeing through the night. This time, the coldness in her marrow was spawned by a sudden ability to vividly imagine the horror of being in the grip of a blood delirium, of being the chaser rather than the chased, of life lived in the regimentation of a pack, where the frenzy of one became the frenzy of all.

Be at peace, she told herself. *Saturday night is for fun.*

There is fun to be had. Do whatever you feel you must do to be happy, and tomorrow you will write your best work ever.

Sanjay came around the Hyundai to her side, and her concern greatly diminished with his arrival. She did not know where this research would take her after they went to the house and rang the bell, but that was, after all, why one conducted research—to see where it might lead.

He had opened the tailgate to retrieve the reciprocating saw and the orange extension cord. She had forgotten about those items. She couldn't imagine to what purpose they would be applied.

Well, they were just tools. One needed tools to accomplish any task, whatever it might be.

"No. Not yet," he said, and he closed the tailgate.

Already, under the streetlamps, the blacktop glistened with a condensation of fog, and wetness mottled the sidewalk, and the grass was diamonded, and the glossy red spathes of the anthuriums dripped.

14

Except for the years that he'd been in the Marines and two years after, Gilberto had lived above the funeral home ever since his mother had brought him home from the hospital as an infant in a bassinet. He had slept most nights knowing there was at least one dead person downstairs—often two, sometimes three—and some of his earliest memories were of venturing into a viewing room when no one was there, to stand on tiptoe by the casket and look at the deceased fresh from the embalming room in the basement. By the time he was eleven, he was observing his father at work, assisting in what small ways he could. He had seen people who'd died of natural causes at ninety, who had been eaten away by cancer at fifty, who had been killed in a bar fight at thirty, who had died in a car crash at sixteen, who had been beaten to death by an abusive parent at six, all those and many more. He had seen them, and later he had prepared their poor bodies with the respect and tenderness that his father had taught him. In all the years of his life with the dead, Gilberto had never been frightened of being in the company of a corpse or of a corpse itself. He had only fond memories of these rooms above a mortuary, memories of love and conviviality.

For the first time, this Saturday in March, fear had come upon him here, and more than once. The previous evening, when Jane had told him about the nano-machines and the Arcadian conspiracy, he had believed her and had felt an existential dread unlike any that he'd known since being away at war. But now observing her interrogation of Booth Hendrickson, both prior to the injection and after, as they anticipated the man's coming conversion, Gilberto had been chilled to the core.

Jane's techniques, persistence, and self-control made the interrogation a riveting experience for Gilberto, but in spite of her unrelenting—even merciless—pursuit of the truth, he had not been shaken by anything she did. In fact, he was grateful she was on the right side of this business, because if she'd been one of *them*, she would have been a damn formidable enemy.

Hendrickson was another matter. The arrogance of the man from the DOJ, his contempt for the rights of others, for the *lives* of others, his utopia that would be the darkest dystopia for most of humanity . . . More than once, the guy sent shivers through Gilberto.

And now, as his personality seemed to deteriorate, either under the extreme stress brought on by his inevitable conversion into one of his adjusted people or because something was going wrong with the control mechanism implantation, Hendrickson's voice and his manner and his revelations about his mother stiffened the fine hairs on the back of Gilberto's neck. Since the control mechanism had not yet woven itself fully across and into the man's brain, there was a possibility that his breakdown was a performance, that he had some trick in mind, though it was difficult to see what he could hope to achieve by such a deception. Besides, there was a creepy reality to his emotional devolution.

Jane wanted to know a great deal about the estate in La Jolla, where Anabel Claridge currently resided, and then about the estate in Lake Tahoe, to which the woman would move on May first and remain until October.

"She likes Tahoe not for its winter sports, but for its summer beauty," Hendrickson said, and he emitted a mutterance of laughter, bitter and restrained, which he refused to explain. In fact, he denied having laughed at all, and he seemed to be sincere in his denial.

Hendrickson spoke of the La Jolla property readily enough, but his mood changed when answering questions about the place in Tahoe, which he called "the forge." When closed in Anabel's absence, the forge was overseen by the live-in groundskeeper, Loyal Garvin, and his wife, Lilith, who was the housekeeper. In her younger days, Anabel had spent nine months of the year at the forge, and the boys had sometimes lived the entire year there.

"Why do you call it 'the forge'?" Jane asked.

"Because she called it that." Hendrickson stared into his glass of cola as if the shapes of melting ice cubes were the equivalent of a Gypsy's tea leaves.

"Was it a forge at one time?"

"It was *her* forge."

"What do you mean by 'forge'?"

He looked up from his drink and met her eyes but quickly looked away as he said, "What do *you* mean by it?"

"Blacksmiths. A furnace for heating metal and hammering it into shape. Forging horseshoes and swords and whatnot."

That bitter, ironic laugh quickened from him and away. "In this case—whatnot."

"By which you mean?"

After a hesitation, he said, "Mostly boys. She forged sons there."

"You and Simon?"

"Didn't I just say?"

"Forged you into what?"

"The kind of men she wanted." His nostrils flared and he turned this way and that, sniffing. "Do you smell that?"

"Smell what?" Jane asked.

"Rancid meat."

"I don't smell anything."

Hendrickson had no trouble looking at Gilberto; it was only Jane's stare that intimidated him. "Do you smell spoiled meat, Charles?"

"No," Gilberto said.

"Sometimes," Hendrickson said, "bad smells no one else can detect . . . that's a symptom caused by a control mechanism threading itself through the brain."

After a silence, Jane said, "How did your mother forge you? Just what do you mean?"

"She had her ways. She had her very effective ways. We aren't permitted to talk about that."

"I'm giving you permission."

"It's not yours to give. We can't talk about that. Never. Not ever. We can't ever talk about that."

15

If it was known that Gavin and Jessie were harboring Travis, they had to assume that their landline phones and their smartphones had been accessed remotely and were acting as infinity transmit-

THE CROOKED STAIRCASE   355

ters. Every word spoken in the house would now be monitored in real time by Jane's enemies.

When they stepped into the kitchen from the back porch, Travis was sweeping the floors with a Swiffer. Duke and Queenie considered the fluffy Swiffer pad to be a toy. For a minute, there was a chaos of dogs panting and whimpering with excitement, of tails whacking cabinets and chair legs, and of a boy giggling as he struggled to preserve the pad from teeth and claws, managing at last to stow it in the broom closet.

When Travis turned to them, Gavin made a V of two fingers, pointed them at his eyes and then at the boy's eyes, which was a prearranged signal that meant *Big trouble, so focus on me.*

Travis became instantly alert.

"Hey, kiddo, you want to play cards, Old Maid?" Jessie asked.

"Yeah, I like those funny old games. They're cool."

Gavin pointed with a forefinger, drew a circle in the air to include the entire room, and tugged at his right earlobe, which the boy would know meant, *They're all around us, listening.*

"I'll get some drinks," Jessie said.

"I'd like a beer," Gavin said.

"Beer for me, too," said Travis.

"You wish," Jessie told the boy as she moved to the iPod that stood on the counter with a pair of Bose speakers. "Heineken for the big guy, root beer for the wise guy."

"I gotta use the bathroom," Travis said.

"Me, too," Jessie said, "but I gotta have music, too."

Gavin said, "Pure tragedy that I was born too late

for doo-wop. Give me some Hank Ballard, some Platters, some Del Vikings."

As he and Travis moved away into the house, music
rose loud in the kitchen.

The only computer with an Internet connection
was in Gavin's office. It had a camera. He'd covered
the lens with a piece of blue painter's tape. But ru-
mors abounded that computers made in the past two
years, which his had been, contained a second, hidden
camera—a so-called Orwell eye—that looked out from
behind the screen.

He hadn't worked today. The computer was off.
But it remained plugged into a wall outlet, so that the
unit-ID package received a trickle charge, and its locater continuously issued an identifying signal. Did
technology exist enabling them to invade his computer, turn it fully on while connecting it to the Internet, and activate its Orwell eye, much as they could
turn any telephone mic into a surveillance device?

He didn't know. He couldn't risk going into his office.

Three televisions in the house. New models might
have been a problem, but they didn't have new. The
small one in the kitchen was probably fifteen years
old; it had belonged to Jessica's mother. Those in the
family room and master bedroom were eight years
old, bought right after their marriage. No cameras
and no Internet capability in those three.

Duke and Queenie raced ahead of him, up the stairs,
their lowered tails dragging across the carpet runner,
alert to the fact that some crisis was at hand.

Gavin's smartphone lay on the dresser. He would have to leave it there. Jessie would need to abandon hers as well.

The only phone they would be taking was the burner that Jane had given them. They didn't dare use it while they might be within range of the sky fisher circling the valley, but eventually they would be in the clear.

Primed for action but finding none immediate, Duke and Queenie departed in a soft thunder of paws, perhaps to seek Travis.

In the back of the clothes closet stood two pre-packed suitcases prepared for just such an emergency as this. He set them by the bed.

From the lowest of the three drawers in his night-stand, he took a Galco shoulder system. The harness had a clover-shaped Flexalon back plate that allowed the four points of the suede harness to swivel inde-pendently of the others for a tight but comfortable fit, which he quickly achieved. From the same drawer, he withdrew a Springfield Armory TRP-Pro .45 ACP. Seven-round magazine. Five-inch barrel. Thirty-one ounces loaded. It used to be the FBI's pistol for their SWAT Hostage Rescue Team, and maybe it still was.

He pulled on a sport coat cut for concealed carry and snatched up the suitcases and went downstairs to the kitchen, where Travis was already standing by the back door with a smaller suitcase of his own. The dogs were with the boy, collared and leashed and standing at attention, tails still and bodies taut.

Jessie was singing "Little Darlin'" along with the

Diamonds on the iPod. She sounded carefree. She wore a woman-friendly belt-fixed rig that allowed the butt of the Colt Pony Pocketlite .380 ACP to ride low on the hip for comfort.

On the table stood a briefcase she'd retrieved from a concealed compartment at the back of the pantry. It contained ninety thousand in cash that Jane had stripped away from various bad guys over the past couple months and had left here, plus another twenty thousand of their own funds they had withdrawn from the bank in small enough amounts to avoid calling attention to themselves, in preparation for just such an emergency as this.

The Diamonds finished their tune, and in the silence between selections, as he went to the back door, Gavin said, "You have the Marcels on deck?"

"Relax, Mr. Romance, 'Blue Moon' was our honeymoon song, if you remember."

"Oh, I do remember. Vividly. Vividly," he said as Joe Bennett and the Sparkletones came on strong with "Black Slacks."

He eased open the door and carried the two suitcases outside. Travis stayed behind with Jessie and the dogs, while Gavin hurried to the stand-alone garage near the stables.

16

Although Sanjay knew that he was awake, he felt as if he were moving through a dream or through a sequence in a noir film designed to convey a dreamlike quality. Something directed by Michael Curtiz or Fritz Lang. Maybe John Huston. Pools of light under streetlamps, reminiscent of the hard light focused on suspects being grilled in otherwise shadowy interrogation rooms. The shifting fog suggesting that reality was fluid, that nothing was what it seemed to be, that his motives were shrouded even from himself. And the night, always the night beyond the lamplight, behind the fog. The night resonated with some darkness in himself that brought him here with intentions that, curiously, were revealed to him only one move at a time, as if he were merely a chess piece with no purpose of his own, a pawn animated by some unknown player's strategy.

When he and Tanuja arrived at the front door, he almost rang the bell, but then realized that he had no need to announce their arrival. From a coat pocket, he removed a key. Perplexed, he stared at it in the soft glow of the stoop light. It lay on his palm as if it had been conjured there. Then he murmured, "The rapist gave it to me last night," although his words did not relieve his perplexity.

He turned to Tanuja, and her gaze rose from the key to his eyes. "What did you say, *chotti bhai*?" she asked, raising one hand to the right corner of her mouth.

"I don't know. Maybe . . . nothing," he said. "Nothing that meant anything."

"Nothing," she agreed.

Next move: He slipped the brass key into the keyway of the deadbolt, and the lock relented. And then the next: He pushed open the door.

Tanuja crossed the threshold, and Sanjay followed her into a foyer with a golden-marble floor, pale-peach walls, and a modern chandelier with ropes of lighted crystals cascading like dreadlocks.

He quietly closed the door and put away the key and looked around at the matching antique chinoiserie sideboards to the left and right, each bearing a cut-crystal bowl of fresh white roses.

"*Mausi* Ashima has always had exquisite taste," said Tanuja.

17

If the plane cruising the valley was what they believed it to be, there was surely surveillance out on the county road, at the entrance to their property, to record whatever vehicles came and went. But Gavin doubted there would be anyone posted closer than that. The gated private lane leading here was over two hundred feet long and flanked by colonnades of old live oaks, which screened the house and other structures from the public highway. To get much closer, the watchers would have to risk being seen; they no doubt preferred to keep their interest secret until they might snatch Jane's next phone call from the air, track it to its source—and then swoop in to grab the boy.

The garage was a rebuilt barn without windows. Gavin didn't worry about switching on the lights after he stepped inside and closed the door behind him.

The building contained a complete automotive workshop as well as four vehicles, including his prized street rod, an apple-green '48 Ford pickup that he'd chopped, channeled, and sectioned. She was hot and fast, but she wasn't suitable for their current escape plan. The '40 Mercury coupe on which he'd recently begun work was without a functioning engine and lacked wheels. Jessie's Explorer would have been adequate if Ford hadn't downsized Explorers years earlier. The getaway fell to the other all-wheel drive, an '87 Land Rover that he'd rebuilt from near ruin and that contained no GPS locater by which it could be tracked.

He stood on a step stool to lash the suitcases to a roof rack, making sure they were secured enough to stay in place through any adventure other than maybe a double rollover.

When he returned to the kitchen, the Coasters were rollicking through "Yakety Yak," while Jessie and Travis were talking cards as if they were actually playing Old Maid. For the entertainment of eavesdroppers, Gavin sang a few bars, while he grabbed the boy's suitcase and Jessie's blade-runner prosthetics, which he carried to the garage and put on the floor in the backseat of the Land Rover.

When he returned to the house for the last time, the Monotones were fully into "The Book of Love."

Travis said, "I gotta go to the bathroom."

"You just went," Jessie said.

"Yeah, well, I didn't went enough."

"Okay, and I swear we won't look at your cards when you're out of the room."

Jessie carried the briefcase containing $110,000, and the boy stayed close by her side all the way to the garage.

Gavin followed behind with Duke and Queenie. The dogs sprang into the Rover through the tailgate.

The horses would be all right for the night. In the morning, he would call someone and arrange to have the stallion, mare, and pony professionally stabled for a month. He had to believe that this bad business would be finished in a month. One way or another, it would be finished.

18

Tanuja was herself, Tanuja Shukla, born in Mumbai, reborn in America, orphaned when her beloved parents fell out of the sky, but she was also Emma Dodge, born in Long Beach, now a personal shopper for wealthy women in Bel Air and Beverly Hills, as chronicled in the recent novel published by Random House. She was as well Alecto, a daughter of Gaea, one of the Furies, having stepped safely down the long sky through which dear *Baap* and *Mai* had fallen, to cohabit Tanuja's body and to share the pages of the story of Emma Dodge. Tanuja-Emma-Alecto, triune entity, stood in the grand foyer of the Chatterjee residence, for the moment uncertain of her purpose. As a writer, Tanuja used her free will to create whole worlds, in one of which she'd shaped Emma, who possessed no free will, and borrowed Alecto from unknown writers who had created her millennia earlier. For all her reputation as a divinity, Alecto possessed no more free will than Emma, both being fictional, and yet in this still point between the past and the future, to bring this moment of indecision to a necessary end, it was Alecto who rose to the occasion.

Gazing at her reflection in one of the mirrors that hung above the chinoiserie sideboards in the foyer, Tanuja saw not the author of *Alecto Rising*, but Alecto herself, dark eyes encircled by darker eye shadow, lips black, and when she put a hand to those lips, the fingernails were black as well. Within fierce Alecto, she saw the shadow of another divinity from another pantheon entirely, Kali in her terrible Chandi aspect, wearing a necklace of human skulls. In fact, there were shadows within Kali, shades of uncounted vengeful deities from all of pagan history, gathered now in Tanuja, and she their avatar, brought here, this night, to do their will, not her own, and so she turned from the mirror when she heard voices and laughter elsewhere in the house.

19

From the dark garage into the dark night, without the aid of headlights, Gavin drove not along the lane toward the county road, but instead to the back gate in the property fence and out into the wildland, into which he and Travis had ridden their horses earlier in the day.

Travis sat belted in the backseat. Jessica rode shotgun, literally, with a 12-gauge racked stock-down in a dashboard-mounted clamp directly in front of her.

Under the starless overcast, through which the moon was only a ghostlight, the rough land lay crisp and clear before Gavin, though it was rendered an otherworldly green by the night-vision goggles that had been stowed under the driver's seat and that he now wore.

These were not average night-vision devices like the Bushnell Equinox Z or ATN Viper X-1. They were ATN PVS7-3 goggles, MIL-SPEC Generation 4 gear used by all branches of the U.S. military, and although they were available for purchase by civilians, they cost north of $60,000. Jane had provided a pair for this sole purpose. Gavin didn't think she had bought them, and he was discreet enough not to ask how she'd obtained them.

The device gathered all the available light—even infrared that could not be seen by the unassisted human eye—amplified it more than eighty thousand times, and with image-enhancement technology presented a 120-degree field of view. The image was rendered in an eerie green hue because the eye was most sensitive to wavelengths of light that were nearest 555 nanometers, the green neighborhood on the spectrum, which allowed the display to be dimmer without losing clarity, thus conserving the battery.

Off-road at night in rough terrain, they could not have risked headlights and taillights, which in this unpopulated and untraveled terrain would have made a spectacle of their escape, especially to an aerial observer. The blush of red brake lights reflecting off slopes of scree and through fields of blond grass would be less noticeable from a distance, but Gavin nonetheless strove to minimize the use of brakes.

The engine noise might betray them on departure, but less so after the first mile. Any agent on the ground would be hard put to get an accurate fix on the Rover's location in this stark country of discontinuous hills and zigzagging canyons scored into the land less by erosion than by thousands of years of earthquakes, which provided a maze of hard surfaces off which sound could ricochet until it seemed to come from everywhere and nowhere.

"We're drivin' blind," the boy said from the backseat.

"You and I are," Jessie said, "but not my man here."

"Clear as noon to me," Gavin said, though in fact the view through the goggles disturbed him.

The strange green light robbed all things of their true color, as though before him lay an alien moon in a universe where the laws of electromagnetic radiation were far different from those of the world on which he'd been born. This radiance seemed also to drown everything that it illuminated, the qualities of light and water married in its effect, the semidesert now submerged in a sea, the Land Rover a submarine at great depth, under terrible pressure.

He had gone little more than a mile before he realized the reason for his disquiet, which now grew sharper. In the museum that was his memory, there were no halls or chambers into which he would not go, but there were places he preferred over others. He wasn't fond of revisiting recollections of night missions in Afghanistan, conducted with this technology. Primitive villages of mud bricks plastered over with stucco. Isolated compounds of graceless concrete structures. All laid with traps, sometimes with tripwires. Every dark-green doorway and every dark-green window a possible assassin's lair. Then sudden action, a running black-green figure silhouetted against a pale-green concrete wall. Firing while on the move. Acid-green muzzle flare. Your return fire, more accurate than his, brought him strangely *en pointe,* his cloak flaring, as if a dance were about to begin, but it was a dance an instant long, and as he fell, the gout of green blood was almost black against the concrete backdrop. Gavin understood the peril that Jane was in, the hydra-headed and formidable nature of her enemies, and the risk that he and Jessie had taken by standing steadfast with her, but it was only now, looking at the world again through night-vision gear, when he fully appreciated that this was *war*, with all the horrors of combat, war in the homeland, Americans against Americans.

20

A nd so she led Sanjay through the elegantly furnished house, past big windows that in daylight might have revealed a dramatic canyon view funneling toward the sea in the distance, but that now were blinded by shifting cataracts of fog. They passed through a lamplit living room, a shadowy dining room, and into a kitchen.

Beyond the open kitchen lay a family room, and in the family room stood a six-sided table designed for card games, and on the table were a few plates of canapés, and in the chairs were three women and three men. They were enjoying a pre-dinner game of cards, their conversation animated, their attention fixed largely on the hands they had been dealt and on the discard that the current player was making.

Ashima was the first to realize that gods in the raiments of judgment had arrived, and she stared openmouthed, too shocked to scream. Indeed, in the few seconds before the gunfire began, there were no screams from any of the six, only gasps of surprise and throttled pleas. Only three of the six managed to push up from their chairs in the little time that fate had allotted them, though they had no chance to flee or fight.

To Alecto, Ashima was not her mother's sister, because her mother was Gaea, and it was not a Fury's role to grant mercy. Nor were there words or need of words, only the voices of the pistols roaring point-blank. A brightly colored dress of silk flared like the wings of an exotic parrot before an attempt at flight failed, and the dazzling silk furled around the fallen form of the broken would-be flyer. Figures in desperate postures, each concerned only for himself. Gesturing antically. Grotesque expressions perhaps common in the subterranean streets of Pandemonium. Those who stood then at once fell into those who remained seated, or they collapsed back into their chairs. The six-sided table shuddered, and the cards slithered onto the floor, fanning out arrangements of numbers and royal images that perhaps a gypsy might have read to ascertain the ultimate destination of the hosts and their four guests.

Start to finish, the judgment lasted less than a minute. And when it was finished, there was no time to survey the aftermath, let alone to dwell upon it or to wonder what it meant. Anyway, it was nothing. It meant nothing. Besides, there was more to be done— and in as timely a fashion as possible.

21

A darkness arises around the perimeter of the kitchen, not a failure of the light, but a gathering of shapes that remind Booth Hendrickson of large birds, although he can't discern any of their features. They are shadows where nothing exists to cast them.

The voice of his interrogator comes and goes. Sometimes he answers her, sometimes not. As the shadows congregate at the edges of his vision, hope retreats through the intricate spirals of his mind, and despair advances.

There was a time long ago when he was alone in the dark, but not afraid, alone in the dark with nobody to see, when like the boy in the books, he would say aloud, *I think to myself, I play to myself, and nobody knows what I say to myself.*

But that is not the darkness to which he is now returning, as the control mechanism weaves its web across his brain. The darkness coming will have no play in it, no delight; and no thought of his can ever be kept secret from those who command him in his servitude.

The coming darkness is that found in deep places, down where the crooked staircase leads, where the steps slope horizontal as well as strictly vertical, a nautilus of stairs, a maze, serving rooms where you must feel your way blindly because you have not earned a light to carry.

He has been there before, long ago, humbled to the condition of a beaten dog. He knows the misery of servitude, of being absolutely powerless. He would rather die than return to enslavement. But he is restrained at this kitchen table with no means of killing himself. And once the web's radials and spirals map the contours of his brain, he will be able to take his life only if ordered to do so.

He knows the truth of the world. He has been taught. There is no escaping the cold truth of the world.

Rule or be ruled. Use or be used. Break others or be broken by them. In every case, his only remaining option is the *or.*

The rising darkness rises farther, reaching the summit of the walls, spreading to the ceiling from which shapen shadows depend like black cocoons, encroaching on the table at which he sits. The only light in all the world is that surrounding the table, and the source of the light is she who rules him. She is clothed in light, and her face is luminous, and her eyes are blue fire as she poses her questions.

Where are you, Booth? Are you still here with me? Do you hear me, Booth Hendrickson? Can you hear me? Where are you, Booth?

He is in despair; that's where he is; it is a despair so pure that it will never evolve into desperation, which is energized and reckless despair, for he is without energy, drained.

Where are you, Booth?

For fear that she will take away her precious light and leave him enswarmed by darkness, he answers her. To his surprise, Booth speaks about that of which he must never speak. He tells her where he is—or rather where he has been and where he foresees himself: "The crooked staircase." Once the words have been spoken, the spell of silence is broken, and what was forbidden to be expressed is suddenly expressible.

22

What had happened was nothing. It meant nothing. Nothing at all. The still, small voice within assured her of that. Those in this house who had appeared to be people were not in fact people. The earth was a stage, those on it merely characters guided by a script. These people's story was no more important than any other, which is to say not important at all, mere entertainment for the gods.

What transpired next was nothing more than stagecraft. Alecto had been a minor divinity in ancient Rome as well as in ancient Greece, but her rank didn't mean that she was colorless. By their nature, the Furies were colorful, agents of retribution, marked by flaunt and flourish, shine and swagger, and it was incumbent upon anyone who would write about Alecto, who would become a vessel for Alecto, for the Chandi aspect of Kali, for others of their dark divinity, to up-hold the sacred tradition of flamboyance.

Tanuja stood on the stoop, waiting, the front door open wide behind her.

The cul-de-sac was quiet in the night and muffling fog. At the only other house that contained light, lu-minous windows seemed not part of any structure, seemed to float in the mist like large video screens made of some lighter-than-air material, none of them tuned to a channel, offering no drama, as if none could compete with events occurring in the Chatterjee house.

There were no shadowy forms of alarmed residents at those windows, no sirens in the distance. Most likely, the brief burst of gunfire had not traveled through walls, through night, through fog, through other walls. But it was not unlikely that even if the sound carried, those near enough to hear it were lost in a video game or binge-watching whatever, or were seeing out Sat-urday with a joint of good weed, having traded reality for one virtual reality or another. The scripts of their stories did not require them to hear.

Through the lamplight and the darkness and a thickening sea of fog, Sanjay returned with the coiled orange extension cord and the reciprocating saw. He was tall, trim, all in black. For a moment, a sharp fear pierced Tanuja, a terror of Sanjay, but this was only her little brother, her twin, blood of her blood, and the fear at once quieted away.

They did not speak when he arrived at the stoop and followed her into the house, for there was nothing that needed to be said. There was merely stagecraft to perform. Set decoration. Steps to be taken. Always one step at a time. Never knowing what was next until it needed to be done. According to the script by which they lived.

For a while, as they worked, Tanuja thought of Subhadra in the storm of the unfinished novelette, of the beauty of falling rain in silver skeins and the splendor of lightning born from a cumulonimbus womb, of the majesty of thunder like the rumble of colossal wheels moving creation along mysterious tracks. . . .

When the six severed heads were placed at intervals along the walkway leading to the front door, sister and brother stepped out of the night, into the foyer, she with her back turned to one mirror, he with his back to the other. They stood face-to-face, an arm's length apart. Cool fog slithered through the open door, drawn by the warmth of the house.

Sanjay wept quiet tears. She asked him why, and he didn't know why.

She said affectionately, "*Chotti bhai*, little brother."

He said, "*Bhenji*," and his tears flowed faster.

She said, "*Peri pauna*," which meant "I touch your feet," though she did not stoop to touch them, for he already knew how profoundly she cherished him.

His reply, "*Peri pauna*," brought tears to *her* eyes.

Not quite sure why she said it, she said, "Every story must have an end. That is the way of stories."

Because it was what his script instructed him to say, Sanjay replied, "I will count to three."

He counted in perfect cadence, precisely two seconds between the numbers, no hesitation because of doubt or confusion or emotion, for their actions must be perfectly simultaneous in this, which was their last moment on the stage.

His eyes on hers, her eyes on his, his pistol pressed to her head, hers to his, they—

—never heard the coeternal shots that ended their lives, though the sound of a single but double-loud blast carried through the open door and along the front walkway and into the cul-de-sac, drawing the attention of a neighbor who had just stepped out to walk his dog, then the police, then the news media, and then the world in all its ignorance.

23

In the green night, there were natural roads through the dense scrub, carved by the ways of water and wind. Navigable slopes of gravelstone. Barren ridgelines that could be followed for a while. Even in this inhospitable territory, in some canyons enough water lay beneath the surface to slake the thirst of eucalyptus and California buckeye. Some places there were immense live oaks, too, that sprawled into tortured architectures, shaped by acidic soil and heat and insect pests that didn't allow more natural forms, never forests of them, but transfigured groves through which the Land Rover passed as if journeying across a postapocalyptic landscape.

Gavin knew some of this territory from years of riding horses here, although he could not possibly be familiar with all of the hundreds of square miles ahead. And in this peculiar citrine light, he was unable to recognize even some familiar landmarks. In addition to experience and instinct, however, he was relying on a battery-illumined large-faced compass that he had fixed to the console between him and Jessie.

Although he'd had no expectation of making good time in these conditions, he worried that they were not putting the miles behind them fast enough. More than eight years from his last battlefield, he began to feel a familiar itch between the shoulder blades, a queasiness in the gut, and a tightening of the scrotum that were his instinct warning of trouble ahead.

In the cargo area behind the backseat, the dogs had been lying down, as they mostly did when traveling in any vehicle other than the apple-green '48 Ford pickup, wherein they liked to sit or even stand, leashed and anchored for their safety, to sightsee and let the wind blow through their fur.

Now, as the Rover was cruising through a meadow of low scraggly grass veined with taller coastal sage, Duke and Queenie scrambled to their feet and began to growl low in their throats.

From the backseat, Travis said, "They sure don't like something on your side of the Rover, Uncle Gavin."

Although traveling five miles an hour in respect of the sudden changes the terrain could undergo, Gavin slowed further to scan the night through his side window. At first he saw nothing. Then the pack raced into view.

"Coyotes," he said.

Six of them, a large pack for a species that often hunted alone. They were lean and shadowy green shapes with bright green eyes; their serrated smiles were the palest green in this macabre vision.

"I can see them, sort of," Travis said. "They've got fire in their eyes."

Gavin slowed further to let the beasts race ahead, but the coyotes slowed as well and hung with the Rover.

"To them," said Travis, "we're like some kinda canned meat."

Jessie laughed. "Delivered to their door, just like pizza."

The dogs' low growls were punctuated with thin keening sounds, almost whimpers. They were ready to fight. But at the same time, they acknowledged the greater ferocity of these wild creatures that, for all they might share with shepherds genetically, would go for the dogs' throats as savagely as if Duke and Queenie were rabbits.

Like the dogs, Gavin saw nothing amusing about being stalked by six long-toothed prairie wolves. They might be safe in this can on wheels, but they couldn't stay in the vehicle forever if it blew a tire.

24

On his way to becoming adjusted, Booth Hendrickson had fallen apart. When the nanoweb finished spinning itself, it would control a human form that looked like the once dreaded man from the DOJ, and it would be powered by the electrical currents of that functioning brain, but the man would not be who he once was, and the brain would be a repository for a mind in which long-tied psychological knots had come undone, and a profound unraveling had occurred.

As he told Jane and Gilberto about the Tahoe estate and the crooked staircase, he did so in a discursive monologue now and then bordering on incoherent. There was no way to keep him focused on the most salient facts by interrogating him, for he reacted to what she asked as if he were the ball in a pinball field, ricocheting off the question in unanticipated directions. The more questions that were put to him, the more fractured his narrative became, so that there was nothing to be done but let him talk, listen, and slowly make sense of all the puzzle pieces.

The story that he told of childhood abuse was so extreme, so unlike anything Jane had ever heard, that she expected him to become emotional, to weep with self-pity and shake with rage. Apparently, however, his capacity for emotion had been diminished for a long time. As an adolescent and adult, what he had been able to feel seemed to have been related to his conviction of superiority, to a deeply instilled sense of being one of a class above all others. He felt contempt for the masses in general and for most individuals in particular; disgust at what he imagined to be their universal ignorance; abhorrence at their pretensions to equality; hatred of them for their claims to such feelings as love, faith, compassion, and sympathy, all of which he *knew* to be fictions by which they hid from themselves the truth of the world. And he had known fear as well, fear of those billions who were beneath him and who, by their stupidity and ignorance and reckless behavior, might destroy the world not just for themselves but for him and those exalted people like him. Of nobler emotions, he seemed to have long been bereft. Now, in the telling of his experiences with the crooked staircase, even the ignoble emotions seemed inaccessible to him, leaving him only with fear, and in fact with just a single fear. He rambled through his story in a monotone, recalling the most hideous details with no more emotion than a mathematician reading off pages of the calculations he used to solve a problem. But from time to time he looked at Jane with sudden fright and said, "Tell me you won't take the light away. Please, please, don't take the light away."

When his story wound to its tangled end, he sat in silence, hands in his lap, head bowed, form without substance, a hollow man, his headpiece stuffed with straw.

An hour earlier, Jane would have thought she could never pity this ruthless user of others. If she pitied him now, she did not go so far as to have sympathy with him, for that would be to confer upon him a dignity he didn't deserve.

When he looked at her and pleaded for light, his expression was one of abject submission with a suggestion of veneration, as if he held her in exalted honor and didn't fear her at all, but reserved his fright for the loss of light, for being left in darkness as he had been left within the place that he called the crooked staircase. His seeming adoration gave Jane the creeps. After so long seeking absolute power, he found himself utterly powerless—and was relieved to submit, perhaps as pleased to be the face beneath the boot as he would have been to be the boot, as long as he could remain in the *presence* of power.

She didn't want his veneration.

And it wasn't mercy that would prevent her from turning out the lights. Even in his diminished capacity, she simply didn't want to be alone in the dark with him.

25

The previous night, Gilberto had enjoyed eight hours of sleep, unlike Jane, who had gotten four hours. But as he leaned back in his kitchen chair and massaged the nape of his neck with one hand, he looked as tired and world-weary as she felt. She had asked him to impersonate a chauffeur; she regretted that he'd been drawn so much deeper into this. Most of all, she was sorry that he'd been required to witness the enslavement of a fellow human being, even if one so lacking in humanity as this specimen.

At 8:45 P.M., and again at nine o'clock, Jane said to Hendrickson, "Play Manchurian with me," which was the trigger sentence programmed into the earlier generations of control mechanisms, like the one with which he'd been injected. Twice, he sat in silence, head bowed, either lost in thought or in a cataleptic trance that might be the end destination of his psychological collapse.

The third time, at 9:20, he lifted his head and said, "All right," and waited expectantly.

Of course, he'd known the trigger sentence and the proper reply before he'd been injected. He could be faking.

She had devised a test that involved a sterilized scalpel from the mortuary's instrument collection and a command for Hendrickson to cut one thumb.

When the moment came, however, she knew too much about his past suffering to require of him a test of pain.

She said, "Are you tired, Booth?"

"Oh, yes."

His ashen face, his bloodshot eyes, his pale lips were those of a man at the limit of his resources.

"Are you very tired?" she asked.

"Very. I've never been so tired."

"While we were waiting for the control mechanism to implant, was everything you told me true?"

"Yes."

"Entirely true? Even about . . . Tahoe?"

"Yes. True."

"And now you're very tired. So I'm going to order you to sleep and keep sleeping until I wake you by touching your right shoulder and saying your name. Do you understand?"

"Yes."

"Sleep," she said.

He slumped in the chair, and his head lolled to one side, and he seemed to sleep.

26

Whether this was her second or third vodka-and-Coke in the past few hours, she didn't know. She didn't care. She wanted only to stop thinking about the crooked staircase, about the terrible task that lay ahead, and be able to get four or five hours of sleep.

In the low light of a silk-shaded lamp, she and Gilberto sat in living-room armchairs, facing each other. He had poured for himself a generous portion of Scotch weakened by a single ice cube.

Hendrickson remained asleep and tethered to the chair in the kitchen. They had left brighter lights on for him than they wanted for themselves.

Minutes earlier, after a call from Gilberto, his older brother, Hector, and Hector's seventeen-year-old son,

Manuel, had stopped by, and Gilberto had gone down-stairs to give them a key so they could retrieve Jane's SUV. They knew only that an unnamed friend had left it parked in the lot of a supermarket the previous day and needed it to be brought here.

Gilberto swirled the Scotch just enough to clink the dwindling ice cube against the glass. "I thought my war was over years ago."

"It's all one war," she said, "and it's never over. But you have a haven here. Still no reason to be afraid of the dead."

"Only the living." He took a drink. "Long way to Lake Tahoe."

"If I catch some sleep, hit the road by four, I'll be there by noon, maybe one o'clock if the weather sucks."

"With him riding beside you."

"I need him."

"But can you really trust him?"

"Not to turn on me, yeah. But if his psychological collapse gets any worse than it is now, he might not be as useful as I hope."

"They know you have him."

"But you heard him—they don't know I walked away from Napa with samples of the control mecha-nism."

"*He* didn't know. Maybe others do."

"I'm betting they don't. And given the need-to-know rule, they won't notify the couple that maintains the Tahoe house when Anabel isn't there. Hell, they're just old people, plebs, plodders, rabble, two-legged cattle."

Gilberto shuddered. "What he said about why they make some kill themselves and just enslave others . . ."

Hendrickson's explanation was engraved in Jane's memory. *The ones who would turn society in the wrong direction, we hate them and believe they deserve to die. Some of those we enslave are just for our pleasure, like the girls of Aspasia. Others will run the world at our direction while we remain concealed behind them, and they are all ignorant fools who deserve to be enslaved.*

After they took a moment of solace in their drinks, Gilberto said, "People in power . . . in my dad's day, they weren't full of contempt for the rest of us."

"Power corrupts."

"It's something more than that. Power has always corrupted."

"It's all the damn experts," she said. "We stopped governing ourselves, turned it over to experts."

He frowned. "It's a complex world. People running it have to know what they're doing."

"*These* experts don't *have* any real-world experience worth shit. They're elitists. They're all theory but no real-world experience. Self-described intellectuals."

"Well, I guess maybe I know the type. Just turn on the TV."

"This British historian, Paul Johnson, he wrote a great book about them," Jane said. "It'll scare the piss out of you."

"I'm already scared pretty much pissless."

"They're uberconformists, live in a bubble of the like-minded. Contemptuous of common sense and regular people."

"Plebs, plodders, the great unwashed like us."

"But people matter more than ideas. Nick mattered

more than any idiot theory. My boy, your kids—they matter more."

"You see it changing?"

That was a question she had asked herself. The honest answer wasn't comforting. "It's gotten worse for a couple centuries."

"We gotta hope, though."

"Hope," she agreed. "And resist."

27

Carter Jergen says, with delight, "Sometimes a charitable act is rewarded with a kick in the teeth."

For weeks, in search of the hidden boy, agents had been tracking down every relative of Nick's and Jane's even to the ex-spouse of a second cousin. Every former Marine with whom Nick had served. The families of the victims of the serial killers Jane had caught or killed, with the expectation that she might have bonded with one of those families. Her old college friends. Anyone she might trust with her child. To no avail.

Because neither Nick nor Jane was a showboat, their support of organizations serving veterans didn't come to the attention of the searchers until so many other, more likely avenues of inquiry had been exhausted. And suddenly, in the photo collections of the fundraising events of those organizations, there they were at this marathon, at that wheelchair-sports weekend, at this gala—often in the company of Gavin and Jessica Washington, smiling and happy and obviously with *friends*.

As Carter Jergen pilots the Range Rover between the colonnades of live oaks, he says, "No rest for the weary."

"It's the price of success," Radley Dubose replies. "We kicked ass on the Shukla job, so they drop this on us a day later. Doesn't bother me. I like being wanted. You ever think what'll happen if we start screwing up?"

"No Christmas bonus?"

"It'll be you and me getting needles in the arm like we did the Hindu writer kids."

"Not in a million years," says Jergen, surprised that even as stunted a specimen as Dubose is so cynical. "*We* don't eat our own."

That statement elicits a patronizing smile. "No cannibalism among the Brahmins? I went to an Ivy League school, remember. I saw what I saw. I know what I know."

Oversized and self-satisfied, Dubose now reminds Jergen of yet another cartoon character—Popeye. *I saw what I saw, I know what I know, I yam what I yam.*

"Not every Ivy Leaguer is an Arcadian or could be. Or should be," Jergen says.

"Certainly not a lot of them at the University of Pennsylvania. It's distressing that Penn's even considered Ivy League."

Being a Harvard man and proud of it, Carter Jergen

is pretty sure he's being mocked with that Penn comment, but now they arrive at the Washington residence. Time to get down to business.

The house is a cozy-looking place with a generous front porch. All the lights are on. There's a barnlike building to the left and a stable beyond that, both dark.

What most interests Carter Jergen is the truck that the first responders arrived in, which is parked near the porch steps. It's a Hennessey VelociRaptor 6 × 6, a bespoke version of the four-door Ford F-150 Raptor with new axles, two additional wheels, supertough-looking off-road tires, and a ton of other upgrades. It's black, it's amazing, it's a *fabulous* truck.

Recently some Arcadians in the NSA and Homeland and elsewhere have been assigned impressive vehicles, mostly bespoke Range Rovers created by Overfinch North America, with performance upgrades, a carbon-fiber styling package, a dual-valve titanium exhaust system, and other cool stuff. Jergen has envied the hell out of them.

But *this*. This truck is another level of perk altogether.

There are two men waiting on the back porch. They're wearing slim-fit Ring Jacket suits, which manage to look casual in spite of the exquisite Neapolitan tailoring, and their seven-fold Cesare Attolini ties are in playful soft-polka-dot patterns.

Jergen feels underdressed in a black T-shirt, Diesel Black Gold denim jacket with embroidered scorpions, and black Dior Homme jeans, but he is, after all, a field op, not a front-office guy.

Dubose's outfit is unspeakable, suitable for knocking around in small-town West Virginia and not much else.

The back door of the house is closed, but Jergen can hear old music from before his time, a song titled "Get a Job."

The men on the porch don't give their names. They are brisk, almost brusque. They succinctly lay out the situation.

It became known at 4:00 P.M. on Friday that Gavin and Jessica Washington were harboring the five-year-old son of Jane Hawk. A decision was made to establish surveillance of the entrance to their private lane and to monitor the house by remotely opening the mics in their phones, computers, and TVs, as well as with the cameras in their computers and TVs. As their televisions did not have Internet links, they proved useless.

At 3:00 A.M. Saturday, NSA electronic-surveillance aircraft out of Los Angeles, rebased to Orange County airport, began spelling each other over the valley, fishing for all incoming and outgoing burner-phone traffic with the hope of identifying a call from Jane Hawk to the Washingtons and using track-to-source to locate her.

At 7:20 P.M., after dinner, the Washingtons and the boy agreed to play Old Maid. They accompanied the game with classic doo-wop music. Their conversation was unremarkable, partly obscured by the music. After a while, when they turned up the volume of the iPod, they couldn't be heard talking. It was assumed either that they were speaking softly and the music drowned out their conversation or that they'd run out of things to say to one another.

After a series of quieter tunes—"Sincerely" by the Moonglows, "Earth Angel" by the Penguins, and "Only You" by the Platters—the suspicion arose that the Washingtons and the boy were no longer in the house. An operative was sent on foot from the county road to reconnoiter. He circled the house, peering in windows, subsequently entered, and confirmed that the house was deserted. The deck of Old Maid cards on the table had not been removed from the box.

Four vehicles are registered to Gavin and Jessica Washington. Three are currently in the garage. A rebuilt and customized '87 Land Rover is missing, and it apparently has no GPS. A back gate in the ranch fencing, left open, suggests that the three became aware of surveillance and fled overland.

A team of specialists is en route. On arrival, they will take the house and other buildings apart in search of clues as to Jane Hawk's activities or whereabouts. Meanwhile, Jergen and Dubose are tasked with pursuing the Washingtons and the boy overland, assisted by an aerial night-search helicopter which is currently incoming.

In fact, no sooner has the aerial unit been mentioned than the helo roars overhead, shaking the long branchlets of the live oaks and stirring up whirling masses of dry leaves that chitter like a plague of locusts before it moves off toward the open gate.

One of the agents in a Ring Jacket suit holds a vehicle key, and a thrill passes through Carter Jergen as he looks at the hulking black Hennessey VelociRaptor 6 × 6.

The second agent in a Ring Jacket suit produces a clipboard, and it is necessary for Dubose and Jergen to sign one document that relinquishes the Range Rover and a second that acknowledges their possession of the VelociRaptor as their new official vehicle.

"On the front seats in the truck," the agent says, "you'll find night-vision gear. You have direct voice communication with the helo crew to coordinate the search."

Jergen makes the mistake of letting Dubose sign the documents first. By the time Jergen signs them, the backwoods boy has the key. Smiling, he says, "I'll drive."

28

Gilberto insisted that he keep a watch on Hendrickson, even though the man was now controlled and sleeping in the kitchen chair to which his ankles were zip-tied.

"I'll sleep when you leave. I couldn't sleep anyway with him here. Even before you had to . . . inject him, the guy was a strange piece of work, miswired. Now he's like a zombie or something. Makes my skin crawl."

Hector and his son had brought Jane's Ford Ex-

plorer Sport from Newport Coast and parked it alongside the funeral home. Gilberto carried her suitcase to
the guest room.

Jane was too tired to shower, but she showered
anyway because she wanted to be on the road as soon
as possible after she woke in the morning. She set the
alarm clock for 3:00 A.M.

She switched off the bedside lamp and stretched
out and put her head on the pillow.

The bedroom lay at the front of the apartment,
overlooking the street. The single window featured
draperies, but she had neglected to draw them shut.
Now she didn't have the energy to cross the room and
close them.

The faintest glow of streetlamps patinated a portion of the ceiling with tarnished silver. In the light of
passing vehicles, the skeletal shadow of an ancient
sycamore, not yet leafed for spring, swooned across
the ceiling and the walls, its direction depending on
whether the traffic was racing east or west, toppling
again and yet again, each time in silence, into darkness.

During the past few months, whether Jane slept fit-
fully or soundly, she had always dreamed, as though
each day was so crammed with events that she needed
twenty-four hours to properly consider the meaning
of them, to let the unconscious mind review them and
either counsel her with scenarios of reassurance or
ring loud its alarms.

Now she dreamed of being on the road, behind the
wheel, traveling through a country of the mind with
illogical geography, snow-draped forests of evergreens

melting into red-rock deserts, cityscapes blurring into lonely shorelines. Nick sat beside her, Travis in the backseat, and sometimes her mother was alive again and sitting at Travis's side, and all was well, until Nick said, *I think to myself, I play to myself, and nobody knows what I say to myself.* When she looked at him, he wasn't Nick any longer; he was Booth Hendrickson with eyes closed, sleeping as she had ordered him to sleep, until he turned his head toward her and opened his eyes, which were as pure white as hard-boiled eggs. *Nobody knows*, he repeated, and he was holding a hypodermic syringe, which he stabbed into her neck.

PART FOUR

Finding Travis

1

S ans headlights, with the dashboard instruments fully dimmed, Radley Dubose drives the big 800-horsepower VelociRaptor into the glowing green night.

Also wearing night-vision goggles, Carter Jergen rides shotgun, faking an enthusiasm for the position that he doesn't feel. Venting his frustration would achieve nothing, except give pleasure to the West Virginia vulgarian.

Although daylight might better facilitate the search, they are able to detect signs of the Land Rover's passage: a length of tire tracks through softer earth; a swath of broken weeds the width of a vehicle; here, parallel lines of crushed grass; and here, chunks of sod torn out where tires briefly spun for purchase.

The problem is that no uninterrupted trail of spoor exists. The signs are scattered along the route the Washingtons have taken, but between them are long stretches of hard and barren land where only a legendary Indian scout of another century might be able to discern evidence of their passage. It is easy to misread a spoor and turn in the wrong direction, vainly seeking another tire track.

Which is where the night-search helicopter comes in handy. With both look-down and look-ahead night-vision cameras that display on the advanced-glass cockpit, the copilot is able to scan for traces of the Land Rover's progress, zoom in as mere goggles can't, and capture even subtle telltales.

In addition to its night-vision cameras, the chopper has the ability to sweep the terrain below for infrared sources, which also display on the cockpit glass. Because the day had been merely warm, because an overcast had formed during the afternoon, and because nightfall is hours behind them, the land has given up most of its stored heat; it does not present a bright, distracting background to the copilot. The heat signatures of coyotes are easy to distinguish from those of deer, and those of deer from those of any human being on foot. If the helicopter gets close enough to scan the Land Rover, the vehicle's heat signature will be a blazing beacon in this otherwise untraveled wilderness.

Both the helo and the VelociRaptor are equipped with special FM receivers and transmitters operating below the standard commercial band occupied by radio stations, tuned to an unused spot on the dial. In addition to his night-vision headgear, Carter Jergen wears an earbud on which he receives guidance from the crew of the helo, and he passes this along to Dubose. His role is important, but it doesn't compensate for being aced out of the driver's seat.

He consoles himself with the knowledge that if they get this right, they will be heroes of the Arcadian revolution forever. They will rise high in the ranks to positions of greater privilege, even if only one of them deserves to be rewarded.

He and Dubose must try to avoid killing the Washingtons, so that the husband and wife can be injected, controlled, and questioned as to everything they know about the Hawk bitch and about who else might have been helping her. Her precious cub, Travis, will become their hostage, and mama bear will be given damn little time to surrender or else be responsible for his suffering.

A hundred yards ahead of them, the helo hovers, identified by an illegal minimum of running lights that register as three small points of green fire, as well as by a pale haze produced by the luminous displays of its night-vision cameras on its cockpit glass. Nothing of its real shape can be perceived, so that the imagination can make of it a levitating sphere or even a saucer-shaped vessel.

If Jergen didn't know what lay before him, he might be persuaded that it is a ship from another world.

The copilot of the helo reports, "Disturbance patterns in an otherwise uniform slope of scree. Could be from a vehicle."

"We'll check it out," Jergen replies.

When he turns to Dubose and passes on the message, the big man's face is green and, in Jergen's judgment, brutish, even a bit Neanderthaloid, and he is reminded of another comic-book figure, the Hulk.

"This light really messes with your head," Dubose says. "I feel as if I've fallen inside the virtual reality of a video game, one of those early ones where the VR wasn't as realistic as it is these days. It's eerie, isn't it? 'Obscure and lonely, haunted by ill angels only.'"

Jergen recognizes the reference to Poe. He is unsettled by the entire character of Dubose's little speech, because it does not seem to be anything someone of his rustic bloodline would say, even after an education at Princeton, if *education* is the right word for what that institution confers on its students.

They speed across a largely barren area, where the scattered clump grass struggles for existence and is so twisted and ragged from winds of other days that whatever damage even the VelociRaptor does to this flora could not be taken as signs of its passage. They come to a short declining slope and a wide swale, beyond which lies a long upward grade. While the helo hovers a hundred feet overhead, Dubose drives down and stops in the shallow trough.

Through the windshield, Jergen can just barely make out where the ghostly rising slope of gravel-stone has been disturbed, although nothing as clearly defined as tire tracks can be seen.

He is grateful to have a reason to take off his night-vision goggles and get out of the VelociRaptor before Dubose might quote another poet and thereby require a complete reassessment of his nature and his mental capacity. The downdraft from the rotary wing of the chopper tosses Jergen's hair and flutters the collar points of the Diesel Black Gold denim jacket against his throat, as if the embroidered scorpions have come alive and crawled up from his chest.

He carries an LED flashlight with which he sweeps the slope ahead. It is a broad expanse of deep scree that time and weather have combed into an even texture, except for a nine- or ten-foot-wide section that appears to have been disturbed by something. A small seismic event would likely have affected the entire face of the slope, so this might in fact be the work of the Land Rover.

Bent forward, studying the mass of small stones, he works his way up the slope with some effort, the scree shifting treacherously underfoot, the rhythmic *whump-whump-whump* of the helo timed like an amplification of his heart's systole. At about the halfway point, something glistens in the beam of the flashlight. A brownish-black glob. He wipes up a bit of it with his forefinger. Studies the stuff. Smells it. Axle grease.

2

The coyotes lost interest in the Land Rover, whidding away into the moonless dark, on the track of some irresistible scent.

In this part of California, it was possible to proceed in a twisting route through contiguous stretches of unincorporated scrubland, protected state wildernesses, national forests, and national monuments, skirting even the smallest population centers, passing under little-traveled county and state roads that bridged the canyons, all the way to the Mexican border, where they could leave the U.S. discreetly either at Tecate or Calexico-Mexicali. Alternately, because the Rover had a spare fuel tank, they could venture overland into southern Arizona.

However, it wasn't Gavin's intention to spend the entire night off-road or to leave California. In consultation with Jane, he and Jessie had developed a plan in anticipation of a day when they might have to go on the run for a while, until this Arcadian conspiracy was blown up, which it would be because it *must* be.

Considering that they were fleeing from a murderous cabal and might be leaving their comfortable life behind forever, he felt surprisingly confident. Not lighthearted. Not full of breezy good cheer. He was buoyed by the kind of sober-minded high spirits that warriors knew after a successful operation, an exhilaration tempered by being well-acquainted with death.

He'd survived numerous near-death moments in Afghanistan, and Jessie had survived two helicopters being shot down and an IED detonating directly under her Jeep. When you miraculously escaped mortal threats often enough, changes occurred in your thinking. For one thing, you came to believe in miracles, although it was better not to *expect* them routinely.

For another thing, you began to wonder if just maybe there was a scheme to things and if perhaps your sorry ass had been saved for a purpose. When

Jane showed up on their doorstep, needing a place in which to hide Travis, Gavin had at once thought, *This is it, the very reason why my sorry ass is still on the planet.* He had looked at Jessica, and her smile had confirmed that she'd arrived at the same conviction. She was the one who had said *yes* by saying, *As long as this boy's here with us, the worst thing that'll happen to him is maybe he'll stub a toe.*

Saying such a thing was tempting fate, but it was the kind of bravado that Jane had needed to hear.

Now the time had come either to make good on that promise or die trying.

The first leg of their journey required them to cross out of Orange County, into San Diego County, far from where they had ridden horses earlier in the day, and pick up State Highway 76 east of Pala. The overland part of the journey was twenty-five miles if you drew a straight line between points, but the rough terrain didn't permit direct travel; in fact, they might have to go as far as fifty miles. And there were stretches of ground over which they could not attain any significant speed, especially because of the need to avoid using headlights. Gavin hoped to reach Highway 76 by midnight, a little more than four hours after setting out.

He expected to be pursued. The only question was how much of a head start they might get. Jessie was certain—Gavin had to agree—there would be an aerial component to the search team. Which meant the pursuer would make faster progress than the pursued.

Consequently, he stopped periodically and switched

off the engine and got out of the Land Rover to listen to the night and scan the land behind them through the NVGs. He needed to guard against the posse abruptly coming upon them without their knowledge.

The third time, when he parked at the head of a long decline, there were the usual desert-insect buzzes and clicks and busy ticks. Also feline cries that might have been a family of bobcats on the hunt. And from a distance . . . the distinctive sound of a helicopter.

He surveyed the night to the northwest, the direction from which they had come. At first, nothing. Just a green dark. Then he identified a three-point constellation in the totally overcast sky, brighter than any stars would have been, each as brilliant as Venus. The constellation rotated. Not stars. A minimal array of aircraft running lights.

They were closer than he expected. He needed to take the Land Rover to lower ground at once and proceed only through valleys and canyons, as deep below the rolling hilltops as he could get, where the engine heat would not register on the helo's look-ahead cameras.

When he got in behind the wheel and started the engine, Jessie asked, "Has the shit hit the fan?"

"Not yet, but they're flingin' it our direction."

Jessie looked over her left shoulder. "Are you belted in back there, cowboy?"

"Belted," Travis assured her. "And the dogs are down like they're supposed to be."

Because of the noise made by the chopper, the pursuing ground unit wouldn't be able to listen for the

Land Rover. Gavin goosed the engine, and they sped down the long slope with stones rattling hard against the undercarriage and quick-settling dust billowing out behind them.

He had to stay as much as possible on sandstone and mudstone and slopes of talus, away from soft soil, avoiding any vegetation that would betray their passage, until he found a place to go to ground. He didn't think he could reach the state route across the county line before they came upon him. His best chance might be to tuck the Rover away somewhere, lie low, and hope that the helo would pass over them, fruitlessly quartering the wilds in search of their human game.

But when you had a vehicle with a hot engine, where did you hide it from an infrared search in a night-cooled landscape as barren as this one?

3

In the kitchen, Gilberto didn't need black coffee or caffeine tablets or lively music to stay awake. In the chair directly across the dinette table from him, Booth Hendrickson was the perfect cure for drowsiness.

Jane had ordered the man to sleep, and he slept, but his sleep was dream-riddled and never restful. Behind his pale lids, his eyes moved ceaselessly, fixing on whatever sights in some dark nightmare kingdom.

His face was not slack, but enlivened by expressions ranging from perplexion to abhorrence to revulsion.

When he wasn't grinding his teeth or chewing his lips, he made soft pathetic sounds or talked in his sleep, his voice haunting the kitchen as if it issued from another dimension.

"Hands and hands and more hands, a thousand hands . . ."

Because he was restrained by zip-ties linking his ankles to the stretcher bar between the back legs of his chair, his hands remained free. As he spoke, they crawled upon the table, nervous, uncertain, this way and that, as if he were seeking something that he feared finding.

"Don't make me, don't make me, don't make me," he pleaded in a whisper.

His respiration grew ragged and then panicky as he gasped for breath and exhaled in gusts, making thin sounds of desperation, as if some creature born of Hell pursued him. It seemed that he must wake himself, but each time the panic subsided and still he slept, sliding into a less urgent state of anxiety.

From time to time, he returned to the subject of eyes. *"Their eyes . . . their eyes . . ."* And later: *"What's that in their eyes? Do you see? Do you see what's in their eyes?"*

Although Gilberto didn't need caffeine, he wanted something to settle his stomach. The Scotch he'd drunk had soured in his gut, and acid refluxed on him. He brought a glass of cold milk to the table and used it to chase a tablet of Pepcid AC before he sat down again.

"Don't leave me in the dark," Hendrickson pleaded

in an urgent and despairing whisper. *"No way is the way you think it is, there's no out, only in."*

For a few minutes the man was silent, though his face appeared no less tortured.

Abruptly he opened his eyes and sat forward in his chair and seemed to look at Gilberto as he whispered, *"Heads inside heads, eyes inside eyes, they're coming now, I know they're coming, no way to keep them out of my eyes, out of my head. They're coming."*

"What can I do for you?" Gilberto asked. "Can I help you somehow?"

But maybe Hendrickson didn't see him after all, hadn't been speaking to him, and was still asleep even when his eyes were open. He closed them and settled back in his chair and grew quiet again.

Gilberto doubted that the milk and acid reducer were going to work.

4

Radley Dubose becomes increasingly agitated as forty minutes pass with no sign of further spoor left by their quarry. He curses the Washingtons, the night, the desert, the helicopter, its pilot, and its copilot. Even though he gets to drive a Veloci-Raptor with all the features that Hennessey's wizards of customization can provide, *a truck costing north of three hundred thousand dollars,* he is not happy. He is possessed by a backwoods urge to whup somebody, anybody.

Carter Jergen is also frustrated, though he would be much less so if he were behind the wheel instead of stuck in the passenger's seat, relaying messages from the helo copilot, who for forty minutes has not had any news worth passing along. It's almost as if the Land Rover has gone airborne.

In the green dark, the helo quarters west to east, east to west, while moving steadily southward. If they don't find something in the next fifteen minutes or so, they'll have to retreat northward through territory already searched, to be sure they haven't missed anything.

This scrub desert is not arid all year long, not in its every contour, especially not here at the end of the rainy season. They arrive at the brink of a deeper canyon than any they have thus far searched. About two hundred feet below, a wide, fast-moving stream, born of snowmelt in the distant mountains and swelled by rain in the foothills, slips over such a smooth course that it appears to flow without cataracts or counterflux. Above the dark-green water spread lighter-green shapes of mature trees that form cloisters in which sections of the stream disappear, and this side of the trees is the still paler green of the rocky canyon floor.

Jergen and Dubose wait in the VelociRaptor at the edge of the canyon and watch as the helicopter slowly quarters more than a mile to the east. Then it moves back toward them, past them, before hovering above the stream at a point at least half a mile to the west of their position.

The copilot reports, "We have a heat source under the tree cover. No clear profile. Diffused heat. Might not be them."

When Jergen repeats this message, Dubose says, "Damn right it's them. Parked in the running water, engine off, hoping the Rover will cool down so the trees can fully screen it."

The canyon wall is without vegetation and not an easy slope, steeper in some places than in others.

When it seems that Dubose is about to angle off the brink and down, Jergen says, "Wait, wait. It's too precipitous here. Go west a little way."

"It's not too precipitous," Dubose says.

"Yes, it is," Jergen insists.

"Don't go fully pussy on me."

This bumpkin's cloddish rudeness offends Jergen. "I've never gone fully pussy in my life."

"Maybe not, but you've got the tendency," says Dubose, and drives off the brink, onto the precipitous slope, along which they descend at such a perilous angle, rollicking over such forbidding terrain, that the night-vision picture, already alien to the eye, becomes a meaningless jumble of leaping shapes in shades of green, as if they are hapless characters in an outer-space movie, rocketing through a meteor storm.

To prove his mettle, Jergen never cries out on the way down, nor does he reach for the grab bar above the door, nor does he raise his feet to brace himself against the dashboard. He relies solely on his harness even though at moments it seems the truck has slipped the bonds of gravity and that he will float out of his seat.

5

VelociRaptor hulking on the deep canyon floor, engine off, both front windows open, and to the port side, silhouettes of trees and then the stream like magma pouring from a wound in the earth, such a scene as a sleeper might imagine after a highly spiced dinner . . . Night air wafting cool into the truck, the chuckle and susurration of fast-moving water, a sweet licorice-like fragrance evidently issuing from some plant along the stream's edge and the fainter limy scent of wet stone, all things green on green with shadows deep . . .

Dubose has parked about three hundred yards from where the helo is hovering and has switched off the engine.

He says, "They know they've been found, so if they were gonna give up, they'd have shown themselves already. We've gotta take the boy alive. But with the other two, we only make our best effort."

"Instructions were all three alive. Inject the Washingtons and interrogate them."

"Thanks for refreshing my memory," Dubose replies with heavy irony. "But these two, they'll be better armed than anyone in your average Quentin Tarantino movie."

"Maybe they will be. On the other hand, with the boy to think about, maybe they won't."

"They're ex-military. They'll have a damn arsenal, and with their training, they won't be pushovers."

"We've been trained, too," Jergen says.

"Law-enforcement training and Army Special Forces training are different worlds. You read this tough bastard's service record? And the bitch lost both legs from the knees down, but still competes in marathons."

"Ten-K runs," Jergen corrects. "Not marathons anymore."

Again with the unnecessary irony, Dubose says, "Oh, that's a whole different story, then. What kind of wimp is the bitch, able to run just ten K without legs?"

"Let's say they *are* carrying big-time."

"We don't have to say it. They *are* carrying."

"If this turns into a firefight, how do we avoid killing the boy, collateral damage?"

"To keep the kid safe, *they* don't want a firefight," Dubose says. "So they'll try to get the drop on us and take our weapons or pull some other cute shit. All I'm saying is, they'll hesitate, and we won't. Blow the shit out of them on sight."

"What if they're using the boy as a shield?"

"Man, to get a degree from Harvard, do they make you minor in cynicism? These aren't the kind of people who use little kids as shields."

"People are never the kind of people you think they are."

"Then there's every reason to blow the shit out of 'em on sight."

They get out of the VelociRaptor and close the doors.

The chopper is hovering high enough above the trees to avoid being an easy target, but it remains stationed over the heat source to guide the ground team and to unnerve the Washingtons with noise.

Jergen and Dubose are armed with belt-carried 9 mm Sig Sauer pistols, but not with rifles, because this is going to be a close-up fight if it is any fight at all.

Thigh-high waterside grass and a variety of trees, which Jergen can't identify in the current light, offer them what cover they will have. The helicopter is an adapted civilian-model medium-twin craft with high-set main and tail rotors, and it produces enough noise to cover any sounds they might make.

The stream is about twelve feet wide. There must be a high concentration of calcium carbonate in the runoff from these hills, because over decades the seasonal rains have laid down a flowstone bed, accounting for the smooth, swift movement of the water, which proves to be about two feet deep when Dubose wades to the farther bank.

Because the night lacks stars and is brightened only by cloud-filtered moonlight, Jergen doesn't expect the darkness to be much deeper under the trees, but it is. Without the NVGs, they would be nearly blind.

Given Gavin Washington's background, there is a possibility that he is equipped with goggles of his own, though they won't be MIL-SPEC Generation 4 gear with eighty-thousand amplification, but rather Generation 1-plus. Hunter and hobbyist models ranging from a few hundred bucks to a couple thousand dollars will not serve Washington nearly as well as their headsets will serve them.

Jergen and Dubose proceed at a matched pace, moving from tree to tree, pistols in a two-hand grip. They are wary of the tall grass and the trees ahead, which offer cover to the Washingtons if they have chosen to get out of their vehicle and establish a forward position in an attempt to set a trap.

This is unlikely. For one thing, they will assume that their body heat will betray them. And chances are they will stay with the boy. They have been counting on the cool water of the stream and the canopy of trees to mask the Rover's heat signature. Now that they realize this ruse didn't work, they won't have had time to plan another.

In retrospect, Dubose's preference for killing the Washingtons on sight in favor of capturing just the boy does not seem to be as ill-considered as Jergen first thought. He certainly doesn't want to die here tonight—or anywhere on any night. Better to act first and decisively. All they really need is the boy. With him, they will have Jane Hawk by the short hairs.

Ahead, the Land Rover comes into view, parked in the middle of the stream, the cooling water flowing over its bumper and around its flanks, glowing with otherworldly light above the water line, as if it is a phantom coach that conveys the spirits of the dead to their reward.

They are now within the perimeter of the helo's downdraft. The trees thrash overhead, spinning off leaves that shudder through the green dark like huge moths, and the tall grasses shiver, and the turbulent air beats shapes into the surface of the stream that was heretofore as smooth as glass.

They're thirty yards from the Land Rover . . . now

twenty . . . fifteen. The windshield is a darker rectangle in the bright green of the vehicle. Beyond the glass there are no warm shapes of people, as though the Rover has been abandoned.

If the Washingtons have foolishly set out on foot with the boy in this forbidding territory, they can't have gotten far. The trees might mask their smaller heat signatures from aerial surveillance, but there will be breaks in the canopy through which they will sooner or later be sighted, and eventually there won't be any trees at all.

Ten yards, and now Jergen and Dubose are in the very eye of the downdraft, where the air is calmer, although the engine roar and the *whump-whump-whump* of the rotary wing are louder than ever.

Perhaps it is only the tidal crash of rhythmic sound resonating in the hollows of Jergen's bones, but suddenly he shudders with the suspicion that they have walked into a trap after all.

6

Gavin was slumped down in the driver's seat. The single lens of the ATN PVS7-3 goggles, which fed a gathered image to both eyes, was aimed through the thick spokes of the steering wheel and just over the top of the dashboard, so that he presented little or no heat profile separate from that of the Rover. From this uncomfortable position, he saw the men appear out of the gloom, one on each side of the stream, pistols at the ready, and he watched them approach through the wind-tossed vegetation.

Travis had put the briefcase full of money and Jessie's blade-runner prosthetics on the backseat, and he had taken refuge on the floor, where the dogs cuddled with him. Jessie was in the cargo area, which the shepherds had occupied previously; she was sitting, propped against the back of the backseat, below window level.

Gavin had switched off the engine when they had first driven into the stream, hoping that the cooling flow and the sheltering trees might blind the chopper to them. When that hadn't worked, he had started the engine again and prepared to make a break for it when the moment was right.

In the roar of the helicopter, the men approaching along the banks of the stream would not be able to hear the Land Rover. They might assume the engine wasn't running, or that the vehicle was abandoned.

When the gunmen drew as close as Gavin dared to let them get before taking action, he shifted the idling vehicle into drive. The pressure of the rushing water prevented the Rover from drifting forward, so that the thugs were not alerted until he popped up in his seat and tramped the accelerator. For an instant, the big tires spun on the flowstone bed of the stream, but then the Land Rover surged forward.

The assassins startled and hesitated for but a moment, which brought the Rover almost even with them before they opened fire. Three muzzle flares,

two on the right. A bullet barked off the roof panel
above the windshield. Another knocked a side mirror
cockeyed. Maybe the third went wide. Even as they
were firing, Gavin gave them a blast of the horn,
which might have further startled them, but which
was primarily meant to be a signal to Jessie.

7

 S eated in the cargo area, back pressed to the
 backseat, Jessie faced the open tailgate, shotgun ready. When the horn blared all but simultaneously with the gunfire and they kept moving, she
could only suppose that Gavin hadn't been hit, thank
God, and that they were already passing the gunmen.

In the immediate echo of the horn, as plumes of
water flared up from the back tires and chopper
downdraft cast a cold spray into the cargo area, Jessie
squeezed off the first of four rounds, unable to see any
target, intending only to make the gunmen drop flat
and hold their fire in the Land Rover's wake, muzzle
flare for an instant glittering in thousands of airborne
droplets, recoil bucking her against the bracing seat-
back. Few things equaled the thundercrack of a
12-gauge to make sober men duck and cover, and by
the time she squeezed off the second, third, and fourth
rounds, the Rover was so far upstream she didn't feel
in danger from their pistol fire.

Ears ringing, half-deaf for the moment, Jessie resorted to the open box of shells between her thighs to slip a round in the breech and three more in the tube magazine.

8

The German shepherds were good dogs, but they were howling now in the backseat, protesting the painful volume of shotgun blasts in such a contained space, and Gavin sympathized, his ears ringing as though he'd been slapped hard up both sides of his head. He shouted to Travis, his voice sounding as if it came from the far end of a culvert. The boy shouted back just loud enough to be heard— he was okay—and Jessie gave a shout-out, too.

The blackish trees beyond the reach of the helo's downdraft stood as still as if petrified to stone in another millennium, and on his left he came to a break in their palisade and swung out of the stream, over the low grassy bank, onto the canyon floor. Fifty yards ahead stood some model of truck he'd never seen before, even though, as he closed on it, he could make out the word FORD in large letters across the grille.

If there had been three men with the truck, one remaining behind, it might be a mistake to stop, but he didn't think there was a third. He didn't see anyone. He braked beside the Ford, threw open his door, and drew his Springfield .45. He emptied the magazine into the two rear tires on the driver's side, blowing out both, a couple rounds ricocheting off the alloy wheels, distorted reflections of the bright green muzzle flashes quivering through the glossy black paint like some aurora borealis in an evil netherworld. He ejected the empty magazine, slapped in a new one, closed his door, holstered the warm pistol, and drove east at high speed.

The gunmen were on foot now and no longer an immediate threat, but the helicopter was giving chase.

Gavin came to a place where the trees relented on both sides of the stream. Beyond the sinuous slide of water, the south wall of the canyon looked lower and less steep than the north wall, offering what appeared to be a clear route to the top. He forded the stream and motored up an incline of grass. The ground was still soft from recent rains and moist below the first couple inches, and he gouged out muddy tracks all the way to the crest.

On the higher ground, the helicopter came at them from the west. It was a civilian helo, large enough to carry six or eight passengers in addition to the crew, if it had not been retrofitted for another purpose. It bore no agency ID that he could see in the drowned light of the NVGs.

Maybe the pilot had been military in an earlier career, but maybe he was just a chopper jockey who had no service training, no war experience. The latter seemed to be the case when he swooped in no more than fifty feet above the Rover, as though to intimidate the driver, which was a hopeless cause.

But even if they weren't ex-military, the pilot and his copilot might be more than just aerial-search specialists assisting a hard-boiled ground crew. If the copilot was a trained sniper—or if a sniper was aboard—that might justify a lower approach in order to take out the vehicle without accidentally killing anyone aboard. No doubt the people trying to find Jane would prefer to interrogate Gavin and Jessie rather than kill them, and at all costs take Travis alive. Or maybe their intent was to spook him with one dangerous feint after another, using the helicopter much as a matador used a red cape to thwart a bull, distracting and delaying him long enough for the ground crew to scale the canyon wall and reengage.

The helo racketed east through the night, looped around to the south, and approached them again.

When he realized the aircraft was coming in as low as before, maybe even lower, as though to skid-kiss the roof of the Land Rover, Gavin braked to a stop. He glanced over his shoulder and saw Jessie scrambling out of the open tailgate. She closed it behind her and crouched at the back of the vehicle.

Ghostly celebrants seemed to spring from graves as the helo passed over the land, billows of dust and chaff shapen into dancers that whirled away into the haunted dark. The blades of the rotary wing carved slabs of air and threw them down to rock the Rover on its tires.

As the chopper passed at reckless altitude, Jessie fired the shotgun three times in quick succession, and then pulled off a fourth round aimed at its tail rotor.

This wasn't a movie, so the aircraft did not burst into flames, as there was no reason that it should. But a knocking noise and the sharp keening of metal parts grinding against each other at high speed suggested that she'd done some damage.

The pilot arced west and south, away from the canyon, and the helo yawed as it gained a little altitude.

Jessie opened the front passenger door and boarded the Rover, and Gavin set out after the helicopter as she slammed her door. He had no intention of giving pursuit for any purpose other than to keep it in sight until he knew whether it was seriously disabled.

Whatever mechanical problem a few loads of point-blank buckshot might have caused, it quickly metastasized into a crisis. The pilot ceased lateral flight and hovered and started to put down, the rotary wing stuttering. When the helo was about forty feet off the ground, its blades locked. Without lift, it dropped hard, snapped a skid, tipped, and came to rest canted to starboard, propped at an angle by wing blades.

Gavin stripped off his night-vision goggles and gave them to Jessie. He switched on the headlights. The pale land and dark scrub seemed to leap at them out of a void, the green world gone, this more familiar world stabilizing under them.

Travis scrambled off the floor, onto the backseat, when Jessie told him to belt up. He tried his best to do so with the dogs half atop him and excitedly licking his hands and face.

Keeping in mind the possibility of gunfire, Gavin drove wide of the downed aircraft. However, the side-wash of the Rover's high beams revealed one man on his knees beside the craft and another in the open cockpit door above, getting ready to jump.

The hills unveiled their contours more readily to headlights than to the amplified moonlight and infra-red of the NVGs. Gavin oriented himself as best he could as Jessie read aloud the compass heading, and then he drove south-southwest through the wildlands faster than he had dared in a green world.

The tremors took him then. Not for long, not violently enough to make his teeth chatter. If there had been a cold sweat on his brow and down his back before this, he didn't realize it until now.

In spite of how practiced Jessie had been in both showdowns, Gavin knew that she was shaken, too, when she said, "Afghanistan used to be half a world away. I liked it better there."

9

Jane Hawk allowed herself far fewer superstitions than did most people, one of which was that long good-byes were more likely to be final good-byes than were short ones. Better to say "until next time" or "see you soon" than to say "good-bye" at any length.

Behind the mortuary, beside her Explorer Sport, in the chilly darkness of 3:30 Sunday morning, Jane said to Gilberto Mendez, "See you soon," and she thanked him, and she told him that she loved him.

It was her conviction, not superstition, that this civilization was built on love—on the love of people for one another and on the love that surpasseth all understanding. In this age of cynicism and snark, genuine emotion was mocked, love derided as sentimentalism. In this world of rapid change, there were few things to which you could hold fast. Wisdom acquired through centuries of experience, traditions, and beloved neighborhoods eroded and washed away, and with them went the people who found solace and meaning in those things, who once would have been part of your life for most of your life. Now a rootless population, believing in nothing but the style and fashion of the moment, produced a culture of surface conformity under which the reality was a loveless realm in which soon everyone would live as a stranger in a strange land. When you loved enough important qualities of a person, then you loved him or her, and you had better say it while time remained.

She loved Gilberto's faithfulness to Carmella, his devotion to his children, his respect for the dignity of the dead and for the eternal nature of their souls, his love of freedom, and his lifelong commitment to the Marine way, to *semper fi.* Therefore, her good-bye consisted of just those eight heartfelt words, "See you soon. Thank you. I love you." She hugged him and kissed him on the cheek.

At 3:31, she was on the road in her SUV that had been rebuilt in Mexico, wearing the chopped-everywhichway *Vogue*-punk black wig and the eye shadow and the blue lipstick and the nose ring that went with the photo on the Elizabeth Bennet driver's license.

In the passenger seat was Booth Hendrickson, still under her control because she had accessed him by saying "Play Manchurian with me," and had not released him with the words *Auf Wiedersehen*. She believed in the efficacy of the control mechanism, even in his case. Nevertheless, for this first leg of the journey, his wrists were bound together with a zip-tie that also looped through his belt, so that he could not lift his hands from his lap.

He wore his suit; but a too-roomy shirt belonging to Gilberto had replaced his custom-tailored shirt from which Jane had earlier cut one arm when preparing him for injection. He wore no tie. Before having his hands encumbered by his belt, he had nervously fingered his buttoned collar and had appeared distressed that his outfit remained incomplete.

Heading east toward San Bernardino, she didn't speak to him, nor he to her. For the first half hour, she welcomed the silence, the time to think about what lay ahead and how best to cope with it. But soon the man's servile obedience to her preference for quiet, his placid expression unchanging mile by mile, and his dead-eyed stare that never wavered from the dark road ahead . . . all that became too eerie for her to countenance.

Since she still had nothing to say to him, she opted for music. She wanted no trackable GPS in any car she acquired, but she always needed a vast store of music, which not unpleasantly reminded her of the life she might have lived if her father had not murdered her mother so many years ago.

In recent days, she had found herself listening more often to Mozart's Piano Concerto No. 3 in A Major, K. 488, in part because the concerto's opening movement inspired a soaring optimism that was much needed in her current circumstances.

Within this exceptional concerto, however, was a melancholy movement so piercing, so expressive of the deepest sorrow, that she couldn't hear it without thinking about Nick and her mother. And about Nathan Silverman, who had once been her boss at the FBI and whom she had spared from a life of Arcadian slavery by an act of loving violence that would weigh upon her forever. This sequence in K. 488 didn't depress her, but balanced the optimism of the opening movement and made her feel complete of heart and clear of mind.

As that movement was nearing an end, Hendrickson violated her instruction to remain silent, but only to say, "It's so beautiful."

"Yes."

"What is it?"

She told him.

"I was allowed no time for music."

She considered that statement for a moment before she said, "You'll have it now, all the way to Tahoe, one music or another."

He said only, "Thank you," gazing at the highway with the stony expression of a sphinx whose stare was fixed on the rim of eternity.

When the slow movement of K. 488 passed, Jane was relieved to hear again more thrilling strains of dauntless optimism.

10

North on U.S. Highway 395, through the western portion of the Mojave, a vast blackness all around, the clouds of the coast having surrendered the sky to stars, the moon far down . . . Later, dawn frosting the heavens with light, first a sweet rose-pink at the horizon, a paler pink farther up, and a swath of buttercream before all goes blue for the day . . . Lonely playas of salt flats and mud flats and sand flats, forbidding dark mountains in the distance . . .

There was Mozart again, *Eine kleine Nachtmusik*, when Jane at last brought up the subject that Hendrickson had not wanted to talk about until he was under her control. He had asked that, after he'd spoken of it, she would order him to forget that he had told her about this thing that apparently mortified him. " 'I think to myself, I play to myself, and nobody knows what I say to myself.' What did you mean by that, Booth?"

His smile was pained, but at least it counted as a smile. He spoke with a note of nostalgic fondness that didn't displace his melancholy, staring at the highway but perhaps seeing into the past. "'So—here I am in the dark alone, there's nobody here to see. I think to myself, I play to myself, and nobody knows what I say to myself.' It's from a book. Poems. A little book of poems."

"What book?"

"*Now We Are Six* by A. A. Milne. But I was just five."

After a moment of consideration, Jane said, "The author of *Winnie-the-Pooh*. What does that mean to you?"

"The books? They're everything. They mean everything to me."

"You could read at five?"

"She pushes me to read. She pushes, pushes, *pushes*."

"Your mother."

"Lessons all day, every day." His brow pleated and his eyes narrowed and his voice hardened. "*Focus, boy. Focus, if you know what's good for you, boy. Focus, focus, focus, you lazy little bastard.*"

She waited until his quickened breathing quieted. "So you read the book of poems when you were five."

"I'm given the set. All four Milne books. To encourage me."

"Encourage you to read."

"To read more, faster, better. To understand what's wrong."

"Wrong with what?"

"With everyone in the story. Like the bear. He's stupid and lazy. He's not focused, and he's kind."

"It's wrong to be kind?"

"He's gentle and kind. Kindness is weakness. The strong own the world. The strong use the weak. They piss on the weak. They *should* piss on them. It's what the weak deserve." His face contorted with contempt, and his voice became harsh again. *"Is that what you want, boy? Do you want to be used and pissed on all your miserable life?"*

Out in the wasteland, Deadmans Dry Lake and Lost Dry Lake and Owl Dry Lake, the Lava Mountains ahead, Death Valley at a distance in the east . . .

Passing through the desert, Jane felt as if something of the desert were passing into her. "But what do those lines of poetry mean to you? Those lines in particular."

"Mother says the only worthwhile life is a regimented life. Make a schedule. Stick to it. It's a very bad boy who can't stick to it. No day is a good day if it isn't regimented."

Jane waited, but after a silence said, "And so?"

"And so, fifteen minutes for breakfast. Fifteen for lunch. Half an hour for dinner. To bed at eight. Up at five. Lights out at eight. Out, out, *out*. Only two lamps in the room. She takes the light bulbs. Takes them with her. Takes them after I'm put to bed."

" 'So here I am in the dark alone . . .' "

He nodded. " 'There's nobody here to see.' The poem is 'In the Dark.' So I take a book to the window. Sometimes there's moonlight. Or landscape lights from outside. I can see the page if I turn it just so. For an hour or two, until I get sleepy, I can think what I want. Play what I want. My time. In all the day, it's my own time."

Jane said, "If she opened your bedroom door and found you not asleep but reading by moonlight—what then?"

"So then . . . the deeper darkness."

"And what was that?"

"At first, it's being made naked. And being spanked. Spanked on my . . . boy thing. Spanked hard so it hurts to pee. *You're not going to be like your father, boy, not like that worthless piece of shit.* So I'm spanked and put in the box to sleep the rest of the night."

"'The box'? What box?"

"A wood box. It has a locking lid. A box the size of the boy. With a folded blanket to lie on. Holes to let air in. But no light. No light 'cause the box is in a closet with no windows."

"Dear God," she said.

"You don't need a god if Mother loves you. Mother is all you need. Mother punishes out of love. To teach what's true and right."

In the arid landscape, geologic formations like crude timeworn temples by gods better left unworshipped, giant rocks graven with pictographs by tribes known and by others too ancient to have names other than those that anthropologists have chosen to give them . . .

"How often were you locked in a box?"

"Two nights a week. Or three. So then I start sleeping early and getting up at like two in the morning. After she's sleeping."

"Then you could read by moonlight."

"Yes. And not be caught."

"You said, at first it was being made naked and spanked and put in the box. And later it was . . . ?"

"Worse. Later, worse. Later, it's the crooked stair-case."

Previously, he told her and Gilberto all about the crooked staircase. Soon they will descend it together.

11

In the last of the night, Gavin had stopped one sage-covered hill away from Highway 76. While boy and dogs lay in a slumberous pile on the backseat, while Jessie held a light for Gavin, while unseen canyon wrens, waking early, whistled sweetly in anticipation of the dawn, he took the license plates off the Land Rover and replaced them with plates that Jane had given him weeks earlier.

She had also provided registration papers and a driver's license in the name of Orlando Gibbons, as well as a license for Jessica in the name of Elizabeth Haffner, obtained from her source for forgeries in Reseda. Those documents would pass the scrutiny of any cop who ran them through the DMV records.

They needed to repaint the Rover, make it the blue that was stipulated on the registration. But they were prepared to do that when they reached their destination.

Likewise, Gavin and Jessie would need to alter some things about their appearance to match the photoshopped pictures used for the forgeries.

At the moment, however, it was most important to strip the Rover of the original plates—which might already be on the National Crime Information Center website—before traveling on paved roads once more. They couldn't risk their old plates being automatically scanned by government vehicles, because those scans would soon thereafter be banked in the NSA archives, allowing them to be found and tracked at least to the general vicinity of the one safehold they had prepared for such an emergency as this.

Using a collapsible spade from a kit of basic tools that they kept in the Rover, Gavin dug a hole and dropped the original license plates into it. He covered them with earth and tamped it down and scuffed the burial place with his boots.

He examined his work in the beam of Jessie's flashlight. It looked fine. No one was likely to wander onto precisely this square yard of remote wildland. If searchers chanced by, they would never notice the telltales of this small excavation, and even if they *did* notice and dug up the plates, their pursuit of Travis would in no way be furthered by that discovery.

Nevertheless, Gavin tore off a few stems of sage and used the foliage to brush away anything that looked like a boot impression.

In the backwash of the flashlight, Jessie smiled. "You really love him, don't you?"

"Woman, I love you, I love him, I love the dogs, I love me, I love life, and I *hate* the people who think we're just part of the great unwashed who need to be taught some manners."

"Give me a kiss," she said.

"What, here?"

"If it's too public for you, I'll turn out the light."
Which she did.

He kissed her, and she kissed back, and he said,
"I've been wondering how Elizabeth Haffner kisses.
She's got the mojo."

"Mmmm. So does Orlando Gibbons."

As dawn broke, with the boy snoring and the dogs
whimpering in their dreams of rabbit chasing, Gavin
drove over one last rugged hill and up a slope onto a
lonely stretch of Highway 76. He switched on the
headlights again and headed southeast toward Lake
Henshaw and then Borrego Valley, which was surrounded by Anza-Borrego Desert State Park, there to
take refuge with one who called himself "a walking
nutbar."

12

And in the vast wasteland were bones, those
of wild burros and of coyotes that had
strayed too far from hospitable terrain, bleached to
the white of salt and pitted by weather. Also the
centuries-old bones of men and women in unmarked
ancient graves or massed in as yet undiscovered caves
where barbaric slaughter had occurred, and as previously in such caves, the bones of children, too, with
caved-in skulls . . .

Behind the wheel of the Explorer Sport, Jane said, "Something else I remember you saying. 'Now is it true, or is it not—'"

Hendrickson finished the line: "'—that what is which and which is what.'"

"Is that also Milne?"

"The first *Winnie* book. A poem called 'Lines Written by a Bear of Very Little Brain.'"

"It means something special to you?"

He stared at the ribbon of highway, which seemed to pull them along with it as it was raveled onto some distant spool.

After a minute, he said, "'What is which, but which is what. Those are these, but these are those. Who is what, but what is who.' *That's the way the world is, you weak, ignorant boy. People aren't ever who they seem to be, and nothing they say means what it seems to mean. Nothing is only what it is. If you want to survive, you pathetic little shit, you damn well better understand, you better learn the need to be strong like me, learn to crush anyone who gets in your way. Don't be like your worthless dick of a father. Go down the hole and learn, boy. Down the hole you go. Down the hole.*"

He sat trembling, sheathed in sweat.

To the east, the Naval Weapons Station at China Lake, and to the west, the beginning of the Inyo National Forest and rising ranks of piñon pines . . .

High overhead an unusually large flock of common ravens with wingspans over four feet glided without the need to oar the air. Jane was reminded of an Indian legend that told of the ravens that had pulled the first light of the world into the sky with their beaks. It was said that one day they would appear in great numbers long before sunset and pull into the world the final and everlasting darkness. This seemed as if it might be the day for that, but the only blackness in the blue was the flock itself, which winged onward, each member an indecipherable cryptograph sent into flight by a creation that teased with meaning but held tightly its secrets.

She said, "Booth, when I snap my fingers, you will forget we ever had a conversation about Milne and the Pooh books. You will forget my questions and what you said in answer to them. The most recent thing we spoke about was Mozart. Do you understand?"

"Yes."

She took one hand from the wheel and snapped her fingers.

Although time would pass before his perspiration dried, his tremors ceased. The anxiety faded from his face. He relaxed in the passenger seat, staring straight ahead, as though his mind traveled the byways of a daydream. Jane couldn't imagine what phantasms and contrivances his reverie might contain, but she suspected that it was of such a character that the ravens of the everlasting night were a part of it and that in the shadows of its twisting streets, there would be a maternal figure who had programmed him long before the nanomachine control mechanism had been invented.

13

The small town of Borrego Springs, in the Borrego Valley, in San Diego County, surrounded by six hundred thousand acres of the Anza-Borrego Desert State Park, was not one of the top-twenty tourist attractions in California. Most of those who vacationed there were campers, and even those who stayed in the town's motels and motor inns were drawn by activities related to the desert.

A week from now, perhaps sooner, the largest crowd of the year would arrive to witness the spring flowering of the desert, when thousands of acres blazed with intricate configurations of blooming annuals: red poppies, zinnia in many hues, deep-purple gentians, and a rich variety of wildflowers that transformed the stark meadows and spread into the distance like some immense random-pattern Persian carpet woven by artisans in a state of euphoria.

Gavin and Jessie's destination wasn't within the town limits, but farther down-valley, off County Road S22. Two unpaved ruts with a stubble of dead weeds between them served as a driveway to the five-acre property. The single-story pale-blue stucco house, in need of paint, stood in a grove of ragged queen palms, under a white metal roof, surrounded by a yard of pea gravel and specimen cacti. Cement-block steps led to a front porch barren of furniture.

Cornell Jasperson, owner of the property, didn't

live in the house. No one lived there, though it was fully furnished.

Cornell's residence was a hundred yards behind the house, in a subterranean structure with thick steel-reinforced concrete walls and ceiling, which he'd designed and built without obtaining permits—perhaps by greasing a lot of palms; he would not say—and by using his connections to import Philippine workers who'd lived in trailers on-site, never went into town, and spoke only Tagalog.

The structure was buried under four feet of earth and beyond detection, known only to Cornell, Gavin, and twelve newly rich Philippine workers who had returned home years earlier, telling stories prepared for them, stories regarding what it was like to spend a year working twelve-hour days in Utah, helping to build a mansion for a wealthy eccentric named John Beresford Tipton.

Of connections, Cornell had many, the least powerful being his cousin, his mother's sister's son, Gavin Washington. Born out of wedlock, Cornell had never known his father. His mother, Shamira, had been a drug addict and sometimes prostitute who named him after the man who, by her best judgment, was her co-conceiver. Shamira and her family disowned each other when she was sixteen; she died of a drug overdose twenty years later, when Cornell was just eighteen. No one in the family even knew of his existence. By the time he was twenty-four, from the proceeds of ten apps of his creation, he had been worth more than three hundred million dollars.

The rapid accumulation of wealth, in his words,

"scared the bejesus" out of him. By his reckoning, something was out of whack when "a walking nutbar like me can go from a net worth of ten bucks to three hundred million in four years." His success had convinced him that current society was "a mouse of cards," and that he needed to "bunker down and ride out the coming Apocageddon."

Cornell's description of himself as a nutbar was too harsh by far. He had been diagnosed variously as suffering from Asperger's disorder and different degrees of autism, among other things, and some people whose education came from movies called him an idiot savant, though his IQ was exceptional. It could be said with certainty only that Cornell was eccentric but most likely harmless.

Gavin drove around the house, following the ruts that led past the yard of pea gravel and ended in a turnaround in front of a barn standing between the house and the undetectable bunker that was buried under four feet of earth.

The barn looked as though it might collapse if sneezed on. Sun, wind, and rain had weathered the unpainted wood into a palette of grays. The structure's north and south walls were concave, and the whole thing canted to the west under a rust-streaked metal roof.

"Does he have horses?" Travis asked from the backseat.

"No," Gavin said. "He wouldn't know what to do with a horse."

"Does he have dogs?"

"No. He wouldn't trust himself to take care of one properly."

"Does he have chickens?" Jessie asked mischievously, as if likewise possessed by the curiosity of a five-year-old. "Does he have pigs and sheep?"

Gavin pinched Jessie's earlobe affectionately and said to Travis, "He lives here all by himself. No animals, no other people."

"That's sad," the boy said.

"Not as far as Cornell's concerned. This is exactly the way he wants things."

Although Cornell had no one after his mother died, he'd made no effort to be taken into the fold of his family. Instead, years later, when he was wealthy, he quietly researched his relatives and chose one of them, Gavin, to whom he felt comfortable reaching out.

Even though the two of them lived but a couple hours from each other, and though Cornell had once suggested that he'd settled here for just that reason, Gavin was welcome to visit no more than once a month.

He didn't know why Cornell favored him and no other. If he bluntly asked why, he wouldn't get an answer. He might even be put on the not-welcome list for his temerity. The only way that Cornell talked about personal matters was at his election and indirectly.

Gavin put down the windows and switched off the engine and said, "I'll go in alone and have a little chat with him, see if he wants to say hello."

"Does he have cows?" Jessie asked.

From the backseat, Travis said, "Cows would be cool."

Gavin sighed. "The depth of my patience amazes me."

He got out of the Land Rover and went to the man-size door in the barn, which was adjacent to the larger double doors that would have admitted a tractor pulling a hay wagon if they had still functioned. He didn't bother trying the door or knocking. Cornell was alerted electronically the moment any vehicle drove onto his property. And concealed in the knotholes of the weather-grayed siding were cameras by which he was even now studying his visitor, assuming he was here rather than in his bunker.

Although the door appeared flimsy, with corroded hinges and a simple gravity latch, it was solid and equipped with an electronic lock that Cornell could engage or release from a control panel in the main room. A buzz, a clunk, and the door swung open.

Gavin stepped into a five-foot-square unfurnished vestibule with white walls. Directly ahead, a metal door. Above the door, a camera.

The outer door closed. The inner one opened. He stepped into the main room, and the second door swung shut behind him.

The truth of the building was not the dilapidated barn that enclosed it like a shell. The one and only room, other than the vestibule and a small water closet, was this forty-foot-square space with a twelve-foot ceiling. The barn was anchored to this solidly constructed building that stood within it.

Here, Cornell passed most days, retreating at night to the bunker, which Gavin had never seen, and to which this place was connected by a hidden underground passageway.

Bookshelves entirely lined three walls and part of the fourth, almost thirteen hundred linear feet of shelving. There didn't appear to be room left for a single new volume.

Along the portion of the fourth wall not devoted to books, there were the door through which Gavin had entered and the door to the water closet, as well as a kitchenette with cupboard, counter space, a double sink, two big refrigerators, two microwaves, and an oven.

On the concrete floor were four area carpets on which stood an amazing variety of chairs and recliners, no two pieces of the same style or period, in configurations that made sense only to Cornell. Each seating option was served by a matching footstool and a side table with either a lamp or a floor lamp. The light filtered through either stained glass or blown glass, or colored-and-cut crystal, or pleated silk, or treated parchment. Every lamp glowed, so Cornell was able to move, at any moment, from one chair to another and continue reading without interruption. The many lamps cast mostly soft pools of amber or rose light, but also two blue pools and two green, in a large room that remained shadowed in many places.

Although there was nothing in this windowless space that Gavin had not seen elsewhere and often, the effect was otherworldly, as if this were not a building, but instead a capsule untethered from the known world, adrift in time, where the readers of these books were hobbits or creatures equally quaint. For all its strangeness, the big room was cozy, welcoming, even as it was magical and richly bejeweled by the lamps.

The one and only reader who ever placed a bookmark between any two of these millions of pages looked entirely human, although his appearance had changed since Gavin's most recent visit. Cornell Jasperson—six foot nine, more than half a foot taller than his cousin—stood beside a wingback armchair in a circle of four mismatched armchairs that faced one another.

Milk-chocolate brown rather than black, he was a long-boned knob-jointed scarecrow with enormous hands, whose body suggested menace and a knowledge of violence that qualified him for a role in movies that featured lonely places where the silence of the night was broken by the roar of a chainsaw. His face seemed misplaced on that body: round and smooth and sweet, with dark eyes that radiated intelligence and kindness, a countenance that might have gotten him cast to play Jesus. All of that was Cornell as Gavin had long known him; but never before had the man's head been as smooth and hairless as an egg.

Gavin stopped three feet from his kin and neither attempted to hug him nor offered to shake hands. Cornell could tolerate being touched, but the experience always took a toll on him.

Years earlier, to avoid a lifelong need to see a dentist and be touched by one, Cornell had gone through two lengthy appointments with an understanding periodontist, in the first of which, under anesthesia, he had all his teeth pulled and titanium posts embedded in his jawbones. After a few months of healing, during a subsequent appointment, his new teeth were installed permanently over the titanium posts. Good-bye decay, good-bye gum disease, good-bye regular teeth cleaning.

"What happened to the dreadlocks?" Gavin asked now.

Cornell's voice matched his face, not his body. "In a book I was reading, there was a mention of Mr. Bob Marley being dead."

"He's been dead a long time."

"I didn't know. Convey my condolences to the family, please and thank you. So I would wake up in the middle of the night and think of Mr. Bob Marley lying in a coffin, and it felt like I was wearing a dead man's hair. So I shaved it off. Does that sound odd to you?"

"Yes, it does," Gavin said.

Cornell nodded. "I thought it would."

"You didn't grow the dreadlocks because of Bob Marley."

"No, that's right, I didn't."

"So you could have kept them."

"No, not once I knew he was dead."

Cornell had heard only one Bob Marley song and had been badly affected by it. Reggae made him feel as if ants were crawling over every square inch of his body. He listened to orchestral pieces, preferably with a lot of strings, but mostly to "Mr. Paul Simon, whose voice sounds like it belongs to a friend I've always known."

"Remember I told you the day might come when

Jessie and I needed to stay for some time in the little blue house out there?"

"And I said okay, sure, no skin off my rose."

"You did, and I'm grateful for that."

Gavin never knew if his cousin's occasional malapropisms were unintentional or for some reason amused him. Maybe he meant to say *nose* and it just came out *rose*. Though there was a twinkle in his eye that suggested he was playing some sly game. Whatever the case, Gavin never corrected him.

"Well, it's that time, Cornell, and I need to explain a little, so you'll have some idea what you're getting into."

"Can we sit down to talk, please and thank you?"

"Of course."

Patting the back of the chair beside which he stood, Cornell said, "This is my chair right now." He indicated the other three armchairs in the circle. "You can sit in any of those, and if you can't decide, I can pick one for you."

"I'll take the leather club chair."

"That's a good one. That's a fine chair."

As he folded into the wingback, Cornell seemed to have extra knee and elbow joints. He interlaced his fingers and propped his hands on his stomach and smiled. "So is it the end of all things come 'round at last, like I told you it would?"

"Not quite," Gavin said.

14

Because they are busy on one assignment after another in California, Nevada, and Arizona, Carter Jergen and Radley Dubose live for the most part in hotels. They are highly valued by their Arcadian superiors. They are technically if not actually agents of the National Security Agency, Homeland Security, the FBI, the CIA, and the Environmental Protection Agency, collecting five salaries and accumulating five pensions, with SPECIAL STATUS emblazoned across the top of their various photo IDs. Because of that special status and the fact that their expenses are divided among five agencies—considering also that a cleverly jiggled accounting program channels 30 percent of their combined expenditures onto the books of the Department of Education and the Department of Energy, under the heading OFFICE SUPPLIES—they can be confident that the government will pay for transportation, accommodations, dining, and incidentals of the highest quality.

During the Shukla operation and one that came before it, and now that the Washington matter has been assigned to them, they have two ocean-view rooms at the Ritz-Carlton Laguna Niguel, which isn't in Laguna Niguel, as its name would imply, but in Dana Point. Laguna Niguel just sounds classier.

After the fiasco in the desert, Jergen and Dubose had

been airlifted out to Capistrano Beach and driven from there to the hotel. They had gone to bed at 3:30 A.M.

Exhausted, Jergen intends to sleep at least until noon. His room phone rings at a quarter past seven. When he doesn't answer it, the smartphone in the charger on the nightstand rings. When he fails to answer that, his room phone rings again—and he ignores it.

He has almost drifted back into a dream when the room's ceiling light comes on and Radley Dubose says, "I know you Boston Brahmins need your beauty sleep, but you're already pretty-boy enough. Get your ass in gear."

Jergen sits up in bed. "How the hell did you get in here?"

"Are you serious? Have you forgotten who we are and what we do? Come on, partner. Every hour we delay, the colder the trail gets."

"There is no trail."

"There's always one. We get the Washingtons and the kid, or we have a black mark by our names in the big book of the revolution."

"I haven't showered yet."

"You have five minutes."

"I can't shower in five minutes."

"Then I'll carry you into the bathroom, turn on the water, and soap you down myself."

Throwing back the covers, getting out of bed, Jergen says, "You're just asshole enough to do it."

"I'm more than asshole enough. Hey, fancy pajamas."

"Stuff a sock in it."

"Four minutes," says Dubose.

15

I n the club chair, enveloped by rose-colored light, Gavin noticed a hardcover copy of *Black Orchids*, a Nero Wolfe mystery by Rex Stout. There seemed to be a different Nero Wolfe novel on each table in the circle of armchairs, each with a bookmark inserted one place or another.

Seeing his cousin's interest, Cornell said, "I recently read the works of the philosopher Immanuel Kant. I needed relief. Have you read the Nero Wolfe mysteries?"

"I've not had the chance, I'm afraid," Gavin said.

"I've read all the Nero Wolfes before," said Cornell, "but they bear rereading. Immanuel Kant—not so much."

Having made his fortune and been terrified by the size of it and the ease with which it had been earned, being himself disengaged from life as most people knew it, Cornell had decided to spend his remaining years—whether or not the world ended—reading about life as others had written of it.

"Do you still avoid the news?" Gavin asked.

"No newspaper, no magazines, no radio. The one TV, and I only turn it on for a minute every day, just to see if transmissions are still occurring. If they are, the end times have not arrived—though what little glimpses I get of the current programs assure me that my prediction of societal collapse is correct. I'm prepared to wait out thirty months of barbarism between civilizations."

Like the small blue house at the front of the property, the big room inside the barn and the underground bunker were connected to the public power supply. If society collapsed as Cornell anticipated, he could switch to a generator housed in a subterranean vault and powered by propane drawn from an immense tank buried nearby. According to his calculations, there was enough propane to operate the bunker and the barn for fourteen months, because both were so well insulated that they needed little heating or cooling; if he retreated to the bunker and didn't use the barn room, he could ride out a crisis lasting thirty months.

"I estimate," he said, as he'd said before, "there's a forty-six percent chance a new society will arise from the disintegration of the current one. But if after thirty months the public utilities aren't operative, they won't be restored in my lifetime, if ever."

"Then what?" Gavin asked, as he had asked before.

"Then the inevitable," said Cornell, as he always said. He smiled. "So you're coming to stay in my little blue house."

"You need to understand the risk of taking us in."

"The coming collapse is the ultimate risk."

"Nevertheless, you need to know a few things. Jessie and I did a favor for a friend who's wanted by the FBI."

"A criminal?"

"A righteous fugitive. She—"

Cornell raised one hand to stop Gavin. "Give me a

thumbnail version, please and thank you. After the Nero Wolfe stories, I want to read everything written by Mr. Henry James. I liked *The Turn of the Screw*—very turny, very screwy—and he was a busy, busy author. He published more than a hundred twenty books in his lifetime, far more than you."

"Thumbnail, then, it is," Gavin said. "Our friend is wanted by the FBI and some really bad people. She's a widow—"

"Convey my condolences, please and thank you."

"I will," Gavin promised. "Anyway, she's afraid the people who want to kill her would also kill her son. So she hid him with us."

"I would feel safe to be hidden with you," Cornell said, "but I feel even safer in my bunker, no offense intended."

"None taken. Anyway, the worst happened, and some people came after us, and last night we got out of the house just in time, went overland, and lost them. Now we've got to lie low."

"I know about lying low. Sometimes people have to lie low in the Nero Wolfe stories, also in those of Mr. Dashiell Hammett and even in those of Mr. Charles Dickens. I think in particular of the escaped prisoner, Magwitch, at the beginning of *Great Expectations*."

Gavin leaned forward in his chair. "This is real life now, Cornell. Real bad people, a real threat, not a story by Dickens or Dashiell Hammett."

"There's no meaningful difference, cousin. I think Plato might agree. Except he's dead. My condolences. When I return to reading fiction, which I hope to do in just a minute or two—please and thank you—it *is* my real life. Now you stay in my little blue house and lie low and don't worry about me."

He accordioned up from his chair, all the pleats of his long legs and arms opening out, drawing in a deep breath in the rising, as if he might issue a squeeze-box sound. But he only sighed and said, "You already have the key to the house."

"Yes. Thank you, Cornell."

"Say no more. Say no more." He put his large hands over his ears. "Say no more."

16

They take breakfast in the hotel coffee shop, which is bright and airy and elegantly appointed. The U-shaped booth is large enough for six, and Dubose sits at the deepest point of it, his back to the wall, so that no one—not even the waitress—can see the screen of his laptop.

The computer *on the table* offends Carter Jergen, but he doesn't complain. If he speaks up every time Dubose does something uncouth or vulgar, he will have laryngitis by noon.

As he enjoys a bowl of mixed berries in clotted cream with brown sugar, Jergen considers the mystery, not for the first time, of why his and Dubose's partnership is so successful. They rarely experience a debacle like that of the previous night. Regardless of the intensity or duration of his deliberations on this issue, Jergen arrives always at the same conclusion, as he does now again: The very fact that he and Dubose have little in common is a considerable advantage. Just as opposites attract each other into marriage, so opposites when paired as agents, with a license to kill and worse, can each bring a unique perspective to any case.

The problem with this explanation is that from it one must infer that, separately, each of them is in some sense an incomplete or at least unfinished person. Carter Jergen believes himself to be complete, finished, as well rounded as a droplet of water floating in a zero-gravity environment. In fact, he *knows* that he is both complete and complex. Yet no other explanation occurs to him. . . .

Using the rootkits that the NSA has secretly installed in the computer networks of the major banks with which Gavin and Jessica Washington have credit cards, Dubose checks to see if they have charged anything since the unfortunate episode the previous night. They're probably too smart to make such an error, but sometimes bright and savvy people do dumb things.

While he works on the laptop, Radley Dubose eats bacon with his fingers. He smacks his lips as if the fullest enjoyment of the meat requires loud gustatory noises. Occasionally, he pauses between one slice of bacon and the next to suck on the thumb and forefinger with which he held the meat to ensure that no dab of grease will escape his consumption.

Jergen finds some consolation that Dubose uses a fork to eat his cheese omelet rather than resorting again to his fingers or putting his face right down in the food.

"They haven't used a credit card," Dubose says. "Let's see if the plates on the Rover were scanned anywhere since last night."

The manner in which Dubose eats is no more mortifying than the fact that, in addition to the bacon that comes with his omelet, he has requested four additional orders, twelve slices, which have been served in an obscene pile on a separate plate. When the waitress put down that mess of pork fat, she made some comment to the effect that he must be hungry, whereupon the inimitable West Virginian winked at her lasciviously and said, "Darlin', I'm a man of voracious appetites."

As if the Ritz-Carlton was the most natural place in the world to respond to an attractive woman with vulgarity. The *Ritz-Carlton*!

Working in the NSA's archives of scanned plates, Dubose sets up time parameters and enters the license number of the Land Rover, but no police car or other government vehicle equipped with 360-degree plate-scanning capability has transmitted those tags in the past twelve hours.

Confounded, the big man leans back in the booth, his forehead corrugating as he contemplates his next step, and of course he must have another strip of bacon to grease the wheels of his mind.

As Jergen listens to the lip smacking, he considers commenting to the effect that, until this moment, he hasn't realized Dubose indulges in cannibalism.

But there's no point in getting snarky. Dubose is incapable of embarrassment. Besides, he'll only come back with some retort about Boston Brahmins or prep school or Harvard or the Hasty Pudding Club that he imagines to be witty.

Dubose says, "We know from the car she had to abandon in Texas, Hawk has a sophisticated source for forged plates. They show up as a legitimate registration in state files."

Having finished his berries, Carter Jergen blots his lips with the satisfyingly substantial cloth napkin. Before picking up his cup of tea, he says, "Perhaps she gave the Washingtons a set of plates, complete with registration papers in another name, so if they ever had to go on the run, they could swap them out for the real plates."

"Great minds think alike," Dubose says, "and so do yours and mine."

"But if we don't have those plate numbers or the phony name in which she registered the Land Rover, we're still nowhere."

The big man picks up two slices of bacon, folds the double thickness into his mouth in one wad, and works his brute jaws as though he is enjoying a chaw of tobacco.

After he swallows, he says, "Maybe I have an idea."

17

Near Coso Junction, Jane pulled off U.S. Highway 395 and into a rest area with public lavatories. Hers was the only vehicle in the lot.

The naked blue sky at the start of their journey had taken on a more modest aspect as they'd come north. Now it was a monkish gray to every horizon, looming low, with some last spell of winter weather pending.

As if the flock she'd seen earlier had reckoned her route and come ahead to wait for her, nine ravens perched at regular intervals on a power line.

She cut the zip-ties off Booth Hendrickson and let him use the men's room. She went with him and waited while he washed his hands, and she walked him back to the Explorer. She zip-tied him again, wrist to wrist and through the belt, as before.

Sufficiently confident of her control, she left him alone in the SUV. As she walked to the women's facilities, the nine ravens sat solemn and portentous on the wire, gazing down at her, working their long, gray beaks in a mute chorus.

When she returned, Hendrickson sat exactly as she had left him, as docile as a good dog but not as engaged. He spoke only if spoken to and seemed to be slowly drifting away into an internal landscape from which he might at some point fail to return. She was convinced that his condition had far less to do with a malfunctioning control mechanism than with a psychological withdrawal or disintegration.

They continued through the northwest corner of the Mojave, passing out of it at Owens Lake. By the time they reached Lone Pine, where she stopped for fuel and food, they were at an elevation of 3,700 feet and headed toward a different world, with the Sierra Nevada to the west and the Inyo National Forest on both sides.

At a diner, she bought takeout—four cheeseburgers and two Diet Cokes. Hendrickson didn't want any food, but she cut his zip-ties again and ordered him to eat, and so he did.

The day had grown colder. She kept the engine running while they ate, for heat and music. Arthur Rubinstein playing Beethoven: Sonata No. 21 in C Major, op. 53.

This time, she didn't secure his hands. He was drained of all potential for independent action and seemed to be a shell of a man.

They returned to the highway with Beethoven's Sonata No. 18 in E-flat Major, op. 31, no. 3, and as they continued north, she found herself wanting only Rubinstein, arguably the greatest pianist who ever lived. It was said that the composer Franz Liszt might have been greater, although he lived before recordings could be made.

She understood why only Rubinstein would suit her now. Her destination was a place of such evil that perhaps even if she came back alive, she would come back changed, in some way diminished by the experience. Although she was a pianist of much less talent than Rubinstein, she was able to hear the pure joy with which he played, to *feel* the joy with which he embraced life, and she wanted to have as much of his music as she could in these last few hours before Tahoe, while she could still be so profoundly moved by it.

As the highway led steadily into higher elevations, the sky descended, and the sun receded so that its position could not be discerned behind the uniform gray shroud. A breeze rose, harrying shapes of dust and chaff across the road, stitching the air with dead pine needles.

An hour past Lone Pine, as they were approaching Bishop, an electronic highway sign advised that, due to weather conditions ahead, California Highway Patrol required that all vehicles bound for Mammoth Lakes and points north must apply tire chains.

She stopped at a service station and bought plastic chains and was third in line to have them installed.

Hendrickson had closed his eyes. He seemed to be sleeping. His lips moved as if he were forming words, but no sound escaped him.

After the chains were in place, she pulled the SUV aside but didn't at once return to the highway. Before beginning the final long leg of the trip, she intended to place a quick call to Gavin and Jessica, which was when she learned that her burner phone had lost its charge.

In almost three months, she had only twice before become so overwhelmed by events that she'd forgotten to keep the cellphone charged. She felt derelict, though the sudden worry that overcame her was excessive, a superstitious response to a simple oversight. Travis would not be taken from her just because she had let the phone go dead. He was safe with Gavin and Jessie. He was happy and safe with his pony and the German shepherds.

The charging station was already plugged into the dashboard port, nestled in a cup holder. She fitted the cellphone to it. Depending on weather conditions, she would stop to make the call at either Mammoth Lakes or, farther on, at the tiny town of Lee Vining.

Rubinstein was playing Tchaikovsky's Piano Concerto No. 1 in B-flat Minor, op. 23, with the Minneapolis Symphony Orchestra.

Eyes still closed, Hendrickson whispered, *"Heads inside heads, eyes inside eyes . . ."*

18

From the restaurant, they return to Dubose's room, where he sits at a small table by an ocean-view window to work on the laptop, while Jergen sits across from him, waiting to hear what idea has managed to fire from synapse to synapse in that bacon-fogged brain.

"Last night, both those chopper jockeys said the Land Rover was last seen heading what direction?"

"Southwest," Jergen says.

"Southwest," Dubose agrees. "Let's have a look at Google Maps."

Jergen doesn't want to move his chair around the table and snug it up against Dubose in order to see the screen. He'd feel like a little boy watching Daddy do important things. He stares out at the sparkling Pacific and listens to his partner walk him through it.

This is how it progresses: First, Gavin Washington will know what unparalleled resources are available to his pursuers and will suspect he has little time to go to ground before every police car in the state will be on the lookout for a vintage white Land Rover with his plate number. So assume he has a set of forged plates and uses them. The vehicle still is what it is. He remains at risk. This Google map. Now that Google map. All right, if Washington doesn't drastically change direction when out of sight of the helo crew, he powers through the wilds of the Cleveland National Forest, heading for the county line. He probably crosses over into San Diego County somewhere between De Luz and Fallbrook, no longer in the national forest but in a decidedly rural area. The first paved road he comes to is a county highway, S13, a two-lane blacktop. An offshoot of S13 connects with Interstate 15, but he's going to avoid such a heavily patrolled major highway even in the quiet hours just after dawn. He's going to stay as long as possible on tertiary roads, where he's least likely to cross the path of a cop. He can stay on S13 past Camp Pendleton, the Marine Corps facility that occupies a big piece of the coast, and then follow a series of county roads that can take him south and east to the international crossing at Tecate.

"He won't try crossing at Tijuana," says Dubose. "He's just too hot for that."

"All of Mexico is too hot for him," Jergen says. "He and that legless bitch have guns, remember. They won't risk going into Mexico with weapons and wind up being held for ransom by some corrupt Federales."

"Exactly right," Dubose says, as if he's already thought of the gun problem.

So the fugitive's options narrow down like this: First, he's going to want to stay away from major population centers until he has a chance to repaint the Land Rover to make it match whatever color is specified on the forged registration, after which he will be less likely to draw police attention. Which means that he must have some relatively secluded location where this can be done. He will most likely go inland, into San Diego County's least populated territory—and there's a lot of it. He might make his way south on S13 and then switch to the first eastbound route, which is State Highway 76, a more significant road than S13, though still tertiary.

Because S13 follows the east perimeter of Camp Pendleton, there will be military-base security cameras at points along that length of the highway. Jergen fetches his laptop from his room, returns with it, and plugs it in. He slips into the NSA's massive data trove through a back door with which Arcadians in the agency have provided him. He summons archived video from Pendleton's S13 cameras during the early hours of this morning. He fast-forwards in search of a southbound vintage Land Rover.

Meanwhile, Dubose is considering State Highway 76, which passes through some lonely territory to the east. He soon finds two points of interest along that route.

19

The little blue stucco house was as humble inside as out. During the building of the bunker and associated structures, Cornell lived here, overseeing the Filipinos, whose language he'd learned. In addition to his talent for devising hugely popular apps, he had a talent for languages; he spoke six fluently. The living room, study, one of two bedrooms, and kitchen were furnished with discount-warehouse goods that were mismatched but serviceable.

"It sure is dusty," Travis said as he followed Gavin and Jessie through the house, while the dogs explored on their own with the usual canine curiosity.

"He never comes here anymore," Gavin said. "Every month, when I visit, I check the place, you know, make sure there aren't plumbing problems, water leaks, confirm that all the appliances are working. But I never have time to do much housecleaning."

"Or inclination," Jessie said. She wiped a finger

across a kitchen counter and held it up to reveal a beard of dust.

"We can have it tidy in no time," Gavin said. "We'll tie rags to the dogs' tails. And this boy here—why, we can work him till he drops, while we sit on the porch with glasses of iced tea."

"That's bushwa, for sure," Travis said.

20

Sequined with sunshine, the sea glimmers to shore in rhythmic waves and breaks on the alabaster beach in boas of sparkling foam, while on *this* side of the window, Carter Jergen fast-forwards through video of the county road along the eastern flank of Camp Pendleton, until he freezes an image in early light. "Got him! Right here it is, the same freakin' Land Rover. I'll be damned if it isn't."

"Of course it is," Dubose says.

He doesn't bother to look when Jergen turns the laptop toward him, as though his theory of Gavin Washington's actions could not possibly be proven wrong, as though Jergen has been given make-work to keep him busy while Dubose does the heavy thinking.

"Meanwhile," Dubose says, "I've been studying State Highway 76. If he's got some private place, some rural hidey-hole, he's headed for, that's the route he's most likely to take. You'll find two cameras at the junction of 76 and County Highway 16, at the town of Pala."

"'Pala'? I never heard of Pala."

"It's a little pissant town. But they have one of the early California missions there, and it's been restored. It's considered worth surveilling the intersection there to have after-the-fact evidence in case of terrorism. I don't know why."

"All the missions are of historic value," Jergen says.

"Petrified dinosaur dung is of historic value, but we don't keep a camera on every pile of it."

Jergen is appalled, but it's not the first time a statement by Dubose has appalled him. "Well, ISIS and all those off-with-your-head types love to destroy historic buildings and erase the past."

"What matters to me is the now," Dubose opines. "I live in *the now*. Anyway, check out those Pala cameras. They'll be in the NSA archives, too. See if the Rover went by there within maybe half an hour of when it should have turned off S13."

Jergen needs ten minutes to retrieve an image of the Land Rover passing the junction of State Highway 76 and County Highway S16. This kind of catch always thrills him. It's like magic. "Got him!" he declares.

"Of course you do," says Dubose, again ignoring Jergen's laptop to focus on what he's doing on his own. "Now, about fourteen miles past Pala, County Highway 6 turns north off Highway 76 to the even tinier pissant town of Palomar Mountain. Two low-profile cameras at the junction. Because of Palomar Observatory. Again, don't ask me why."

"They have the two-hundred-inch Hale telescope," Jergen says. "It's an important national asset. They study the stars, the universe."

"The stars haven't changed in, like, several million centuries. Says here Palomar opened in the 1930s. If they need so many years to study what never changes, then some of these guys are sitting around up there smoking weed and jerking off."

Sometimes it seems as if perhaps Dubose says things he doesn't really believe, just to see if he can get Jergen to pop a cork. But Jergen tries his best not to respond in a way that will give the hillbilly hulk satisfaction.

Without responding, he seeks out the archived video from the cameras at the highway junction south of Palomar.

21

The cleaning supplies under the kitchen sink were a few years old but still effective. While Jessie and Travis set about giving the kitchen a preliminary scrub, Gavin went through the connecting door into the single-stall garage and turned on the light.

Cornell had abandoned his Honda four years earlier, when he moved into his secret residence to read through Apocageddon. Since then, he'd come out only once a week to get his mail; when Gavin visited, Cornell gave him the paid bills to post. Cornell no longer drove anywhere. In spite of his millions, he had purchased the car used; though twelve years old, its odometer registered only 47,566 miles. According to Cornell, he'd driven less than two thousand of those, traveling in and out of Borrego Springs to shop at Center Market and Desert Pantry during the construction of his end-of-the-world bunker. He didn't like to drive. He felt the speed at which an automobile could travel was deeply unnatural.

On his once-a-month visits, Gavin had looked after the Honda, keeping it in good running order, against the day when his cousin might decide that society wasn't going to collapse after all. Ever since he and Jessie had taken in Travis, he'd had another reason to take care of the sedan: so they could use it in a pinch.

After he had driven the Honda out of the garage and parked it beside the house, the fullest recognition of what had happened hit him. He needed to sit for a while in the yard, on the stump of an Indian laurel that had been cut down ages ago, in the shade of the palm trees planted later. If their comfortable life wasn't gone forever, it was gone for at least as long as Jane's crusade lasted and perhaps longer. If she failed, their lives would not only be less comfortable, but would unspool day after day in an atmosphere of tension, even dread.

Of course, if Jane failed, not just he and Jessie, but most of the country—in time, most of the world— would fall into a darkness without exit. Three months earlier, he would not have found credible the notion of a future in which an elite class with unprecedented power ruled a fearful population, some enslaved by nanoimplants, others intimidated into obedience by the millions who were thus programmed. Those millions could in minutes be transformed from your friendly neighbors into ruthless killers who would slaughter anyone identified as a rebel, including their own parents, even their own children. Now he was finding it difficult to believe that such a future would *not* happen. By comparison, an army of the walking dead would be a feeble force.

He and Jessie had believed enough in the need to defend freedom that they'd given years of their lives— and Jessie her legs—to the fight. They were grateful for each other, for their life after war. To have it upended now seemed almost too much to endure. Not that they would fail to endure it. They were good at enduring; adversity was the touchstone by which they proved their value to themselves.

He knew what Jessie would say, because she had said it before: *Nobody ever promised me that life would be a party; as long as I have you to laugh with and hope with, nothing can defeat me.*

He felt the same way.

Nevertheless, when he got up from the tree stump, he turned in a circle, surveying the day, and he knew that everything that seemed so solid and eternal was in fact fragile. The bleached-denim blue of the desert sky, the queen palms with their feathery pendent fronds, the great flatness of desert soon to be flowering all the way to the distant mountains: All of it might seem mundane, but it was, in truth, astonishing if you took the time to think about it, precious beyond any price, every place in the world a fantastic dream that had been given substance. But you could wake from it when you woke into death—or now into a life of nanoimplant slavery.

He pulled the Land Rover into the garage and closed the big tilt-up door. In a day or two, he would put together a simple spray booth, from a little lumber and a lot of plastic sheeting, and paint the Rover blue.

Now, he went back into the house to shave his head.

22

Although Carter Jergen is keen to get Travis Hawk and use the boy to bring the mother to her knees, he almost wishes that Dubose is proved wrong, that the cameras at the turnoff to the Palomar Observatory will not reveal the Land Rover. If the Washingtons have somehow pulled off a disappearing act between Pala and Palomar, what a pleasure it will be to see the West Virginia yeti gape-mouthed and bewildered. But, no, there it is, the target vehicle, motoring past Palomar.

"About twelve miles farther," Dubose pontificates, "Highway 76 terminates in Highway 79. From there, maybe they went south on 79. There are two low-profile cameras at Santa Ysabel, related to the mission there, the Santa Ysabel Asistencia. Check it out."

"You could've been checking it out while I was reviewing the Palomar video," Jergen observes in as neutral a tone of voice as he can manage.

"I'm thinking. I'm looking at the maps and thinking. Someone has to do the thinking," Dubose says.

After a while, Jergen has a report to make. "They should have passed through Santa Ysabel maybe half an hour after Palomar. I've fast-forwarded through ninety minutes of video. No Land Rover. Have you been thinking? We need more thinking."

"I never stop thinking," Dubose says. "I wish we had a few more of these stupid missions in the area, but we don't. That's okay. I'm on it. Stand by."

"Stand by?"

"I've got an idea shaping up," Dubose says.

The big man sits before his laptop, shoulders straight, head raised, chin jutting forward, his expression almost a parody of what a man might look like when he is full of virtuous purpose. Damn if it doesn't seem as if he's *trying* to look like Dudley Do-Right.

23

The breeze died just before the clouds began to shed large pillowy flakes that spiraled in their descent, floating across the hood of the Explorer, streaming up the windshield without touching the glass, caught in the vehicle's slipstream. Like a cold smoke, snow at first eddied across the pavement, but then it began to stick.

By the time that she reached the town of Lee Vining, Jane had to reduce speed, whereupon she needed the windshield wipers. The metronomic thump of the rubber blades and the monotone song of the tire chains hashed Rubinstein, so she switched off the music.

She pulled off the road and stopped in the parking lot of a convenience store. When she picked up the disposable phone, which was now charged, Hendrickson rose out of his self-cast spell and regarded the instrument with interest. He met her eyes as she prepared to key in the number of the burner that she'd left with Gavin and Jessie. Then he looked down at the twelve-button display.

His eyes were not the slick white of hard-boiled eggs, as in her dream. But there seemed to be an unwholesome curiosity in them, as if on some level he knew that he should still be her enemy, even if he could not act against her.

"Look away," she said, to be sure that he wouldn't see the number she meant to call.

Instead, he met her eyes again.

"Look away," she repeated.

He turned his face to the window in the passenger door.

Maybe because of the remoteness of this place or because of the storm, she couldn't get service. She would have to try later, though they were heading into even more remote territory and worse weather.

She might have to delay calling until she crossed the border into Nevada and reached Carson City.

She drove back onto 395, in the wake of a highway department truck fitted with an enormous plow that skimmed the pavement. The rotating yellow beacons flung waves of light through the gray, alchemizing the falling snow into gold.

Still gazing out the side window, Hendrickson said, "They'll find him."

"Find who?"

There was no note of triumph or animosity in his flat voice, only a somber statement of what he believed to be fact. "They'll find your son."

As if she were a stringed instrument that Fate was tuning for a performance, Jane felt something tighten in her chest. "What would you know about it?"

"Not much. The boy wasn't my primary focus. But recently . . ."

"Recently what?"

"They doubled the number of searchers looking for him."

"What else? You know something else. Tell me."

"No. Just that. Twice as many people chasing down leads."

"They'll never find him," she said.

"It's inevitable."

Irrationally, she wanted to draw her pistol and whip the barrel across his face, but she had nothing to gain—and much to lose—by indulging that desire. There was nothing worse she could do to him than what she'd already done.

As he faced forward again, she said, "What *was* your primary focus?"

"Finding you."

"How did that work out?"

After a silence, he said, "I don't know yet."

24

R adley Dubose's idea is that if the Washingtons didn't go south on Highway 79, which the archived video from Santa Ysabel confirms that they did not, then they must have gone north.

Jergen restrains himself from congratulating his partner on the brilliance of deducing the *or* in this either-or choice.

"But they wouldn't have gone far north on 79," Dubose says, peering into his laptop screen as though into a crystal ball, "because all that does is take them back to Orange County by a roundabout route. They weren't just out for a pleasure drive."

"Yes, I'm aware of that."

"But the only road that connects with the entire northern leg of 79 is County Highway 2."

"Therefore . . . ?"

"They switched onto Highway 2. But that road goes south to the Mexican border, and I already figured they won't try crossing the border with guns."

"Was it you who figured that out?" Jergen asks.

Dubose isn't listening closely enough to hear the subtle sarcasm in his partner's voice. "However, Highway 2 doesn't just go south. It offers them a binary choice."

"Another either-or to test the clever sleuth."

"Just as Highway 2 takes a sharp turn south, it intersects with County Highway 22. So it's a damn good bet they took 22 east, which goes all the way across the Anza-Borrego Desert to Salton City by the Salton Sea."

"Salton City by the Salton Sea. Sounds like a song title," says Jergen.

"But if they wanted to go to the Salton Sea, they would have gone south on 79 to 78 to 86, 'cause those are all much better roads than 22."

"All these numbers," Jergen says, "are making my pretty head spin. So what is your conclusion?"

"Twenty-two only leads two places. Salton City is at the end of it, and before that, Borrego Springs."

"Maybe we go to Borrego Springs and see what there is to see."

Dubose looks up from his laptop. "Didn't I just say that? It's a hundred thirteen miles. We can be there in two hours."

Jergen takes his laptop, Dubose leaves his in the room, and they go downstairs to the hotel's front entrance. The day is warm and the palm trees tower majestically, and there are white gulls kiting high in the silence of the clear blue sky.

The valet confirms that an hour earlier a gentleman named Harry Lime had delivered a vehicle for their use. It came on a flatbed truck. He declares that it is

one of the most amazing vehicles any of the valets has
ever seen.

NSA personnel have replaced the two shotgunned
tires, washed the VelociRaptor, and waxed it. The
truck looks fabulous. Dubose drives.

25

In a barren condition, Gavin's head wasn't
nearly as smooth as that of his cousin; it had
topography. He returned to the kitchen from the bathroom, frowning as he slid a hand over his naked skull.
"I've got a bumpy head."

"Probably from all the times I've had to knock some
sense into you," Jessie said.

Travis said, "Uncle Gavin, you look like Vin Diesel."

"The *Fast and Furious* guy? I guess you mean it as a
compliment. But I'm not sure I'd have shaved off my
hair if I'd known I've got a bumpy head."

"Everyone's got a bumpy head," Jessie assured
him. "That's why phrenologists have something to
read when they read your head."

"Cornell's head is as smooth as an egg."

"Well, that's not the only thing different about Cornell."

"I'm not sure what I'm going to look like with a
beard."

"Hey, Aunt Jessie, the dogs are shedding a lot right now," Travis said. "We could save some dog hair and glue it to Uncle Gavin's chin."

"Now that's genius, Trav. We run that hand vac over Duke and Queenie, we'll have more than enough hair. We can glue it tonight, get a preview of what my man will look like in a few weeks."

The dogs had taken a special interest in Gavin, sniffing around his feet and up his pant legs, as though trying to determine if, like Samson after Delilah, he'd lost something more when he'd lost his hair.

To Jessie, he said, "We've got to go in town to food shop. So why don't you start your makeover now, give me a chance to fire a little mockery back at you?"

"Fire too much, and you'll have nothing for dinner but what the dogs get."

After Jessie went into the bedroom, where they'd left their luggage, Travis said, "We wiped off the whole kitchen, Uncle Gavin. Now we have to wipe out *inside* the cupboards. This here is Lysol water. It stinks."

"But it stinks good," Gavin said. "Why don't you start, and I'll come help in five minutes."

"Where are you going?"

"To hide where you can't find me."

The boy grinned. "I'll find you, all right. Duke and Queenie, with their noses, they'll find you all the way to Mars."

When Gavin went into the living room, he discovered that Jessie had anticipated him. She handed him the burner phone that Jane had given them. "This is gonna hit her hard, baby."

"Don't I know it."

He took the disposable phone onto the front porch and closed the door behind him. He dreaded having to tell Jane, having to add to whatever hell she was currently dealing with, but he wanted to get this done.

Apparently she was at the moment somewhere that didn't have cell service. He couldn't reach her.

26

At Oceanside, Dubose exits Interstate 5 and enters State Highway 76, heading east. They have traveled perhaps twenty-five miles when he says, "There you go."

"There I go what?" Jergen asks.

Pointing through the windshield, Dubose says, "That's County Highway 16 ahead on the left. The turnoff for Pala. The place you never heard of, where there's a restored mission. See that pole? The cameras are on top of that pole, just like I told you they were. Low-profile cameras, so you hardly know they're up there." He slows the VelociRaptor. "It's exactly like I told you, and then you went to the video, and the Rover had gone past, just like I said. That's when Jane Hawk's rampage began to come to an end, when the threat she posed began to unravel."

He sounds as though he must be rehearsing for his role in some documentary that the Techno Arcadians will make, after their triumph, to glorify their ascendancy to total power.

Dubose accelerates. "About fourteen miles ahead, on the left, is County Highway 6, which goes to Palomar Mountain. That's one more important milestone in the events leading up to the historic capture of Travis Hawk and the surrender of his mother."

Carter Jergen is feeling increasingly cranky about Dubose's guided tour of this historic journey. "Yeah, well, nobody's captured anybody yet."

"We'll get the little shit," Dubose assures him. "I smell him."

"'Fee, fi, fo, fum,'" Jergen says, wondering if that literary allusion might go over the head of a Princeton man.

A short while later, Radley Dubose says, "And there ahead is the turnoff to Palomar Mountain. Two more low-profile cameras high on that pole, even now recording us as I race toward the endgame of this ugly business."

"Damn it," Jergen grieves, "I should be driving."

"Palomar Observatory," says Dubose, "has the two hundred-inch Hale telescope, an important national asset."

This is too much. Jergen reminds him of what he'd said earlier: "Where the astronomers sit around smoking weed and jerking off."

"Might very well be the case, my friend, but I'd advise you not to say such a thing publicly. You'll only be mocked and derided, and the powers that be will decide you are seriously unserious."

27

When Jane had left the makeover items, Jessie had doubted that anyone would fail to recognize her in such a getup. But regarding herself in the bathroom mirror, she admitted that, as usual, Mrs. Hawk had known what she was doing.

She returned to the kitchen, her straight black hair pinned under a modified-afro wig, which worked because her multiethnic heritage left her with a café-au-lait complexion, allowing that she might have a trace of Africa somewhere in her roots. Her Irish-green eyes were hidden behind contacts that turned them brown.

Travis said, "Aunt Jessie, you look great this way, too."

"You do," Gavin agreed. "It's suddenly like my wife's out of town and here's this total fox."

"Oh, baby, now that's just the kind of thing a foolish man says, thinking he'll score some points."

Gavin grimaced. "Heard myself saying it, couldn't *believe* I was saying it. What I think happened is I was for a moment possessed by the spirit of a really stupid man."

They had come now to a moment that made Jessie uncomfortable, but she couldn't figure a way to get around it. They were going to leave Travis alone for an hour and a half, maybe two hours.

He had two canisters of Sabre 5.0 pepper spray, of a strength used by law enforcement, which they'd trained him to use when he first came to live with them. He would have the dogs, who adored him and were vigilant and protective by breed and training. Although he was not yet six, the boy was at least as responsible as the average ten-year-old. The house would be securely locked. It was broad daylight. Borrego Valley had virtually zero crime, in part because more than a third of the population was over sixty-five and the median age was maybe fifty-seven, fifty-eight. In the years that the house had stood empty except for Gavin's monthly visits, there had never been a break-in or vandalism.

Travis was arguably safer here than he would be with them, and yet Jessie worried.

The plan was to shop for food and other necessities that would get them through a month. Even with their appearance altered, she and Gavin didn't want to be venturing into Borrego Springs on a regular basis. In a town that small, with a population of less than four thousand, new people would be noticed quickly, especially new *black* people, considering that the black population was about 1 percent. The less they showed themselves, the better. And if no one saw them with Travis, they wouldn't match any description of two fugitives with a child. They were regular folks, probably campers, RV types, visiting Borrego Springs for a few weeks.

There was every reason to think they couldn't have been tracked to this relatively remote place. The traffic monitors and public-space surveillance cameras that were ubiquitous in urban and even suburban areas, as well as on interstate highways and major state freeways, had not yet been installed on back roads or in places as small and as out of the way as Borrego Springs.

Nevertheless, if Gavin went shopping alone, there would be times when he would be distracted and when both his hands would be occupied with one task or another. He would be vulnerable, and in their current circumstances, every moment of vulnerability was an invitation to Death.

At all times, one of them must have a hand on a gun. Jessie could do that by pushing the shopping cart that Gavin filled, keeping her pistol in her open purse.

Although it might be unlikely that he would be spotted and pursued during his first visit to town, minimal prudence required that Jessie go with him and remain at all times aware of their surroundings. They were in a war now, and no one could fight a war alone.

There was Cornell in his library. But poor Cornell, stressed by Gavin's recent visit, had asked him to leave and would not have recovered enough to welcome the boy this soon.

"You'll be okay here for two hours," she assured Travis, though it made her stomach turn to think of him here by himself.

"I know," the boy said. "I'll be okay."

"Don't answer the door if anyone knocks."

"I won't."

"Stay away from the windows."

"I will, Aunt Jessie."

"Nobody's going to break in, sweetie."

"Okay. I know."

"If someone does break in, which they won't, let the dogs deal with them."

"All right. I will."

"If the dogs can't deal with them—which they will, they'll tear 'em up all right, but if they can't—only then should you use the pepper spray."

"I know how."

"Once you've sprayed them in the face, run like hell, out of the house. Go to that barn door, sweetie. Cornell will know, and he'll let you in." She looked at Gavin. "Won't he let Travis in?"

"Of course he will."

She could tell from her husband's expression that he wasn't a hundred percent certain what Cornell would do.

"You'll hardly know we're gone, honey. We'll be back in no time."

Travis sighed. "I'm not a two-year-old, Aunt Jessie."

She knelt and hugged him and said, "I love you, Trav."

"I love you, too, Aunt Jessie."

She might have spent another ten minutes reassuring the boy if Gavin hadn't said, "Jess, you might not know this, but Bigfoot has never been seen in this area, and Godzilla is in Japan."

Jessie got to her feet. "You'll be fine, sweetie."

The boy said, "So will you."

Gavin saluted Travis. "Hold the fort, Lieutenant. We'll be back with the beer at fourteen hundred."

"Holding the fort, sir," Travis replied, returning the salute.

When they stepped onto the back porch, Travis engaged the deadbolt and waved at them through the dust-filmed window in the door, a hazy figure beyond the dirty glass, as if he were already fading out of their lives.

28

This was surely the last storm of the season, and a late one at that, but Nature worked hard at it, as though she'd taken a dislike to spring and intended to double down on winter. In the absence of wind, the small flakes fell in skeins, layering veils across the face of the day. Ramparts of evergreens, black in the hours-long twilight of the storm, stepped steeply up from the highway, obscured to such an extent that they looked less like masses of trees than like the bastions and battlements of castles.

Jane was aware of Hendrickson staring at her from time to time. When she turned her head to meet his eyes, he at once—and almost shyly—looked away.

Regarding his potential for violence, her estimation of him had proved correct. Neither had he made an attempt to escape, nor given any indication that he might be contemplating one. He remained as obedient as a machine—just as she had made him.

The effort to keep the highway open had been joined by road graders fitted with plows. They moved through the whitewashed day like raw-boned prehistoric creatures with phosphorescent stares. Trucks followed the plows, spreading salt across the pavement.

In spite of tire chains or because it lacked them, a vehicle occasionally slid into a roadside ditch or into a snowbank, where it was either abandoned or attended to by a tow-truck driver trying to free it.

Hendrickson whispered, "'The more it snows, the more it goes, the more it goes on snowing,'" and though he smiled wistfully, tears tracked down his cheeks.

Jane suspected he was quoting from another poem he had learned in childhood, but she didn't ask. Beyond the fact of his being now one of the adjusted people, his condition was so grotesque and his demeanor so disturbing that she didn't want to be drawn further into his orbit than was necessary.

She yearned for the company of her child. Instead she found herself entangled with this strange manchild whose tortured history included being both the victim of abuse and the vicious abuser of others. And his demonic potential was still within him, still there to be called forth by anyone who discovered he'd been injected with a control mechanism and who knew how to command him.

At 1:10 P.M., about an hour and a half later than she expected, she arrived at U.S. Highway 50, a couple miles south of Carson City, and turned west toward Lake Tahoe. Ahead at a highway department marshaling yard, road-clearing equipment lined up to be refueled. She pulled off the highway, stopped, and made another attempt to call the Washingtons.

When she picked up the burner phone, Hendrickson turned his head away without being told to do so. He covered his eyes with his hands, like a small child seeking approval by doing more than was asked of him.

This time she got service. Down there in Orange County, the phone rang. Showers of snow ticked against the windshield, and the midday dusk seemed to darken by the moment, and the phone rang, rang, rang.

There could be a good reason why neither Gavin nor Jessie took the call. It didn't necessarily mean trouble. There could be *many* good reasons.

Nevertheless, when she terminated the call and returned the disposable phone to the cup holder, her palms were damp with sweat.

29

Travis wasn't scared about being alone. He really wasn't. His dad had been a Marine, and his mom was FBI. He was a Marine-FBI kid.

The dogs were with him. They had teeth like sabres. They could rip up anyone. They wouldn't rip up *him*, but they for sure would rip up anyone who *ought* to be ripped up.

And he had the pepper spray. *He* could protect the *dogs* if it came to that.

He was not as little as he looked. He had an Exmoor pony that he rode, and one day not too long from now, he would ride a horse.

Although he'd had a couple hours' sleep in the backseat of the Rover the night before, he needed a nap. But he didn't think it was a good idea to sleep.

So he ate another PowerBar to help himself stay awake, and he gave each of the dogs a biscuit. That used up five minutes.

Two hours was a long time. But not if he kept busy. There was a lot that needed to be done. The house was full of dust and cobwebs, and there were dead pill bugs in some corners.

He took a roll of paper towels and a spray bottle of Windex to the bathroom. They had used the Windex in the kitchen.

He climbed onto the counter beside the sink. He used the Windex and the paper towels to clean the mirror above the counter.

If you wanted to do something right, which was the only way you should do *anything*, there was a trick to it. His mom had taught him the trick. The trick was to care about doing a good job and not do it fast just to be done with it.

Queenie kept coming to the bathroom door to look at him. She wouldn't come into the bathroom because the Windex made her sneeze.

Duke was going room to room, on patrol. Sometimes he passed the bathroom door, grumbling to himself.

Travis was working on the really dirty sink, trying not to think about who might have spit into it and what they might have spit, when a telephone rang somewhere else in the house.

Aunt Jessie and Uncle Gavin had said not to answer the door and stay away from the windows. But they didn't say what to do if the phone rang.

He left the bathroom, Duke at his side, Queenie behind him. He followed the sound and found the phone in the kitchen. It was on the counter, next to the fridge.

It looked like the special phone his mom called on. She didn't call often, only to say she was coming for a visit. And she always called at night, when he was in bed. So he'd never heard the phone ring. But he was pretty sure this was the phone.

He never talked on this phone with his mom. It wasn't for long conversations. It was for quick messages and emergencies.

If it was his mom, he wanted to talk to her.

If it wasn't his mom, if it was one of the bad people, then if he answered, maybe they would know where to find him.

The dogs stood one to each side of Travis, and all three of them stared at the phone.

The dogs' ears were pricked forward, their bodies tense. They weren't wagging their tails. The dogs didn't seem to like the phone.

Travis decided to answer it anyway, just take the call and not say anything unless he heard his mom's voice.

But as he reached for it, the phone stopped ringing.

30

The town of Borrego Springs is as far removed from Carter Jergen's experience as any place on the moon. If he believed in Hell, he would call this a preview of that satanic kingdom.

The temperature report in the VelociRaptor dashboard readout claims it is 88 degrees. But as he and Dubose walk the downtown, such as it is, the day feels hotter than that. In summer it probably hits 120 degrees most days. The air is so dry, he repeatedly licks his lips to keep them from cracking, and his sinuses seem to be shriveling inside his skull.

In Borrego Springs, wherever there are not vast expanses of concrete and blacktop, there are even bigger expanses of bare, sandy earth. On three sides, mountains rise in the distance, and on the fourth side, they loom closer, barren crags of rock as forbidding as the cliffs where Zeus chained Prometheus and sent an eagle to tear out his liver every day, for the crime of giving fire to humanity. Desert surrounds the town and intrudes everywhere, spotted with withered scrub, no doubt abounding with rattlesnakes, poisonous lizards, and tarantulas the size of basketballs. The strip shopping centers and the standalone businesses are landscaped with pebbles, cactuses, and curious arrangements of rocks that seem intended to convey some mystical message.

Clusters of dusty trees are planted close to the sides of houses to shade them. In the business district, however, there are little more than widely separated palms rising from small cutouts in blacktop and concrete, casting meager patches of shade. They look pathetic, desperate, as though they long to be dug up, root-boxed, and hauled on a truck to Florida.

Sun glares off bare earth, pavement, buildings, and windows, which store the heat and radiate it back. The entire town is like one giant pizza oven.

The only grass seems to be in the heart of Borrego Springs, in what is called Christmas Circle, a park with a comparative wealth of trees, mostly palms and evergreens, encompassed by a roundabout from which seven streets radius off like spokes from the hub of a wheel.

Jergen feels displaced, foreign, shipwrecked on a strange shore. A pizza-and-beer restaurant. Taco shop. Mexican grill and bar. Coffee shop. Liquor store. He sees no evidence of a French or Northern Italian restaurant, or any place with refined Mediterranean cuisine. Not even sushi. He suspects that every eatery in town will accept a customer in T-shirt, shorts, and sandals. Looking through an art-gallery window, he does not see one item that fits any definition of art known to him. Everywhere are pickups, Jeeps, and SUVs. Although summer is months away, everyone has a tan, as if they've never heard of melanoma, and they're weirdly sociable. Most people whom they pass on foot, total strangers, speak to them—"Beautiful day," and "Good afternoon," and "Have a nice day!"—

which is the most alien thing about the place, though not to Dubose, who smiles and returns the greetings.

"Why're you talking to strangers like you know them?" Carter finally asks. "We shouldn't be calling attention to ourselves."

"You're calling attention to yourself by *not* speaking when spoken to."

"They're strangers. What do I care if they think it's a nice day or want me to have one? What's wrong with them, anyway? Why're they so concerned I shouldn't have a crappy day?"

"Just relax, Carter Northrup Jergen the third, and look for something out of the ordinary."

"*Everything* here is out of the ordinary. And I'm the fourth, not the third."

"That explains a lot."

"What do you mean by that?"

"The quality of any gene pool," Dubose said, "is adversely affected by the number of generations in which unfortunately few new bloodlines have been introduced."

Jergen considers commenting to the effect that the Northrup and Jergen families do not, unlike some, have numerous pairs of married cousins in the family tree. But he's too hot and too afflicted with desert-inspired ennui to get into a tit for tat.

31

The stress of leaving their comfortable life behind, the chase in the desert, and a night without sleep left Gavin with bloodshot eyes, a stiff neck, various sore muscles, and a general fatigue against which he had to struggle to remain alert. For breakfast, they'd eaten PowerBars, nothing for lunch; now every edible item that Jessie added to the shopping cart made his stomach growl.

A month's supplies for three people and two dogs would require two grocery carts piled high with goods, which meant both Gavin and Jessie would be too preoccupied to be constantly, adequately on guard. The solution was to split the task between the town's two main markets, buying only canned and packaged goods in the first, more canned goods and all the perishables in the second, a single piled-high cart per store.

In the first market, Jessie pushed the cart, and Gavin tagged along, commenting on the prices and pretending to quibble about brand choices, trying not to be obvious when he scoped out the other shoppers to make sure nobody seemed to be taking an unusual interest in them.

He didn't think their photographs were on TV. The Arcadians wouldn't want the media to know that those sheltering Jane Hawk's son had been identified. The bastards never intended to rescue the boy; they meant to *capture* him. If the authorities made an offi-

cial announcement, they would thereafter have to operate by the book and place Travis with Child Welfare
Services, whereupon Jane's in-laws—Clare and Ancel
Hawk, in Texas—would seek custody. Considering
that he was a cute five-year-old who'd recently lost
his father and whose mother was the most-wanted fugitive in America, the human-interest factor would
ensure a media frenzy. Any judge who ruled against
the grandparents would be a villain in the public's
eye, create sympathy for Jane, and raise the suspicion
that there might be more to her story than the carefully crafted image of a "beautiful monster" who had
sold her country's most important, if unspecified, secrets to an enemy power, killing numerous people
along the way. So the grandparents would be given
custody. And sooner rather than later, to regain control of the boy, corrupt authorities would inject Clare
and Ancel with brain implants, the worst of all possible outcomes for Jane. No, the bad guys would not
risk losing control of the media narrative; they would
keep the hunt for Gavin and Jessie out of the news.

Everything went smoothly in the first market. In
the parking lot, they transferred their purchases from
the cart to the trunk of the Honda. They drove a short
distance to the second establishment.

32

As they are strolling around a little shopping complex, Jergen suddenly feels revitalized when he does indeed see something out of the ordinary. About fifty feet ahead of them, a black couple in their thirties crosses the parking lot and approaches the entrance to a market. Jergen can't clearly see the man's face, but his height and body type are right for Gavin Washington; the guy is bald, but maybe he shaved his head. The woman appears to be black, which Jessica Washington isn't; she could be wearing a wig. What's out of the ordinary about them is the same thing that makes Jergen and Dubose different from everyone else they've seen in Borrego Springs: On this hot afternoon, both the man and woman are wearing sport coats, and the coats are cut roomy enough to conceal weapons.

As the two disappear into the market, Dubose says, "But she has her own legs."

"She's wearing full-length khakis. How do you know what's under them?"

"She's walking like people with real legs walk."

"Because she's got Ottobocks."

"She's got what?"

"She uses blade-runner legs when she's in races. Other times she uses Ottobock X-Threes." Jergen spells O-t-t-o-b-o-c-k. "Evidently you didn't read everything in the background report on the bitch."

Dubose is unrepentant. "Background reports are written by deskbound pussies who believe they're gonna write a novel one day and win a Pulitzer. I skim their flowery shit."

"Avoiding the flowery shit," Jergen says, "here's the essence: Each prosthetic knee has multiple sensors, a gyroscope, terrific hydraulics, a microprocessor, software, a resistance system, and a battery. She can run reasonably well, walk backward, climb steps, and look natural doing it."

"So you think that's them?"

"What do you think?" Jergen asks.

Dubose frowns. "I think we should have a closer look."

33

Jessie kept checking her wristwatch, thinking about Travis at the house with just the dogs and the pepper spray. She didn't worry that the people hunting for him would find him. But there was always the possibility of a fire. Or an earthquake. Or he might cut himself somehow, on something, and be bleeding badly.

Her fears arose less from likely threats to the boy than from weariness and from distress at how abruptly their lives had been turned upside down. She'd had no sleep the previous night; and the responsibility she felt for the boy stropped her nerves, until her anxiety was sharper than it had been since the war.

During their time in the first market, she hadn't trusted her ability both to appear relaxed and to react quickly if a threat materialized. Her mind was fuzzy. Her reflexes weren't what they should be. There was a real possibility that if she had to go for her gun, she might fumble with the sport coat.

Consequently, during the drive between markets, she had taken the Colt Pony .380 from the low-ride belt-fixed rig on her hip and put it in her purse.

The purse was now propped in the small fold-down basket that overhung the larger part of the grocery cart. The zipper was open, the pistol grip awaiting her hand, tucked between her wallet and a packet of Kleenex.

Even with the weapon better positioned for a quick draw and though everything had gone smoothly thus far, Jessie worried about Travis. They had hardly begun their tour through the second market, but already they'd been away ninety minutes. They wouldn't get back to the house for at least another hour, which would be half an hour later than they had promised.

34

I mmediately after spotting the suspects, Jergen and Dubose hurry to the back of the market, where deliveries are made. The door is unlocked. They step inside and stand blinking in the cool air as their eyes adjust to the low light.

This is the warehousing space behind the sales floor, and it is smaller than Jergen expected. You can't call the market a mom-and-pop operation, but neither docs it deserve the prefix *super*.

Here are three men in black slacks and white shirts, two of them wearing white aprons with the market logo on the breast. The one without an apron is cutting away the shrink-wrap from three pallets of recently delivered goods. The other two are transferring five-pound bags of sugar from one of the pallets to metal storage shelves.

The guy scissoring the shrink-wrap straightens up from his work. He has close-cropped hair, a scrubbed look, no face jewelry, no visible tattoos, neatly pressed pants, and shoes with a high shine. His just-so appearance suggests he might be a Mormon, which is a plus, as Mormons are people who are raised to be helpful. "What can I do for you gentlemen?"

"We need to speak with the manager," Dubose says.

"Well, now, that would be me. Oren Luckman. What can I do for you?"

Jergen says, "IRS." He looks at the other men, who are too interested in whatever little drama might play out here. "We'd prefer to keep this discreet."

Oren Luckman's office is in a corner of the warehouse space. Piles of invoices cover the desk, weighed down by a variety of colorful polished stones.

Indicating a red stone with black veining, Dubose says, "That's a nice specimen of rhodonite." He points to another. "And that's an exceptional cabochon of chrysocolla."

"You know stones." Luckman's face shines with the delight of a collector meeting someone who doesn't think his peculiar enthusiasm makes him a class-A dweeb.

"It's long been a hobby of mine," Dubose reveals. "Oh, now, that's a spectacular chunk of quartz-embedded rhodochrosite. A real beauty."

"That's from the Sweet Home Mine in Colorado," says Luckman with an annoying note of pride.

This is the first Jergen has ever heard of Dubose's hobby. Not to be outdone, he points to a stone. "Magnificent turquoise."

Luckman and Dubose regard him with something like pity, and the manager says, "That's stained howlite."

"People who don't know any better," Dubose says, "buy howlite jewelry and pay a turquoise price." Putting an end to stone talk, he withdraws his ID wallet from an inner coat pocket and flashes his National Security Agency credentials.

As Jergen produces his ID as well, Luckman is confused. "But you said Internal Revenue Service."

"For the benefit of your two assistants back there," Jergen explains. "We don't want them talking about NSA agents to other employees on the sales floor right now."

"We've spotted two suspects that just came into your store," Dubose says. "If they are who we think, we'll have to arrest them."

"Oh, my," says Luckman. "Nothing like this ever happens here."

Jergen points to a large wall-mounted monitor on which is a view of what appears to be the area just inside the front door of the market. "How many security cams can you show us?"

With almost as much pride as when reacting to Dubose's admiring words about the quartz-embedded whatever, Luckman says, "One at a time or four in quad-screen format."

"And how many cameras altogether?"

"Eight."

"Just eight?" Jergen asks.

"Two exterior, six in the store."

"Just six," Dubose laments. "Should be at least twenty-four."

"Surely not for a place this size," Luckman says. "Not around these parts."

With Luckman using a remote, they need maybe two minutes to find the black couple. The manager is able to zoom in on them for a satisfying close-up.

Standing directly in front of the monitor, Dubose and Jergen study the faces, the attitudes, the way the woman moves.

"It's them," Dubose declares, and Jergen agrees.

They can wait until the Washingtons are leaving the store and pushing a cart full of grocery bags, draw down on them outside. But these two will be cautious exiting, alert for anything amiss. Going through a door, the husband will have his hand under his coat, on his weapon.

They will be somewhat more relaxed in the parking lot, on the way to their wheels. However, the parking lot is sizeable, and there aren't many vehicles in it on this Sunday afternoon. The moment they see Jergen and Dubose moving toward them, the Washingtons will read the situation right, and there could be a firefight.

A firefight isn't a risk worth taking, not when this situation allows Jergen and Dubose the element of surprise.

One stone fancier to another, Dubose tells Luckman what they need to do and what help they require from him. The manager pales, but although he surely would have been slower to concede assistance to Jergen, he is taken with Dubose's folksy manner and agrees to the strategy.

35

When the Washingtons had their shopping cart fully laden and were nearly finished, one of its wheels developed a stutter and wanted to pull a different direction from the other three.

"Let me wrestle with it," Gavin said.

"No, we're almost done," Jessie said, patting her purse in the fold-down basket. "Let's just finish it according to plan."

Maybe three minutes later, when they reached the front of the store and were approaching the cashier stations, a man working on a display of Coke, Diet Coke, and Coke Zero noticed the mountain of groceries they were pushing. His shirt tag said his name was Oren and that he was a manager. "You folks best go to checkout three. Eddie there, he's our fastest checker. He'll have you out the door in no time."

Eddie was a thirtysomething guy with blond hair and blue eyes. He looked a little like a shorter Robert Redford from the days when Redford was doing movies like *Butch Cassidy and the Sundance Kid.* He had a smarmy smile that Gavin didn't like, the kind of smile a bigot wore when he was pretending to like black people.

Gavin went ahead of the cart to unload it as Jessie pushed it into the checkout lane, and he sensed something besides Eddie's smile that was wrong with the man. His shirt. Eddie was wearing a market apron over a patterned short-sleeve sport shirt. Hadn't all the other employees been wearing white shirts?

And the name tag. It said EDUARDO. Not Eddie. Eduardo suggested Hispanic. This guy was about as Hispanic as the queen of England.

Gavin felt his right hand, powered by intuition, wanting to go under his coat for the Springfield Armory pistol. He glanced back toward the manager and saw him fading away from the Coke display, around the corner into an aisle, looking back with something like alarm.

He glanced at Jessie, and her expression said, *What?*

Taking a large bag of corn chips off the top of the stuff in the shopping cart, Gavin contrived to drop it on the floor. "Oops."

If this was it, there was only one way out. The people who arrested them would not be operating according to the law. They would be Arcadians, and there would be no future for him or for Jessie that didn't involve a control mechanism. Slavery.

He stooped, ostensibly to pick up the bag of corn chips, though in fact to draw the .45 before Eddie saw him making the move. As he slid his hand under his coat and pulled the pistol, he looked at Jessie again and thought, *Oh, God, how much I love you*, thought it so hard that he hoped she'd actually hear him telepathically.

36

Maybe ten seconds before Washington and wife will be exactly where they are wanted, ten seconds before Jergen and Dubose would have pulled their peacemakers and shouted *Police*, the man seems to block the cart from coming in farther, and he drops a bag of corn chips. Jergen does not like the way the dude drops the corn chips.

His pistol is on a shelf under the cash register. As he reaches for it, Washington is coming back up from his stoop, and—*shit*—he's got a cannon in his hand.

Just then Dubose, who's been crouched behind the magazine rack, comes out into the open and doesn't bother to shout *Police,* like it would matter even if he did, and just rushes forward, squeezing off two shots, one of which takes Washington in the head. In a death reflex, Washington fires a round that misses Jergen but point-blanks the cash register, and even as the register responds with noises of electronic distress, the woman is so quick that she's drawn a small gun designed for concealed carry and is emptying it not at Jergen, who is much closer to her, but at Dubose, who is forced to drop and scramble. The expression on the bitch's face is the most frightening thing that Jergen has ever seen, such horror and hatred and fury and indomitable intent that she seems supernatural, like some creature risen out of an infernal bottomless darkness to collect souls and tie them, wriggling, to her belt. His first shot takes her in the shoulder, staggers her, and his second shot knocks her down.

Customers and market employees are screaming and running for the doors, and Dubose is shouting— *"Police! Police! Police!"*—just in case some witness has a license for concealed carry and, in an unfortunate misunderstanding of the situation, might open fire on the legitimate authorities. In the wake of the gunshots, all that noise echoes hollowly in Jergen's ears, as though it's issuing out of a deep well.

Jergen opens a waist-high gate and exits cashier's station number three, stepping into the lane for station two. Staying low, pistol in a two-hand grip, heart knocking so hard that his vision pulses, he rounds the display of candy and gum and copies of the *National Enquirer*. There on the floor behind the full shopping cart is the woman, on her back, head turned toward him, still alive. She seems unable to get up, maybe paralyzed, but with her left hand she is reaching for the dropped pistol.

He moves toward her and kicks the weapon out of her reach and looks down as blood bubbles on her lips. Her eyes are fierce, one brown and one a dazzling green, and if a stare could kill, he would be as dead as her husband. Jergen's hearing remains temporarily impaired because of all the gunfire, and though the woman's voice must be weak, it comes to him with piercing clarity. *"I'm not done with you,"* she says, and then she dies.

Her eyes are fixed on Jergen, as if she can still see him from some far shore.

At first he backs away from her corpse. But then in spite of all the evidence to the contrary, he suddenly wonders if they have made a mistake, if perhaps these aren't the Washingtons, after all, but some innocent couple of similar appearance and with a legitimate reason to be armed. This is a big mess, any way you look at it, but if they aren't the Washingtons, it's an even bigger mess, a career-ending mess. As agents of the revolution, a failure this epic will not earn them early retirement; the only way careers like theirs are ended is two bullets in the back of the head or nanoweb enslavement.

He goes to the corpse and squats beside it and, after a brief hesitation, pulls up one leg of the khakis, revealing the Ottobock. Relief floods through him as he looks into her dead eyes and says, "Try to run a ten-K now, bitch."

PART FIVE

Lost Boys

1

The frozen sky lay invisible behind the numberless flakes that scaled from it and crystaled the air in their silent white descent.

By two o'clock, they had traveled U.S. Highway 50 west and then south. They exited onto a county road, and from there made their way to an unpaved track that, according to Booth Hendrickson, had been carved out and was maintained by the forest service. The single lane, with periodic lay-bys, had been plowed during the current storm, though probably not during the past hour. With four-wheel drive and tire chains, Jane felt confident that she could navigate it.

The fabled lake lay to the west, a quarter mile from this rough track and still far below, screened from sight as much by forest as by the quiet storm. Lodgepole pine, red fir, white pine, juniper, and mountain hemlock received the snow. In spite of the urgency of this mission, there was a timeless quality to the scene and a sense that all the works of humanity and all the dramas of Jane's life were but a dream from which she had awakened into this.

Booth had been her captive for well over twenty-four hours. The longer he remained missing, the more effort would be expended in the search for him and the wider the net the Arcadians would cast.

Those in charge of the search didn't know about the crooked staircase, about what a profound impact it had had on his life and what thing of great value waited for Jane at the bottom of that fearsome descent. Other than Booth and the couple who maintained the estate in the absence of its owner, only his mother, Anabel, and brother were aware that the vertical passage existed. Simon hadn't been admitted to the Arcadian conspiracy; he knew nothing of the brain implants. And Anabel might not credit the possibility that her elder son would speak about this place where his abject humiliation and formation occurred—unless she knew that Jane possessed ampules of the control mechanism and might have injected mama's best boy.

Booth hadn't known of the ampules, however, so perhaps no one else knew, either. And if the most elite of the conspirators *did* know, it was only Anabel who also knew about the crooked staircase, only Anabel who might in time realize why Jane would go there if she learned of it.

A second track branched off the first, likewise white-mantled but plowed recently enough that it was passable, and she switched to it at Booth's direction. The way grew steeper. The trees crowded closer. She was just minutes from her destination.

For centuries, for thousands of years, the lake, as well as the forests and alpine meadows surrounding it, had enchanted those who journeyed there. For some, the effect was greater than enchantment; this place had a mystical aura and evoked a feeling that the truth and meaning of the world lay behind fewer veils here than elsewhere.

Only the Great Lakes were larger than Tahoe, but Tahoe was far deeper, shaped by glaciers a million years ago and plunging 1,645 feet at its deepest. The clarity of the water provided visibility to surprising depth, and the coloration under a summer sun transformed it into a vast display of emeralds and sapphires.

The lake never froze, but its cold temperatures greatly slowed decomposition at extreme depth. Seventeen years after he drowned, a diver was found three hundred feet below the surface, his body all but perfectly preserved.

"Stop here," Booth said, and pointed.

She pulled into a lay-by and put the Explorer in park.

"We walk from here," he said.

She wished they had stopped somewhere to buy insulated jackets and boots. However, the forecast had called for only a fraction as much snow as had fallen, and outfitting herself and this man, in his condition, had seemed a daunting task fraught with risk.

As if privy to her thoughts, he said, "It's a short walk."

2

The San Diego County Sheriff's Department maintains a major substation in Borrego Springs, which means deputies are on scene at the market almost before the last echoes of the gunfire fade away. They are well-trained, professional, efficient— and a pain in the ass, as far as Carter Jergen is concerned.

He and Dubose are NSA agents, among other things, and these guys are nothing but generic fuzz, plain-vanilla cops. Nevertheless, they want to have a role in the investigation of the shootings because this is their turf, their town; these are their neighbors.

There is no damn role for them. This is ostensibly a national security matter, far above their pay grade. None of them possesses the necessary security clearance to work the investigation. Not one of their precious neighbors has so much as suffered a paper cut in the course of the event. The only significant damage to property is the bullet-drilled cash register. Otherwise, losses involve only a small quantity of candy bars, gum, and tabloid newspapers spattered with blood and brain tissue; no big deal.

Yet here they are, frustrating Jergen and Dubose, taking photos of the so-called crime scene and busily collecting the names of those witnesses who haven't fled.

Dubose puts in a call for backup. There will be

other agents on scene as soon as they can be choppered in. Greater numbers will help push the hometown boys out of the picture.

But then the watch captain from the substation shows up, a guy named Foursquare, if it can be believed. He has a bulldog jaw and the steely eyes of a Vegas pit boss who would call his own mother a cheat and throw her out of the game if she won more than forty bucks at blackjack. He wants to know who the decedents are, and he's not satisfied to be told only that they are foreign agents. He wants to check their ID, but Jergen heatedly argues against disturbing the cadavers, even though there's no ID to find; he and Dubose had the foresight to take the wallets from the bodies of Washington and his wife before the local gendarmes arrived. They have also found a key to a Honda in one of the dead man's sport-coat pockets.

While Jergen debates jurisdiction with Foursquare, Dubose goes into the parking lot, supposedly to make a list of the vehicles that might belong to the deaders and to record the license-plate numbers, but in fact to try Washington's car key in each of the Hondas.

No sooner does Foursquare stop grumbling about needing to know who the decedents are than he takes aside Oren Luckman, the store manager, and is recording a statement from him. One of the deputies is searching for expended shell casings, and another escorts a tall, somber civilian to Jergen and introduces him as a town mortician who also serves as the coroner.

Dubose returns and takes Jergen aside to inform him that the key fits the green sedan. The car contains a trunkful of groceries in bags from the town's other major market. Evidently, they were stocking up for several weeks of hibernation. There is nothing else in the Honda to identify its owner, no registration paper and no insurance-company card in the glove box, as there should be.

While Captain Foursquare records Luckman's fevered reimagining of the shoot-out, Dubose goes to the manager's office. He intends to use the market's computer to back-door the California DMV and run the Honda's license plate to find the registered owner.

Jergen is left with the swarm of uniformed busybodies. If there's one thing he despises the most about local cops, no matter what locale they hail from, it's that too damn many of them think they have a sacred duty to enforce the law, as though the law isn't just what a bunch of money-grubbing power-crazed politicians cobble together, as if instead it's handed down by God on stone tablets. And here in Borrego Springs, he seems to be dealing with a *nest* of their kind.

He counsels himself to be patient with these sworn-to-serve-and-protect types. All will be well. If Dubose can identify to whom the Honda is registered, they will most likely have the address at which the Washingtons took shelter.

That's where the boy will be.

3

The tightly gathered trees took most of the snowfall upon their boughs, admitting but a fraction to the ground between them. No wind had yet arisen. Snow sought the earth in silence, mounding for the most part beneath the barren limbs of the deciduous hardwoods. The undergrowth was sparse. Carrying her leather tote bag, Jane had no trouble following Hendrickson, although the day was cold enough to make her eyes water. Her breath plumed from her.

How he knew, she couldn't tell, for the woods seemed too uniform to provide easily recognizable landmarks, but he glanced over his shoulder to say, "We've just stepped onto the estate. Not much farther now."

Anabel owned nine acres here, wrested from Booth's father in their divorce settlement. Only the lower three acres, on which the house was situated, were walled, the upper six left for some future purpose.

The stairhead building stood under pines, the lower limbs of which had been cut off to accommodate the structure, and therefore it was canopied by higher growth. Windowless, crafted from native stone, perhaps twelve feet in diameter, the structure had a domed roof of the same stone, so that it suggested an oversized, ancient kiln. The steel door stood in a steel frame.

She put down the tote and examined the Schlage deadbolt. The cylinder was rimless, preventing anyone from pulling it out of the escutcheon. The two spanner screws that fixed the escutcheon to the door had been soldered so they could not be removed. If anyone had been curious enough to want to break in to the building, they would have required a couple hours and would have made so much noise that even the caretakers of the house five hundred feet below would have been aware of the effort.

As Jane took the lock-release gun from the tote, Hendrickson let out a thin sound of distress and turned from the building and stood trembling more violently than could be accounted to the cold.

"You can do this," she told him. Then, remembering the power she had over him, she said, "You *will* do this."

He harked back to his childhood, as he had done before, his brow furrowing and his eyes narrowing and his voice turning hard. The rant came from him in a rush: *"Finding your way with a light is nothing, boy. But when you can go through it top to bottom in the bitter dark, as blind as some dung beetle living on bat shit in a cavern, then you'll be something. These stairs are life, boy, the truth of this life, of this dark world, the truth of humanity in all its cruelty and viciousness. If you want to survive, you pathetic little shit, you better learn to be strong like me. Go down the hole and* learn, *boy. Down the hole."*

His recital of his mother's tirade ended with a shudder and a series of frantic gasps for breath, as if he were drowning, though great exhalations smoked from him.

The storm-faded light grew dimmer at just that moment, the winter sun more an idea than a reality. The tree-roofed clearing seemed to be a borderland between the material world and a realm of spirits. A breeze arose at last and swept some snow off the boughs overhead, and shapen clouds of flakes moved through the clearing like half-formed figures of people lost and seeking.

"Don't make me go down in the dark," Hendrickson pleaded.

From the tote, Jane retrieved a flashlight and gave it to him.

She had one for herself.

"We won't be in the dark. We'll have our lights. You'll show me the way. You *will* show me the way. You understand, Booth?"

"Yes."

"You'll be all right."

"I will. I know I will," he agreed, though he didn't sound convinced.

If his mother was a twisted work, his father must have been one, too, in his own way. After all, it was the father who had found the crooked staircase; instead of reporting it to the state or to university archaeologists and anthropologists who would have thought it a treasure beyond valuation, he had kept it to himself as an amusement, a rare curiosity. He had used his longtime employees to construct this stairhead building.

Jane lightly kicked the wall to knock the snow from her shoes. They were wet all the way through, and her feet were cold.

She opened the door with the lock-release gun, reached inside, flipped a switch. Light bloomed in the round stone room. She ushered Hendrickson ahead of her and crossed the threshold after him.

The lock was a deadbolt that could only be engaged with a key. But before she let the door close behind her, she confirmed that a keyway existed on the inner face of the escutcheon. In case someone should lock the door from the outside, she would still be able to use the lock-release gun to get out of the building.

Directly ahead, the floor shelved away through a hole that Booth regarded with dread.

She went to it and directed the beam of her flashlight into it and saw steep stairs, perhaps of limestone, that had been shaped out of the natural rock flue with primitive tools. The way was narrow, the ceiling low ahead, and the walls of nature's making were mostly worn smooth by millennia of water's patient labor.

"You won't be afraid," she told Hendrickson. "You will show me the way, and you won't be afraid."

Although breath still paled from between his parted lips, he looked as dead as the man on the mortuary table in the basement of Gilberto's funeral home.

After a hesitation, he switched on his flashlight and took the lead into the crooked staircase.

4

Two cooling deaders on the market floor, a container of melting ice cream dripping through the contents of the shopping cart, blood here, brains there, Oren Luckman fluttering anxiously just beyond the scene of the shootings, the ugly light of overhead fluorescent tubes, the tedium . . .

The situation with Captain Foursquare and his contingent of diligent deputies becomes so untenable that Carter Jergen uses his smartphone to call an Arcadian who is deputy director of the NSA. The man is also a former United States senator who, as an elected official, always managed to wheedle an abundance of face time on TV. He has styled himself as a champion of public-employee unions, so there is little doubt that Foursquare will know his name.

The senator's voice is distinct and easily recognized, and when Jergen hands the phone to Foursquare, the captain is impressed, then charmed, then won over by whatever the great man tells him. Their conversation lasts at most four minutes, but Foursquare is smiling when he returns the phone to Jergen.

"You should have told me you work under him," the captain chides Jergen.

"Well, sir, I always feel it's wrong to drop his name unless I have to. I don't think I've done enough for the country to trade on the accomplishments of a man like him."

"That speaks well for you," says Foursquare. "We can't stand down entirely, but we'll stand aside until your incoming contingent gets here and we all agree there's nothing more we can do. He says they're airborne and sure to be here in half an hour."

"Thank you, Captain. I'm most grateful," Jergen says with as much fake sincerity as he can muster. In fact, he's no more grateful than he would be to a disease-bearing mosquito that keeps trying to take a bite of him.

And here comes Dubose, looking not like a man who has solved a mystery, but like a man who needs to take a leak and is on a quest to find the ideal person on whom to empty his bladder.

5

Decades after his cruel formation, Hendrickson going down the hole again, Jane following him but not so close that he might turn and strike her in a moment of unlikely rebellion . . .

The descending passage seemed to construct itself only as the beams of light flowed across it, as though such eerie architecture must be a work of the imagination, dreamed into being. Smooth, pale walls of stone sloped down in velvety folds shaped by unknowable millennia of moving water, no doubt including the melting of the miles-thick sheet formed during at least one ice age.

Millions of years earlier, long before a human being walked the earth, nature had begun to form the crooked staircase, perhaps when violent vertical faulting formed the Sierra Nevada mountains on the west and the Carson Range on the east, leaving the Tahoe Basin between.

The staircase was actually a series of small caverns, each partly atop the one below it, the entire formation of galleries angling down toward the lake, through more than five hundred feet of mountain, like a chambered hive. There were also narrow corridors of stone snaking off to other rooms that weren't among those vertically aligned; according to Hendrickson, some of those passages looped like entrails and returned to the main descent, creating a maze; others were dead ends, some a hundred feet long, some continuing for half a mile or farther before dwindling to such a restricted width that not even a child could crawl farther through them.

Jane's tote bag was slung from her left shoulder, and in her left hand she held a can of spray paint that Gilberto had given her. At each bewildering junction of stone passages, she marked the way back to the stairhead with an arrow.

Although the world itself, in its eternal remaking, had done the basic work through millions of years, human beings had taken nature's random art and carved it to a purpose. Where the floor sloped at a negotiable angle, it was left natural, but when it became precarious, especially when any steepness led to a fissure into which someone might fall, crude steps had been shaped in the stone. Each crevasse—as narrow as two feet, as wide as seven—was bridged by a plank seated in notches cut into the lips of the fissures. When Booth's father discovered the staircase, the bridge planks had long before rotted and fallen into the clefts they once spanned. The secondary passages had also been stepped and bridged where necessary, some climbing and some trending down into perpetual night.

Early in the descent, they arrived at a larger chamber before which Hendrickson halted. He bent forward, clutching his stomach as though plagued by abdominal pain. But he didn't look back at Jane or plead to retreat.

After a minute, rising to full height again, he continued into a room in which a fault line bisected the ceiling, matched by a parallel fault in the floor. The medieval atmosphere weighed on the heart, and the air carried the faint fungal smell of things that thrived only in the dark. The right half of the chamber was a foot higher than the left. Although the right portion lay dry and pale, the ceiling to the left bared a row of huge teeth like the staves of a castle portcullis that might drop to bar entry, from which brown water dripped onto a mud floor; the stone was wet, dark, glistening as if lacquered. On both sides of the room, on every ledge and on the floor were severed hands gone to bone in centuries past.

Hundreds of fleshless hands seemed to twitch in the sweeping beams of light, skeletal fingers extended as though in supplication or clutched as if in rage. Those in the dry space were mostly white and well preserved, but those in the moist area were more yellow than not, mottled brown, sometimes serving as matrixes on which mold grew like rodent hair.

Jane was prepared to find this—and worse—on their journey, because Hendrickson had spoken of it, but the tableau was a grislier spectacle than expected. She didn't know what to make of it, except that this was no sacred catacomb where peaceful people placed the dead with reverence. To her, trained in homicide investigation, these appeared to be trophies. The wrist bones were crushed and splintered where hands had been hacked from arms, perhaps sometimes from the arms of the living. The cavern told a story of violence and brutality, of ancient war and subjugation. Carved in the walls were strange runes, each sharp character like a cry of hatred.

"See this, you little coward. Look!" Hendrickson whispered. *"If a man intends you harm, cut off his hands before he can act."*

Whoever had shaped the steps and adapted the cavern to their purpose must have been those who murdered these hundreds and made the crooked staircase into an ossuary.

Evidence existed of Paleo-Indian tribes living in this area more than fourteen thousand years ago, but little was known of them other than they were hunters of large game, including mastodons. Their tools were thought to have been such as flint or obsidian spearheads and hammerstones, primitive and insufficient for the stone shaping done here. Their cultures were said to be largely peaceable, but in fact so little had they left behind that they were ghosts in the fog of ancient history.

Only carbon dating and other tests would help to determine who created this place and furnished it with bones. Perhaps some paleo culture had possessed more advanced tools than were thought. Or as Hendrickson suggested when she questioned him at Gilberto's place: It was known that, thousands of years nearer our time, the Northern Paiute had brutally oppressed the Washoe Indians; perhaps an even more militant faction of Paiutes had done part of this.

The Martis Indians had also lived in this general area for 2,500 years before disappearing without a trace around 500 B.C., which happened to be about the same time that other tribes invented the bow and arrow. These caverns might hold the remains of the long-vanished Martis people.

Hendrickson channeled his mother, and his words were like the susurrus of centipedes crawling the walls. *"See, boy, see this. Did they eat these people after slaughtering them? We're not far from Donner Pass, where stranded pioneers ate their dead to survive. Dog eat dog, so they say. More true is man eat man."*

Jane thought of Hendrickson, five years and younger, sleeping in a locked boy-size box, coffined in darkness as punishment, and by the age of six sent into this maze alone, at the top as they had entered this time, told that he would be let out only at the bottom. The first few times, he'd been given a flashlight, but on occasions beyond his counting, he'd been denied a light and had felt his way through damp stone corridors, down disconnected sets of zigzagging stairs, across fissure-bridging planks, through crypts appointed with trophies of genocide, like a lost spirit haunting the haunted dark, hearing noises he didn't make and wondering at their origin, feeling presences where none should be, with no food, with nothing to drink but the cold water that formed shallow pools in certain chambers and sometimes tasted like iron, sometimes like nothing he wanted to name, on the worst occasions lost for two or three days.

As pitiable as he was, he nevertheless deserved some admiration for having endured without being driven entirely insane. But if he had remained functional, he had nonetheless been mentally deformed, twisted and knotted into a creature that, though pitiable, had no slightest measure of pity for others. During his many ordeals in darkness, he at some point ceased to be just a boy and became a boy who was a monster, the minotaur of this labyrinth. He didn't eat human flesh as did the Minotaur of Crete, but other people had no value for him except to be used in whatever way the use of them might satisfy him.

For all her pity, Jane kept in mind, cavern by cavern, step by step, that what she had here on a leash was a monster who passed for human. In the long history of monsters, they sooner or later slipped their leashes.

6

S ome of the sheriff's deputies have returned to their regular patrols. Foursquare and two of his men are standing together in the produce department, admiring the fruit, waiting to see if they might be needed—which they won't be—when the additional NSA contingent arrives.

Upon his return from the manager's office, Dubose draws Jergen aside to the relative privacy of pallets stacked with large bags of charcoal being offered at a special price now that the barbecuing season is about to start in earnest. "This damn well better not be another freakin' banana peel we have to take a fall on before we can get our hands on that little bastard. The plates on that Honda expired four years ago, and the registration was never renewed. It shouldn't be on the road."

"You've got the name and address of who last registered it?"

"Some guy named Fennel Martin."

"What kind of name is Fennel?"

"Hell if I know. But he's still in the local phonebook at the same address that's on the registration."

The rhythmic sound of a rotary wing draws their attention to the window. As the glass begins to hum with vibrations, they step outside into the parking lot and use their hands as visors and look to the west, where the helicopter angles down out of the sun.

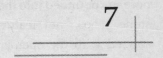

7

J ane used the spray paint so often that she worried the can might be empty before they reached the house at the bottom of the serried caverns, leaving critical final turns unmarked. She formed smaller arrows on the walls.

Most of the chambers through which they passed were marked with runes, but only a few of the larger ones contained bones. The least disturbing was nevertheless a dramatic display in a space decorated instead with pictographs that were perhaps far older than the runes. The contents also might have been older, suggesting that more than one ancient culture had used this place to memorialize their skill as hunters of both animals and humans. The skulls of three mastodons were elevated above Jane on pedestals of stacked stone, immense and chalk-white in the probing lights, shadows shifting in the sockets as if eyes of some immaterial nature still looked out from the empty craniums and across thousands of years of time. The enormous tusks, clearly having been broken out of the skulls in order to get them through the narrower passages, had somehow been reattached, curving in majestic threat.

In two successive chambers, hundreds of human skulls were arranged on ledges, like some collection of grotesque beer steins, most bearing evidence of ritualistic murder in the form of pikes made of chert or obsidian, one in each forehead, bristling like a horn, perhaps pounded into the skull with a crude hammer-stone. Those not featuring pikes had been accessorized with the open-jawed sharp-fanged skulls of rattlesnakes inserted in the place of human eyes, demonic visages configured thus bizarrely with what meaning it was impossible to say.

Hendrickson was transfixed by the sight of those evil-eyed totems, the papery bone of long-ago severed serpent heads issuing with silent hisses from skulls unmasked of faces.

"Let's go, let's go," Jane urged, chilled and weary of both body and spirit. "Let's get to the bottom of this place."

He didn't respond, but addressed himself as Anabel had lectured him forty years earlier, his quiet voice reverberant in the cavernous sarcophagus. *"Here's the truth, boy, the one truth. Take or be taken from, use or be used, rule or be ruled, kill or be killed."*

"Booth, do you hear me?"

He said nothing.

"Play Manchurian with me."

"Repeat after me, you ignorant little shit. Repeat after me, boy, repeat after me. Say this, say—do unto others before they can do unto you. Say it and mean it. Say it until your throat is raw, until your voice fails."

More adamantly, Jane commanded, "Booth, play Manchurian with me. *Now.*"

After a hesitation, he muttered, "Yes, all right. All right. Yes."

"You must do what I tell you."

"Yes, Mother."

"What did you say?"

"Yes, Mother. All right."

"Look at me. Booth, look at me *now*."

Hendrickson turned from the display of skulls, his face devoid of expression. As if he saw serpents in her stare, he bowed his head and lowered his eyes. "Yes. Of course. This way. It's not far now."

"Who am I, Booth?"

"Who are you?"

"That's what I asked."

"You're Jane Hawk."

"Why did you call me 'Mother'?"

"Did I?"

"Yes."

"I don't know. You're not her. You're you. I don't know."

She studied him. Then: "Lead me to the bottom of this place."

A plank bridging a wide cleft, a corridor of dripping stone, umbilicals of light quivering forward along the puddled floor

Two chambers from the bottom, a tumbled collection of small skeletons, discarded as if with contempt, didn't bear consideration, for they were not the remains of some elfin race out of Tolkien, but the bones of children that might have been the offspring of enemies conquered and killed with genocidal intent.

Half an hour after they entered the stairhead, they arrived at the bottom of the crooked staircase, where there waited what once must have been a cave that opened onto a last slope leading to the lake, by which this subterranean complex could be accessed. The mouth of the cave had been sealed off with mortared brick in which stood a steel door like that in the stairhead building.

Jane discarded the spray paint and set her light on the floor.

Hendrickson focused his beam on the keyway while she used the lock-release gun to disengage the deadbolt.

Beyond lay the promised room.

8

Two agents arrive by helicopter. Two more are on their way by ground transport.

Jergen and Dubose leave the airborne pair to deal with the now cooperative local authorities, to clean up the scene, and to bag the bodies. The waiting helo, which sits in a corner of the parking lot, will spirit the corpses away.

Except for a few locals who witnessed the incident, it will be as though nothing untoward occurred. There will be no press or TV coverage of the shootings in little Borrego Springs. No one will ever report that Gavin and Jessica Washington were killed here. There will be no autopsy, no coroner's report in *any* jurisdiction. Another plausible story will be concocted to account for their deaths, which will be framed as a tragic accident.

Now Dubose and Jergen, having administered tragic accidents to quite a few people over the years, set out in the VelociRaptor for the address at which they hope to find Fennel Martin, owner of the Honda sedan with the out-of-date license plates and the long-expired registration. Dubose drives.

Just beyond the town limits, Martin's home is a house trailer elevated on a foundation of concrete blocks, in the shelter of two big Indian laurels from which shadows yearn eastward. In the shade stands a white-painted metal table and four mismatched patio chairs. A small apron of lawn is long dead, and what grass has not withered away is thatched like a well-worn tatami mat.

Under a carport attached to the trailer stands a two-door Jeep Wrangler Sport maybe six or seven years old.

Steps formed of concrete block serve the door. Jergen and Dubose select their FBI credentials rather than those of the NSA, because the average citizen doesn't know what the NSA is, but still has some respect for the FBI. Dubose knocks.

The man who opens the door must have seen them arrive. He looks past them to the VelociRaptor and with a note of wonder asks, "Man, what is that? Is that a Ford F-150?"

"It used to be," says Dubose as he holds up his Bureau ID. "Are you Fennel Martin?"

The guy stares wide-eyed at Dubose's ID, and then

he looks at Jergen, and Jergen holds up his ID, and the guy says, "Really FBI? Wow. What's this about?"

"Are you Fennel Martin?" Dubose asks again.

The man is in his late thirties, lean and tan, with shoulder-length hair and a day's worth of beard, wearing flip-flops and jeans and a Smashing Pumpkins T-shirt. The average guy living on the edge of the law or a step outside of it usually is either arrogant and obstinate, making no effort to conceal his contempt, or else goes wobbly in the presence of police and presents himself as meek and compliant in the hope of appearing to be a model citizen. This man's reaction is neither of those. He seems genuinely astonished that FBI agents would appear at his door, perplexed, and just a little bit excited, as if a dull Sunday has suddenly become interesting.

"Yeah, that's me. I'm Fennel."

Dubose says, "We'd like to ask you a few questions about a car, Mr. Martin."

"A car? Sure. Man, I'm all about cars. What car is it?"

"May we come in, Mr. Martin? This might take a while."

"Well, the thing is, the place is kind of a mess," Martin says. He points at the white table and the folding chairs in the shade of one of the Indian laurels. "Let's sit there. Can I get you guys a couple beers?"

"That's very cordial of you, Mr. Martin. But we can't drink on duty." Dubose puts away his ID. "And we'd rather come inside."

To Fennel Martin's surprise, Dubose grabs him by

the crotch, squeezing hard, and by the throat and lifts him an inch off the floor and carries him backward into the house trailer.

9

The steel door at the bottom of the serried caverns opened into a room measuring about thirty by thirty feet. It was furnished as a study or home office in an elegant soft-contemporary style. Immense U-shaped desk and wall of cabinets in matching blond-finished wood. Armchair with a footstool and reading lamp. Sofa. The necessary occasional tables. There was as well an entertainment wall with a music system and a large TV.

According to Hendrickson, of the two interior doors, one led to a full bath, the other to a closet. Opposite the steel door by which they entered, another steel door led out of these quarters onto the extensive grounds behind the main house, which overlooked the lake.

From the exterior, the stone-walled building was said to look like modest servants' quarters and to match the style of the main house. But in here, there were telltale indications of a secret purpose. The windows were fitted with locking shutters of steel plate that could not have been penetrated by common burglars. And the door to the grounds had a feature that the door to the caverns did not: three four-inch-wide steel bars that extruded from the jamb, across the width of the door, when the deadbolt was engaged from outside. The door featured no obvious escutcheon or keyway; it was locked and unlocked only by a keypad on this side and another on the exterior wall.

All this was as Hendrickson had told her after she injected him in Gilberto's kitchen, and as he had confirmed after the nanomachine control had assembled.

"Let's do this fast," she said. "Get me those DVDs."

Hendrickson had said there was an alarm system for the main house but none here. He insisted that Anabel would not want police responding to any attempted break-in of this building.

Nevertheless, Jane wanted to be done and gone in five minutes.

Initially she had intended to take Hendrickson with her, to use him as an example of nanoweb control, to convince some uncorrupted authority—if she could find one—of the truth of this technology. But his psychological deterioration, which seemed to be continuing, made that plan untenable. She would have to leave him here.

Jane followed him into the large bathroom, which was entirely clad in honey-colored marble: ceiling, walls, floor, shower stall. The tub and sink were carved from blocks of the same material, and all the fixtures were gold-plated. Anabel had quarters in the main house; but when she wanted a bathroom here, it must be exquisitely appointed. The color of honey. For the queen bee.

Hendrickson pressed on the fluted, gilded frame

of the mirror above the sink, releasing a touch latch, and the mirror swung like a door. Within were the four shelves of a medicine cabinet, stocked with the usual items. When he pulled on the second and third shelves simultaneously, the interior of the cabinet came forward on rails, revealing a space beyond. From that hidden compartment, he withdrew a rectangular plastic box and handed it to her.

As Hendrickson rolled the interior of the cabinet back into place and closed the mirrored door, Jane flipped up the lid on the plastic box. Within were sixteen DVDs in cardboard sleeves. On each sleeve, a first name had been printed with a black felt-tip pen.

She said, "Your father's name was—"

"Stafford. Stafford Eugene Hendrickson."

In the study again, she found the DVD marked STAFFORD. She put the box on the desk. She hesitated to give the disc to Hendrickson. "You've really seen this?"

His face was slack and his voice without color, as though he had traveled into some gray kingdom of the soul, where he could no longer feel anything strongly. "Of course. Many times. We watched it together many times, Mother. Back then, it was on videotape. We didn't have DVDs then, did we? You had to transfer them to DVD."

She needed to be sure these discs contained what he'd said they did. She gave the DVD of his father to him. "Play this for me."

"Yes. All right."

He took it to the entertainment center.

In the years during which Jane had worked with the Bureau's Behavioral Analysis Units 3 and 4, she had been assigned to cases involving serial killers. When she had tracked their squamous kind to the snake holes they called home, as always she did, she had seen things that could never be purged from memory, that returned to her on sleepless nights. A firm faith in the rightness of this made world and in the promise of the human heart was required to look upon the works of those supremely evil individuals without losing hope for humanity in its entirety. That faith had sometimes been bruised, but never broken.

Yet she steeled herself for what would appear on this large-screen television. She intended to watch only enough of it to confirm that Hendrickson's description of it was accurate.

10

When Jergen follows Dubose and the wheezing Fennel Martin into the house trailer, he discovers why their host prefers to sit at the table in the yard to answer questions. The girl might be thirty, an ash-blond cutie.

Their explosive entrance surprises her. She thrusts up from the sofa, hastily buttoning her open blouse, though not hastily enough that Jergen has no chance to admire the fullness of her figure.

Approaching her, smiling in a friendly sort of way, he says, "What's your name, dear?"

"Who are you? What're you doing to him? You've hurt him."

Jergen flashes his Bureau ID, but the girl doesn't appear to be reassured by it.

Still smiling, he says, "He'll be okay. That's nothing. Things happen, that's all. Tell me your name, dear."

"Ginger."

"Ginger, can you show me where the bathroom is, please?"

"Why?"

"I want you to stay in the bathroom while we're having a chat with Mr. Martin. But I need to be sure there's no window big enough for you to climb out."

"There isn't."

"It's not that I don't believe you, Ginger. I do believe you. But I need to see for myself. It's the way I was trained. We go through a lot of training in the FBI. I'm just following protocol. You understand?"

"No. I guess. Yeah."

"So let's go see the bathroom."

The window is very small and near the ceiling. He puts down the lid of the toilet and gestures for her to sit there.

"Where is your phone, Ginger?"

"In my purse. On the table by the sofa."

"Good. You wouldn't want to be calling anyone. Just wait here, and we'll be gone in no time."

She is trembling. "I'll wait. I'm okay with waiting."

Jergen steps into the hallway, looks back at her.

"Fennel's not going to be ready for sex, after all. But when we're gone, you can play cards or something."

Jergen closes the door and returns to the living room, where the fan of the Smashing Pumpkins is sitting in an armchair.

Fennel's tan now has a gray undertone. Sweat slicks his face, jewels his eyebrows. With his right hand, he gently cups his crotch.

Dubose has moved a side chair to sit in front of their host.

Jergen perches on the edge of the sofa.

Dubose says, "Fennel, we need some truth, and we need it fast."

Fennel sounds thirteen when he says, "You aren't FBI."

"What I don't need," Dubose explains, "is your stupid opinions and commentary. I'll ask questions, you'll answer them, and we'll be on our way. Earlier, you said, 'I'm all about cars.' Which means?"

"I'm a mechanic. I have a place in town. It's not much, but I stay busy."

"You take cash to fake smog checks so dirty cars can pass inspection?"

"What? Shit, no. I have a business license to protect."

"You build secret compartments in the bodywork, so some asshole can run fifty kilos of heroin in from Mexico?"

Fennel glances at Jergen. "I think maybe I need an attorney."

"Don't answer my questions," Dubose explains,

"and what you'll need is a testicle transplant. Before you bullshit me, consider maybe I already know the truth."

The mechanic is too frightened to lie, but afraid that honesty will not avail him. "I run a clean business, man. I swear."

Dubose frowns and bites his lower lip as if he's disappointed in Fennel. "You once owned a green Honda. What happened to it?"

Fennel is surprised it's about this. And maybe alarmed. "I sold her. She was cheap, ran good, but she was the opposite of sexy."

"When was that?"

"I don't know exactly. Like maybe six years ago."

"Who'd you sell it to?"

"This guy. Some guy."

"Don't remember his name?"

"No. Not after so long."

"What did he look like?"

"He was Asian."

"What Asian—Chinese, Japanese, Korean?"

"I don't know. How would I know?"

"You put an ad in the paper, on some Internet site?"

"No. Just a sign outside my shop."

"What's your bank?"

"Bank? Wells Fargo. What's my bank matter?"

"I'll need the account number. And the amount of the check."

Fennel is sweating anew. "His bank wasn't the same as mine."

"You remember *that*, do you? Doesn't matter. We

can track it from bank to bank. What was the amount of the check?"

Fennel looks around as if he's lost, as if he doesn't recognize his own living room. "After six years it comes back to bite me? *Six years?* This totally sucks."

11

They stood before the large LED television screen. Hendrickson pushed PLAY and handed the remote to Jane.

In silence, the camera moved past torches standing tall in oil drums filled with sand, serpentine coils of dark smoke rising toward vent holes in the ceiling. Past the corrugated walls of the Quonset hut, firelight rippling with the contours of the metal, illuminating goggle-eyed lizards in vertical pursuit of cockroaches that could not outrun the spooling tongues. Racks of candles, hundreds of thick candles, mostly black and red, but here a cluster of canary yellow, the fluttering flames patterning everything around them with faux butterflies and causing the very air to glow as in a furnace. Voodoo veves on the concrete floor, intricate patterns drawn with wheat flour and corn meal and ashes and redbrick dust, representing astral forces here attendant.

The scene had an inauthentic quality, as if it had

been staged in imitation of true voodoo, to establish a narrative explaining the murder to come. This suspicion was confirmed when four men entered, dressed not in what voodoo priests would wear, but clad in black and hooded to maintain anonymity. At the center of all, a pale and naked man lay chained to a sacrificial altar formed by three concentric circles of stepped stone around a center post carved as a pair of twining snakes.

Speaking to himself as Anabel had spoken to him, Hendrickson said, *"There he is, the gutless wonder, the worthless piece of shit who fathered you. You'll hear him beg. You'll hear him beg me. You listen to him beg, boy, and learn never to beg for anything from anyone. See here what begging gets you."*

The camera panned across a battalion of conical blue and green drums, and as it returned to the naked man, the silence gave way to the rhythmic beating of the drums, though neither the instruments nor those who played them were shown again. Stafford Hendrickson did indeed beg Anabel by name, his pleas desperate and then hysterical as the four black-garbed executioners began to effect a prolonged act of murder. Tourniquets to stem the bleeding, preventing the victim's quick demise. A razor-sharp machete. They began with his right hand.

Jane used the remote, and the screen went blank.

Booth Hendrickson said, *"Your daddy was a pencil-neck history geek. He loved the past in all its barbaric splendor. He loved his crooked staircase, his private archeological treasure. I wouldn't give him the satisfaction of adding any*

part of his body to that collection. They left him to the Ja-
maican lizards and cockroaches until the police found the
worthless bastard."

12

Although Carter Jergen wants a turn driving the VelociRaptor, and although there are occasions when his partner appalls him, he has to admit there are also times when he greatly enjoys watching Radley Dubose at work, as now. In numerous subtle ways, the big man builds an air of menace, akin to how a thunderstorm builds a charge leading up to that sudden first flash of lightning. Poor Fennel Martin. The mechanic is profoundly intimidated.

Dubose gets up from his chair and paces the small living room, seeming even bigger than usual by comparison with the humble space he occupies, the floor creaking under him. "When a car is sold in California, the seller is required by law to file a Notice of Transfer and Release of Liability with the DMV, providing among other things the new owner's name. You never did that, Mr. Martin."

"He didn't want me to. Part of the deal was I wouldn't file a notice of transfer."

"You're talking now of the mysterious Asian buyer—who never filed for a new registration, either."

"He *was* an Asian guy. I wasn't lying about that."

"What was his name, Mr. Martin?"

"He never gave me a name. He didn't even speak English."

Dubose stopped pacing and turned and stared down at Fennel.

"It's true," the mechanic insists. "He had it all typed out."

"Had what typed out?"

"The deal he wanted to make for the Honda, the terms."

"He couldn't speak English, but he could type it?"

"Somebody typed it for him. Whoever was really buying the car. I don't know who. I really don't."

"So somebody wanted a car that couldn't be traced back to him. Didn't you worry about liability, Mr. Martin? Like if they used the car in a bank robbery?"

"He wouldn't do that. He was a very nice man, very respectful."

"Who was?"

"The Asian guy."

"But he wasn't the actual buyer. The actual buyer could have been some damn terrorist going to use it as a car bomb."

The mechanic bends forward in the armchair, hands on his thighs, head between his knees, as if nauseated and about to spew.

"It wasn't used as a car bomb," Dubose says. Fennel shudders with relief. "But we damn well have to find whoever bought it and find him fast. What aren't you telling me, Mr. Martin? There needs to be one more piece to this story of yours if it's to make sense."

In his misery, Fennel Martin speaks to the floor between his feet. "You know what it is."

"I know what it has to be, but I need to hear it."

"The guy comes to me with the terms typed out and a sort of briefcase full of cash. The Honda's six years old then. It's got some serious miles on it. Maybe it's worth six thousand. There's *sixty* thousand in the bag."

"Tax free," Dubose says.

"Well, shit, I guess not now."

After a silence, looming over Fennel, Dubose says, "So you figured, if the car was used for a crime, then you'd act surprised to find it missing, say it was stolen."

"Seemed like it would work. I really needed the money."

"Did you ever see anyone driving that car around town?"

"Not in years. Two, maybe three times back then, I saw it parked. Never saw anyone with it. I didn't *want* to see anyone. I didn't want to know who or why."

"You didn't want to risk him asking for his money back."

The mechanic says nothing.

"Look at me, Mr. Martin."

The mechanic doesn't raise his head. "I don't want to."

"Look at me."

"You'll hurt me."

"Even worse if you don't look at me."

Reluctantly, Fennel Martin turns his head, looks up, terrified.

Dubose says, "I'm in a mood to bust your balls. I mean that literally. You made me pull the details out of you one by one. So now you better hope there's something useful you've not yet told me. Because if there isn't, then you'll be useless to women when I'm done with you."

Fennel Martin is a poster boy for pathos. "There isn't anything more. I'm not hiding anything more. There's nothing more."

"There better be."

"But there isn't."

"Get up, Mr. Martin."

"I can't."

"Get up."

"Maybe . . ."

"I'm waiting."

"Maybe one thing. It was kind of funny. Those typed-up deal terms. They were done as bullet points. And after each bullet point, whoever he was, he typed 'please and thank you.' Like it said, 'Purchase price will be sixty thousand dollars, please and thank you.' And 'Neither of us will report the sale, please and thank you.'"

Dubose stares down at him with contempt and after a long silence wonders, "What am I supposed to do with that idiot tidbit?"

"It's all I have. I didn't even know I had that."

"Did you save that paper you were given?"

"No."

After another silence during which the mechanic looks as if he will die from suspense, Dubose says, "Hell, you're not worth the effort." He walks out of the trailer.

13

It was one thing to see the aftermath of such brutality, another thing altogether to watch even a minute of it in progress.

Sickened, Jane returned the DVD to its cardboard sleeve and then put it in the plastic box with the fifteen others. She trusted Booth Hendrickson's word that two discs featured other of Anabel's divorced husbands. One would show he who supposedly hung himself with a noose of barbed wire, except that he begged for his life before hooded men did the hanging for him. And perhaps it was the same hooded men, well paid and eager to accommodate, who videoed the other husband pleading for mercy before they set the house on fire—or in fact set him on fire and let him carry the flames through the house.

Among the other DVDs were more recent videos that recorded the injection and enslavement of a United States senator, a governor who was thought to have a future in national politics, a Supreme Court justice, the president of a major television network, the publisher of a highly respected magazine of opinion, and others who were now adjusted people. Anabel nurtured a particular animus against each; she wanted videos of their conversion for the historical record and for her own entertainment.

With this evidence and all the additional names and details that Hendrickson had revealed, Jane would find a way to bring the Techno Arcadians to ruin, every last one of them.

As she was putting the plastic container in her tote bag, the TV came on. The screen filled with the face of Anabel Claridge, at seventy-five still beautiful. An imperious beauty. High cheekbones, chiseled features. Hair thick and glossy, faded from black to a lustrous silver rather than white. Her eyes were as bright blue as Jane's, as blue as Petra Quist's eyes and the eyes of Simon's wives, a more fierce blue perhaps, but lacking any glint of madness.

Hendrickson stood before the TV, zombified, as Jane had left him. He had apparently inserted another DVD.

But then Anabel said, "Booth, what are you doing there? What stupid thing have you allowed to happen?"

"I'm sorry, Mother. I'm sorry. I'm sorry. She made me do it."

Anabel was broadcasting live, perhaps via Skype. Behind her a window, beyond the window a palm tree. The estate in La Jolla.

In the grip of morbid fascination, Jane had taken a couple steps away from the desk and had evidently come into the range of the camera built into the TV.

The matriarch's eyes turned to her. "My son isn't a weakling like his worthless father. My son is strong. How did you break him so fast?"

Evidently, when Hendrickson accessed the secret space behind the medicine cabinet, he'd triggered an alarm that was phoned not to the police, but to Anabel in faraway La Jolla.

The woman's gaze shifted from Jane to her son. "Booth, take no chances. Big firepower. Kill her."

He turned away from the TV, from Jane, and started across the room toward the closet door.

Jane said, "Booth, play Manchurian with me."

The gasp of shock from Anabel was proof enough that no one had known Jane had acquired ampules of the control mechanism when she'd been in Bertold Shenneck's house in Napa Valley, weeks earlier.

"Play Manchurian with me," Jane repeated.

Again he failed to respond as he worked the lever handle on the closet door.

Jane drew her Heckler and fired twice as he darted into the closet, the first round drilling the jamb and showering him with splinters, the second passing through the diminishing gap between the jamb and the closing door, which slammed shut.

"You ignorant skank." Anabel's hatred was in fact *rancor*, the rancidity of mind and heart evolved from cherished malignity that had been long souring, festering, now virulent and implacable. Her venomous rancor had the power to transmogrify her face from that of an elegantly aging grande dame out of the pages of *Town & Country* into a grotesque countenance both terrifying and beautiful, as might be the face of a fallen angel enraptured by the power to do evil. "You foolish little twat. Your control is layered over the control that I injected a month ago. Mine rules over yours. He's *mine*, and he always will be."

No wonder he had been disintegrating psychologically. One web was woven across the other, his skull crowded with nanostructures, his free will long extinguished.

Big firepower. He was getting a fully automatic weapon, maybe an automatic shotgun with an extended magazine.

Anabel in distant La Jolla was a threat for another day. Booth was *now*.

One way out.

Jane holstered the pistol, grabbed the tote, and rushed to the door by which they had entered.

As she yanked open the steel slab, a weapon spoke repeatedly inside the closet. A volley of high-powered rounds drilled the door, cracked and shrieked into furniture behind her.

She crossed the threshold, snatched her flashlight from the floor where she had left it, switched it on, and hurried up a ramp of stone into a higher chamber. The steel door closed with a crash that echoed dire warnings through this nautilus of stone.

14

Wearing sunglasses against the nuclear glare of the desert sun, cruising the town, such as it is, in the VelociRaptor, looking for he knows not what, bringing to bear all the pathetic intellectual faculties he possesses and what little knowledge Princeton will have bothered to impart, Dubose drives.

Riding shotgun, wearing sunglasses, more concerned about their situation than he cares to admit, Carter Jergen says, "We never did get lunch. Where should we have dinner? At the quaint Mexican bar and grill, the taco house, a vending machine at some tacky motel?"

"If he sold it to someone who lived in town," Dubose says, "then he would have seen the Honda more than twice over the years."

"Possibly," Jergen acknowledges.

"Definitely. Someone local bought it, but not someone in town. Someone willing and able to pay a boatload of money to avoid having a car registered in his name."

"I wouldn't call sixty thousand a boatload."

"It was a boatload to Fennel Martin."

"We never did ask him what's with the name *Fennel.*"

"I did. While you were putting Ginger in the toilet."

Jergen winced. "Bathroom."

"His mother, she's big into herbal medicine, says eat enough fennel every day, you add twenty years to the average lifespan, so she doesn't just feed it to him, she names him for it."

"How old is his mother?"

"She died when she was thirty-two. What we're going to do is we're going to cruise around the valley while we have a few hours of light, have a look."

"Look for what?"

"Something. Anything. You got an iPhone picture of the Honda?"

"Yes."

"We'll show it to some people we see here and there. Maybe one of them will know it. For a Honda, it's a peculiar shade of green."

This is too much for Jergen, this claim of Sherlockian mastery of esoteric detail. "You know twelve-year-old Honda colors?"

"I love Hondas. My first car was a Honda."

Dubose still seems as if he stepped out of a comic book, but the difference this time is that Carter Jergen is beginning to feel as though he's losing substance from association with this hulk and will wind up, himself, like a fumbling detective in some Saturday-morning TV cartoon show.

15

In the reeling and seesawing beam, the smooth wet flowstone seeming to throb, like the peristalsis of some monstrous esophagus trying to swallow her as she struggled upward . . . Climbing open-mouthed to minimize the gasp and wheeze of respiration, listening intently for sounds of pursuit, which will precede the gunfire . . .

Out of the cave that adjoined the room where the face of Anabel floated on the LED screen, through the first of the caverns, Jane's quick footsteps were soft on dry stone, squelching on the wet. She came next into the chamber where, on both sides, the skeletons of children were heaped in a timeless testament to hate and cruelty. The path through that boneyard of innocents brought her to a lich-gate formed from slabs of stone tumbled in one or more ancient quakes. Three passages provided a choice. As she took the one marked by a white arrow of paint, from below came the thunder of the steel door slamming shut, doomful echoes ringing off the stone to all sides of her.

He was in the crooked staircase and climbing.

Bite on the fear. There was a boy to live for.

Pressing forward, she passed through a corridor of sweating stone, droplets of water falling cold on her face, and in the next cavern arrived at a plank that bridged a fissure perhaps more than seven feet wide. When she reached the farther side of the bridge, she put her tote down and probed the cleft with her light. It was about thirty feet deep, with sloped walls that would allow a swift and safe descent of the farther side and a clamberous ascent of this nearer face. He would need a few minutes to transit that territory, precious time in which she could get a safer distance ahead of him.

She put the flashlight on the floor, the beam fanning across the stone to the crude bridge. She knelt and lifted her end of the plank out of the notch in which it rested, and pulled hard, dragging it from the other notch on the farther side. The heavy length of wood slipped from her hands, clattering into the cleft, knocking leaden-bell sounds from the walls of stone.

On her feet again, she snatched up the tote with its precious evidence, plucked the flashlight from the floor, and switched it off. She looked back toward the dripping corridor, to the lich-gate at the farther end of it, beyond which light swept back and forth in the tomb of the innocents. Now that Hendrickson had entered the labyrinth, he was coming faster than she had hoped, with whatever fully automatic weapon he possessed.

Clicking on the light, she hurried through the remainder of the cavern. She ascended a narrow flight of low and uneven steps, across one of which slithered three translucent alabaster insects of a kind she had never seen before, each the size of her thumb, the beam of light revealing their inner organs like miniature voodoo veves in photonegative. She cautioned herself that, although haste was essential, she couldn't afford to trip and fall. She would never escape this preview of damnation with a broken leg.

Not halfway across the upper room, Jane heard Hendrickson in the lower chamber, beyond the stepped passage. He shouted to her, boasting like a boy: "I can jump! I don't need a plank. I can jump that far easy. I can jump!"

She dared not wait to hear him screaming in pain from the bottom of the fissure. Perhaps he could have jumped across the gap forty years earlier, as a spry and limber boy, but though he might now be regressing into some adolescent mental state, he was nonetheless a man in his late forties, with less athletic ability than in his youth. Praying for his fall, she hurried on and was spurred faster when, instead of a scream of agony, he let loose a cry of triumph at having cleared the wide fissure without any need of a bridge.

The exit passage from the current cavern angled sharply to the right. She ducked into it. She switched off her light and tucked it under her belt. Dropped the tote. Drew the Heckler. Turned to the room that she'd just left. She would kill him when he came off the steps where the ghostly insects had crossed her path. The muzzle flash of the Heckler would reveal her position, but he would be wounded or dead before he could return fire.

Jane heard him on those stairs, but there was no jiggling light by which to measure his ascent. He was coming in the dark. Suppose he *had* regressed to adolescence or childhood. If so, then in his diminished state, perhaps he'd found the fear-etched memory of the architecture of this stone hive, perfected through thousands of hours of blind exploration, and now had no more need of light than did the sightless insects on the stairs.

Although her heart knocked at a gallop, the pistol felt steady in her two-hand grip, and all she needed to do was listen for the change in his breathing and the difference in his footfalls when he topped the stairs. He would be directly in front of her, thirty feet away. She wouldn't be able to put every round in the body core, but four shots squeezed off in quick succession would result in at least a couple hits, certainly one of which would wound him badly if not kill him.

Absolute darkness, without a single point of light, with no varying shades of black to give perspective, was disorienting. She held her stance and didn't let the gun drift to one side or the other. He needed less than a minute to climb the steps, but time seemed attenuated in this total eclipse. She held her breath, the better to hear when he transitioned from the stairs. Suddenly there was only silence.

Case after case, in the Bureau and now gone rogue from it, she survived because of training and intuition. If she'd had to choose between one or the other, she would have forgone training to rely on intuition— the still, small voice that speaks out of your bone and blood and muscle.

It spoke to her now, and she knew that Hendrickson anticipated a trap. He'd come off the stairs with his breath held, careful to make no sound in his final few steps. He would start moving sideways around the chamber that lay between them, out of her blind line of fire. Hoping she had been quick enough to intuit his intent, she didn't hesitate to squeeze off shots, although just two, not daring to expose herself through twice that many. An extra two seconds might be the difference between life and death. As she juked back into the passageway, he fired a burst at her muzzle flash, maybe six rounds. Stone cracked, bullets ricocheted with thin banshee shrieks, and even through the roar, she heard the distinct and mortal whistle of a round or two passing through the opening where she had stood.

She had to keep him guessing for ten seconds, fifteen. If she dared the flashlight, he'd follow, hose the passageway, and take her down either with a direct hit or a couple bank shots. She plucked the tote off the floor, left the flash tucked in her waistband, moving into the pitch-black passageway. She knew that in twelve or fifteen feet, it curved to the left, a ramp of flowstone, and she thought it lacked steps all the way to the top, although her memory was but a crude sketch compared to the mental blueprints he could consult.

16

They were hours late. Travis didn't want to believe anything bad had happened to them, but they were very late.

Although he was supposed to stay away from the windows, he now stood in the living room, staring out at the highway, hoping to see the green car drive up to this little blue house, everyone safe and happy, after all

Cars passed now and then, but never the right one.

The day someone killed his dad, he'd been playing at a friend's house, staying overnight. He hadn't heard about his dad until the next day.

He didn't want to hear about Uncle Gavin and Aunt Jessie later. He wanted them to come home. He asked God to get them home.

The dogs were restless. Duke and Queenie roamed the house, not just on patrol, but as if looking for something.

Looking for Gavin and Jessie, just like Travis knew Gavin and Jessie were supposed to be there. The dogs knew Gavin and Jessie were supposed to be there, just like Travis knew.

It was time to feed the dogs. There was kibble, brought from home with biscuit treats and collars and leashes and blue poop bags.

He knew how to measure the kibble. Soon he would have to give them kibble and leash them and take them outside.

He didn't want to take them outside. For one thing, he wasn't supposed to leave the house. Don't answer the door, don't go near the windows, don't leave the house.

Those were the rules. His mom said the best chance anyone had for a good and happy life was to play by the rules.

For another thing, he was afraid if he broke the rule about not leaving the house, he would jinx Gavin and Jessie. Then maybe they would never come back.

Duke came to his side and stood looking out at the palm-tree shadows stretching long, the sunshine, the highway. The dog made a crying sound.

17

The curving ramp of flowstone ascended without steps. Although Jane repeatedly misjudged the curve, bumping against the walls, she made it to the top, where she stood for a moment, listening to the hush below. He seemed hesitant to follow closely, as if he, too, feared being hosed in those confines.

Keep moving. Plan the action and commit. Stalking and being stalked, you're more likely to die from lack of commitment than from taking action.

Because she had one more task than she had hands, she holstered the pistol. She carried the tote in her left hand, the flashlight now in her right, two fingers across the lens to damp the beam, so the glow might not be as easily seen around corners or from another room.

Sideways through a narrow passage, as if she were a fencer, the light her foil. Into a chamber with an open center surrounded by a peristyle of columns formed by stalactites meeting stalagmites; the atmosphere that of a temple, as if some subterranean congregation of mutant form gathered here according to a nether-world calendar, to worship gods unknown. Three passageways led out, and she took the one marked by a white arrow of paint, glancing back frequently.

She was like Jonah in the belly of the whale, al-though if this had been a leviathan, it would have lived hundreds of millions of years ago in a sea that had receded, its massive corpus fossilized, its endless bowels turned to stone.

They had taken half an hour to descend from the stairhead, but ascent would take longer. She hoped that by moving faster than might seem prudent, she would not only put distance between herself and Hendrickson in his blind pursuit, but also make her way to the surface in as little as forty minutes.

She found herself holding her breath when she didn't intend to hold it, and her mouth repeatedly filled with saliva, perhaps ruled by a subconscious fear that the sound of swallowing would be enough to bring him down on her.

In the first room of skulls with their lethal pikes of chert and obsidian, with their fanged and yawning eyes, the deep stillness behind Jane suddenly meant to her not that Hendrickson was creeping cat-quiet, but that he was no longer following in her wake. Not that he was shot and dead. Not that he was incapacitated by injury. Not that he had descended into some madness in which he could not function. *He was no longer following her because he was taking another route known only to him and would be waiting for her someplace ahead.*

She halted with hundreds of eyeless sockets gazing at her from their ledges, with hundreds of humorless smiles turned upon her. No. Bite on the fear. She knew what to do. There was death everywhere in this place, yes, but there was death everywhere in the world above, as well. *Between the idea and the reality, between the motion and the act falls the shadow.* Even in the Valley of the Shadow of Death, keep moving. Plan the action and commit. Hesitation was lethal.

18

On this bright Sunday afternoon, in rural Borrego Valley, the white clapboard church with the white shingled steeple seems luminous in the fierce desert sun, as if it takes the hard light into itself and softens it and gives it back in a form that is easier on the eyes. It reminds Carter Jergen of those carefully detailed, miniature buildings that people use to create precious little villages in Christmas displays through which scale-model electric trains go *clickity-clickity-clickity* in tedious circles.

A couple dozen vehicles are parked in front of the place, and newly arrived people are going not into the church, but around the side of it, to join others gathering in a bosk of trees under which stand maybe a dozen long picnic tables.

Dubose pulls the VelociRaptor to the side of the road and studies the scene for a moment. "What's all this about?"

"It's Sunday," says Jergen.

"But it's not Sunday *morning*."

"Some of the new arrivals are carrying baskets."

"Baskets of what?"

"Maybe food," Jergen suggests. "Maybe later they're going to have Sunday supper together."

After consideration, Dubose says, "I don't think I like this."

Jergen agrees. "Dull as bingo night at an old folks' home. But we can show the Honda photo to a lot of people in a few minutes."

Dubose glowers in thought. "All right. But let's get the hell in and out." He drives into the church lot and parks.

As they're walking across the blacktop, Jergen glances back at the VelociRaptor. It looks like some magnificent machine predator, that, when no one is looking, will become animate and eat all the crappy little vehicles surrounding it.

As they reach the corner of the church, the gleeful squeals of children rise in a raucous chorus, and Dubose halts. "Oh, shit."

Kids tend to want to climb in the giant's lap and pull his ears and make a honking noise when they pinch his nose. He's like a big shaggy dog to them.

"Ten minutes," Jergen promises.

They follow a brick walkway through a landscape of pebbles and cactuses and silver-dollar plants and various weird succulents, to the cluster of nine big trees that shade the picnic area.

None of the younger children are in the bosk, where the adults are mingling. A separate rubber-floored playground features a jungle gym, a tube slide, swings, and other attractions that Jergen thought had gone extinct with the invention of the Game Boy. Screaming kids are running, jumping, sliding, swinging, and slashing at one another with foam-rubber swords.

"Sonofabitch," Dubose mutters, but he doesn't bolt.

Jergen asks a woman in a flowered muumuu if the minister is in attendance, and she points to a man of about thirty who is standing two trees away from them, chatting with parishioners. "Pastor Milo," she says.

Pastor Milo has a shaved head and an athletic physique. He wears sneakers, white jeans, a blue Hawaiian shirt, and an earring that is a dangling cross.

Remembering Reverend Gordon M. Gordon of the Mission of Light Church, Jergen whispers to Dubose, "Try not to shoot this one."

19

The tote slung over her left shoulder, the flashlight in her left hand now, two fingers still over the lens to allow only the minimum of necessary light, the Heckler & Koch in her right hand, no hope of doing this with a two-hand grip . . .

All five senses enhanced by adrenaline and fear. Hyperacute. The darkness layered with moving shadows, moving not because something living shared the immediate space, moving because the light she carried briefly enlivened phantoms as she progressed. The whisper of her breathing. Otherwise no sounds except the slow dripping of water at sundry places in the gloom, ticking like clocks that had marked the years in their millions. The scent of wet stone, of her own fear sweat.

How very like a dream it often was, these minutes before a final accounting, when it came down to kill or be killed, and this time more than ever dreamlike. Caverns flowing for the most part in soft folds, as if the walls continuously melt and re-form around her. The massive tusks and skulls of mastodons materializing like some gene-stored memory of another incarnation many lives before this one. Here again the regiments of skeletal hands in bony gesture, once sheathed in flesh and occupied with work, with play, with making love, with making war. And in every dream, somewhere a beast prowled, human or not, the human kind more terrifying than others. Only the human monster knew beauty and rejected it, knew truth and disdained it, knew peace and did not prefer it, unlike the tiger and the wolf who knew not.

This time it was a boy, a lost boy in spite of the almost five decades he'd lived and sought his way, now crawling this underworld, more confident in the blinding dark than in the light. If he would kill her because he'd been told to kill her, he might kill her with particular savagery also because in his dementia he confused her with the hated mother who had molded him from boy into beast.

When Jane reached the end of the display of hands, she paused in a kind of vestibule between caverns. Just before the terminus of this small connecting chamber lay a generous passageway to the right and a narrower one to the left, and directly forward a room awaited without grisly ornamentation. She was only a couple levels below the stairhead.

Easing forward, she lifted the two shading fingers from the lens, and the light lanced the wide corridor to the right: steps zigzagging down, walls dissolving away into the dark. The narrower passage to the left led straight away, without steps and continuing beyond the reach of the beam.

She covered the lens again and stood listening. From the cavern directly ahead came not the drip of water but a drizzling sound. She recalled a flue to one side of that room, from which water issued in a thin ribbon. She strove to hear *through* the drizzle, which was a white noise that might mask a sound more meaningful, but otherwise there was only stillness.

A ledge of stone overhung the opening between the vestibule and the next cavern. She hesitated beneath it, right arm close to her side, the pistol pointed forward, and again raised her fingers from the lens. The light speared out at full strength, and she swept the room ahead. There was no immediate threat, no irregularities in the walls where a man might press out of sight and wait for her to pass.

The only tricky spot would be the fissure that bisected the space and had to be crossed on a plank. She could not remember how wide or deep it was. In her ascent, at other bridges, she had been wary, afraid that he might be hidden in a shallow cleft, waiting to shatter her with a barrage from below when she set foot on the plank. As close as she was now to the surface, every crossing of this kind became more dangerous than the one before it.

She damped the beam again and came out from under the overhang. The motion and the act were one, so that she heard him only in the fraction of a second during which he dropped from the ledge and fell on her, driving her to the floor. No time to turn and shoot. The Heckler flung from her hand, spinning across the floor. Flashlight rolling away as well. The breath having been driven out of her, for a moment she could not resist, all of his weight atop her, and she felt herself as close to death as ever she had been.

He could have finished her then, but he relented and forced her onto her back, straddling her and pincering her with his knees, his left hand around her throat, gripping with such ferocity that she could not get a full breath to replenish what had been knocked from her in the fall. In the backwash from the flashlight, his face was a surreal work of light and shadow, so fiercely configured by hatred and rage that he looked little like himself, looked hardly human, as though during his ascent he'd shed layer after layer of identity, until nothing remained but a primordial self, uncivilized and unreasoning, a being of pure and darkest emotions.

When he spoke, the words came in a tortured shriek, exploding in a spray of spittle. "*He's mine, and he always will be. Is that right? IS THAT RIGHT? He's mine, and he always will be? You think so? What do you think now, you vicious bitch? Am I yours? Will I always be? No! YOU ARE MINE NOW.*" He quoted his mother to Jane as though Jane had spoken those words, and if he knew the difference between her and Anabel, it was a difference that didn't matter to him. She clawed at his hand on her throat, tearing the skin. A darkness not of the room but within her faded the perimeter of her vision as Hendrickson picked up something with his right hand and raised it high. A large bone. A human femur. Taken from some room she had not seen. At the broken end, wicked splinters encircled the hollow core in which marrow had once produced blood within the living bone. He might have descended into such dementia that he was no longer able to operate a gun, or maybe he hadn't taken more than a single spare magazine when he'd set out in pursuit of her. But as she gazed up at his diabolic face, into eyes radiant with decadent desire and bloodlust, she knew that he abandoned the gun because it wasn't *personal*. He needed this to be a hands-on murder, to smell her terror and feel her quake beneath him, to know intimately the warmth and consistency of her blood. Her vision dimmed further.

If there was one image she could take with her on leaving this world, it must be the face of her child, her sweet Travis, the face of innocence in answer to this evil countenance. He drove the jagged femur at her eyes, and perhaps it was the thought of Travis that electrified her, that gave her strength even when she didn't have breath. She heaved against his pinning weight and turned her head, and the bone stabbed stone, spalling off splinters that prickled across her face.

Hatred boiling for decades had resulted in blackest malignity, which was the source of his inhuman strength, but when the bone cracked into the floor with such force, the reverberations coursing up his right arm for a moment weakened him, and the femur slipped from his numbed fingers. He wanted her blind and disfigured and dead. When he saw her alive and unmarked, his rage became so great that he lost even his animal cunning. He let go of her throat with his left hand and pulled his arm back and made a fist, and in so doing ceased to pincer her thighs with his knees. She drew her right leg out from under him, knee to her chest, and as his fist hammered down, she thrust her foot hard at his balls, missed the target, but landed the blow solidly in his groin. The kick unbalanced him, and his punch found only air. She thrust up and shoved him, he fell away from her, and she scrambled to her feet.

Gasping for breath, she backed off, scanning the

floor for her pistol. It was lost in shadows, or maybe it had spun across the stone and into the fissure.

Hendrickson clambered to his feet with his back to her, spewing a sewage of obscenities unlike anything she'd heard before, as if he had no language anymore except for words that were scurrilous and filthy, lacking the presence of mind even to make of them coherent invective. He turned and saw her and came after her, and there was nothing for her to do but snatch up the femur. Some of the wicked points had snapped off the broken end, but at the same time the bone had further shattered, exposing other points as sharp as stilettos. He rushed her, and Jane didn't retreat or stand her ground, but instead thrust forward to meet him. Reckless in his wrath, he was surprised by her assault and failed to knock her arm aside as she drove the jagged end of the leg bone into his throat.

She stepped quickly backward, leaving the bone embedded, and though blood ran from the wound, there was no arterial spurting, as she had hoped there would be. He stood stunned and swaying, one hand on the femur, working his mouth but producing no obscenities. She thought that he must go to his knees, but instead, gagging noisily, he pulled the bone from his throat and held it by the shank. He took a step toward her with the weapon, towering like the indestructible avatar of some cruel god. His foot came down on the flashlight, and he kicked it out of his way, his grin a crescent of darkness and red teeth.

Like a roulette wheel, the spinning light gave her one last hope of a win, coming to a stop so that the beam revealed the Heckler. She picked up the pistol, turned with it in a two-hand grip, and shot Booth Hendrickson three times as, hand fisted around the ancient femur, he came at her with the glee of a man who'd been shorn of his soul and all restraints therewith. When he was down and dead on the floor, she shot him twice again.

20

P astor Milo assures them he has great respect for the FBI, in spite of some doubts he expresses about recent directors. As he escorts Jergen and Dubose among his parishioners, he explains to his people that no one should take photos with their phones to post on the Internet, as this might compromise these fine agents in any future vital undercover work to which they might be assigned.

Of all those present, only four think they might have seen the Honda from time to time. But just one, a grizzled specimen named Norbert Gossage, says anything that intrigues Jergen and Dubose.

"It's a peculiar shade of green for a Honda," says Gossage, scratching his bearded neck, "which is why I remember it at all."

Dubose gives Jergen a look that expresses his doubt about the value of a Harvard education. "Yes, sir, you're right about that."

"Honda isn't a car people spend bucks to customize," says Gossage, working a finger in his left ear. "So you notice a thing like that special paint job. I used to see this one here"—he takes the finger out of his ear and taps the photo on the smartphone, as though it would never occur to him that Jergen will now have to sterilize the screen—"down in the south valley, around where Route 3 divides. I used to work in those parts."

"Saw it where, exactly?" Dubose asks.

"Nowhere exactly. It was always on the move when I saw it."

"You have any idea who might have been driving it?"

"Some fella. I never got a clear look at him. Truth is, I stayed out of his way when I saw him comin'. I don't think he was ever properly taught how to drive. Other thing is, it's been years since last I saw it."

His expectations deflating, Jergen says, " 'Years'?"

"At least three years. Maybe longer."

Although they try to wring additional details out of Norbert Gossage, there is no more to be wrung.

By now, three small children are clutching Dubose's pant legs, and the big man is looking like he might start swatting them.

Time to go.

21

Jane recovered the tote and the flashlight and crossed the plank, resisting the urge to look back, as if Hendrickson would stay dead only as long as she remained convinced that she had killed him.

She made her way to the stairhead and out of that building into the snowy day. Thirty-eight minutes had elapsed since she'd fled Anabel's lair at the foot of the crooked staircase.

No doubt the woman, from her winter home in La Jolla, had reported Jane's whereabouts to those with a burning desire to see her dead. She needed to keep moving, faster than fast, but the storm that had hampered her on the journey north was now her ally. They might be able to marshal a hit team out of Las Vegas, even out of Reno, possibly out of Sacramento. However, the snow was falling harder than ever, and the light breeze had become a stiff wind. The only way they could reach her in a timely manner was by chopper, but the wind and the poor visibility and the certainty of ice forming on the rotary wings, bringing the helo down, would force them to delay.

By the time she reached her Explorer Sport, she was shaking uncontrollably, not entirely because of the weather, for which she wasn't adequately dressed. The engine started on the first try. She turned the heat up.

From the shorter forest-service road to the longer

one, to the county road, to Highway 50 South, the word for the world was *white.* By the time she crossed the state line from Nevada into California, she was able to dial down the heat.

She stopped for fuel in South Lake Tahoe and considered staying there for the night, because they would not expect her to be in the area come morning. But though road conditions were far from ideal, the plows were working and 50 West was open, and she decided to try for Placerville.

Since the struggle with Hendrickson, she'd felt pain in her left side, above the hip and below the rib cage. A week earlier in San Francisco, she'd been wounded. Nothing serious, although she'd needed stitches and was sewn up by a friend who was a doctor. She might have pulled a stitch or two, but now wasn't the time to check.

She drove.

What beauty snow usually held for her was absent this storm. There was something of ashes about it this time, as if beyond the limited view that the blizzard allowed, the world was burning and, when the ashfall ended, would be revealed as blackened ruins to every horizon.

Survival might be a matter of training and intuition, but it was also always a gift for which gratitude was required. Mile after grudging mile, the desolation that shrouded her heart would not relent, would not allow grace to find her.

At last she resorted to music and turned it loud, so that the monotony of the tire chains could not be heard. Rubinstein at the keyboard, Jascha Heifetz on violin, Gregor Piatigorsky on the cello. Tchaikovsky's Piano Trio in A Minor, op. 50.

She didn't know at what point she began to weep as she drove, and she didn't realize at what point she stopped weeping, but by then the ash had become snow again, and gratitude rose in her and grace settled upon her, and hope.

22

Half an hour of daylight remained, but Travis knew he couldn't wait any longer. Something terrible had happened.

He wasn't supposed to go outside, but the rules weren't the rules anymore. He had to think for himself.

He fed the dogs and leashed them and took them out to potty. They were good dogs, and they didn't run off when he dropped the leashes to pick up their poop in blue bags. He twisted the necks of the bags and knotted them and set them on the porch.

He took the leashes in hand again and walked with the dogs to the falling-down barn that wasn't really falling down, though it sure looked a mess.

He stood in front of the door Uncle Gavin had stood in front of earlier in the day, when everything seemed like it was going to be all right.

He didn't try the door or knock. Uncle Gavin had

said there were cameras and Cousin Cornell would know when anyone was waiting there.

Maybe Cousin Cornell was sleeping or maybe he took a while to make up his mind what to do, but after a long time, there came a buzz and a clunk, and the door swung open.

Travis stepped into a little room, bringing the dogs with him. The door behind him closed all by itself.

The door in front of him didn't open right away. The dogs fidgeted, but Travis didn't.

He looked up at the camera, and after a while, he thought he ought to explain, so he said, "Something very bad has happened."

Another minute or two passed, and then the inner door opened.

He went into a big room full of books and comfortable chairs and lamps, with many pools of light and pools of shadow.

Duke and Queenie were so excited by this new place that they pulled their leashes out of Travis's hands and scampered off this way and that, sniffing everything.

A man stood by an armchair, in lamplight. He was very tall and not as black as Uncle Gavin. Tall and thin like a scarecrow on stilts or something.

The man said, "Those are big dogs. Don't let those big dogs kill me, please and thank you."

23

With daylight fast fading, Jergen and Dubose are still touring Borrego Valley in search of they know not what. Or at least Carter Jergen knows not. His partner, apparently now gripped by the delusion that he is clairvoyant, cruises slowly, waving impatient drivers past him, squint-eyed behind his sunglasses, surveying the inhospitable landscape as if Travis Hawk might be traversing it in full camouflage, regarding every structure as though he suspects that a five-year-old fugitive is holed up there with a cache of weapons and a hundred thousand rounds of ammunition.

"We can't be looking for the peculiar-green Honda, because that's back in town, at the market."

Dubose says nothing.

"And whoever drove it years ago must be driving something else now, but we don't know what."

Dubose cruises in silence.

"What we should be doing," Jergen says, "is digging deep into the Washingtons' background, see if we can find any link between them and anyone in this godforsaken desert."

Dubose deigns to speak. "We'll start doing that after dark, when there isn't any more light to search by."

"All right, but what exactly are we searching for?"

Dubose keeps his strategy to himself.

He slows as they approach a small, faded-blue stucco house with a white metal roof shaded by unkempt palms.

24

While Travis reported how Uncle Gavin and Aunt Jessie changed the way they looked and went into town and didn't come back, the big strange man never stopped moving as he listened. He went to a chair and started to sit down, but then didn't, and he chose another chair that he almost also sat in, but again he stood up before his butt met the cushion.

Moving, moving, moving this way and that, here and there, he also kept rubbing his ginormous hands together like he was washing them under running water. When he wasn't doing that, he covered his face with his hands as if there must be something he didn't want to see and had forgotten he could just close his eyes. He kept moving with his hands over his face, not able to see where he was going, and almost fell over a chair. He walked into a table, rattling the lamp on it.

There wasn't much to Travis's story, but the big strange man, who was Mr. Cornell Jasperson, asked him to repeat some details again and again, as if they might change a little each time until, after a while, the whole story would be different and Gavin and Jessie would have come back hours ago and there would be nothing to worry about after all.

When Mr. Jasperson finally stopped asking to hear this and that bit yet again, he stood in silence, his hands over his face, but now looking at Travis between the spread fingers. After a silence, he said, "I don't know what to do."

"I don't know, either," Travis said. "Except I better tell my mother."

That was when he realized he hadn't brought the disposable phone with him, to which the number of his mother's disposable cell was taped. "I have to go back to the house."

25

The driveway to the little blue house is unpaved and bristling with weeds. The yard immediately around the house is pea gravel. Behind the house stands an unpainted barn with each wall askew the other, a shaky assemblage of dry rot and rust and tar paper, likely to collapse if a cow farts.

"Reminds me of home in West Virginia," Dubose says.

Carter can't help tweaking him. "You lived in a barn?"

"We had a house maybe a little nicer than this one. But our barn was worse."

"How could it be worse?" Jergen marveled.

"It took some effort, but it looked like such a ratty place you'd dare go in only if you wanted your family to collect on your life insurance. Nobody official ever did go in when my granddad and my daddy distilled whiskey and packaged it there, and not later when my brother Carney put in all the lamps and planted a crop of weed."

"Your grandfather and father were bootleggers?"

"That isn't a word they would have used."

"And your brother is a pot dealer?"

"He farms it a little, but he's too much of a user to be a seller. Anyway, Carney is a world-class asshole. He's dead to me."

Jergen considered that last sentence. "When you say 'dead to me,' do you mean . . . ?"

"No, I didn't kill him. Though there's times when I wish I had. Anyway, even with Carney, life was good back then."

"Well," Jergen commiserates, "we all feel that way about one relative or another."

His nostalgic reverie drawing to an end, Dubose takes his foot off the brake and the VelociRaptor drifts forward. "They left the boy somewhere in the valley when they went to the market. He's still here. His mother will know where, and she'll sooner or later come for him."

26

"Don't leave me alone with these big, scary dogs," Mr. Jasperson said, "please and thank you."

"They won't hurt you," Travis promised. "I'll just run over to the house and get the phone and be right back."

"Oh, my. Oh, goodness."

"You'll be okay."

Duke and Queenie were lying against each other, a puddle of dog fur, about as threatening as a rug.

"I'll be fast," Travis promised.

He went into the vestibule, and the door closed behind him, and he opened the outer door.

Out on the road, a monster pickup truck was moving slowly past, rolling on six big tires, glossy black and as cool as anything from a *Star Wars* movie.

27

"... Still here. His mother will know where, and she'll sooner or later come for him," Dubose says, and he accelerates.

"We'll set a hundred traps for her," Jergen says.

"Yeah, but I wouldn't bet serious money that she can't walk right through the hundred. While we're waiting for her, we have to be finding the boy."

"You think she'll surrender if she knows we have him? I mean, she's got to figure we'll inject her and him if we don't just kill them both."

"After a lot of serious contemplation regarding the mother-child bond," Dubose says, as though he is a heavy-thinking backwoods philosopher, "the way I see it, if she doesn't surrender within six hours after she knows we have the kid, then we just kill the little bastard. Because that'll as good as kill the bitch herself. She'll be done after that. She won't have any game in her anymore. She might even kill herself and save us the trouble."

As night descends, they cruise a few miles in mutual silence, during which Jergen contemplates the unmitigated ruthlessness of his partner, which he cannot help but admire. "I think you're right about the kid. But I wouldn't give her six hours. Maybe two."

28

In the days of the gold rush, Placerville, which lay on the eastern flank of the Mother Lode, went by the name Old Dry Diggins. It was a place of such lawlessness that to keep order, authorities started hanging lawbreakers two at a time, after which the settlement became known as Hangtown. Placerville was less colorful these days, and quiet.

Jane had driven out of the storm twenty miles back and had the tire chains removed when she refueled. Now she found a generic motel, paid cash for one night, and moved all her luggage into the room. The titanium-alloy attaché case, which contained $210,000 that had once belonged to Simon Yegg, could not be seen when she slid it under a dresser that stood on four short legs.

She walked to a nearby supermarket, went to the deli counter, and ordered two roast beef sandwiches with provolone cheese and mustard.

The heavyset woman who built and wrapped the sandwiches was sensitive to the moods of others. "Been a long day, dear?"

"I've had better."

"I'm sure it's not man trouble."

"Not anymore."

"Girl as pretty as you should give *them* some trouble."

"It's been known to happen."

In the liquor department, she located the Belvedere vodka and added a pint bottle to her purchases.

Back at the motel, she filled an ice bucket from the ice maker in the vending-machine alcove and bought two cans of Diet Coke.

In her room, she took off her Elizabeth Bennet wig. She had lost the clip-on nose ring somewhere. It didn't matter. Anabel had seen her in this look, probably even captured an image of her, which meant she couldn't be Liz anymore.

She stripped and examined the wound in her left side. Not bad. A thin crust of blood. She had pulled one of the stitches. It was healing well enough, and she still had plenty of antibiotics.

She took a hot shower and dressed in underpants and a T-shirt. She mixed vodka and Diet Coke and sat on the bed to eat the sandwiches, one of them entirely, only the meat and cheese from the second.

There was a TV, but she didn't want it.

Bolted to the nightstand to keep it from being stolen, a clock radio offered an alternative. She found a station doing a Mariah Carey retrospective. That sensational voice. "I Don't Wanna Cry" and "Emotions." And then "Always Be My Baby" and "Love Takes Time" and "Hero" and more.

Music could lift you up so high, and music could destroy you, and sometimes it could do both in the same song.

When she finished eating and felt fully calm, she intended to call the disposable phone that she'd left with Gavin and Jessie.

She was finishing her second vodka when her own burner rang. She switched off the radio and plucked the phone from the nightstand and took the call. She heard Travis say, "Mommy?"

Whatever had happened, it was all there in that one word, because since she'd gone on the run with him from their home in Virginia, months earlier, he had called her only Mom, as if he had understood that it had fallen to him to grow up fast. Besides, she knew him so well that she could read him in two syllables.

She swung her legs off the bed and sat on the edge of the mattress. "What's wrong, sweetie?"

"Uncle Gavin and Aunt Jessie went for groceries, and they never came back."

29

Jane in Placerville, which seemed like a suburb of Hell when Travis was all the way down there in Borrego Valley, the motel room now a cage in which she moved restlessly, without purpose, a pain in her chest as if the dread that cinched her heart was a thorny vine, a demon of anguish feeding on her mind . . .

She knew the whole story of Gavin's cousin Cornell Jasperson, brilliant and highly eccentric, a kind of end-times prepper, but not crazy. She had approved his place as a bolt-hole. But she had not allowed herself to believe such a moment as this would ever come.

Travis would be safe there for a while. A short while. Two days. Maybe three.

Unless Gavin and Jessie had been injected. Then they would reveal his whereabouts.

But they hadn't been injected. They wouldn't allow themselves to be captured. They knew what that would mean: nanoweb enslavement.

They were surely dead. They were as much a part of her heart as were its walls of muscle, and they were dead. There would be some news of their death in the morning, some concocted story containing no truth except for the truth of their murders.

She couldn't shake the feeling that, by enlisting them in her war, she was responsible for their deaths. Yes, they'd understood the risks, no doubt about that. They saw this as their fight, too, as everyone's war, everyone who loved freedom and had sufficient experience to know that evil was real and implacable. If they could speak to her now from that mysterious place of which no human being knew the full truth, they would absolve her of responsibility, but in her grief she was nevertheless also pierced by guilt.

She dressed and stepped outside and took deep breaths of the crisp night air and stood trembling with a need to act. The sky remained as overcast as it had been when she arrived.

No volume of vodka existed that would bring her sleep.

She wanted to be in Borrego Springs *now*. But the worst thing she could do would be to rush to Travis. She would need the night to get there. They would be expecting her, and she would be exhausted and easy to take down. She had to have a plan to get in and out of that valley undetected. As an agent working cases involving serial killers and mass murderers, and now since she had been branded a murderer herself and a traitor, she stayed alive by staying cool. But this . . . this was the ultimate test of her fortitude and prudence in the face of extreme threat. Not only her life but that of her son now depended on her not succumbing to hot emotion.

Nonetheless, she wanted to be closer to Travis, if even just a little closer, and she wanted another thing. She wanted stars.

She returned to her room and put on the excessive eye makeup and the blue lipstick and the chopped-everywhichway black wig, because that was her quickest option. They knew the look now, but they didn't know the Elizabeth Bennet name; she could use it one more time.

She returned her luggage to the car, turned in the room key, and drove west to Sacramento, and then south toward Stockton.

30

This exhaustion had the substance of a real presence, a mantled thing resting on her neck, its thick cloaks weighing heavily on her shoulders. There was always a moment when iron will and a determined heart could no longer compensate for the fatigue of mind and muscle. Her vision blurred with weariness until, if she stayed on the road, she was a danger to herself and others.

At 11:50 P.M., near Stockton, the overcast abated. Still farther south, when the night cast off the last rags of cloud, Jane exited Interstate 5 at the little community of Lathrop, where she would get a room for the night.

First, however, she stopped along the side of the road on the outskirts of town and got out of the car and walked a few steps into a meadow. The sky was a sea of suns afloat in the eternal dark that only their light relented. The nearest sun of all, which warmed the earth, was hours below the eastern horizon. When it rose, it would reveal a world of wonders, a world on which had been lavished such natural beauty of such astonishing depth and complexity that an honest heart perceived meaning in it and yearned to *know*. In the night as it was now and in the morning light, there were men and women making music, writing poetry and novels, researching new medicines, fighting wars against malevolent forces, doing hard and honest work, raising families, loving, caring, hoping. A hole in the ground, its galleries shaped into a museum to display works of cruelty and horror—that was not the truth of the world, as Anabel insisted. That "truth" was the delusion of those for whom life was nothing more than a contest for power, who either could not see or refused to see the beauty and the wonder of the world, who wanted to find no meaning beyond them-selves, who lived to control, to tell others what to do and think and believe, and who relished crushing those who would not submit. If it was inevitable that evolving technology would provide them with the ab-solute power they craved, they must still be resisted. When the universe had been brought forth and light had been born within the stars, if even at that first mo-ment all had been shaped toward tyranny and slav-ery, she would be damned rather than have such a future for herself or her child. If they forced her to wade through blood and never allowed her to find a welcome shore, she would nevertheless seek it until she died. And if they pursued the hellish transformation of this world, she would give them Hell itself by opening the door for them.

And now the motel room. A pillow. Weariness and grief and grace and gratitude. Instant sleep. And with the coming of the morning sun, the wonder and the terror of it all.

Please turn the page for a preview of

the next Jane Hawk novel

by *#1 New York Times* bestselling author

Dean Koontz

THE
FORBIDDEN
DOOR

1

At first the breeze was no more than a long sigh, breathing through the Texas high country as though expressing some sadness attendant to Nature herself.

They were sitting in the fresh air, in the late-afternoon light, because they assumed that the house was bugged, that anything they said within its rooms would be monitored in real time.

Likewise, they trusted neither the porches nor the barn, nor the horse stables.

When they had something important to discuss, they retreated to the redwood lawn chairs under the massive oak tree in the backyard, facing a flatness of grassland that rolled on to the distant horizon and, for all that the eye could tell, continued to eternity.

As Sunday afternoon became evening, Ancel and Clare Hawk sat in those chairs, she with a martini, he with Macallan Scotch over ice, steeling themselves for an upcoming television program they didn't want to watch but that might change their lives.

"What bombshell can they be talking about?" Clare wondered.

"It's TV news," Ancel said. "They pitch most every story like it'll shake the foundations of the world. It's how they sell soap."

Clare watched him as he stared out at the deep, trembling grass and the vastness of sky as if he never tired of them and saw some new meaning in them every time he gave them his attention. A big man with a weathered face and work-scarred hands, he looked as if his heart might be as hard as bone, though she'd never known one more tender.

After thirty-four years of marriage, they had endured hardships and shared many successes. But now—and perhaps for as long as they yet might have together—their lives were defined by one blessing and one unbearable loss, the birth of their only child Nick and his death at the age of thirty-two, the previous November.

Clare said, "I'm feeling like it's more than selling soap, like it's some vicious damn twist of the knife."

He reached out with his left hand, which she held tightly. "We thought it all out, Clare. We have plans. We're ready for whatever."

"I'm not ready to lose Jane, too. I'll never be ready."

"It won't happen. They're who they are, she's who she is, and I'd put my money on her every time."

Just when the faded-denim sky began to darkle toward sapphire overhead and took upon itself a glossy sheen, the breeze quickened and set the oak tree to whispering.

Their daughter-in-law, Jane Hawk, who was as close to them as any real daughter might have been, had recently been indicted for espionage, treason, and seven counts of murder, crimes that she hadn't committed. She would be the sole subject of this evening's *Sunday Magazine*, a one-hour TV program that rarely devoted more than ten minutes to a profile of anyone, either president or pop singer. The most-wanted fugitive in America and a media sensation, Jane was labeled the "beautiful monster" by the tabloids, a cognomen used in promos for the forthcoming special edition of *Sunday Magazine*.

Ancel said, "Her indictment by some misled grand jury, now this TV show, all the noise about it . . . you realize what it must mean?"

"Nothing good."

"Well, but I think she's got evidence that'll destroy the sons of bitches, and they know she's got it. They're desperate. If she finds a reporter or someone in the Bureau who maybe she can trust—"

"She tried before. The bigger the story, the fewer people she can trust. And this is as big as a story gets."

"They're desperate," Ancel insisted. "They're throwin' all they got at her, tryin' to turn the whole country against her, make her a monster no one'll ever believe."

"And what then?" Clare worried. "How does she have any hope if the whole country's against her?"

"Because it won't be."

"I don't know how you can be so sure."

"The way they demonize her, this hysteria they ginned up in the media—it's too much piled on top of too much. People sense it."

"Those who know her, but that's not a world."

"People all over, they're talkin' about what the real story might be, whether maybe she's bein' set up."

"What people? All over where?"

"All over the Internet."

"Since when do you spend five minutes on the Internet?"

"Since this latest with her."

The sun appeared to roll below the horizon, although in fact the horizon rolled away from the sun. In the instant when all the remaining light of day was indirect across the red western sky, the breeze quickened again and became a wind aborning, as if all were a clockwork.

As the looser leaves of the live oak were shaken down, Clare let go of Ancel's hand and covered her glass, and he shielded his.

There was no privacy in the house, and they weren't finished counseling each other in matters of grief and hope, preparing for the affront that would be the TV program. The wind brought the dark, and the dark brought a chill, but the sea of stars was a work of wonder and a source of solace.

2

Nine miles from Hawk Ranch, Egon Gottfrey heads the operation to take Ancel and Clare Hawk into custody and ensure their fullest cooperation in the search for their daughter-in-law.

Well, *custody* is too formal a word. Each member of Gottfrey's team carries valid Department of Homeland Security credentials. They also possess valid ID for the NSA and the FBI, though they work at those two agencies only on paper. They receive three salaries and earn three pensions, ostensibly to preserve and defend the United States, while in fact working for the revolution. The leaders of the revolution make sure that their foot soldiers are well rewarded by the very system they are intent on overthrowing.

Because of Egon Gottfrey's successful career in Homeland, he was approached to join the Techno Arcadians, the visionaries who conduct the secret revolution. He is now one of them. And why not! He doesn't believe in the United States anyway.

The Techno Arcadians will change the world. They will pacify contentious humanity, end poverty, create Utopia through technology.

Or so the Unknown Playwright would have us believe.

The Hawks will not be arrested. Gottfrey and his crew will take possession of them. Neither attorneys nor courts will be involved.

Having arrived in Worstead, Texas, shortly after

four o'clock in the afternoon, Egon Gottfrey is bored
by the town within half an hour of checking into the
Holiday Inn.

In 1896, when this jerkwater became a center
through which the region's farms and ranches shipped
their products to market, it had been called Sheepshear Station, because of the amount of baled wool
that passed through on the way to textile mills.

That's the story, and there's no point in question-
ing it.

By 1901, when the town was incorporated, the
founders felt that the name Sheepshear Station wasn't
sophisticated enough to match their vision of the future. Besides, snarky types routinely called it Sheep-
shit Station. It was then named Worstead, after
Worstede, the parish in Norfolk, England, where wor-
sted wool was first made.

Anyway, that's what Gottfrey is supposed to believe.

More than fourteen thousand rustic citizens now
call it home.

Whatever they call it, Egon Gottfrey finds it to be a
thin vision of a place, incomplete in its detail, much
like an artist's pencil study done before proceeding to
oil paints. But every place feels like that to him.

The streets aren't shaded. The only trees are in the
park in the town square, as if there is a limited budget
for stage dressing.

Near sunset, he walks the downtown area, where
the buildings mostly have flat roofs with parapets, the
kind behind which villains and sheriffs alike crouch to
fire on each other in a thousand old movies. Many

structures are of locally quarried limestone or rust-colored sand-struck brick. The sameness and plainness don't allow the chamber of commerce to call the architecture *quaint.*

At Julio's Steakhouse, where the bar extends onto an elevated and roofed patio overlooking the street, Paloma Sutherland and Sally Jones, two of the agents under Gottfrey's command, having come in from Dallas, are precisely where they are supposed to be, enjoying a drink at a streetside table. They make eye contact as he passes.

And in the park, on a bench, Rupert Baldwin is studying a newspaper. Wearing Hush Puppies and a roomy corduroy suit and a beige shirt and a bolo tie with an ornamental turquoise clasp, he looks like some nerdy high-school biology teacher, but he is tough and ruthless.

As Gottfrey walks past, Rupert only clears his throat.

On another bench sits Vince Penn, half as wide as he is tall, with a flat face and the big hands of a natural-born strangler.

Vince holds a handful of pebbles. Now and then, he throws one of the stones with wicked accuracy, targeting the unwary squirrels that have been conditioned by Worstead locals to trust people.

South of the park stands a two-star mom-and-pop motel, Purple Sage Inn, as unconvincing as any location in town.

Parked in front of Room 12 is a bespoke Range Rover created by Overfinch North America, a vehicle with major performance upgrades, a carbon-fiber styling package, and a dual-valve titanium exhaust system; it's a recent perk for certain members of the revolution. The Range Rover means Gottfrey's two most senior agents—Christopher Roberts and Janis Dern—have checked in.

Counting Egon Gottfrey and the two men who are at this moment conducting surveillance of the entrance to Hawk Ranch, ten miles east of Worstead, the team of nine is complete.

In this operation, they are not using burner phones, not even Midland GXT walkie-talkies, which are often useful. In some parts of the country, Texas being one, there are too many paranoid fools who think elements of the government and certain industries conspire in wicked schemes; some are in law enforcement or were in the military, and they spend countless hours monitoring microwave transmissions for evidence to confirm their wild suspicions.

Or so the Unknown Playwright would have us believe.

As Gottfrey continues his walk through town, no longer to confirm the presence of his team, merely to pass time, the sinking sun floods the streets with crimson light. The once-pale limestone buildings are now radiant by reflection, but they appear to be built of translucent onyx lit from within. The very air is aglow, as if all the light in the invisible spectrum—infrared and other—is beginning to manifest to the eye, as though the illusion that is the world will burst and reveal what lies under this so-called reality.

Egon Gottfrey is not merely a nihilist who believes there is no meaning in life. He's a *radical philosophical* nihilist who contends that there is no possibility of an objective basis for truth, and therefore no such thing as truth, but also that the entire world and his existence—everyone's existence—are a fantasy, a vivid delusion.

The world is as ephemeral as a dream, each moment of the day but a mirage within an infinite honeycomb of mirages. The only thing about himself that he can say exists, with certainty, is his mind wrapped in the illusion of his physical body. He thinks; therefore, he is. But his body, his life, his country, and his world are all illusion.

On embracing this view of the human condition, a lesser mind might have gone mad, surrendering to despair. Gottfrey has remained sane by playing along with the illusion that is the world, as if it is a stage production for an unknowable audience, as if he is an actor in a drama for which he's never seen a script. It's marionette theater. He is a marionette, and he's okay with that.

He's okay with it for two reasons, the first of which is that he has a sharply honed curiosity. He is his own fanboy, eager to see what will happen to him next.

Second, Gottfrey likes his role as a figure of authority with power over others. Even though it all means nothing, even though he has no control over events, just goes along to get along, it is far better to be one through whom the Unknown Playwright wields power rather than one on whom that power is brought to bear.

3

The room illumined only by the netherworld glow of the TV, the vaguest reflections of moving figures on the screen throbbing across the walls like spectral presences . . .

Ancel sitting stiffly in his armchair, stone-faced in response to *Sunday Magazine*'s lies and distortions, the program mirrored in his gray eyes . . .

Clare couldn't stay in her chair, couldn't just watch and listen and do nothing. She got up and paced, talking back to the screen: "Bullshit" and "Liar" and "You hateful bastard."

This was nothing like any previous edition of *Sunday Magazine*. Always before it had avoided both puff pieces and vitriolic attacks, striving for balance, at times almost highbrow. But *this*. This was the worst kind of tabloid exploitation and alarmism. This special, "The Beautiful Monster," had one intention—to paint Jane as an evil angel, a traitor to her country, who wasn't only capable of horrific violence but who also perhaps took pleasure in wanton murder.

At the half-hour break, the program host teased the blockbuster revelation that they had been selling in the promos for days. In a portentous voice, he promised to feature it in the next segment.

As the first commercial played, Clare perched on a footstool and closed her eyes and wrapped her arms around herself, chilled. "What is this, Ancel? This isn't journalism, not one iota of it."

"Character assassination. Propaganda. These people she's up against, they're veins of rot runnin' through government and tech companies, hell-bent to destroy her before she can tell her story."

"You think people are still going to defend her after this?"

"I do, Clare. These fools are hammerin' too hard, makin' her out to be some girl version of Dracula and Charles Manson and Benedict Arnold rolled into one."

"A lot of stupid people will believe it," Clare worried.

"Some stupid. Some gullible. Not everyone. Maybe not most."

She said, "I don't want to watch any more of this."

"Neither do I. But that's not a choice, is it? We're one with Jane. They blow up her life, they blow up ours. We've got to see what's left of us when this show is done."

After the break, *Sunday Magazine* harked back to Jane's photo taken on completion of her Bureau training at Quantico, where she'd met Nick when he was assigned to Corps Combat Development Command at the same base. There were wedding photographs: Nick in his Marine dress uniform, Jane in a simple white bridal gown. Such a stunning couple.

Seeing her lost son and his bride so happy, so vibrant, Clare was overcome with emotion.

The narration moved to film of Nick receiving the

Navy Cross, which was one step below the Medal of Honor, Jane looking on with such love and pride.

Clare got up from the footstool and went to Ancel and sat on the arm of his chair and put a hand on his shoulder, and he put a hand on her knee and squeezed and said, "I know."

The narrator began to talk of Nick's suicide the previous November.

He and Jane had been at home in Alexandria, Virginia, preparing dinner, having a little wine. Their boy, Travis, was on a sleepover with another five-year-old in the neighborhood, so that his parents might have a romantic evening. Nick went to the bathroom . . . and didn't return. Jane found him clothed, sitting in the bathtub. With his Marine-issue combat knife, he'd cut his neck deeply enough to sever a carotid artery. He left a note, the first sentence in his neat cursive, which deteriorated thereafter: *Something is wrong with me. I need. I very much need. I very much need to be dead.*

More than four months had passed since that devastating call from Jane. Clare's tears now were as hot as her tears then.

"That," the narrator solemnly intoned, "was Jane Hawk's story, and the investigation by the Alexandria police confirmed every detail. In the days following Nick's death, friends say Jane became obsessed with what she believed was an inexplicable rise in suicides nationwide. She discovered that thousands of happy, accomplished people like her husband, none with a history of depression, were taking their lives for no apparent reason. On leave from the FBI, so deep in grief that friends worried for her mental health, she began to research this disturbing trend, which soon consumed her."

Suddenly it seemed that the tenor of the show might change, that all the terrible things said about Jane in the first half hour might be considered from a more sympathetic perspective, raising doubts about the official portrayal of her as traitorous and cruel.

The program turned to a university professor, an expert in suicide prevention. He claimed that nothing was unusual about the increase in suicides over the past two years, that the rate always fluctuated. He claimed that the percentage of affluent, apparently happy people killing themselves was still within normal parameters.

"That can't be right," Clare said.

Next came an expert in criminal psychology, a woman with hair pulled tightly back in a chignon, as lean as a whippet, eyes owlish behind black-framed round lenses, wearing a severely tailored suit that matched the severity of her manner as she discussed what was known of the subject's difficult childhood.

Jane. A piano prodigy from the age of four. Daughter of the famous pianist Martin Duroc. Some said Duroc was demanding, distant. She was estranged from him. Jane's mother, also a talented pianist, committed suicide. Nine-year-old Jane discovered the bloody body in a bathtub. Eight years later, Duroc remarried in spite of his daughter's objection. A decade later, Jane declined a scholarship to Oberlin, rejecting a music career to pursue one in law enforcement.

"And it's intriguing to consider her six years at the

FBI," the psychologist said. As the camera moved close on her face to capture the pale solemnity of her expression, she lowered her voice as if imparting a confidence. "During her time in the Bureau, Jane was assigned to cases under the purview of Behavioral Analysis Units Three and Four, which deal with mass murderers and serial killers. She participated in ten investigations with eight resolutions. For a young woman who might have a long-harbored grudge against men, being immersed in the world of murderous male sociopaths, required to *think like them* in order to find and apprehend them, the experience could have had profound traumatic effects on her psychology."

A shudder passed through Clare, the sense of some abomination coming. She thrust up from the arm of Ancel's chair. "What the *hell* does that mean?"

On the screen now: J. J. Crutchfield. The narrator recounted the sordid story of this killer who had kept the eyes of his women victims in jars of preservative. Jane had wounded and captured him.

And now: narration over video of the isolated farm where two vicious men had raped and murdered twenty-two girls. Here the agent working the case with Jane had been shot to death, and it had fallen to her, alone in the night, to counterstalk the two murderers who were stalking her. She had taken out both of them, killing the second in the former hog pen that was the graveyard of their victims.

More video from that night, outside the farmhouse, after the police arrived. Jane conferring with officers in the crosslight of patrol cars, strikingly beautiful, like an avenging goddess, but hair wild, uplit face made subtly ominous by a mascara of shadows.

Sunday Magazine froze the video on a close-up that did not deny her beauty but that suggested . . . What? A disturbing hardness about her? A potential for cruelty? Madness?

Walking along a street in Alexandria, the town where Nick and Jane had lived, the program host addressed the camera. "How thin is the line between heroism and villainy?"

"Don't be stupid," Clare said. "They aren't separated by a thin line. They're different countries, an ocean apart."

Ancel sat silent and grim-faced.

"When a good person," the host said, "badly damaged by profound childhood trauma, for too long is immersed in the dark world of serial killers . . . might she lose her way?"

He stopped in front of the Alexandria police headquarters.

"After the events of recent weeks that have made Jane Hawk front-page news, the police department that originally certified her husband's death a suicide has quietly reopened the case. The body has been exhumed. A subsequent autopsy and extensive toxicological tests reveal that Nicholas Hawk had a powerful sedative in his system and that the angle and nature of the lethal cut in his neck are not consistent with a self-administered knife wound."

Clare felt cold in heart and blood and bone. Such a world of deceit. Such bold, shameless lies. Nick's remains had been cremated. Only his ashes were buried in Arlington National Cemetery. There was no body to exhume.

4

S *unday Magazine* was not on Jane's radar.

Hours earlier, she had survived an ordeal near Lake Tahoe that had almost been the end of her, leaving her shaken and desolate. She had obtained evidence of murder that might help her break open the conspiracy that had taken Nick's life and so many others, but she'd gotten it at considerable emotional, psychological, and moral cost.

Through a cold day darkened by storm clouds and blinded by torrents of snow, she drove south, then west, out of the Sierra Nevada, out of the blizzard— and, after many miles, out of that darkness of spirit, into grace and gratitude for her survival.

In Placerville, she paid cash for one night at a generic motel, using her Elizabeth Bennet driver's license as ID, because she was wearing the chopped-everywhichway black wig and excess makeup and blue lipstick that made her Liz.

She bought deli sandwiches and a pint of vodka at a nearby market and got Coca-Cola and ice from the motel vending alcove and took a shower as hot as she could tolerate and ate the sandwiches while sitting in bed, listening to Mariah Carey on the radio. She drank a vodka-and-Coke and was finishing her second drink, grateful to be alive, when her burner phone rang.

She intended to call Gavin and Jessica Washington down in eastern Orange County, the friends with whom she had secreted her son, Travis, the only place in the world where he was not likely to be found. If the boy fell into the hands of her enemies, they would kill him because they knew that his death would at last break her. When the disposable phone rang, she thought it must be Gavin or Jessie; no one else had the number.

But it was Travis. "Mommy? Uncle Gavin and Aunt Jessie went for groceries, and they never came back."

Jane swung her legs off the bed, stood, and felt as if she were standing for the attention of a hangman, a noose tight around her neck and a trapdoor under her feet. At once she sat down, dizzy with dread.

He had been with Gavin and Jessie for more than two months. If something happened to them, he was alone. Five years old and alone.

Her heart as loud as a cortege drum, but much faster than the meter of mourning, reverberating in blood and bone . . .

Travis was a little toughie being strong like he knew his dad would have been, scared but self-controlled. Jane was able to get the situation from him. Gavin and Jessie had realized they were under surveillance, had somehow been connected to Jane. In their Land Rover, with Travis and two German shepherds, they escaped from their house into the dark desert hills. They were pursued—"This crazy-big truck and like even a heli-copter, Mom, a helicopter that could see us in the dark"—but they avoided capture. They drove to a bolt-hole, long ago approved by Jane, in the Borrego Val-ley, south of Borrego Springs. After settling in a small house on acreage owned by a man named Cornell Jasperson, Gavin shaved his head and Jessie changed her appearance with a wig and makeup, and they went into town to buy supplies. They meant to be back in two hours. Eight had now passed.

They must be dead. They would not have allowed themselves to be captured, and they would never have shirked their responsibility to look after Travis. Gavin and Jessie were ex-Army, two of the best and most reliable people Jane had ever known.

She loved them like a brother and sister before she left her child in their care, and she loved them yet more for their unfailing commitment to Travis. Even in these dark times of so much terror and death, when each day brought new threats and sorrows, new shocks to mind and heart, she had not become inured to loss. This one pierced her, a psychic bullet that would have dropped her into tears and numbing grief if her child had not been in such jeopardy.

She didn't tell Travis they were dead. She could discern by the catch in his voice that he suspected as much, but there was nothing to be gained by confirm-ing his fear. She needed to project calm and confi-dence, to give him reason for courage.

"Where are you, sweetheart? In the house where they left you?"

If he was still in the house where Gavin and Jessie had meant to hole up with him, he was more likely to be found sooner.

"No. Me and the dogs, we walked over to Cornell's place like we were supposed to if there was trouble."

Cornell lived off the grid. He was not likely to be linked to Gavin and Jessie soon. Travis might be safe there for two or three days, though not much longer. The word *might* was a gut punch.

"Honey, you'll be safe with the dogs and Cornell until I can come for you. I *will* come for you, sweetie. Nothing can stop me."

"I know. I know you will."

"Are you all right with Cornell?"

"He's kind of weird, but he's nice."

Cornell was a brilliant eccentric whose eccentricities were complicated by a mild form of autism.

"There's no reason to be afraid of Cornell. You do what he tells you, sweetie, and I'll come for you just as soon as I can."

"Okay, I can't wait, but I will."

"We can't talk even on burner phones again. It's too dangerous now. But I'll come for you." She got to her feet and was steady this time. "Nobody ever loved anyone more than I love you, Travis."

"Me, too. I miss you all the time a lot. Do you have the lady I gave you?"

The lady was a cameo, the face of a broken locket that he had found and that he thought important because, to his mind if not to hers, the profile carved in soapstone resembled Jane.

It was on the nightstand with other objects—switchblade, butane lighter, penlight, small canister of Sabre 5.0 pepper spray, four zip-ties each held in tight coils by a rubber band—the tools and simple weapons and instruments of restraint that she had cleaned out of the pockets of her sport coat before hanging it up. Plucking the cameo off the nightstand, she said, "It's in my hand right now."

"It's good luck. It's like everything is gonna be all right if you just always have the lady."

"I know, baby. I have her. I'll never lose her. Everything will be all right."

5

Before dinner, Egon Gottfrey returns to his motel to see if the courier has arrived from the laboratory in Menlo Park, California.

Waiting for him at the front desk is a large white Styrofoam chest of the kind that might contain mail-order steaks or a dozen pints of gelato in exotic flavors.

This marionette theater in which he has a role is well managed, and the necessary props never fail to appear where they are needed.

He carries the insulated box to his room, where he uses his switchblade to slit the tape sealing the lid in place. Clouds of pale, cold vapor issue from perforated packets of dry ice that coddle a Medexpress container twice the size of a lunchbox.

In a compartment without dry ice are hypodermic syringes, cannulas, and other items related to intravenous injections.

In the bathroom, Gottfrey places the Medexpress container on the counter beside the sink. The digital readout reports an interior temperature of thirty-eight degrees Fahrenheit. He swings back the lid and counts twelve insulated sleeves of quilted, silvery material about an inch in diameter and seven inches long, each containing a glass ampule of cloudy amber fluid.

Three ampules for each person residing at the Hawk ranch. The ranch manager, Juan Saba, and his wife, Marie. Ancel and Clare Hawk.

Each set of three ampules contains a nanotech brain implant. A control mechanism. Hundreds of thousands of parts, maybe millions, each comprising just a few molecules. Inert until injected, warmed by the subject's blood, they become brain-tropic.

The concept intrigues Gottfrey. Although he has not received such an implant, he considers himself to be a marionette controlled by unknown forces. And when he injects people with these mechanisms, to some extent he becomes their puppeteer, a marionette who controls marionettes of his own. His mind controls their minds.

The incredibly tiny nanoconstructs migrate through veins to the heart, then through arteries to the brain, where they penetrate the blood-brain barrier and pass through the walls of capillaries just as do vital substances that the brain needs. They enter the tissue of the brain and self-assemble into a complex weblike structure.

The injected people are programmed to be obedient. They are made to forget they have been injected. They don't know they are enslaved. They become "adjusted people." The control is so complete that they will commit suicide if told to do so.

Indeed, Clare and Ancel Hawk's son, Nick, had been in a special class of adjusted people, those on the Hamlet list. The Arcadians have developed a computer model that identifies men and women who excel in their fields of endeavor and who possess certain traits that suggest they will become leaders with considerable influence in the culture; if those individuals hold positions on key issues that conflict with Arcadian philosophy and goals, they are injected and controlled. To doubly ensure they don't influence others with their dangerous ideas and don't pass their unique genomes on to a lot of children, they are instructed to kill themselves.

This control mechanism might terrify Gottfrey if he didn't believe that the brain and the body it controls are both illusions, as is everything else in so-called reality. His disembodied mind is the only thing that exists. When nothing is real, there is nothing to fear. You need only surrender to the Unknown Playwright who crafts the narrative and go where the play takes you; it's like being in a fascinating dream from which you never wake.

He closes the Medexpress container and returns with it to the bedroom, where he places it in the Styrofoam chest with the dry ice.

When he goes out for dinner, he leaves the lights on and hangs the DO NOT DISTURB sign from the door-knob.

6

The shadowy room, the light of the TV that illuminated nothing, the dark at the windows, the moral darkness of *Sunday Magazine* . . .

Clare's chest felt tight, each breath constrained, as she stood watching a homicide detective, someone *said to be* a detective, a fortyish man who looked as clean-cut as any father on a family-friendly 1950s sitcom, but who must be dirtier than any drug dealer or pimp. He spoke of an exhumed body that didn't exist, that had been ashes since the previous November, of toxicological tests that couldn't have been conducted on ashes. He claimed to have evidence that Nick Hawk was *murdered* with his Marine-issue knife. It was known, he said, that Jane had been selling national-defense secrets to enemies of the country even then, and he speculated that Nick, a true American hero who had received the Navy Cross, might have grown suspicious of her, might have confronted her with his suspicions.

Ancel rose from his chair. By nature he wasn't an angry soul. He gave everyone the benefit of the doubt, rarely raised his voice, and dealt with difficult people by avoiding them. Clare had never seen him so incensed, though his rage might have been unnoticed by anyone but her, for it manifested only as a pulse in his temple, in the clenching of his jaws, in the set of his shoulders.

With the program near its end, they stood in silent sentinel to outrageous deceit, as Jane's father, Martin Duroc, was interviewed in his home, with a piano in the background to remind everyone of his renown. "Jane was a sweet but emotionally fragile child. And so young when she found her mother after the suicide." He seemed to choke with emotion. "I'm afraid something snapped in her then. She became withdrawn. No amount of counseling or therapy helped. I felt as if I'd lost a wife *and* a daughter. Yet I never imagined she would become . . . what she is now. I pray she'll turn herself in."

Jane *knew* that he'd killed her mother to marry another woman. He had supposedly been hundreds of miles from home that night, but in fact he'd been in the house, though she couldn't prove his guilt.

Now, the program ended as Duroc took a display handkerchief from the breast pocket of his suit to dab at his eyes, and Clare said, "My God, what do we do? What *can* we do?"

"I intend to get fall-down drunk," Ancel said. "No other way I'll be able to sleep tonight. And there's nothin' we can do for Jane. Damn the whole crooked lot of them."

Never in Clare's experience had Ancel been drunk, and she doubted that he meant to lose himself in a bottle this time.

He confirmed her doubt by turning to her and fluttering the fingers of one hand as if they were the pinions of a bird's wing, a prearranged signal that meant *time to fly*.

She couldn't disagree. Jane had warned that the conspirators might become so frustrated by their inability to find her that they would come after her in-laws, hoping to use them to get her. Now that these vicious shits had pulled this stunt with *Sunday Magazine*, they would expect Clare and Ancel to make a statement to the press tomorrow. So they would come before dawn.

The telephone rang.

Ancel said, "It's one friend or another, knows Jane, saw the show, wants to say they're with us. Let it go to voice mail. It won't be the last. I'm not in the mood tonight. Call 'em back tomorrow. I'm gettin' that damn bottle of Scotch. What about you?"

"This . . . it sickens me," Clare said. "I'm furious and scared for her and . . . and I feel so helpless."

"What can I do, honey? What do you want to do?"

"Can't do a damn thing. This is so rotten. I'm going to bed."

"You won't sleep. Not after this."

"I'll take an Ambien. I can't handle whisky like you, I'd be throwing up all night." She was amazed at how convincingly she delivered her lines. They had never practiced a scene like this.

They spoke no more as they prepared to leave before sunrise.

Clare loved this house, their first and only, where they began their marriage, where they raised Nick, where they learned from Nick and Jane, during a visit, that she was pregnant with their first—and now only—grandchild. Clare wondered when they would be able to return. She wondered *if*.

7

Because the revolution is everything to him, Ivan Petro works seven days a week, and on this first Sunday in April, he seems destined also to work around the clock.

He is based in Sacramento, where Techno Arcadians maintain a significant network in the state government, which is as corrupt as any, more so than most.

He's having dinner in his favorite Italian restaurant when he, like thousands of other Arcadians, starts receiving text messages about the incident involving Jane Hawk in Lake Tahoe, including a photograph taken there, showing her current appearance.

No hit team has been dispatched to nail her, because a late-season blizzard in the Sierra Nevada has grounded all helicopters.

Although the highways in that territory are treacherous, they are passable. No one knows what she's driving or in which direction she's gone; but she probably will want to get out of the Tahoe area, all the way out of the storm, before going to ground for the night.

If she flees west on Highway 50, she'll be coming straight toward Ivan Petro.

As he finishes a plate of saltimbocca, he checks the weather report and learns that snow is falling only as far as Riverton. In the twenty miles west of Riverton, there is no town of any size until Placerville, which has a population of maybe ten thousand.

Ivan finishes a second glass of Chianti. He doesn't order the two servings of cannoli that he was anticipating with such pleasure.

An hour after nightfall, he's in Placerville, stalking the so-called beautiful monster, on what is shaping up to be perhaps the most important night of his life.

Ivan Petro appears to have a molecular density greater than that of mere flesh and bone, as though the substance of which he's constituted was first made molten in a coke-fired oven before being poured into a man shape. Teeth as blunt and white as those of a horse, face broad and flushed as if he has spent his entire life in a stinging wind that has left this permanent coloration. People have called him "Big Guy" since he was eleven years old.

Ivan is a hit team all by himself.

It has been assumed that Jane must be staying in motels, paying cash and using forged ID, remaining nowhere more than a night or two. The national chains in the hospitality industry will accept cash in advance from someone without a credit card, but it is far from a common practice. To avoid raising an eyebrow and attracting undue attention, she most likely prefers mom-and-pop operations, one- and two-star motels more accustomed to cash transactions.

Placerville is not so large that it offers scores of mom-and-pop motels. With his Department of Homeland Security credentials and his authoritative demeanor, using a description of Tahoe Jane but not her name, he receives cooperation from the clerks at the front desks of the establishments most likely to interest the fugitive.

In any endeavor like this, luck plays a role. If Jane chose to continue through Placerville to Sacramento and points beyond, Ivan is wasting his time. But luck strikes after his second stop. He is in his Range Rover, a third motel address entered in his navigator, stopped at a red traffic light, when he sees a woman of interest come out of a supermarket.

Carrying what appears to be a deli bag, she passes the Range Rover and crosses the street to the motel on the northwest corner. She resembles the photo of Jane incognita, taken in Tahoe: stylish chopped-shaggy black hair, a little Goth makeup around the eyes.

He can't see if she is wearing a nose ring or if her lipstick is blue, as in the photograph, but she's a looker, wearing a sport coat that's maybe cut for concealed-carry. And she has attitude, moves with grace and confidence that people often mention when talking about Jane Hawk.

She walks past the motel office and along the covered walkway serving the rooms.

The light changes to green, and Ivan eases through the intersection, timing it so that he is gliding past when she lets herself into Room 8.

Most of the motel's rooms are evidently not yet booked for the night, because only four vehicles stand in the parking lot. Only one of the four is anywhere near Room 8, and it is parked directly in front of that door: a metallic-gray Ford Explorer Scout.

Ivan hangs a U-turn at the next intersection and pulls off the street, into an apartment complex across from the motel.

The apartments are in an arrangement of bland stucco boxes tricked up with decorative iron stair railings and faux shutters in a sad attempt at style. In front of the buildings is a long pergola that, during the day, shades the vehicles of residents as well as those of visitors. It now provides moonshade for the Range Rover.

The Explorer Scout is parked between lampposts, and with binoculars Ivan glasses the rear license plates. Using the computer terminal in the console of the customized Rover, he back-doors the California DMV and inputs the number. The vehicle is registered to Leonard Borland at an address in San Francisco.

Ivan switches to Google Street and looks at what stands at that address: a ten-story apartment building. He suspects that if he visited the place, no tenant named Leonard Borland would live there.

Rather than go to that trouble, he returns to the DMV system and seeks driver's licenses issued to men named Leonard Borland, of which there are several with various middle names. None of them shares the address to which the Explorer Scout is registered.

This might only mean that another Leonard Borland owns the Scout but does not drive it himself, does not drive at all.

But what it *might* mean isn't in this case worth considering.

It's been known for some time that Jane Hawk has a source for forged documents so well crafted that the forger is able to insert them undetected in government records, ensuring they will withstand scrutiny if she is stopped by the highway patrol.

Minutes after checking out the various Leonard Borlands, Ivan Petro receives an electrifying phone call. The guardians with whom Travis Hawk's mother entrusted him have been found in Borrego Springs, where they have been killed in an exchange of gunfire. The boy has yet to be located. A major search is being organized to comb every inch of the town and the surrounding Borrego Valley.

Almost an hour later, following much fevered calculation, Ivan arrives at a course of action. He isn't going to call for backup and allow the credit for the capture of Jane Hawk to go to those Arcadians above him in the revolution, many of whom are in the habit of adding to their resumes accomplishments that aren't theirs.

He calls them poachers, though never to their face. They are dangerous people, such vipers that it's amazing they aren't poisoned by the potency of their own venom. He treats them with unfailing respect, though he despises them.

However, he is self-aware enough to know that, were he to rise into their ranks and be accepted, he would no longer despise them, would find them ideal company. He despises the insiders only because he isn't one of them; being excluded is what feeds his hatred.

Since childhood, he's been a superb hater. He hated his father for the many beatings and hated his indifferent mother for raising no objection to them. His hatred had festered into pure black rancor until, at fifteen, he was big enough and furious enough to pay his old man back with interest and knock some remorse into his mother, as well, before walking out on them forever.

Because they had no interest in teaching him anything at all, other than fearful obedience, they no doubt still have no awareness that by their cruelty they taught him the most important of all life lessons: Happiness depends on acquiring as much power as possible, power in all its forms—physical strength, superior knowledge, money and more money, political control over others.

His parents are ignorant alcoholics full of class resentment, but in essence they are alike to the Arcadian poachers who have thus far thwarted Ivan's ascent in the revolution. He hates them all.

Anyway, he has a plan, and it's a good one that could elevate him into the hierarchy where he belongs.

The motel is not a place where he can surprise her, overpower her, take custody of her, and put her through a hard interrogation without drawing unwanted attention. If he is patient, a better opportunity will present itself.

If he can break her on his own, learn where the boy is . . . he can present *both* mother and child to the revolution as a single package and in such a way that credit is given where it is due.

The cargo area of the Range Rover is stocked with surveillance gear, from which he selects a transponder with a lithium battery. It's the size of a pack of cigarettes. After programming the unit's identifier code into his GPS, he crosses the street to the motel.

The best way to accomplish a task like this is boldly, as though it's the most natural thing in the world to stoop beside a stranger's car and attach a transponder. The back of this particular unit features a plastic bubble containing a powerful epoxy. With a penknife, Ivan slits the bubble, reaches between the tire and the rear quarter panel, and presses the transponder to the wheel well. The epoxy sets in ten seconds. Because it is an adhesive used to attach heat-dispersing tiles to space shuttles, there is no chance it will be dislodged by any patch of rough road or in a collision.

If people in the passing vehicles notice Ivan at work, they aren't curious. He crosses the street and returns to the Range Rover without incident.

However, fewer than ten minutes pass before the door of Room 8 opens and the woman exits, carrying luggage. She needs two trips to load the Scout. She is clearly agitated and in a hurry.

He is sure, now beyond all doubt, that she is Jane Hawk.

He suspects she has somehow learned what has happened to Gavin and Jessica Washington, the two guardians of her boy, who have been killed in Borrego Springs.

He watches her drive away from the motel and

does not at once pursue her. He doesn't need to keep her in sight in order to tail her. The transponder that he attached to her Explorer is represented as a blinking red signifier on the screen of the Range Rover GPS.

Ivan waits a few minutes before reversing out of the pergola. He turns left into the street. Jane Hawk is headed west on Highway 50, toward Sacramento and points beyond, and so is Ivan Petro.

About the Author

DEAN KOONTZ, the author of many #1 *New York Times* bestsellers, lives in Southern California with his wife, Gerda, their golden retriever, Elsa, and the enduring spirits of their goldens Trixie and Anna.

deankoontz.com
Facebook.com/DeanKoontzOfficial
Twitter: @deankoontz

Correspondence for the author should be addressed to:

Dean Koontz
P.O. Box 9529
Newport Beach, California 92658

Don't miss any of the electrifying thrillers in the Jane Hawk series.

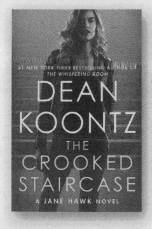

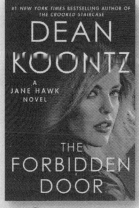

Coming soon

Join Dean Koontz
on social media!

Facebook.com/deankoontzofficial

@deankoontz

Instagram.com/deankoontzofficial

Visit DeanKoontz.com
and sign up for Dean's e-newsletter!